STRANGE
BEDFELLOWS

By the Author

Holy Rollers

Strange Bedfellows

Visit us at www.boldstrokesbooks.com

STRANGE BEDFELLOWS

by

Rob Byrnes

A Division of Bold Strokes Books

2012

STRANGE BEDFELLOWS
© 2012 By Rob Byrnes. All Rights Reserved.

ISBN 13: 978-1-60282-746-2

This Trade Paperback Original Is Published By
Bold Strokes Books, Inc.
P.O. Box 249
Valley Falls, NY 12185

First Edition: September 2012

Credits
Editors: Greg Herren and Stacia Seaman
Production Design: Stacia Seaman
Cover Design by Sheri (graphicartist2020@hotmail.com)

Acknowledgments

Thanks as always to my agent, Katherine Fausset; my editors, Greg Herren and Stacia Seaman; my partner in crime, Becky Cochrane; and my partner in life, Brady Allen. And thanks to David Green, Greg Crane, and Illyse Kaplan for bravely reading early drafts; and to Nick Donovan for letting me fictionalize him... or did I?

To Anthony Weiner, in appreciation for the inspiration

CHAPTER ONE

Most times, a sneeze wouldn't have been that big a deal. Most times, it was something that just happened. But most times a guy didn't sneeze while he was standing in the after-hours darkness of a store he was robbing and pretending to be a mannequin while a cop trained a flashlight near him through the plate glass window.

Which is why it sort of became a big deal when Chase LaMarca sneezed.

"Shuddup," said a hiss from the shadows. That hiss came from his partner, Grant Lambert, who said it so quickly Chase could hardly see his lips move. Which was the point.

Chase waited until the beam from the flashlight moved away from him before he said, "I didn't do it on purpose. It was just a sneeze."

"Sounded like a trumpet."

"For someone concerned about making noise, you're sure talkin' a lot."

"Shh!"

They fell back into silence and froze as the light made another sweep across the room. When it was trained away from them, they could see the silhouette of the cop outside on the sidewalk.

Chase felt his pants pocket vibrate. "Now my phone is buzzing."

"Shh."

Out in front of the store, the cop was talking into his radio. They couldn't hear the words but knew that was never a good sign.

"We're gonna have to make a break for it," said Grant. "If he's calling for backup, we don't wanna be standing here when they arrive. The minute this guy turns away…"

Which is when the cop aimed the beam back into the store. And directly into Grant Lambert's eyes.

❖

The patrolman held the flashlight in one hand and the hand mic wired to a radio clipped on his belt in the other and said, "I don't see anything. Except maybe the ugliest mannequin in mannequin history."

"That's why Jackson Heights ain't Madison Avenue," said the dispatcher on the other end of the radio. "If everything looks secure, move on."

"Coulda sworn I saw something move in there, though."

"Probably your eyes playing tricks on you. Move on."

The patrolman flicked off his flashlight, then—just to reassure himself one more time, 'cause it sure as hell looked like something had moved in there—walked to the front door and tugged. It was locked tightly. Yeah, must have been his eyes playing tricks.

But one more look through the glass couldn't hurt...

"Think he's gone?" asked Chase, trying to spot movement in the darkness on the other side of the window.

Grant, still frozen, again talked out of the corner of his mouth. "I think so."

"'Cause I'm vibrating again."

"Ignore it." Still seeing nothing outside, Grant started to let himself breathe.

"But if someone is trying that hard to get in touch with me—"

"It can wait." He froze again when he saw the silhouette of the cop reappear, then nudged Chase, who also froze.

The beam reappeared, slowly sweeping the store's interior. This time, Grant turned his head slightly, so the light wouldn't blind him again.

That was probably a mistake.

The patrolman clicked the button on his handset and said, "A mannequin moved."

"What's that?" asked his dispatcher.

"This mannequin. One minute the light's in his eyes, the next minute he's looking away from me. Meaning that's a *man*, not a mannequin."

It took the dispatcher a few beats to follow. "You say 'a man, not a mannequin'?"

"Ten-four."

"Gotcha. I've got backup on the way."

"You hear sirens? I hear sirens."

Grant parted his lips slightly. "I hear 'em. Is the cop still outside?"

"Yeah," said Chase. "Standing by the front door."

"Let's get the hell out of here." He backed up a few feet until he was hidden behind a rack of cheap suits, where the bottom of a rope ladder dangled. He began climbing.

Below him, Chase said, "I'm buzzing again."

"Shut up and move."

Up above the drop ceiling, they stood precariously on wooden beams and hauled up the ladder, rolling it into a tight coil before carefully navigating those beams to a cheap aluminum vent cover on the wall. It wasn't screwed into the wall—they knew that, since they'd been the ones who'd unscrewed it to gain access—so Grant kicked it aside and, on hands and knees, crawled through the opening into a narrow staircase leading to the apartments upstairs. Chase, still holding the rolled-up rope ladder, followed.

A single bare forty-watt bulb hung from the ceiling, the only illumination in the hallway. Through the murkiness, they began to descend the stairs but stopped as the pulsating red light from a patrol car flooded the foyer below them.

"That was faster than I anticipated," said Grant.

"Up," said Chase, who was already climbing the stairs toward the roof.

Now two police officers trained their flashlights through the shop window, and—judging by distant sirens growing nearer—more were on the way. They'd again tried the door to the shop, and again found it locked, so looking through the window was the only immediate option that occurred to them.

"You're sure one of those mannequins moved, right?" asked the new officer. "*Absolutely* sure?"

"Not one of *those* mannequins," said the first officer. "The one that moved isn't there anymore."

"That right?"

"That's right."

"So where'd it go?"

The cop who'd first interrupted Grant and Chase while they were trying to make a dishonest day's living sighed in exasperation. "What I've been trying to tell everyone is that it wasn't a mannequin that moved. It was a *man*."

They stared through the window for another thirty seconds. "So what did the mannequin look like?"

"Man."

"Yeah, okay."

"Beat up," the first officer reported. "Sort of old and beat up. Gray hair...needed a shave."

The second officer took his beam off the interior and shined it on the first officer's face. "Wait a minute. Are you tellin' me you see a mannequin in there that looks like some kind of bum and you think it's a mannequin, and not a bum?"

"Not once he started moving."

"I mean before that."

The first officer shrugged. "Figured maybe they were going for the gone-to-seed look." When the second cop frowned, he added, "Hey, guys that look like bums gotta buy their clothes somewhere, right?"

"I guess."

The second officer turned his flashlight back to the interior and waved it around until he at last found something that didn't seem right.

"Up there," he said, as the beam danced along the ceiling. "That ceiling panel's been pushed aside."

The first cop's flashlight found the target. "Think that's where he went?"

"I don't know. But if he's still up in the ceiling, we'll get him out."

Minutes later, Grant and Chase caught their breath and watched from the roof as three more patrol cars rounded the opposite corners—one heading the wrong way down the one-way street—before pulling to a stop in front of the store.

"This isn't good," said Chase.

"No, it isn't," Grant agreed.

"And now I'm buzzing again."

Grant scowled. "I'm about to throw your phone off the roof. How'd you like *that*?"

Chase ignored him, took the phone from his pocket, and glanced at the screen. "It's Jamie Brock."

"I knew it wasn't important." Grant took another look five stories below, to where seven or eight cops now stood in front of the store, some with their guns drawn. He grabbed Chase's arm when he saw a few of them break off and approach the door to the stairway. "We've gotta get out of here, lover, so put your toy away."

Chase held out the coiled rope ladder. "And what do you want me to do about this?"

"Keep it. We might need it to get off this roof." He took another look over the side of the building. "Well…it could mean the difference between a sixty-foot fall and a fifty-foot fall, so I guess that's something."

They darted through the darkness across the roof, then vaulted over a thigh-high brick wall onto the next roof, repeating the process twice more until they were nearing the end of the adjoined buildings.

It was when they were crossing the second to last roof that two large men emerged from the shadows. Even in the open air, Grant and Chase could smell marijuana. They froze for a moment, until they realized they were looking at a couple of teenagers. Very *big* teenagers who looked like they could pull both their heads off their shoulders without effort, but still teenagers.

For their part, the teenagers didn't quite get that they weren't dealing with run-of-the-mill middle-aged white guys who just happened to be dashing over the rooftops of Jackson Heights, Queens.

"Got any money, gramps?" one of them asked Grant.

"Get out of our way," was Grant's terse reply.

"My friend asked if you had any—" The second punk stopped mid-sentence when Grant stared at him, then backed up a few steps. "Okay, man, we don't want no trouble."

Chase, who was tired of carrying the rope ladder, tossed it at the second kid's feet. "Here. You might need this to get down."

Grant and Chase crossed over one more rooftop before coming to an abrupt stop. On the other side of the last thigh-high brick wall was a sixty-foot drop to a trash-strewn alley.

"Sure could use that ladder about now," said Grant.

"Oh, Grant, paralysis is not necessarily better than death."

They looked behind them, barely noticing the stoned teenagers who'd been disarmed by a single stare from Grant Lambert.

It was hard to be certain in the darkness, but it sure as hell sounded like there was activity coming from where they'd started. Which probably meant the cops were just a few rooftops behind them.

Without a word or another glance, Chase grabbed the nearest doorknob and was pleasantly surprised that not only was it not locked, but it opened into another barely lit stairwell. Grant followed him through the door and quietly shut it behind them.

They made it down to the third-floor landing when an apartment door opened. An older man with fussily curly white hair stepped into the hall, not noticing them at first. In one hand he held a trash bag; in the other, a small blue plastic bag and a leash attached to a cocker spaniel. His eyebrows jumped in alarm when he saw Grant and Chase behind him on the stairs.

His first and only reaction was to plead, "Don't hurt me!"

Grant gave him a look that was considerably less intimidating than the one he'd given the teenagers. "Hurt you? Now why would we do that?"

The man seemed slightly hopeful he wasn't about to be mugged. "You're not with those ruffians who hang out on the roofs? Those... those..." His hands made a little flourish. "Those *gangstas*?"

Grant shook his head. "Nah, but we're borrowing your stuff."

"My stuff?" The man looked confused. "What?"

Chase flashed his wallet too quickly for anything inside to be visible. "NYPD. It's all okay, buddy. We'll take it from here." He leaned down. "C'mere, Fluffy."

"Mitzi," the man corrected him.

"Mitzi, then." He took the leash out of the not-quite-convinced man's hand. "Come outside in five minutes. We'll leave Mitzi tied to a tree."

"But..."

Chase flashed him an ingratiating—yet somehow authoritative—smile. "The safety of the public depends on this, sir. There are some dangerous characters out there pretending to be cops."

"Right," said Grant as he liberated the trash bag from the man's other hand. "So we're gonna outsmart 'em by pretending to be civilians. Kind of like a double-cross."

Chase, half dragging the cocker spaniel—who wasn't at all sure she wanted to follow the stranger—and Grant, carrying the trash bag, began descending the steps as the man looked on.

"Will my Mitzi be all right?"

"More than all right," Chase reassured him, taking the stairs two at a time without turning around, leaving Mitzi no choice but to keep up with his pace. "This is a hero dog. Probably get a photo in the *Post*."

"And anyway," added Grant, "what could go wrong?"

"Well…" Grant and Chase were almost to the second floor when the man thought to call out. "Wait!"

Grant kept going, but Chase turned as the man hurried down the steps and offered him the blue bag. "You'll have to clean up after her."

"We won't need her that long," said Chase, giving the leash a bit too much of a yank, if Mitzi's growl could be considered a complaint.

They were almost to the first landing—almost out of that building and on their way to safety—when the man called out, "And you'll get rid of those *gangstas*, too?"

"Top of my list," Grant called back to him.

Out on the sidewalk, two teams of cops strolled by as Grant emerged from the doorway with the bag of trash. Chase and Mitzi followed closely. No one probably would've looked twice at them if one of the cops hadn't tried to pet the cocker spaniel.

She nipped him.

"Mitzi, no!"

"No harm done," said the cop who'd been nipped, while his buddies giggled. "Better watch yourself. Looks like there was a burglary down the street."

Chase's hand went to his mouth. "Burglary! Oh my! That explains all the police officers."

One of the other cops nodded toward Grant, toting his trash bag away from them at a fairly rapid pace for trash bag-toting. "You know that guy?"

"Yeah, he's my neighbor. Mr.…Mr. Mitzi!"

The cop made a face. "Mitzi? I thought that was the dog's name."

"I…uh…he…I named her after him. He's sort of like the dog's godfather."

Implausibly, that seemed to work, because the cop yelled, "Hey, Mitzi, hold up there!"

The cocker spaniel barked. Grant kept moving.

The cop tried again. "You with the trash! I said to stop right there!"

Grant finally stopped, and then he turned very slowly. "Can I help you?"

"What's in the bag?"

"Uh…trash?"

While the cop jogged up to him, Grant undid the twist-tie and hoped the man in the hallway wasn't the best-disguised heroin dealer in the neighborhood. The cop hovered over the bag and sifted inside for a few seconds with his nightstick before motioning for Grant to close it.

"One word of advice," the cop said. "Ease up on those frozen éclairs."

"I'll do that, officer."

"Trust me on that, my friend. See this gut?" The cop patted his own stomach. "Two years ago I couldn't see my feet. I was hooked on those things. But I gave 'em up, and now I'm a new man. Understand?"

Grant nodded. "Absolutely. Consider these my last frozen éclairs."

The cop patted Grant on the shoulder. "I know they're creamy and chocolaty and just about the best-tasting treat ever, but—"

"Got it."

The cop felt his stomach one more time, then half turned until he could see both Grant and Chase. "Okay, then. In that case, please call nine-one-one if you see anything suspicious."

"Come to think of it," said Chase, "there are some gangstas on the roof right now."

"*Gangstas*?"

"Yeah. They're on the roof. With a rope ladder."

The cops looked at each other in wonder that this crime-solving tip had just fallen into their laps. Seconds later they were bounding up the staircase.

Although the one cop did have to stop and lecture the old guy with the fussily curly white hair when he passed the third-floor landing and caught him eating a frozen éclair.

The good news with trying to pull a job so close to home was that they could walk back to their apartment, so even though they'd gotten out of there with nothing, at least they weren't out the cost of a couple of subway fares. And Chase kept trying to convince Grant that their flight up and down stairs and across rooftops even counted as getting fresh air and exercise, a fine point Grant didn't seem to appreciate. He didn't much care for fresh air and exercise.

But there really *was* something to be said about not getting caught. They both tried to keep that in mind. It not only kept their perfect record of not getting caught intact after almost twenty years together—and a few more than twenty for Grant in this particular business—it also meant they wouldn't be going to The Tombs that night.

They were approaching their apartment building and Grant had almost worked himself into a normal mood—meaning not happy, but not as unhappy as he'd been when the cops had interrupted their job—when Chase again announced, "I'm vibrating."

Grant sighed. "Jamie Brock again?"

Chase fished the phone from his pocket. "Jamie Brock again. Should I answer it?"

"No," said Grant.

"Yes," said a voice that wasn't Grant's.

They turned, and there stood Jamie Brock. In the flesh.

CHAPTER TWO

Jamie Brock smiled and ran a hand through his tousled hair, no doubt recently cut at an expensive Manhattan salon and, knowing Jamie, no doubt paid for in something other than cash. He wasn't much younger than they were, but there was something annoyingly boyish about him that could always be counted on to set Grant off. And it did.

Yeah, Jamie had a weathered look to his face. But it was the weathered look of someone who'd spent too much time in the sun and wind—in other words, the *weather*—as opposed to the OTB parlor or corner bar. And he more than overcompensated for his lived-in complexion with the trendiest hair and clothing styles, which—coupled with that annoyingly boyish demeanor—made his real age indecipherable to most people.

But Grant Lambert could decipher it, and while it was bad enough that Chase, Grant's partner of eighteen years, looked much younger than him, Jamie's ability to pass almost as his son—or at least much younger brother, and at least in very bad lighting—was almost too much to bear at times. Especially times like this, when Grant's mad dash across rooftops only to return home with empty pockets contrasted so unfavorably to Jamie's facile charm and mysterious sources of income.

So Grant did what Grant tended to do and pretended he didn't have a problem, although—when dealing with Jamie—that was always easier said than done.

"What the hell are you doing here?" His tone wasn't really a clue that he had a problem with Jamie; he talked to most people that way. "Last I remember, you couldn't find your way out of a paper bag, let alone Manhattan."

Jamie smiled, and damn if he didn't rub it in again—by now Grant was convinced he was doing it on purpose—by rumpling his hair. "I'm getting around a lot more. Spreading my wings! Moving all over this big, beautiful city without a care!"

Grant ran his eyes up and down the street until he spotted the bright yellow car parked with its lights out a few buildings away. "You took that cab, right?"

"Uh…Yeah, okay. Anyway, I've been trying to reach you guys."

"We know," said Grant. "You kept bothering us while we were working."

"You were on a job tonight? Sorry. I didn't know. How did it go?"

"Perfect." Anyone who wasn't Jamie Brock could have seen through that lie by reading the sour expression on Grant's face, but Jamie would *never* be that perceptive.

Chase, sensing an eruption was coming if he didn't defuse the situation, diplomatically stepped between them. "So what's the problem, Jamie? You seem sort of desperate."

Jamie looked perplexed. "Do I?"

"Uh…yeah, a little." Chase pulled his cell phone from his pocket and scrolled through the list of missed calls. "You tried to call me fourteen times."

"And you showed up *here*," added Grant. "In front of our house. In the middle of the night." He looked back down the street. "In a cab."

Jamie glanced at his watch. Grant noticed it looked like a Rolex and was sure it wasn't a *real* Rolex. "It's not the middle of the night. It's only 1:00 a.m." He tossed a smile at Grant. "You sure are getting old, Grant."

"Shuddup."

Chase tried to get the conversation back on track. "So, you're here because…?"

Jamie glanced up and down the almost-treeless street. "Can we go up to your apartment and talk in private?"

"No." There was a firmness in Grant's voice. Which wasn't unusual.

"Okay, then." Jamie shrugged. "I think I have a job for you."

Grant's head dropped. "When you bring us jobs, they don't seem to turn out all that good. So I'm gonna say no."

"But…"

"No."

"But…"

"No!"

Chase, again the peacemaker, stepped up to his partner. "Grant, let's hear this out. And *then* we can say no. Jamie? Please continue."

Jamie scuffed his loafers against a crack in the sidewalk. "Well… okay, I know some things have gone a little bit wrong in the past, but this one can't miss." Seeing they remained unconvinced, he hurried to continue before the definitive refusal came. "This is a simple breaking-and-entering job. Get in, get the goods, bring them back to the guy who's hiring us—"

Grant cleared his throat. "Us?"

"Us."

"You mean you're going on the job with me and Chase?"

"Well, no. Of *course* not. But I'm bringing you the job, so I'm a part of it. Anyway, you steal this thing, bring it to the guy, and collect our money. Maybe three or four hours out of your life, and we'll make ten grand."

Grant raised an eyebrow. "Someone's paying ten thousand dollars for a few hours to do a simple retrieval operation? In that case, it don't sound so simple."

Jamie dropped his voice and kicked again at the sidewalk. "It's a simple job. But it's important. See, there's this congresswoman I've become friends with—"

"Huh?"

Chase was going to try to stop Grant's cynicism, but let it go. Because he was wondering the same thing.

"And how does someone like you become friends with a congresswoman?"

Jamie shrugged, as if the answer was obvious. "We travel in the same circle of friends out in the Hamptons."

Grant shook his head. "I think I get it. You and your fellow Hamptons bloodsuckers met a little old lady with a lot of money who happens to be a congresswoman—"

"No!" Jamie thought for a moment. "Well…okay, yes. But you're making it sound really tawdry."

"It *is* really tawdry."

Again, Jamie ran his fingers through his hair. The highlights picked up a glow from the one working streetlight on the block, and Grant thought he might scream.

"Whatever. Anyway, she's retiring when her term is up at the end of this year, and her son-in-law is running in the election to replace her. Follow?" Grant nodded noncommittally. "Triple-C just loves him, but there's a little problem. You see—"

Grant held up a hand to silence Jamie. "Wait a minute. What's a Triple-C?"

"I think it's a bra size," Chase guessed, but he wasn't sure because he hadn't seen a bra that wasn't being worn by a drag queen in almost thirty years.

Jamie set them straight. "No, Triple-C is the congresswoman. Catherine Cooper Concannon. Triple-C. Get it?" Grant snarled; Jamie either missed it or ignored it. "So she loves the idea that her son-in-law will replace her. See, there's the whole family dynasty thing going on, and the son-in-law's the last link. Still follow?"

"Close enough. But why don't you skip ahead to the part that has to do with me and Chase so I can say no, throw you off my stoop, and get some sleep."

Jamie tossed off a knowing smile that put Grant about twenty seconds away from punching him in his probably-courtesy-of-surgery-perfect nose.

"Well, it *is* sort of important how all these people go together."

"Not to me."

Jamie sighed. Sometimes Grant Lambert had no appreciation for the narrative, which is why he'd always be a small-timer. Jamie was dealing with congresswomen, and Grant was dealing with fences and chop-shops. But if Grant wanted to know about the job, and *only* about the job, Jamie would jump ahead to the job.

"So Austin—Austin Peebles; that's Triple-C's son-in-law—got himself in some trouble with his Twitter account."

While Grant tried to figure out what that meant, Chase—who understood *exactly* what that meant—stepped forward.

"I think Jamie means this Peebles guy sent, uh, risqué pictures of himself to someone, Grant."

"Right," Jamie confirmed. "Dick pics!"

"I get that," said Grant, who hadn't the slightest clue until Chase sort of explained, and still hadn't fully embraced the concept. One day he was going to have to learn to use that machine. "So this Triple-C is paying ten thousand dollars to get back this Twitter thing?"

Jamie smiled and rolled his heavily lidded eyes in Chase's direction, giving him a "your partner is so out of touch" look that decreased the time in which Grant wanted to punch him in the nose from twenty seconds to that immediate moment. But Chase stared him down—it wasn't a Grant Lambert stare, but it did what it had to do—so he let it go.

Chase's words were calculated to rein in Jamie while minimizing any embarrassment Grant might feel for being trapped in the 1980s when it came to technology. And yes, there were still times when Grant said "telex" when he meant "fax," and did anyone even *fax* anymore? Grant probably thought they did.

"So let me see if I have this straight, Jamie. This Peebles fellow used his camera phone to take an inappropriate photo, then uploaded that photo to his online Twitter account, where other people could see it."

Jamie wondered why Chase was speaking so slowly and awkwardly. His own answer was quick and concise. "Right. He tweeted a dick pic to the world!"

"What's that?" Grant again felt as if he was learning a new language.

"A picture of his penis."

Chase blocked them again. "I think Grant was wondering what a tweet is." He patted his partner's arm. "He already knows what a dick is."

"I sure do," Grant said evenly as he stared at Jamie.

Chase kept pretending everything was fine. "When you send a message on Twitter, it's like an e-mail…sort of. But it's out in public, and anyone can see it, and it's called a tweet."

"Why's that?"

Chase closed his eyes and sighed. "Just punch Jamie and get this over with."

Which Grant considered while Chase *re*considered and turned back to Jamie to wrap up the situation as he understood it. "So this guy tweeted a dick shot and his mother-in-law wants it gone. Is that the story?"

"Not her. I don't know what she even knows. But there's an intermediary—"

"So this son-in-law—"

"Peebles. Austin Peebles."

"He's the intermediary?"

"No, the intermediary is someone else."

"Whatever. Peebles is paying the ten grand?"

"No," said Jamie. "Austin doesn't have that kind of cash lying around. His wife controls the purse strings. His wife controls *everything*."

Grant, having finally mostly figured out what the hell they were talking about, brought himself back into the conversation. "So do you want to tell me who's paying up?"

"The campaign committee."

Grant didn't like that. "I don't like that. Plus, I don't usually work for other people. I'm what you call an independent businessman."

"Are you sure? We're talking ten grand—well, minus my finder's fee, of course—for only a few hours of work. You'd be able to pay your rent on this place for the next year and never break a sweat."

"With you," said Grant, "things are never as easy as they sound. And they always involve sweat."

"Sometimes that's true," Jamie agreed. "But this time, I've brought you a piece of cake."

Again, Chase took over the conversation. "Okay, Jamie, suppose we do take this job—"

"We ain't taking it."

"But suppose we do. What is there about it you aren't telling us?"

Jamie shrugged. "Everything *I* know, *you* know."

"That's what scares me," muttered Grant.

"No, seriously." Jamie again ran a hand through his hair; again, Grant resented it. "It should be an easy job. I'd do it myself, but I'm not really a b-and-e kind of guy."

"Which doesn't mean your hands aren't dirty," snarled Grant.

Jamie was agitated. "You know, Grant, I could just grab my cab over there, go back to Manhattan, and find a *better* crook. A more *cooperative* crook."

"But still you're here. Bothering us."

"Well…" Jamie's expression clouded over, and his foot started playing with the crack in the sidewalk again. He'd come without a Plan B and only now realized that was a mistake. He said "Well…" again and then shut up.

After he'd let Jamie twist for an uncomfortably long period, Grant said, "Okay. Ten thousand dollars. You *say* a few hours' work, but what makes you so sure?"

Jamie rebounded quickly for a man with no Plan B. "Triple-C's chief of staff is also her son-in-law's campaign manager. *He's* the intermediary. Follow?"

"I not only follow, I'm already getting a headache."

"So this guy—Kevin; Kevin Wunder—well, I've gotten to know him on the Hamptons circuit, and—"

Grant stopped him. "Is he gay?"

"Kevin Wunder? No."

"Is this Peebles guy gay?"

A smile crossed Jamie's lips. "I *wish*! But no. Why?"

"Just trying to figure out what you have on these people."

Jamie seemed to be offended. Almost. If he wasn't so casually superficial, it might have worked.

"Grant, I'm *shocked*!" One hand went to his chest; the other, of course, to his hair. "I'm *friends* with Kevin Wunder, and I've *met* Austin Peebles, but I have no interior motives!"

Grant cocked an eyebrow. "*In*terior?"

Jamie tried to stare him down and failed miserably. "Not the right word?"

"*Ul*terior."

If Jamie had known the word "pedantic," he'd have used it at that moment. But he didn't, so he brushed it off.

"Interior...ulterior...close enough. Anyway, I'm just helping Kevin—and Triple-C, and Austin Peebles—as a friend. That's all. No sex. No drugs. No...no scams." Grant and Chase both noticed that brief verbal stumble. "Nothing like that."

"Uh-huh." Grant let his gaze drift down the row of beat-up brownstones lining the block before returning it to Jamie. "So this Wunder guy. Why'd he ask you?"

"I guess he figured I knew people."

Grant allowed himself a smile. "That means he's made you. Which means your latest Hamptons scam is almost over. Once you've helped them pull this job, you'd better find yourself a new carcass to feed on. Here's some free advice: Keep a little something on these people. Don't give it all up or you'll be finished." *And that*, he left unsaid, *is the nicest I've ever been to you, and the nicest I ever* will *be.*

Jamie ignored him—Grant was *so* negative sometimes—and turned to Chase. "So I suppose you're still good on a computer? Because I think we'll need someone who's good on a computer."

"I'm not ready to run an IT department, but I've got skills."

"Get to the point, Jamie," said Grant before Jamie had a chance to ask what IT meant. Or before Grant could, for that matter.

Jamie bit his lip. "It'd be easier if I let the guy explain it."

"The guy?"

"The guy who wants to hire you. The intermediary! Kevin Wunder!"

Grant scowled. "This Wunder better live up to his name."

CHAPTER THREE

Chase began his day early the next morning, leaving Grant embracing nothing but empty sheets while he went off to make an honest living. His job as assistant manager of the Groc-O-Rama in Elmhurst was soul-deadening and unfulfilling, but crime didn't pay bi-weekly and it was nice to know that there'd be a paycheck—albeit a small one—when times were lean. Plus there were benefits, another thing his side job didn't include.

Most people simply called it "The Gross," but while the market certainly lived down to its nickname, Chase was a loyal employee and had tolerated it for almost two decades. By him, and pretty much only him, the ratty store was always referred to by its full name.

If Groc-O-Rama left a lot to be desired besides the paycheck, benefits, and frequent interaction with inspectors from the departments of Health and Consumer Affairs, it still held a sentimental appeal to Chase. It was there he'd met Grant all those years ago. It had been kismet: a magical moment. They had both planned to break into the safe on the very same night, and met for the first time in the dark bakery aisle outside the manager's office. After the initial shock wore off, they'd teamed up, split five thousand dollars in loot, and been inseparable ever since.

Chase punched out eight hours later, collected Grant, and—just after nine o'clock that night—met Jamie in Manhattan at the entrance to an eight-story white-brick office building on Second Avenue in the low East Sixties a few blocks north of the Roosevelt Island tram station.

There was no guard on duty—it was the type of building where no guard had been hired to *be* on duty—so Jamie pushed the buzzer marked "U.S. Rep. Catherine C. Concannon District Office" a few times. They waited until the panel buzzed back at them, then pushed the front door open. On the other side of the door, the sparse lobby was adorned with utilitarian white-and-gray tile on the floor and a badly faded aqua paint job on the walls. Even Grant and Chase—longtime residents of a hardscrabble block on a rough edge of quickly gentrifying Jackson Heights—weren't impressed.

But that was the deal on the Upper East Side of Manhattan. There was a lot of wealth, but there was also a lot of ordinary. It was a hunting ground for social scavengers like Jamie Brock, and it definitely held a certain professional allure for people like Grant and Chase, especially when their favorite chop-shop was looking for a Mercedes. But a lot of the real estate was affordable. Despite the neighborhood's reputation as home base for Old Money, the Upper East Side's dirty secret was that Grant and Chase could have managed to scrape up the cash to live there if they had to. Fortunately for the residents who prized their cars, artwork, jewelry, electronics, furniture, and collectibles, they sort of liked Jackson Heights.

The elevator—barely big enough for the three of them and painted a faded aqua to match the lobby walls—slowly ascended to the fourth floor before it stopped, and they stood in silence for what seemed like hours but was more like seven seconds. When the door finally opened, a short, dark-haired man in his late thirties, wearing a blue pinstriped suit and red tie with gold eagles on it, stood in front of them, holding open a door off the hallway. He looked Grant and Chase over without bothering to hide his contempt and turned to Jamie.

"Inside."

Jamie smiled. "Grant and Chase, this is—"

"Inside," the man commanded again and walked into the office.

Grant hadn't caught a good look at much more than the tie, but when the man walked away, he could see a large round bald circle on the back of his head. That, and he was—as they say—broad in the beam.

"Wunder," Jamie whispered, a smile playing at the corner of his mouth.

"Figured that," Grant whispered back, with no smile playing anywhere.

The door had almost closed behind Wunder before it occurred to them to follow, and Chase caught it moments before they were locked in the hall. They entered a large reception room, big enough to comfortably hold a dozen disgruntled constituents of U.S. Rep.

Catherine C. Concannon, or more likely a comparable number of lobbyists.

Wunder kept walking, following a worn pattern on the cheap carpet, and they filed behind his broad beam through the shotgun layout of the suite of offices. He would flick a light switch, lead them into a room, lock the door behind them, and proceed to another room, where he'd repeat the process. The rooms themselves were basic—messy desks, battered filing cabinets, more than a few tiny American flags waving from decorative coffee cups—but that's not what interested Grant.

He eyed the locks.

They didn't look like they came with the office rental, and it seemed like Wunder was opening them with different keys. That was probably something he'd never *need* to know, but it was still *good* to know. And as a halfway decent lock man, he took a professional interest.

They went through the pattern of unlock-light-lock four times before reaching the last room. Grant noted the one door they'd bypassed, which had a classier brass knob and lock plate and a semicircular throw rug on the floor outside, and less wear to the carpet. He guessed it led to the congresswoman's private office. He also guessed she didn't spend too much time there. Again, it was probably something he didn't need to know, but sizing these things up was part of his character. Sort of like how he couldn't walk down a street without checking out which cars looked ready to steal, even if he wasn't shopping for a car at the moment. Those habits just came with the vocation.

In any event, once the lights were on and they'd been ushered into that fourth and final room, it was clear this was definitely *not* the congresswoman's office. It could have been a large closet if not for the small desk pushed into one corner, with four metal folding chairs arranged in front of it. Behind the desk was a decent-sized window that, the best Grant could tell in the darkness, seemed to overlook the windows across the alley and nothing else. Two walls were hidden behind floor-to-ceiling bookcases, with shelves bulging from heavy loads of law books, folders, and what looked to be lengthy computer printouts jammed haphazardly into whatever space they'd fit.

There was also a Derek Jeter bobblehead on one shelf, wobbling slightly in its plastic Yankees uniform from the movement in the room. Grant had no use for baseball, but—as a longtime resident of the Borough of Queens—still felt a vague sense of pride in the Mets. Meaning the bobblehead Yankee counted against this guy.

Wunder motioned for them to take seats. They did—although it was warm outside, the metal chairs were cold—and then he perched on the corner of the desk.

In the brief silence that ensued, Grant tried to figure out what tied Jamie to this guy. He didn't know what Jamie liked in a man, but Wunder—barely five foot six, if that; balding; sort of intense—didn't seem to fit the bill. Not on the surface, at least. Then again, Jamie was a scamming moth drawn to the flames of wealth and power, so who knew? Hadn't he had a fling a few years earlier with a much older Russian billionaire who was also a mobster? Yeah, Grant thought he had heard that rumor, so anything was possible where Jamie Brock was concerned.

The silence ended when Jamie leaned forward on his chair. "So these are the guys I was telling you about."

"I figured." Wunder looked at Grant and Chase, frowned, and got down to business. He was no-nonsense; Grant appreciated that. "Here's the deal." Even though they were locked behind four doors, he dropped his voice to a near whisper. "First thing, you should know who I am."

"I know," said Jamie, and Wunder's sneer erased any thought from Grant's head that there might be something between the men.

The "shuddup" that Wunder and Grant said in unison also provided them with an instant bonding experience. That moment was fleeting; after the briefest of smiles, Wunder turned that sneer on Grant.

Wunder smoothed his lapels and gave Jamie one last sneer before turning his full attention to Grant and Chase. "The name is Kevin Wunder." He tried to affect a tough-guy look, but it didn't really work on his small, doughy frame, especially while wearing a red tie with gold eagles on it. He pegged Grant as the leader, so he spoke mostly to him. "And you are?"

"Call me Grant. This here's Chase."

"Last names?"

"Doubt you'll need to know 'em."

Wunder's lips pulled back, exposing a glimpse of perfect teeth which were a few shades too white, and he chuckled. It was too throaty and labored to be convincing. "Fair enough, and good to meet you. I'm serving two masters here. First, I'm here as Representative Concannon's chief of staff—"

"You mean the congresswoman?" asked Grant.

Wunder's smile was dim. "*Representative*, if you please. It's the twenty-first century; we don't use gender-specific terms like 'congresswoman' anymore." He swallowed hard and tried to remember that some people evolved more slowly than others. "Anyway, I don't know how much Jamie has told you—"

"Nothing useful. Just enough to get us here."

Wunder chuckled; again, it was throaty and forced. "I assumed. Well, *Representative* Concannon is retiring at the end of her term, and her son-in-law is running to succeed her. Did Jamie tell you that?"

Grant nodded. "He tried."

"Bringing me to the second reason I'm here: I'm also that son-in-law's campaign manager."

Chase said, "In other words, you're neck-deep in whatever's going on."

"More than neck. Try 'over my head.' If we were just talking about my neck, I probably wouldn't need you."

"Maybe it wouldn't seem so bad if you were taller," said Jamie. "Then your head would be…" Grant thought it was supposed to be a joke, but maybe not. In any event, Jamie realized he'd gone too far and stopped talking, instead running one hand through his tousled hair. Grant tried not to notice.

Kevin Wunder cleared his throat, gave Jamie one more unappreciative sneer, and continued. "Here's our problem. Representative Concannon's son-in-law—*our* candidate for Congress—has gotten himself into a…well, into a compromising position."

Grant was tempted to let Wunder drag it out just to watch for any slip he might be able to use later, but he was more eager to move on and get to work. "We know, Wunder. This Peebles guy got himself a girl on the side. He tweetered some, uh, twits he shouldn't have. Now he's being blackmailed and you want the picture back, right?"

Wunder wasn't surprised Grant knew the basic story, figuring Jamie would have needed a hook to bring them in. He also wasn't surprised Grant had mangled the terminology. In mere minutes together, it had been easy to peg him as a technophobe. "Yes, he's been sexting."

"Been what?"

"Sexting."

Grant glanced at Derek Jeter on the bookshelf. He hated to admit he didn't know something—let alone do that repeatedly—so it was best to do it to a bobblehead.

"I give. What's sexting? Is that like twittering?"

Jamie was only too eager to answer, and Wunder was only too eager to let him answer. "That's what we've been talking about! Sexting is texting plus sex. It's when you take a naked picture of yourself with your camera phone and send it to someone."

"I get that, but I thought you said this Peebles was twittering."

"*Tweet*ing. But text or tweet, it's the same concept."

"So you can use your phone or tweeter or whatever to take pictures of your junk and just send it out to...*anyone* with an Internet?"

The others nodded emphatically, ignoring Grant's mangled concept of the Internet as an owned item.

Grant was having a hard time grasping the purpose of all this self-exposure. Since he'd spent his entire adult life off the grid, that wouldn't surprise those who knew him. "People really do that?"

"Yeah!" Jamie was a bit too enthusiastic.

Chase leaned forward, talking to his partner but keeping one wary eye on Wunder. "Remember that Internet, uh, *job* we were pulling for a while?"

"The one with the provocative pictures?" He tried to keep it vague, because there was no reason for Wunder to know more than he had to.

"That's the one. Well, a lot of those guys who sent us pictures were taking them with their camera phones. Get it now?"

"Huh." Grant frowned. "This is just another reason for me to not like phones." He looked Chase in the eye. "You text a lot. You ever do that sext thing?"

"Of course not," said Chase as his ears slightly reddened.

Grant frowned. He didn't miss a lot, and he had definitely not missed Chase's red ears. "We'll talk about that later." Then he finally returned his attention to Wunder. "Okay, so this guy's got some pictures out there you don't want anyone to see."

"Correct."

"And you want us to get 'em back, because if anyone sees them, he's not getting elected to Congress."

"Correct."

"Let me see the picture."

A phone was produced from Wunder's breast pocket. He punched a few buttons and handed it to Grant.

After he studied it for a few seconds—with Chase and Jamie looking over his shoulder—Grant finally said, "Yeah, that's a penis, all right."

"Sure is," Chase agreed.

"A nice one, too," said Jamie.

"Shuddup, Jamie." Grant looked away from the genitalia on the phone's screen. "But how are people gonna connect this penis to your candidate?"

Wunder took the phone, manipulated the screen, and handed it back. Now they could see the rest of the image…the part with a head.

"I don't think I should be looking at this. How old is this guy? Twelve?"

The politician heaved a sigh. "Twenty-seven. He only *acts* like he's twelve sometimes."

Grant thought about that. "If he's dumb enough to do something like this, maybe he doesn't even belong in Congress."

Wunder cleared his throat. "I'm not going to argue that point with you, Mister…?"

"We'll worry about my last name if I decide to take the job."

"Okay, *Grant*." Wunder's head was throbbing slightly as he took the phone back and set it behind him on the desk. He wasn't sure why this wasn't going more smoothly. "Austin Peebles is a smart enough man. He's very young—and therefore very impulsive—but he's smart enough. Unfortunately, even smart people do stupid things every now and then. And this is one of those times."

Grant understood. He'd had his own moments…especially whenever he took a job referred to him by Jamie Brock. "So who's got the photos now?"

"The opposition."

Grant's brow furrowed. "Like…China?"

Wunder chuckled again. That fake chuckle was starting to annoy Grant. "This isn't exactly an international incident. What happened is, Austin meant to send the picture to someone with whom he'd been having a flirtatious—but entirely platonic—online relationship, but accidentally sent it to the wrong person. He realized his mistake right away, but unfortunately not before an enemy—a *political* enemy— saved a copy. And now this *woman*"—he spat out the word—"is trying to use the photo to force Austin out of the race."

Chase, who was feeling left out of the important parts of the conversation, put himself into it. "So we have to get the photo away from this woman. The opposition."

"Correct. June Forteene."

Grant was puzzled. "Wait, it's September. You don't want us to pull this job until next summer?"

"No, June Forteene is the woman who has the photo."

"That can't be a real name," said Grant. He paused. "Can it?"

Wunder shook his head. "Her real name is Hillary Morris. She calls herself June Forteene. Named herself after Flag Day, obviously. She got no attention as Hillary Morris, but she gets tons of press, publicity, and speaking engagements as June Forteene, so now…she's not Hillary Morris anymore. She's become her blog."

"Her what?" Grant asked. "Blog?"

Wunder looked at Chase, then Jamie. "Is your friend stuck in 1995?"

Chase cast an indulgent smile at Wunder. "He's not really a computer guy. A blog is just a website, Grant. People have them to discuss food, travel, the media…whatever."

"And politics," added Wunder. "Lots and lots of politics. In this case, politics are her obsession. Specifically, jingoistic, flag-waving, right-wing politics. Hence, Hillary Morris's pseudonym: June Forteene. Get it?"

Grant shrugged. "Okay. Keep talking."

Wunder leaned back against the desk. "She hates Democrats, and she *really* hates the Concannon and Peebles families, and she *especially* hates Austin Peebles. I'm not sure there's much more to say. I need you to get into June Forteene's office, remove the photo of a certain penis from her computer, and…that's that. Although…"

"What?" asked Chase, when the pause dragged on too long.

"I will need to insist that you bring the photo back to me."

"What for?" asked Chase.

"Proof you actually got into her office and did what I'm paying you to do." He tried to smile; it didn't work. "If you don't bring me back proof, then I only have your word to go by. And, no offense, but you're professional criminals. I'm not sure how much I trust you."

Grant smiled, which wasn't really a reassuring look but was more reassuring than whatever had just flickered across Wunder's face. "You're a *politician*, Wunder. So how much should we trust you?"

"Touché, sir." Kevin Wunder stood, but his diminutive stature gave him only a few inches of advantage over the criminals seated before him on metal folding chairs. "I guess this is one of those cases where we'll have to operate on blind faith. I'll have to trust you, and you'll have to trust me." He extended his hand to Grant. "Deal?"

Grant looked at the outstretched hand. Then at the wrist. *Nice watch*, he thought.

"Before we shake, we should discuss terms. This sounds like a twenty-thousand-dollar job."

Wunder knit his brow and his extended hand slowly retracted to his side. "I was thinking more like five."

"Jamie told us ten." Grant and Chase folded their arms across their chests and settled back in their chairs. It was a synchronized move that was even more planned out than it appeared; they used it as a demonstration of solidarity and insistence whenever someone was giving them a hard time, especially about money. It didn't happen often, but it happened.

The politician studied their body language for a moment and decided to push the issue.

"Jamie heard wrong."

"What?" Jamie squawked and shifted in his folding chair. "I'm *sure* you said—"

Grant cut him off. "Maybe you should find yourself some cut-rate crooks, Mr. Wunder. The city is full of 'em."

"You have to understand..." Wunder affected a reasonable tone as he propped his wide ass back on the edge of the desk, which actually gave him a little bit more height and authority. "This is a political campaign. We're not in the pre-Watergate years anymore. We don't just have a stash of cash lying around. We have to run lean and mean, and every penny has to be accounted for."

"You make a good argument," said Grant. "But it's still a twenty-thousand-dollar job. Plus, we're only here because we were promised ten thousand dollars."

Wunder felt his forehead dampening. "Would you *take* ten?"

"No."

That reasonable tone began to crack and was peppered with an undertone of pleading. "You have to understand we're under constant scrutiny from the FEC and the media. *Constant.* I'd really like to ask you to cut me a break here. Do the job for five thousand and maybe down the road, after he's elected, future Representative Peebles will be helpful to you."

"You keep this up," said Grant, "it'll be a thirty-thousand-dollar job."

"All right, all right." Wunder threw up his hands. "I'll split the difference. Ten thousand."

"Ten is what brought us to the table. Now it sounds like twenty."

"Like I said, split the difference. Ten!"

Grant sighed. "First, I know my math. Ten thou ain't splitting the difference. Twelve-five would be splitting the difference between five and twenty. Ten thou is you trying to screw us. Second, the cost for our services is twenty."

Wunder shook his head. "I only need you to steal one tiny picture off a computer." He dropped his head, probably trying to seem boyish even though his boyish days were a solid decade in the past, as underscored by the bald circle he unknowingly revealed when he dropped his head. "One teeny, tiny picture."

"C'mon, Wunder." Grant frowned. "We both know it won't be that easy. I might not know what globs are—"

"Blogs," said Jamie.

"Shuddup. I might not know that, but I know that this photo is very valuable to you. I also know that if this July Fourth dame—"

"June Forteene," said Jamie.

"Did you not hear me tell you to shut up?" Jamie nodded. "Then shut *up!*" Grant turned his attention back to Wunder. "If this picture's that valuable—to you *and* to her—then you can bet she's got copies all over the place. That means we're gonna have to go through every computer file she's got, and maybe even her phone. That's the kind of thing that takes time, and time increases risk, and risk means..."

"More money." Wunder was deflated.

"More money," Grant agreed. "*You* see a five-thousand-dollar job and all we have to do is slip in and out. *We* see a twenty-thousand-dollar job that's gonna take time and involves a lot of risk." He paused, giving his words time to sink into Wunder's head. "So do we have a deal? Or do we walk?"

Kevin Wunder mulled that over. "I suppose so," he finally said.

"Twenty thousand?"

Wunder sighed. "I'll find it somewhere." This time when he extended his hand, Grant accepted it.

"Now that's out of the way, where do we find this July Fourth?"

"June Forteene." He'd accepted the higher price for their services, so Kevin Wunder was done playing games. Not that he was all that sure Grant was playing games, but still...

"Her office is on Eighth Avenue." He grabbed a notepad and jotted down the address, then handed it to Grant. "You know the Hell's Kitchen area?"

Chase took the piece of paper from Grant's hand and smiled pleasantly. "We know Hell's Kitchen."

"And where does she live?" Grant asked as he watched Chase pocket the slip of paper.

Wunder shrugged. "I don't know. Somewhere on the East Side, I think. Maybe Turtle Bay. Why?"

Chase answered for Grant. "She might have a backup of the picture at home. Meaning we might have to, uh, pay a visit to her apartment in order to complete this job, if you know what I mean." He smiled at Wunder and waited for a nod. He got it. "Can you get us the address?"

"I can try."

"It'd be helpful."

"It's *essential*," Grant said. "Because if she's hiding computer files in her apartment..."

Wunder started thinking for himself again. "Using that logic, couldn't she have a copy on a thumb drive locked in a safe deposit box, too?"

Grant nodded. "That's always a possibility...in which case you're on your own. Twenty K covers a sweep of her office and home, not a bank. A bank job will cost you, oh..." He pretended to calculate, although he was really mentally reciting song lyrics to himself, because there was no way anyone was breaking into a bank over this. If Wunder could've read his mind, Grant thought he might appreciate that.

Finally, when enough time had passed to make it seem as if he'd put real thought into it, he said, "A bank job will run you at least three hundred thousand. Maybe more."

Wunder swallowed hard. So hard that not only did the humans hear it, but even the Derek Jeter bobblehead moved.

"I understand."

"And," Grant added, "If we find anything in her apartment we want, we get to keep it."

"Uh, I..." Wunder felt his brown dampen again. "Okay."

Grant shook his head. "Sounds like you found yourself one hell of a candidate, Wunder."

Kevin Wunder's head hung low. "Not that it's any of your business, but that's how it works out sometimes. If I had been the candidate, none of this would have happened. But my last name isn't Peebles and I'm not married to a Concannon, so..." He looked up with a resigned half smile. "So I play the cards I'm dealt."

Since there was nothing else for them to discuss, and since Grant and Chase needed to get home and start figuring out how they were going to burglarize June Forteene's home and office, and since they were both getting a little jittery behind four locked doors, Grant decided it was time to get out of there.

"So if we could just get the deposit…"

Wunder hiked an eyebrow. "Deposit?"

"Yeah, the deposit. Fifty percent now, the rest when we bring you the photo."

"You're kidding, right?" Wunder laughed until he saw Grant wasn't kidding. "You don't understand the way this works. I thought I made it clear that we *don't* have cash on hand. This has all got to conform to the election laws and hold up to media scrutiny."

"So…" Grant tried to process that. "So how were you expecting to pay us?"

Wunder held his composure. "It's easy. After the job is done, you'll submit an invoice for consulting fees. You won't be itemizing the services you provided, of course. I'll make sure it's processed through the campaign committee right away, and you'll receive a check in four to six weeks."

Grant held up one hand. "Wait. Four to six weeks?"

"Yes."

"A *check*?"

"Why, of course."

Grant turned on Jamie. "Didn't you explain to this guy how things are done in our business?"

Jamie hunched his shoulders. "It didn't occur to me. But what's wrong with a check?"

"Checks leave a paper trail. Next thing you know, I'll have to pay taxes."

Wunder scrunched up his face. "Well, of *course* you'll have to pay taxes. It's earned income."

"It is, but it isn't."

"What Grant means," said Chase, his voice calmer but still every bit as alarmed as his partner, "is we don't want the IRS snooping into our business. Business that is sort of illegitimate, by government standards."

"Not to mention the standards of most of the rest of society," added Grant. "Except people who do what we do. Or people like you who hire people like us."

Kevin Wunder sat back down on the edge of the desk. "Gentlemen, you have to understand this from the campaign's perspective. There are laws—"

"Some of which you want us to break," said Grant.

"Look, maybe I can get the check expedited—"

"It ain't about the timing." Grant looked at a blank wall, which seemed to calm him. "I've waited longer to be paid for a job. I didn't like it, but I waited. This is not about the wait, it's about the way you want to pay us."

"Can't do it that way," Chase agreed.

"Well, then…" Wunder's voice drifted off and he stared at a yellowing ceiling tile somewhere above the wall Grant stared at. "It sounds as if we've just wasted each other's time."

They were all in reluctant agreement…until Jamie had a thought. "I can do it."

They looked at him and Jamie's face brightened. He liked being the center of attention.

"You could do *what*?" asked Grant. "Steal the picture?"

Jamie brushed his words away. "Not that. But I can be the middleman."

"Huh?"

"Sure! I'll invoice the job and the campaign can send the check to me. Then I'll make the payoff to you guys"—he indicated Grant and Chase—"and everything will look nice and legit."

Grant eyed him with a heightened level of suspicion. "What's your angle?"

"No angle. All I get out of the deal is my twenty percent finder's fee."

"Huh? You think it's worth four Gs just to process a check?"

Jamie shrugged. "I mean…I *assume* I'm getting a finder's fee for bringing you the job, right?" When Grant didn't answer, he mistakenly took that as agreement. "So think of this service as a bonus I'm providing you for no extra fee."

"I think of it," said Grant, "as Jamie Brock getting twenty percent for not doing a damn thing. That's how *I* think of it."

"I really wish you'd look at the positives here." Jamie ran a hand through his hair, making Grant grip the edge of his seat so tightly his knuckles turned white. "You'll still get sixteen thousand dollars. Tax-free!"

"And you're paying the taxes out of your share?"

"Nah. I always operate a couple of businesses at a loss, so *I* won't end up having to pay taxes either."

"*You* have businesses?" That made no sense to Grant. "*You're* a businessman?"

Jamie made a little motion with his head in the direction of Wunder. "I'd rather not go into all that right now."

"I wouldn't worry about that," said Grant. "I figure this guy's got your number already."

For his part, Wunder held up his hands to stop the back-and-forth, and was more than a little surprised it worked. "I really don't need to know these details." He stood again, growing shorter in the process. "Just make this happen."

Grant turned to Chase and didn't bother to mute his voice. "Think we can trust Jamie?"

"I think we have to." Chase stared down Jamie. "Of course, if he tries to screw us, we know where he lives."

Grant frowned but nodded at Wunder. "I guess we've got a deal."

Those beads of sweat that had been forming on-and-off on Kevin Wunder's brow had been on again, but now he happily wiped them away. "That's great. I'm sure you'll do a fantastic job, Mister…?"

"First names will do, Wunder. You just find out where this June whatever lives, and hopefully you'll never have to trouble yourself with any of the details."

Kevin Wunder readily agreed it would be better that way.

CHAPTER FOUR

When the criminals were finally gone, Kevin Wunder poured a generous dollop of sanitizer on his hands and rubbed briskly. The worst part, he realized, was that after almost two decades in politics, they weren't even the seamiest characters he'd ever dealt with.

He'd raised a lot of campaign money from Bernie Madoff. He'd negotiated legislation with Jack Abramoff. He'd even come far too close to being an alternate delegate for John Edwards at the 2004 Democratic National Convention.

No, these criminals weren't the seamiest by far.

He almost had to give them credit for being more up front than many of the memorable people who'd been part of his political life. There was none of the backslapping, "how-the-hell-are-you" bonhomie that masked an agenda. None of the wink-and-nod quid pro quo. None of the tell-you-one-thing-do-another outright lying.

The criminals had been very direct and straightforward: They would do a job, and they would do it for twenty thousand dollars. In a very begrudging way, he had to respect that.

The difference was that Kevin Wunder *understood* political treachery and double-dealing and backstabbing and promises that were never intended to be fulfilled. He'd been immersed in it for almost twenty years, after all, and a person didn't survive an immersion in politics if he didn't understand the rules.

But he did not understand the rules of the underworld in which these criminals plied their trade. He was sure there had to be a set of rules—even crooks needed to operate with some basic order—but those were beyond his comprehension. Fortunately, he had no desire to learn them, which was why this job had been outsourced.

He began the process of turning off lights and locking doors behind him. It had been a long day, and he was looking forward to spending the rest of his evening in solitude at his apartment, which was only a twenty-block walk away.

Kevin Wunder always did his best plotting in solitude.

With "Wunder" as his surname, it was inevitable that people would call him "Boy Wunder." That taunt had started in grade school, continued through high school, and probably would have hit a peak in college if he hadn't gotten involved in politics, which is where the nickname peaked instead.

Kevin Wunder had been a young man in a hurry when he arrived on the New York political scene as a college senior and was tagged "Boy Wunder" within the first five minutes of his first campaign. For a while, he'd tolerated it with good humor on the surface. In time, though, as his connections solidified and he gained a reputation as a political operative—along with an increasing degree of political power—he grew much more comfortable expressing his displeasure at the nickname.

Soon, people called him "Boy Wunder" only behind his back. They still used the nickname as frequently as ever; he just didn't hear it, and therefore didn't know about it, and therefore was fine with the situation.

As predictable as the nickname was, in recent years it wasn't all about the predictability. Sometimes it was about the irony. As time passed, the term "Boy Wunder" began to take on an increasingly biting tone. Now that he was in his late thirties, balding, and could stand to lose a few pounds, Kevin Wunder was no longer a young man in a hurry, let alone a boy. Time had caught up to him and threatened to pass him by. Now he was more or less a conventional political operative and strategist, his status no different from any of several hundred other thirty-something men and women who were doggedly good at their jobs but not individually exceptional.

Kevin Wunder had lost the exceptionalism that defined his twenties. He was no longer a rising star. He was no longer a Young Turk. He was even starting to edge out of the late bloomer demographic. Now he was just…average.

Not only was there nothing "boy" about him, there was little wonderful about him anymore but his surname.

It was bad enough that he knew it. It was even worse that everyone else did, too.

Those years in the not-too-distant past—when his name was on everybody's lips as an up-and-comer and the term "Boy Wunder" had not yet acquired such cruel irony—were his glory days. He still found himself reliving them in his head more often than was probably healthy. He was becoming the white-collar equivalent of the high school quarterback who was unable to let go of Big Game memories as he settled his middle-aged bulk into a La-Z-Boy with a six-pack of Bud and two canisters of Pringles.

During those glory days, the conventional wisdom predicted he'd soon be elected to the state legislature, or maybe even a congressional seat. He'd most likely have a long and powerful career ahead of him. And while no one actually *said* the words "President of the United States" out loud, Kevin suspected they had thought it. He certainly knew *he* had.

But every life has its twists and turns. Kevin Wunder's life had been no exception.

The biggest twist that stymied his advancement was incumbency. Every elected official in his base on the Upper East Side of Manhattan seemed determined to remain an incumbent until death, or until they could figure out a way to hold their seats *after* death. The state legislators and congressional representatives had no term limits, and the city council members kept finding a way around them. And the voters, well…the voters *loved* their incumbents—mostly because they recognized their names—and kept returning them to office over and over and over again.

The incumbents would remain in office forever. The incumbents would never die. Occasionally, one might get indicted, but the incumbents usually beat the rap. The path to career advancement veered away from him at every turn, effectively shutting him out.

Still, Wunder had to try to position himself for the future—just in case—so he accepted a job as Representative Catherine Cooper Concannon's chief of staff. Which soon became his second obstacle, because once he'd become a behind-the-scenes player for Triple-C, he became invisible.

It wasn't Triple-C per se. It was the nature of the job. She'd been a Member of Congress since her husband died, and *he'd* been a Member of Congress since his *father* died, and so on. The Concannon legacy extended back through generations, and their aides—even talented aides like Kevin Wunder—were looked on as little more than family mouthpieces.

The words out of his mouth were the words she wanted him to convey. His positions on the issues were her positions. The campaigns he advised were for her candidates. And even in those extremely rare moments when he spoke his own mind, it was just assumed that he was speaking for Triple-C. The years and his ties to the Concannon political dynasty had conspired to change him from a young man in a hurry and an *un*ironic "Boy Wunder" into little more than a talented servant with a bald spot and bulging midsection.

It was hard not to be bitter.

He contented himself by believing that there would be a payoff. Triple-C wasn't getting any younger, and thanks to fertility problems she was almost the last member of the Concannon bloodline. She had one daughter, but Penelope—very attractive and just thirty years old—had almost no interest in politics.

Better yet, Penelope was already making a fortune in the financial sector, thanks in no small part to the family ties that landed her the job and kept her connected to a pool of wealthy investors. It was inconceivable she'd give up a high seven-figure annual salary to humble herself in elected office simply to carry on a family tradition that began during the New Deal.

Which meant Kevin Wunder's payoff would, one day, be Catherine Cooper Concannon's congressional seat. Triple-C had all but promised it.

"Kevin," she'd say every now and then as they rode the Acela home from Washington, "you would make a very effective Member of Congress."

Okay, so that wasn't exactly a formal endorsement. But it was a step in the right direction.

Then the career train again jumped off the rails. Penelope had the bad sense to meet Austin Peebles, the young son of one of Triple-C's close colleagues in the House, and Kevin Wunder's last hope for relevance vanished in less time than it took to say "I do."

That seemed to have happened so far in the past that Wunder frequently had to remind himself that Austin had been in his life—in *all their* lives—for less than two years.

The bastard.

Austin was the scion of the Peebles family, Mainline Philadelphia's answer to the Concannons of the Upper East Side of Manhattan. Austin's father had been in Congress since 1981, when he succeeded *his* father, first elected the same year Jack Kennedy won the presidency.

That also happened to be the year Triple-C's father-in-law—Langdon Concannon Jr.—was first elected to the House of Representatives. Apparently 1960 had been a watershed year for the advancement of that most marginalized sector of the American public: members of East Coast political dynasties.

Like the Concannons and Kennedys, the Peebles' roots in public life extended decades into the past. But no one would have pegged Austin—like Penelope Concannon, the last of the genetic line—as a likely candidate to carry the family tradition of noblesse oblige into the future. Even the Peebles family didn't expect that.

And certainly *no one* would have ever expected young Austin to be the man destined to combine the Peebles *and* Concannon legacies. That two of the most politically powerful families in the Northeast had been unified was improbable; that Austin Peebles would become their standard bearer was nothing short of bizarre.

It certainly wasn't unknown for very young people to be elected to office—even the United States Congress—but there was nevertheless a process to be followed. Dues had to be paid, even when a candidate bore a name like Peebles or Concannon. There were issues to be studied, advisers to be consulted, good deeds to be done, political grunt work to be grunted out. The young Kennedys and Concannons and Peebleses who had been elected to office were educated, thoughtful, and dedicated to the ideal of public service. They carried a certain air of gravitas, even if they were only twenty-something years old.

That was the way Kevin Wunder had played the game when "Boy Wunder" was still an apt nickname instead of a laugh line. Except, in his case, he lacked an important and storied surname. The Wunders of Metuchen, New Jersey, were unfortunately not known as a dominant family on their block, let alone in American politics.

But a grasp of the issues, a coterie of advisers, a history of good deeds, an air of gravitas…Austin Peebles had none of that when he met Penelope Concannon. And, if possible, he had less of it even as Triple-C determined he should be the heir to her congressional seat. For some reason known only to herself—an unknown reason Wunder found galling—Catherine Cooper Concannon thought her callow son-in-law was "charming" and "a natural leader."

What Kevin Wunder saw was quite different. Austin was twenty-seven years old and acted younger. He had been an average student at Brown, which was hardly a disqualification from public office but also didn't quite establish him as a burning intellect whose ideas would transform Washington DC and eventually lead to economic stability and world peace. He had not discussed important issues at the knee of his father and grandfather—Austin had been too busy with video games and downloadable porn—and even as he began his campaign for Congress, his positions were reflexive, unformed, and generally naïve.

And as for charitable interests and good deeds, well...

Kevin Wunder's first job as campaign manager—a job he'd taken on at Triple-C's direction and performed with a professional gusto that masked his loathing for both the task and the candidate—had been to send him out as a volunteer for a soup kitchen, figuring that, at least, would be something the campaign could point at when the inevitable questions arose about the candidate's commitment to those less fortunate than his pampered self. Somehow, Austin had managed to forget the obligation in the two hours between the scheduling of the shift and the actual shift, and instead took Penelope to Per Se for one of the most expensive dinners served that evening in the developed world.

The incident actually caused a minor scandal when a camera crew showed up at the soup kitchen and discovered Austin Peebles was missing in action. The charity's director tried to cover—mostly because Triple-C had not only been a generous individual donor over the years, but she had also funneled hundreds of thousands of federal dollars into the program—but Austin's absence was seized on by his primary election opponent, an uncharacteristically ethical—but characteristically self-righteous—state legislator who was perhaps the only person more frustrated about the Peebles candidacy than Kevin Wunder.

The Peebles campaign went into damage control mode and the next day the front page of the *Daily News* featured a photo of Austin reading to blind orphaned puppies. The public uttered a collective *awwww*, the state legislator almost had an aneurysm, and two weeks later Austin Peebles won the Democratic primary election by a four-to-one margin, all but ensuring his victory in November.

Until the photos of his penis—with Austin's smug smile in the background—surfaced a few months later.

The most frustrating thing, Wunder thought as he neared his apartment building on East Eighty-first Street, wasn't the candidate's callowness. Nor was it the lack of maturity and judgment that would lead a grown man, let alone a candidate for the United States House of Representatives, to take a photo of his erection—and face—and tweet it into the ether.

No, the most frustrating thing was the way everyone seemed to *love* him.

He may have been a hollow shell, but he was a hollow shell that drew people in. Every mother wanted to protect him…every father wanted to play catch with him…every young woman wanted to muss his hair…every young man wanted to be his best friend—unless they were gay, in which case they wanted to be his best friend *and* muss his hair.

Everybody just loved Austin Peebles.

Everybody *except* Kevin Wunder.

Although…it was not *just* Kevin Wunder who had a problem with Austin Peebles. Not every day, at least.

For a few days, United States Representative Catherine Cooper Concannon did *not* love Austin Peebles. In fact, she barely liked him.

He had hurt and embarrassed her daughter, and that made her angry. It was a natural, motherly instinct. Penelope was, perhaps, far more materialistic than she'd raised her to be, but she was still her only daughter. And she knew this much: For all Penelope's knee-jerk, selfish, "it's mine" approaches to life and public policy, when her daughter hurt, Catherine Cooper Concannon hurt.

Once, decades earlier, her late husband Newley Concannon—then a congressman himself—had cheated on her with a secretary in her early twenties improbably named Arabetta *Something* who worked for Tip O'Neill. It took her years to forgive him.

Catherine was also disappointed on another, more personal level. Austin was not only her son-in-law, and he was not only the son of her close colleague. He was also her hand-picked successor. Fairly or not, his immature actions reflected unfavorably on her. If the news got out, it would almost seem as if Catherine Cooper Concannon condoned taking photos of one's engorged genitals and putting them on the Internet.

Not to mention, she was now the person who had to clean up the mess.

Thank God she had Kevin Wunder—loyal Kevin!—to help.

For a few days, Austin slipped quietly around the edges of her life. She appreciated that he understood he was in the doghouse and why he was there, and that he had the good sense to try to be invisible in her presence. It showed a sense of good judgment so sorely lacking when he'd taken that photo.

But Catherine Cooper Concannon was, ultimately, a forgiving woman. She'd forgiven Bill Clinton, Henry Hyde, Newt Gingrich, Anthony Weiner...As an Episcopalian, she felt she had no choice but to forgive the repentant. Not immediately, of course—she was no Unitarian—but sooner, rather than later.

There was no reason she couldn't forgive Austin, too.

Plus, well...She caught a glimpse of the young man—her son-in-law; her *heir*—before he could duck out of sight when she exited the library of the sprawling Park Avenue pre-war co-op she owned and shared with Penelope and Austin. *Look at him*, she thought. *He's such a naïve puppy.* And that reminded her of how he'd read to the blind orphaned puppies, which made her think, *Awwww.*

"Austin!" He'd almost managed to disappear into the kitchen when her patrician voice stopped him half-in, half-out of the doorway. He froze. "Come here, Austin."

He did, hanging his head to convey shame as he slowly trudged toward her. She guided him back into the library and pushed the Department of Homeland Security report she'd been reading to the floor before motioning him to join her on the couch. She'd read most of it and was sure Janet Napolitano would fill her in on anything she'd missed.

She wasn't quite certain how to start the conversation, so she opted to be direct, blunt, and tough. "You were a very naughty boy, Austin Peebles."

He lifted his head and his lashes fluttered. His voice was soft and penitent. "I know, Catherine."

Well, that *wasn't so difficult*, she thought, and a slight twinkle came to her eye. "I thought we agreed you'd call me 'Mother.'"

His smile was one of relief. "I know, *Mother.*"

"That's better." She sighed. "So about that photo that's causing such a commotion around here..." She was almost seventy years old and a little too decent to describe it in further detail.

He shook his head; limp hair fell over his forehead. "I was just fooling around. I never thought it'd become an ish."

He'd lost her. *"Ish?"*

"Sorry. *Issue.*" He stood, placing his hands on his narrow hips covered by jeans that seemed to the United States Representative to be a full size tighter than skintight. "I promise it won't happen again, Mother."

She wanted to believe him, even as she recognized his impulsive nature was part of the charm that had attracted Penelope and who knew how many other women. "I hope not, Austin. You hurt some people because of this escapade."

He looked at her with brief confusion. Then he got it. "Oh, right. *Penelope!*"

"Who is, remember, your wife. *And* my daughter."

Austin's eyelashes fluttered again. "Right. Yeah, that was bad. She's still not talking to me."

Catherine wanted to defend her daughter's anger, but…really, what *was* Penelope's problem? Any woman knew that when you married a younger, charming, slightly caddish man like Austin Peebles, you were introducing a bit of devilry into the union. Penelope should have seen that going in and prepared herself to roll with the occasionally choppy waters.

"I'll try to talk to her," she heard herself say, and—when her brain caught up with her mouth—decided that *yes*, she would! Penelope had married a fine young man—a bit of a devilish cad, perhaps, but nevertheless a fine young man—and she'd have to learn to appreciate him as he was.

And honestly, her daughter had been acting so negatively toward Austin ever since he'd made his mistake. True, taking the time to pull down your pants and snap a photo of your genitals, then sending that photo to a total stranger, was a bit more egregious of a mistake than forgetting to buy eggs at the market, but Penelope's petulance was over the top. She knew what she was getting when she married Austin—the good *and* the bad—and now it was time to be a Big Girl and move on with life.

In a sense, she was acting very much like Kevin Wunder had acted when he first brought the blackmail attempt to Catherine's attention and showed her the picture. She'd instructed him to take care of the problem, but he had demurred.

"Austin created the problem. He should be the one who cleans it up," Kevin had said.

Catherine Cooper Concannon had no idea why Kevin seemed to be so hostile toward Austin. Maybe he was going through some personal problems. He was pushing middle-age, balding, overweight, and alone, so it wasn't out of the realm of possibility.

But she took control and changed her request to a demand. Still, he claimed he had no idea how to get the photo back from that loathsome blogger. Fortunately, nine full terms in the House of Representatives—

plus that extra seven months after Newley died—had given her a worldliness he seemed to lack.

"You don't have to do it yourself, Kevin. This city is full of grifters and criminals. Hire a professional!"

"But how am *I* going to find a criminal?"

It took her no more than ten seconds to come up with an answer. "Remember that Jimmy fellow I couldn't get away from last summer when I was in Montauk? The one I kept hiding my jewelry from? I'm sure you met him."

He scratched his ear. "Jimmy? Not ringing a..." Then the memory kicked in. "You mean *Jamie*? Jamie Brock?"

She smiled. "That's the one. I can guarantee he associates with the type of person you need to look for."

She hated that she always had to do *all* the thinking. That was one reason Kevin would never be in Congress, even if she did occasionally humor him during long train trips between New York and Washington. He had no imagination. No *charisma*!

Austin, though...well, *he* had it! Once he settled down—and she had no doubt Penelope would eventually domesticate him—he'd be a fine public servant. He needed discipline but had charisma in spades. One could learn discipline, but charisma was a God-given gift. It could not be learned.

As a young woman, her father-in-law—an earlier Congressman Concannon—had introduced her to Jack Kennedy. *He* had it. So did Bill Clinton and Ronald Reagan. When they talked to you, it felt as if the two of you were the only people in the room.

Austin Peebles had it, too.

The U.S. Representative patted her son-in-law with the God-given gift lightly on the shoulder.

"I'll talk to Penelope."

His smile was shy; his thick lashes fluttered again. "Thank you so much, Mother."

He's such a fine young man, she thought again. *We're lucky to have Austin Peebles in our lives.*

If anyone had asked Austin why he'd taken and tweeted the picture—asked in words other than "Why the hell did you do that?" that is, since plenty of people had asked *that* way—he doubted he'd be able to come up with a better explanation than "I just wanted to."

It wasn't as if sexting was anything new to him. Sometimes he did it because he was bored; sometimes because he was horny. He'd been sexting since prep school and saw nothing wrong with it. It was just another manifestation of his sexuality.

As a sexual creature—a *highly* sexual creature—Austin Peebles had been seeking new experiences and repeating old ones for over a decade, ever since he was fifteen years old and lost his virginity during a visit to the Cannon House Office Building to a much older woman with the improbable name of Arabetta who used to work for Tip O'Neill. Afterward, when she'd come to her senses and realized she'd committed the statutory rape of a congressman's son, she begged him not to tell anyone. She needn't have worried; he didn't kiss and tell then, and still didn't twelve years later.

The thing was, he could afford to kiss and not tell. Austin was born with a natural self-confidence that gave him a sort of immunity from social pressure. From a very young age—well before the romp with Arabetta in a supply closet—he knew who he was, and he knew people were drawn to him. He knew he was a sexual creature before he even knew what sex was. He had nothing to prove—to himself or anyone else—so while there was every reason to kiss, there was never a reason to tell.

That uncomplicated attitude about sex did, on occasion, lead to complications. Often his partners were less able to just let go than he was. Sometimes he was struck by the seriousness others brought to the act when his attitude was so casual. And every now and then it blew back at him.

The most recent sext was one of those times.

When sex had negative ramifications, he was usually comfortable moving on. The partners who wanted more eventually got used to the fact that what they'd had was all they were going to get, and those who turned the act into something of great importance were easy to forget as he walked away. If a naked camera phone photo happened to get passed around, he really didn't much care, as long as he looked good in the picture. Since he always photographed well, that was never really an issue.

But this latest image had gotten into the wrong hands, which changed the dynamic. And he was no longer just "a guy"; he was a congressional candidate. Suddenly, it was no longer an indiscretion he could nonchalantly walk away from. Now everyone wanted to make a big deal about it.

Especially his wife.

When they'd married two years earlier, he suspected it was a mistake. She didn't seem to share his values, and although his first instinct was now proving correct, it was far too late to do anything about it. Yes, they'd had fun when they were dating, but Penelope was hardly a tigress in bed. She was a cuddler, and needy, and clingy, and, well...*serious*. In short, she was the embodiment of everything he'd walked away from since the fling with Arabetta.

But suddenly he was engaged, and a few short months later he was married. And now they were stuck with each other.

And he barely understood how any of that had happened. Just that it was his father's fault. His father's *and* Mother Concannon's.

Their parents had been friends since Catherine was elected to replace her husband following his massive heart attack during an impassioned speech on trade policy with New Zealand. Newley Concannon had obviously been the only person in Washington to feel passionate about trade with New Zealand. Ever.

Their desks were next to each other on the House floor, and eventually they became inseparable whenever Congress was in session. Some of the more gossip-oriented members and staffers thought the widow and widower might even be in a relationship, but nothing could have been further from the truth. They respected each other and liked each other's company, but that was as far as things went or ever would go.

Since their son and daughter—the last of the Peebles and Concannon lineages, respectively—were roughly the same age, the Representatives took some of the same energy they used to serve a combined total of more than one million Americans and funneled it into matchmaking. No one but them saw it as a natural fit—Penelope was a few years older and serious-minded; Austin was aimless and a little too confident for his own good—but no one else had a vote on the matter. Representative Concannon (D-NY) and Representative Peebles (D-PA) had made the decision, voted on it, and signed it into law.

In fact, the decision was not made cavalierly. Catherine Cooper Concannon thought Penelope needed to loosen up, and Neil L. Peebles III thought Austin needed some grounding. By pairing them up, the parents hoped that each child's strengths would help balance the other child's weaknesses.

Left to themselves, the romance would have quickly faded. Austin and Penelope liked each other enough, just not passionately enough to marry. But forces beyond their control propelled them forward, and the decision was out of their hands.

After the wedding, the newlyweds moved into the Concannon home on Park Avenue. Penelope went off to earn a lot more than a living, and Catherine took the time to slowly groom Austin to be her successor at some point in the indefinite future. She quickly learned he had no aptitude for substantive public policy, but couldn't think of a reason why that should hinder him. She'd been in Washington long enough to know that no one had ever been held back in the House of Representatives for being a policy lightweight.

Which was how Austin Peebles became a fixture in the Concannon family and Manhattan. If Penelope was career-driven, emotionally distant, and increasingly passionless, at least he had a nice place to live, great clubs to visit, and a clear career path whenever his mother-in-law decided to pack it in and retire.

He also had his indomitable self-confidence.

And his camera phone.

When he was locked into his apartment on East Eighty-first Street, Kevin Wunder made three calls.

The first was to Catherine Cooper Concannon, who was relieved to know he'd found some people who could make their problem go away and urged him to do so at once. He reassured her he was on it.

The next was to the campaign treasurer. She'd have to know an invoice would be forthcoming from Jamie Brock's sham company.

That the campaign treasurer's name was Penelope Concannon Peebles—daughter of Catherine, wife of Austin—didn't especially bother him. Quite the contrary, given present circumstances. If he was destined to be frustrated, it was nice to have company.

"Let him rot," said Penelope when Wunder explained about the invoice. "My husband got himself into this mess, and he should get himself out."

"I understand how upset you must be—"

"No!" Even though he couldn't see her, he knew Penelope's stylish blond hair was being thrown around furiously. "You can't possibly understand. And now you want to pay a group of criminals twenty thousand dollars to save his ass?"

He chose his words judiciously. Penelope was upset at that moment, but she'd probably soften over time. It wouldn't do him any good to say something in this phone call that could come back to haunt him a few days, or months, or even years down the road.

"This is your mother's idea." He said it reverently, as if an idea conceived by Catherine Cooper Concannon could only be brilliant.

"My mother has an inexplicable old-lady crush on that horny little twerp."

For her benefit, he acted as if she hadn't said a word, even as he memorized each syllable. "You know how important the family name is to her. It may not seem like it right now, but this is her way to protect you, not Austin."

There were few moments of silence finally shattered by Penelope's strangled "Argh!" Muffled primal scream behind her, she calmly said, "Okay, fine, I'll do what I have to do. But I'm still not talking to him!"

"Who could blame you?"

Wunder ended the call and then dialed a third number. A third woman.

The most important woman he'd speak to that evening.

CHAPTER FIVE

Good morning, and welcome to *Sunday Roundtable*. I'm your host—Morton Miller the Third—and joining me to review and debate the week's hot topics are…"

Miller ticked them off:

"Former City Councilman Garrett Drew." The half-asleep older man leaning away from the desk on Miller's far right managed to raise an eyebrow in recognition of his name. He'd once been an energetic public official…and John V. Lindsay had once been mayor.

"Marilyn Belkin, executive director of the Northeast Policy Center on Economic Freedom." The prim woman next to the half-asleep former councilman forced her mouth into something resembling a cartoonist's squiggle. From her discomfort, the casual viewer would never suspect that under the cover of Internet anonymity, she was a far-right pit bull who'd been banned from scores of websites.

"Father Louis Appanello, president of Americans Against Evolution." On the host's far left, the young priest winked inappropriately at the camera and flashed movie-star teeth. He wasn't known as Father Hollywood for nothing.

"And finally, to my left, prominent community activist and blogger June Forteene."

When the camera found June Forteene, she stared directly at it, as if it were an enemy. Her face, framed by long black hair, bore an expression that was no friendlier. It was a face her mother used to say would be *so pretty* if she'd only take a Xanax and chill the fuck out. Which were often her mother's exact words as she popped her second Xanax.

Morton Miller III, a staple on this television station since early in the second Eisenhower Administration, pulled at the knot in his expensive tie, cleared his throat, and brushed away the thought of how much he disliked every single one of his guests and had for at least the past decade. Finally he scrunched his mouth in an approximation of a smile that made the squiggle on Marilyn Belkin's face look positively glowing.

"Thank you to the members of our panel for being here this morning. I'd like to start off our discussion by asking for your thoughts on one of the biggest and most controversial news stories of the week—"

"The Times Square Mosque."

The host frowned slightly and looked at his guests to see who'd interrupted him. His eyes settled on June Forteene.

"Actually," he said, his ordinarily smooth baritone edged with more than a hint of disdain, "I was referring to the city's new plans for bike lanes on the Long Island Expressway."

June Forteene didn't care about his disdain. Her Daily Affirmation was "Bulldoze ahead." She turned to face him, her hair unmoving and dark eyes staring him down. "With all due respect, *Morton*"—the emphasis she put on his first name suggested everything *but* the due respect he figured he deserved from this whippersnapper—"the most important news story facing this city is the Times Square Mosque."

Miller's already tenuous smile faltered, but he rallied it back to his lips. "According to polls, this mosque—which, I should add, is being built on Eleventh Avenue and Fifty-fourth Street, several long blocks west from Times Square, and several more blocks north—has substantial community support, whereas the bike lanes—"

"The Times Square Mosque is an affront to all New Yorkers." The segment producer, not used to people interrupting Morton Miller, was late in cueing the camera operator, so they only caught her as she finished. "A finger in the eye of decency."

Former Councilman Garrett Drew stirred a bit. "I'd like to talk about the bike lanes."

June offered up an icy smile and shook her head so slowly it couldn't have been more apparent she was mocking him if she'd announced it. "Of course you would. The power structure in this city— from the mayor on down—would love nothing more than to distract New Yorkers from contemplating the danger posed by the Times Square Mosque."

Miller tried to take back the conversation, swiveling toward former councilman Drew. "The bike lane proposal has been quite controversial—"

"You want controversy, Morton?" The host sighed and reluctantly swiveled back. "Think of how controversial it'll be when eight million New Yorkers are forced to live under Sharia law."

He closed his eyes for a brief moment and decided to fire the person who booked *Sunday Roundtable* guests the minute the cameras were off. "I don't think—"

"That," she continued, thumping one lacquered nail against the desk, "is the problem. No one in power is *thinking*."

Morton Miller III turned to the panelists on his right. "Does anyone else have thoughts on the bike lanes? To me, it seems dangerous to install bike lanes on the Long Island Expressway. Does anyone agree?"

Uncomfortably, Father Appanello piped up from his seat on the far left, even though Miller wasn't looking at him. "Well...it does. Yes, it does seem like a very dangerous situation. Bicyclists, fast-moving motor vehicles—"

"More dangerous than Sharia law?" The priest, physically cut off from the other, slightly less aggressive panelists, was at June's mercy. "Are you prepared to be stoned for your beliefs, Father?"

He began sweating. "Well...uh...I think the Muslims also oppose the teaching of evolution, so we have a commonality of..."

"That's *not* what I mean!"

A tic had developed under Morton Miller III's left eye. He glanced at Mrs. Belkin, who sat next to him and seemed to want to disappear. "Any thoughts on this subject before we change topics?"

"No." She was scared. This wasn't the Internet. Later that day she'd boot up her computer and take up June's cause under several of her screen names, but she'd *never* be so crass and unladylike to do it on camera.

"Good."

"I want to talk about bike lanes," said former councilman Drew before June Forteene leaned forward into the desk, turned her head in his direction, and shut him down with a piercing stare.

Morton Miller III sighed. "Okay, now that we've covered the Eleventh Avenue Mosque—"

"The *Times Square* Mosque."

"—and the bike lane proposal, let's move on to a new topic. Last

June, voters across the city selected candidates for congress in primary elections, and a few interesting races are shaping up. Councilman Drew, as the only member of our panel with experience in elected office, do you have any thoughts?"

Drew managed to open his eyes, although they started to slowly droop back to that half-closed position as he spoke. "Yes, I do. As usual, most of the incumbents running for reelection will be back on the ballot. But there are a handful of interesting new faces this year."

"Such as?"

"I'm sort of impressed by young Austin Peebles, who's campaigning to replace his mother-in-law—Catherine Cooper Concannon—on Manhattan's East Side. As you know, Morton"—the host didn't mind the familiarity from *him*; they were practically contemporaries—"the Concannon and Peebles names have been prominent in national politics for decades, and Austin Peebles now has an opportunity to make his own imprint on Washington. He's very young, of course, but he also seems smart and enthusiastic. He has the potential to go places."

June piped up. "Morton."

He ignored her and kept his attention on the former councilman. "Interesting. But couldn't he also be considered to be too inexperienced?"

Garrett Drew again managed to raise his eyelids and chortled. "Weren't we all young once, Morton? One can legitimately think Austin Peebles is *too* young—I don't happen to share that view—but no one can say he doesn't come from a long legacy of—"

"Austin Peebles isn't going anywhere!"

Recognizing June Forteene's voice—they *all* recognized it by now, and would probably hear it in their sleep—the host and other panelists sighed and tried to find something interesting to look at on the floor.

"And legacy shmegacy!" she added, bulldozing ahead.

Ten seconds of silence followed before Miller finally lifted his head, and only then because such a long interlude of silence made for very bad television and an even worse radio simulcast. "Okay, why not?"

She allowed herself a smug smile, which didn't make her nearly as pretty as her mother's second Xanax would have, but was an improvement.

"I can't tell you. Not yet. Let's just say you should watch my blog for a bombshell that will be coming in the next few days."

Morton Miller III hoped this woman was making the most of her appearance on *Sunday Roundtable*, because she wouldn't be coming back to his show.

Well…not unless she brought viewers. He made a mental note to check the show's ratings before making any final decisions.

Sitting together on a couch that had seen better decades in their apartment in Jackson Heights, Grant looked away from *Sunday Roundtable* on the big-screen television they'd recently picked up from Costco for a steal. Literally.

"So that's the one, huh?"

Chase nodded. "Yep. And she's about to spill the goods on Peebles, so if we want to make our twenty thousand—"

Grant corrected him. "Sixteen thousand. Remember Jamie's cut."

"Right. Sixteen thousand. Anyway, we'd better get to work."

They stared at the TV for a few minutes longer, watching as June turned what should have been a panel discussion into a monologue.

"So what's the deal with this mosque?" Grant finally asked. "She's sure worked up about it."

"Sure is. She's either really pissed that it's being built, or she's using it for attention. Or maybe both."

"From what I've seen of her, I'll put a grand on attention. Wanna take the bet?"

"Hell no."

Grant found the remote under a cushion and clicked off the TV, fading June to black as she went into another rant and the rest of the panel looked uncomfortably at the floor. There was blessed silence for a few minutes after June Forteene disappeared from their living room, but soon Grant got back to business.

"Here's what I'm thinking. We drug her."

Chase squirmed. "Drug her? I don't know—"

"It should be harmless enough. Somehow put something in her drink, wait for her to pass out, and ransack her office. Get what we need and get out."

"Maybe." Chase was unconvinced. "It's just that…"

"What?"

"Well, we've never drugged anyone before. We don't want to kill her or anything."

"If it shuts her up—"

"Grant!" Then, realizing it was *probably* a joke, Chase said, "I really think we need to come up with a different plan."

"I might know someone who can help." Grant stood and reached for a jacket hanging over the arm of a chair before Chase could do much more than sputter vague objections. "I'll be back in an hour."

Sure enough, less than an hour later, Grant returned home. He produced a baggie from his jacket pocket and held it out for Chase to examine. A chalky powder coated the inside of the plastic.

"What's that?"

"Guy I know says this should do the trick."

Chase stared skeptically at the baggie. "And not kill her?"

"Nah. It'll just put her under for a few hours. That should give us plenty of time to take care of business *and* clean out her apartment before she comes to."

Chase began pacing, weighing the consequences in his head and not liking the way the scale kept tipping. "I'm still not comfortable with this."

"This guy says nothing can go wrong. She'll sleep like a baby. Probably never even realize she's been drugged when she wakes up." He looked at the baggie. "That's what the guy says, at least."

They continued their conversation at a slightly higher volume when Grant walked into the kitchen.

"I dunno," said Chase, still pacing the living room. "Maybe we should just call Wunder and turn down the job."

Grant seemed to be ignoring him. "Any clean coffee cups?"

"Next to the sink." Chase leaned in the doorway between the rooms, where he could see Grant's back. "I mean, think about it. Is sixteen grand worth maybe killing someone?"

Grant didn't answer, so Chase finally retreated to the couch. A few minutes passed before Grant returned. He was holding two full coffee cups.

"Here," he said. "Drink up."

"I don't want coffee."

"You'll want *this* coffee."

"No, I don't…Wait a minute." Chase stared into the cup. "Did you drug my coffee?"

Grant smiled crookedly. "Just a little bit. Mine, too. I'm gonna prove that there's nothing to be worried about. We're gonna be our own guinea pigs."

"Now *this*…" Chase stared into the cup again. "*This* is a very bad idea."

Grant ignored him and lifted the cup to his lips. "Bottoms up!"

And he drank.

A few minutes after he felt his legs buckling, Grant woke up on the couch. Through a fog that used to be thoughts, he struggled to remember what had happened.

Something in that fog was making noise. He blinked a few times until his vision was finally clear enough to sort of kind of vaguely make out Chase, who sat several feet away and stared at him.

Grant started to realize the noise was coming from Chase's mouth.

And he was saying…what? Grant listened until the noise started to make sense.

"Grant? Grant, honey? Grant?"

He smacked his dry lips a few times and tried to answer, but what should have been a crisp "I'm fine" came out sounding something like "Friviliffer."

Still, Chase was relieved. If Grant's eyes were open and he was trying to speak, then he wasn't dead. Up until that moment, Chase had his doubts about how this experiment was going to end.

More time passed, and Grant was finally able to speak and be more or less understood. "See? That was nothing. Just a short nap."

"A short nap?" Chase looked at his watch. "Maybe. If by short you mean eleven hours. I had to call in sick for my shift at the Groc-O-Rama, so I hope you're happy."

Grant managed a lopsided smile at Chase's joke. Until he realized that Chase wasn't smiling.

He looked at the window and saw blackness. He'd downed the laced cup of coffee around noon, which meant…

Eleven hours?

"Eleven hours," repeated Chase as if reading Grant's thoughts. "You're one hundred eighty pounds—"

"Hundred seventy-two."

"If you say so. Anyway, so you're one hundred *seventy-two*

pounds, and I figure that June woman is maybe one-twenty max. Meaning that dose you gave yourself would've probably killed her."

Grant shifted on the couch until he could swing his legs off the edge and sort of feel his feet touch the floor. "How about you? You got the lighter dose and you're what, one-sixty?" Chase nodded. "How long were *you* out?"

"You think I'm some kind of idiot? *I'm* not gonna drink that stuff."

Bracing his arms against the couch, Grant attempted to stand. He quickly realized that wasn't going to happen, so he settled back into the cushions and tried to will his body to start working again.

"Maybe coffee would help," he said finally. "Coffee without drugs in it, please."

"Can't remember the last time I heard you say please." Chase walked to the kitchen, returning less than a minute later with coffee reheated in the microwave.

He sat next to Grant on the couch. "Now don't be mad, but I have something to tell you—"

"Talk." Grant took the cup of coffee, holding it tightly in case his hands decided to imitate his legs. He was happy to discover the hands were shaky but held a grip.

"Jamie's on his way over."

Grant frowned. Then he sniffed at the cup. Just in case. "And I'm sure you're gonna tell me there's a good reason that social-climbing idiot is coming to our apartment."

"Just that he called and said he wanted to discuss this June Forteene job. It was while you were out, so I couldn't exactly ask you. And anyway, I was getting a little concerned, since you'd been under for so long. I figured some company wouldn't be a bad thing, especially if I was gonna need help moving a body."

"True love," Grant mumbled.

"Not for nothing, but you *did* OD on whatever was in the baggie."

"Oh, so this is *my* fault."

"Well…" Chase wanted to agree, but knew better. "Of course not. It's just that Jamie knows these people—Kevin Wunder and the congresswoman—"

"*Representative*," Grant remembered.

"Right. That. Anyway, he knows them, so I figured if he's got something to say, maybe we should listen."

Grant was going to disagree, even though it was too late for that. It didn't matter because the door buzzer sounded the moment he opened his mouth. So instead he took a long sip of coffee and hoped he wasn't about to go down for another eleven hours. If that happened, Chase would pay for it the moment his legs were strong enough to hold up his one hundred-eighty-four pounds.

He'd barely finished that thought—thinking being one of the many things the drug slowed to a crawl—when Jamie Brock was standing in their apartment. It wasn't as if that had never happened before, but it still didn't mean Grant had to like it or be especially polite about being a host.

"Hey, Grant!" Jamie said by way of greeting.

"Mmmph," was the reply.

"You okay?" Jamie sensed that Grant was not quite himself, which probably had something to do with the way his numb ankles were turned in against the floor and he held a coffee cup in two shaky hands like he was afraid it'd run away from him.

"Whaddya want?" was the gruff response.

Jamie, unfazed, planted his frame on a chair across from Grant and smiled. "I think I know a way to increase the take on this job."

"You do, huh?"

"Sure! All you have to do is steal the picture from June Forteene and get that twenty thousand dollars from the Peebles campaign—"

"Correct me if I'm missing something," snarled Grant. "But isn't that already the plan?"

Jamie bounced a little in his chair, a demonstration of enthusiasm he was already far too old to pull off. "Yes, yes, but here's my idea. After you steal the picture and return it, and after we get the twenty grand, you steal it again and sell it back to June Forteene! Then we can make more money off it! Maybe Kevin Wunder will even hire you to steal it back again, and we can make even *more* money!"

Grant started to shake his groggy head but stopped when he thought he could actually hear his brain bump against the inside of his skull. "There are quite a few things wrong with your great idea. But here's the big one: Every time you mention stealing something, it's a job for me and Chase. Every time you mention collecting money, it's me, Chase, and *you*. Seems you're spending an awful lot of time thinking up ways to make me do more work so you can line your pockets."

"That's because I'm an *idea man*!"

"Oh fer chrissakes…" Grant looked for a place to set the coffee cup down, saw nowhere close enough to avoid using his shaky legs, and instead tightened his grip.

"I wish you'd think about it. This could turn into a real cash cow, Grant." Jamie sat back, still smiling.

"I'd appreciate it if you'd wipe that smile off your face, 'cause your plan has so many holes even *you* should be embarrassed. For one, don't you think June Forteene is gonna wonder why a bunch of crooks are bringing her a picture that was already stolen from her? Don't you think she's gonna call the cops right away?"

Uncertainty crossed Jamie's face. "I hadn't really thought of that. I just figured she'd want it—"

"And don't you think Wunder and Peebles and those people are gonna know we had something to do with it if that picture makes its way back to her? You think they're stupid enough to hire us again to steal something we've already stolen? Hell no. They're gonna call the cops. They may be sleazy politicians, but they're not as stupid as you are."

"Hmm." Jamie tried to affect thoughtfulness by scratching at his chin. "Maybe there are some aspects to my plan that need to be refined." He took a self-affirming pause. "But I still think it's a great idea."

"You know *my* great idea?" Grant asked. He looked at Chase, his face deadpan. "Baby, why don't you get Jamie a cup of coffee? I'd like to talk about my great idea with him."

Jamie glanced at his fake Rolex. "Coffee? But it's almost midnight. I don't think…"

Grant smiled, baring teeth. "Oh, but *I* think you should have a cup of coffee. It's very important to me. I wanna make sure you're sharp and alert when I tell you about this idea of mine."

"Well, if you're sure."

"*So* sure."

Jamie still wasn't sure—in fact, he was starting to regret taking the expensive cab ride out to Queens in the first place—but he saw wisdom in placating Grant, so…

Chase cleared his throat, and Jamie saw he was looking disapprovingly at Grant. "Can I talk to you about this?"

"Nah." Grant waved him away. "Remember the coffee you didn't touch earlier? Why don't you throw it into the microwave for Jamie."

"I really don't think…"

Grant again bared his teeth. After eighteen years, Chase understood. "I'm trying to be a very nice host to our very good friend. So I'm afraid I have to insist."

The next noise in the apartment was the beep Chase LaMarca's finger produced when it pushed a button on the microwave.

CHAPTER SIX

Jamie slept for only five hours, so they figured they'd come up with what was probably a safe enough dose for a woman of June Forteene's stature. Which meant Grant and Chase were now free to go about their business with relatively clear consciences. Since Jamie and Chase were roughly the same weight, Grant sort of regretted that they couldn't have determined the safe dosage earlier. But it *had* been fun to see Jamie collapse in his living room, which more than made up for that.

The next morning, Grant put on a brown UPS uniform he had stashed in the back of his closet for occasions like this and went to work. Unlike most UPS deliverymen, though, he went to work on the subway. In uniform.

He rode a 7 train into Manhattan and walked a few blocks up Eighth Avenue from the Port Authority until he found the address Wunder said housed June Forteene's offices. The building was old and drab, a washed-out brown ten-story box with offices above an adult video store advertising *Live! Nude! Girls!* sharing the ground floor with the lobby.

There was no doorman, but a steady stream of people moved through the lobby. Grant pushed open the front door and checked out the building directory. A lot of talent managers; a few design firms; a few tenants that sounded sketchy, even to him…and June Forteene Enterprises on Floor 5.

He took the elevator to the fifth floor.

He'd been under the assumption June Forteene ran a one-woman operation—now that he'd been brought up to speed on globs or blogs or whatever, that seemed to be the nature of the business—so he was thrown off when the elevator doors opened and a pale young man looked up from a desk positioned directly in front of the elevator. Behind him, the wall was adorned with a red-white-and-blue, American-eagle-emblazoned banner with the words "June Forteene: An American Crusader for Freedom."

The eagle was gold, like on Kevin Wunder's tie, and Grant thought, *Must be a trend.*

The pale young man sized him up. Grant hoped he wouldn't notice the old UPS uniform was fraying and didn't fit so well anymore, but the tone in the kid's voice indicated he'd already been read loud and clear.

"Can I *help* you?"

To even things out, Grant took a good look back at him. He looked college age, at most, and sported stylish eyeglass frames he probably didn't need, since people who wore frames like that seldom did. He also wore a red sweater vest, which helped Grant feel confident that, if it came to it, he could probably take him in a fair fight. Not that it was part of the plan; it was just an impulse he had when he saw the red sweater vest and hipster frames.

Emboldened, Grant squared his thin shoulders and did his best to project authority. He *was* the UPS guy, after all. "So where's this dentist office?"

"Dentist office?" The young man in the sweater vest furrowed his brow. "There isn't a dentist on this floor."

"That's what I'm saying. How come they told me the dentist was on five, when there ain't no dentist on five?"

"Who told you that?"

"The guy."

"The guy?"

"The guy downstairs."

The kid clucked disapprovingly. "*Which* guy downstairs?"

"Like I told ya, the guy who said the dentist office was on five."

The young man shook his head. Not a single hair moved. "Look, I don't think there's a dentist in the entire building, but there's definitely not a dentist on the fifth floor. Maybe you should go back downstairs and ask again."

"Ask who?"

"The guy."

"*Which* guy?"

The kid sighed. "Whoever sent you…" He sighed again. "Look, I'm sorry, but there's no dentist on this floor." He looked longingly at his sudoku puzzle, half-buried under a manila folder. "And I'm very busy."

Grant eyed the room that opened up behind the young man. An old wooden door frame—old wooden door still attached, with a half-open transom across the top—outlined the entrance. He couldn't see anyone moving around in there. "So what kind of place is this?"

"It's a…it's a place that wouldn't interest you." The young man sensed something was wrong beyond the UPS man's seedy appearance and took off his probably unnecessary glasses. "Don't you have deliveries to make?"

"Sure. To the dentist." Grant scratched his head. "Mind if I take a quick look?"

"*Yes!* Yes, of course I'd mind!" Finally he stood, puffing out a pipe-cleaner chest. "I already told you there's no dentist on this floor. We're the only fifth-floor tenant."

Grant scratched his head again. "Who's 'we'?"

"June Forteene Enterprises." He nodded at the banner on the wall behind his desk. "This is a media office. *Not* a dentist."

"Never heard of this June Forteene."

The young man huffed. "That doesn't surprise me."

But Grant had seen enough. This wasn't going to be as easy as drugging June Forteene and robbing the place. It was going to be a lot more complicated.

It always was.

He probably should've checked that out before almost overdosing, but it had given him an excuse to drug Jamie, so at least there was that.

"Thanks for your time." Grant turned and pushed the elevator button. "Guess the guy was wrong about the dentist."

The kid frowned and didn't answer.

On the way back to the lobby, he considered what he now knew. This certainly wasn't a one-woman operation, and June Forteene Enterprises appeared to rent an entire floor. He'd greatly underpriced the job.

Out on the sidewalk, he swallowed hard, took his phone out of the pocket of his fraying uniform, and dialed. Much as he hated to do that.

When Chase answered, Grant kept it short. "Meet me in Manhattan."

Kevin Wunder, a bag over one shoulder, stepped out of the white brick office building on Second Avenue and made a beeline for the curb, intent on hailing a cab and making his lunch appointment five minutes before his guests. His plan was to wrap up a real estate developer's support—personally and financially—for Austin Peebles's congressional campaign over steak frites at Smith & Wollensky. There was really nothing like red meat to complement the blood sport of politics.

He'd barely raised his hand for a cab when he heard someone call his name.

He squinted against the bright sunlight and saw them. It was those criminals. And they were standing just yards away from him on the sidewalk in *broad daylight*!

And the sort of scary older guy was wearing a *UPS uniform*! An *ill-fitting, faded, fraying* UPS uniform!

He waved off a cab that slowed at his hail. "What the hell are you doing here?"

Grant's eyes were hidden behind generic sunglasses he'd picked up one night at the tail end of robbing a CVS. "We need to talk."

"Not here!" Wunder's eyes darted around, looking for a secluded space where they wouldn't be seen. He settled on the alley at the side of the building that led back to the trash bins. He started for it, waving over his shoulder for Grant and Chase to follow.

When they were tucked between two Dumpsters, Wunder snapped at them.

"What's the meaning of this?"

"This job is bigger than we thought." Grant said it evenly, not reacting to the outburst. "This June woman doesn't work alone, for one thing."

Wunder shook his head. "I never said she worked alone. That was *never* part of the deal."

"Yeah, well now it is. We can't do the job for twenty grand."

"What do you…?"

Chase, whose own sunglasses looked like they were from Versace but were really from a guy who sold knock-offs on a corner a couple of blocks from Versace, said, "This is at least a thirty-thousand-dollar job."

Wunder huffed. "*Thirty?* You're lucky we're willing to pay twenty! There's no way the campaign will authorize a thirty-thousand-dollar expenditure for this."

Grant and Chase shrugged in unison, a variation on their cross-armed projection of solidarity.

"It's too big a risk for twenty grand," said Grant, shoving his hands deep inside the pockets of his UPS uniform. "Plus, we might need to bring in another person. Therefore, the job is gonna cost more."

Kevin Wunder wasn't having any of that.

"No way. Twenty thousand or nothing. In fact…In fact…" He began sputtering. "In fact, take the twenty thousand off the table!"

"Huh?" said Grant.

"You heard me! Kevin Wunder does not bend over for bullies. You…you…you *bullies*! Now it's a *five*-thousand-dollar job!" He thumped a fist against his chest. "Take it or leave it!"

The bluff didn't work.

"Okay, then."

Grant and Chase turned and began walking back to the sidewalk.

"Wait!" Wunder scrambled after them. He hadn't really expected them to take a fifteen-thousand-dollar pay cut, but he was surprised they'd just walk away from the job without trying to negotiate. "Where are you going?"

"Home," said Grant. "And you'd better find yourself a couple more criminals if you want to get those pictures back."

"But—"

"*Cheap* criminals," added Chase. "Just remember: You get what you pay for."

They were half a block away when Chase asked, "How soon?"

"Any second now. In fact," Grant cocked his head slightly, "I think I hear the pitter-patter of Kevin Wunder's little size-seven feet coming up behind us right now."

"I was thinking size eight."

"Nah, definitely seven. Listen."

Sure enough, Wunder caught up with them, looking slightly disheveled for the short trot. Sweat and motion didn't do his thinning hair any favors. It stuck out at a half dozen angles, all unfortunate.

"Okay, okay." He was out of breath, so the words came in short gasps.

"Okay what?" asked Grant.

"Okay, I'll find thirty thousand dollars. *Somehow.*"

Grant nodded graciously, and once again they shook hands. It was a deal.

On his cab ride to Smith and Wollensky, Wunder decided he'd better not only tap the real estate developer for support, but make him the chairman of a new fund-raising committee: Real Estate for Peebles.

Because it was becoming increasingly apparent there was going to be a new need for some significant campaign cash.

Speaking of which...

He dialed Penelope from the cab and went straight to voice mail, which he told, "I think we have a problem with these jokers. Now they want thirty instead of twenty. This doesn't feel good to me, but I'll monitor the situation closely."

He was smiling when he disconnected.

They sat on a bench in the plaza—technically the city called it a park, but it was really a plaza—next to the Roosevelt Island tram. Chase was half looking at the pedestrians strolling up and down Second Avenue, while Grant, still in his UPS uniform, idly watched traffic pour off the Queensboro Bridge. Neither was really focused on what was in front of them, though. They were too busy thinking things through.

Finally Grant spoke. "It's those people that bother me."

Chase stretched his arms, working out a few kinks. The bench wasn't as comfortable as it looked, and it didn't look all that comfortable to begin with. "Which people? The ones who work for June Forteene?"

"Those are the ones. If this was a one-woman operation it'd make things much simpler." He focused on his visit to her office that morning, trying to recall every detail. "It's an old building, so getting inside ain't gonna be a problem. So long as those people aren't around."

"I'm sure they go home at the end of the workday. It's a job, not a dormitory."

Grant played with a thread that had come loose on the uniform pants. "You're probably right, but something feels wrong about the setup. Take the elevator, for example. It opens right into her office."

"She's got a private elevator?"

He shook his head. "Nah, it's the regular building elevator. Except she rents the entire floor, and when you step off there's this desk right out in the hall. That tells me the building staff either locks the elevator and stairwells at night, or—more likely, 'cause I can't imagine a crappy building like that locking up so tight—they've got at least one person in that office pretty much around the clock."

"Hmm." Behind his fake Versace sunglasses, Chase thought that over. "I see what you're saying."

They fell into silence again.

"What we'll need to do," said Grant, after several quiet minutes, "is be prepared in case my gut is right about this."

Chase didn't like the way that sounded. "We're not talking about physical violence, are we?"

"That's not my plan." Chase began to exhale with relief, but stopped when Grant added, "But—"

"Aw, c'mon. We're both too old for that stuff. And weren't very good at it when we were younger."

Grant let the comment hang in the air. "I also think we're gonna need to spread around some of the extra ten grand we just squeezed out of Wunder to bring in another person."

"Jamie?"

"Hell no. We'll need someone who's competent." He thought it out a bit more. "I figure we go one of two ways. Someone big who can take care of business in case things get tricky; or someone small and wiry who can move through tight spaces."

"Tight spaces?" Chase wrinkled his nose. "What tight spaces?"

Grant stared off at the bridge traffic. "I'm just preparing for contingencies, is all. If someone is standing guard at June Forteene's office when we break in, a big guy should be able to take care of it. But a big guy won't be much help if we need dexterity instead of muscle."

"Why not get one of each?" asked Chase. "One big goon; one small wiry guy. Then we're covered, no matter what."

"Maybe." Grant did some quick math in his head. "It depends who's free tonight, and how much they charge."

Chase sat up straight on the bench. "*Tonight*? Did I hear you say *tonight*?"

"Yeah, tonight. When we pull the jobs." He was briefly tempted to laugh at the expression of surprise on Chase's face. "The clock is ticking, lover. If we don't get that picture before she makes it public, we're out thirty grand. I don't know about you, but I don't want to risk waiting until it's too late."

Chase sat back against the bench. "Thanks for giving me a lot of warning."

Grant shrugged. "That's the nature of the business. You should be used to it by now."

❖

The decision was made for them by availability. All the big guys they knew were either unavailable or they were locked up, which made them *very* unavailable.

So, for that matter, were most of the small, wiry guys. With one exception.

Chase closed his cell phone and looked at Grant. "Nick Donovan can do it."

"Oh, jeez…" muttered Grant, accompanying the mutter with an abbreviated eye roll.

"I thought you liked Nick."

"He's all right. For a kid. But…"

"But what?"

Grant returned his gaze toward the traffic coming off the Queensboro Bridge. "Ever since his mother went legit she's wanted nothing to do with the business. And she doesn't want Nick to have anything to do with it, either. He's probably out of practice."

"How out of practice can you be if you're small, thin, and limber?"

"You'd be surprised."

Chase set his phone on his lap. "I don't know what to tell you. If you want me to keep trying to find a big, intimidating accomplice, I'll call Paul Farraday again, but he sounded pretty adamant the *second* time he hung up on me. Otherwise, we can either try to pull two jobs in one night by ourselves or bring Nick Donovan in on the job. Those are our only options."

A pigeon wandered near them until Grant stared at the bird and sent it flying away in a flurry of feathers.

"Okay," he said, after mulling over the equally unattractive options. "Just make sure the kid doesn't tell his mother. I don't want to deal with that."

While Chase rang Nick back, Grant glanced at his watch. It was still early afternoon, but they had business to attend to. When the call was over he decided they should head off to scope out June Forteene's home address a few miles south on Second Avenue.

Because if they were going to pull off two jobs that night, they'd better know what they were getting themselves into.

While the criminals were walking at a brisk pace down Second Avenue, intent on casing her apartment building, June Forteene was across town in her Eighth Avenue office and staring with disgust at an erect penis.

It wasn't that erect penises disgusted her—far from it, although it had almost been too long since she'd seen one to remember clearly—but the one on her computer screen was a different story. Because, of course, it was attached to Austin Peebles.

She zoomed out. First his taut, slim body appeared; then his face. There was a trace of a smug smile on his thin pink lips, and she almost punched the monitor.

A woman of great certainty about everything from her breakfast cereal to her political beliefs, June was not quite certain what it was about Austin Peebles that set her off. It wasn't for a lack of reasons; it was because there were so many.

He was the son of Neil Peebles, the soft Mainline WASP who, having inherited a fortune, was now at work in Washington betraying his class by taxing and spending everyone else's money.

He was the son-in-law of Catherine Cooper Concannon, the wealthy patrician who'd just assumed she deserved her husband's seat in Congress when he died, and whom no one had been willing to turn down.

He was the husband of Penelope Concannon Peebles, a filthy-rich money manager who was quickly amassing a fortune by playing on her family connections.

And then there was Austin Peebles himself.

At twenty-seven years of age he had never held a real job. He was too good-looking; not in a Ronald Reagan kind of way, but in that way which made everyone want to take care of him. Hooded eyes, pouty lips…Everyone wanted to take Austin Peebles home and mother him.

Which would have been enough, but now, as a final insult, he had been anointed as a congressional candidate.

June Forteene took a deep breath to clear her head and reminded herself he was also undisciplined and irresponsible and promiscuous, as witnessed by the erection on her monitor.

Austin Peebles embodied everything that disgusted June Forteene.

An immoral, immature child of privilege who married into more privilege was expected to be elected to high public office with no attributes or accomplishments to speak of except connections, looks, and charm. It was infuriating, and she knew he had to be stopped.

It was true that Austin Peebles had a lot in his favor. Ordinarily, it would be almost impossible to stop the Peebles-Concannon juggernaut before his coronation.

But June Forteene now had that photo of his penis.

And *that* was a game changer.

She zoomed back in until she could see every vein. Then she zoomed out again to look at that smug smile attached to that face attached to that head attached to that slim body attached to that penis, before zooming back in on the money shot.

"Oh, my!"

She turned and saw Edward—her most junior assistant, who was in only his fourth day at June Forteene Enterprises—avert his eyes from the giant erection on her monitor. June was fairly certain he had seen his fair share of them—she got that impression when she interviewed him, and today's outfit of hipster frames and a red sweater vest didn't do much in her eyes to burnish his masculinity—and so made no effort to diminish the image.

"What is it, Edward?" There was boredom in her voice.

Overcompensating by making a point to avoid looking at the image on the screen, he handed her a small package. "UPS just dropped this off."

She took it from his hands. "Thanks."

"By the way," he said, still looking away, "the Cuban guy is the regular UPS deliveryman for this building, right?"

"Raul? Yes, why?"

Edward continued to speak away from the monitor. "It's nothing, really. Just…this morning there was a different guy—an older white guy—who showed up in a UPS uniform. He said he was looking for a dental office."

She narrowed her eyes. "There aren't any dentists in this building."

"That's what I told him."

After a slight moment of suspicion—June was suspicious about a lot of things, and usually for good reason—she shook her head, and it went away. "He probably just had the wrong address."

Edward nodded his agreement. "That's what I figured. And frankly I'm surprised UPS would send a driver out in such a shabby uniform. It doesn't reflect well on the company. Now take Raul; *his* uniform is always crisp and…"

She stopped him. "What was that?"

"The first UPS man. The white guy. His uniform didn't fit and it was fraying. He looked very shabby."

She tried to tell herself she was paranoid...but paranoia was part of her nature. It was a dangerous world, and if people let down their guard they'd soon be living at the business end of a rifle held by the Muslims, Russians, Chinese, radical homosexuals, Washington power elite, Wall Street bankers, labor leaders, ACORN, Mormons, illegal Mexicans, and Indian telemarketers. Or maybe all of them, joined together in a vast conspiracy she had not yet been able to draw together.

Then again, maybe it was nothing.

"Thank you, Edward," she said, dismissing him. "And please let me know if he shows up again."

Edward said he would and then, when her back was to him, took a nice long look at Austin Peebles's erection.

The building June Forteene called home was on Second Avenue near East Forty-second Street, not too far from the United Nations. And that, Grant soon realized as he surveyed the area, could present him with a problem.

The timing of this job was full of trouble, but all of the timing had been out of their hands.

First, Wunder had called them in at the last possible moment, giving Grant and Chase just a few days to pull off the job. If June Forteene got a bug to publish the photo before they had a chance to pull things off, they'd be out thirty grand.

Then, because the job was so rushed, they hadn't had time to put together a team that Grant could feel comfortable working with. Nick Donovan was okay...but just okay. He wasn't Grant's idea of the sort of support that would put his mind at ease.

And now, well...Once again, the timing sucked on this job. Because there were a hell of a lot of cops in the general vicinity. He could only hope there'd been some awful accident.

The situation needed to be checked out. First, though, Grant had to pay a visit to the lobby of June's apartment building to size things up. While he was there he managed to have a little talk with the super, mostly because he couldn't find June Forteene's name on a mailbox and couldn't remember her real name. The super—far too friendly, meaning he was bored—directed him to the box labeled *H. Morris.*

"Got a package for Hillary?" the super asked as he stood next to Grant at the mailbox. "I can sign for it."

"I'm not sure." Grant tried to appear conscientious, figuring the average UPS driver wouldn't let just anyone sign for anything. Also, he needed her apartment number, and it wasn't on the mailbox, so...

"Can you confirm her apartment number?"

The super smiled broadly. "Seven-F!"

Grant decided to press his luck, since the poor schmuck seemed to want to talk more than he seemed to want to filter out what he shouldn't talk about. "Seventh floor? Is that the top floor in the building?"

"No, that would be eight."

"Of course." Grant mumbled something about grabbing a package and returning at some vague point in the future.

When he walked back outside, there were no fewer cops.

"You figure out why there are all these blue uniforms?" he asked Chase.

"Nope. But more seem to be coming."

Somewhere nearby, a patrol car's siren let out a loud *whoop*. Instead of standing, watching, and guessing, Grant figured he'd try to figure out what was going on.

The building super was still in the lobby, and still eager to help.

A few minutes later Grant Lambert and Chase LaMarca stood at the corner of Forty-second and Second, a half block from the apartment building, and looked on as dozens of uniformed police officers stood guard or tried unsuccessfully to move traffic in every direction of the intersection.

Grant sighed. "So this is what the United Nations area looks like when the General Assembly's in session." He watched a half dozen NYPD motorcycles roar up. "This is gonna make things interesting."

Chase frowned. "Great timing."

"Just what I've been thinking." Grant took another look over the sea of blue uniforms. "Maybe we should call Wunder and tell him we can't—"

"Hey, you!"

They pivoted toward the shout and found themselves looking at a police lieutenant, who in turn pointed unhappily—and directly—at Grant. In their line of work having a cop point at you was never good, but since they hadn't done anything—yet—they figured the guy was trying to get someone else's attention.

He wasn't and shouted, "Hey!" again.

Grant finally jabbed a finger at his chest and mouthed, "Me?"

"Yeah, you! Move your damn truck before we tow it! We've gotta clear the streets for the Secretary-General's motorcade!"

Grant was confused until he saw a brown UPS truck double-parked at mid-block…and remembered he was still wearing the uniform.

"Well," Chase said as they approached the truck. "At least we don't have to take the subway back to Jackson Heights. That's *one* good thing that's happened today."

Grant grunted as he climbed into the driver's seat. "You keep telling yourself that."

The key wasn't in the ignition but Grant Lambert knew a half dozen ways to get around that. It was part of the business.

CHAPTER SEVEN

Ordinarily, Chase LaMarca's instincts would have been on the money when he told Grant that the office was likely a workplace, not a dormitory. With the exception of national emergencies—say, a terrorist attack, or Barack Obama caught in a lie, or news that a Muslim or Mexican had been caught committing a crime, no matter how petty—June Forteene and her staff treated that office on Eighth Avenue in Hell's Kitchen as a workplace, and nothing more. By 6:00 p.m.—maybe 6:30 p.m. on a busier news day—they locked it up, set the alarm, and went home.

Even June, who barely had a life outside her blog, kept her hours there to a realistic limit.

The desk placed in the hallway outside the elevator—the desk that had so concerned Grant—wasn't important at all. They didn't even bother locking it; no one was quite sure where the keys were anymore. They would stow the laptop in the main office, but that was the full extent of their security measures for Edward's desk. If a building employee wanted to help himself to some paper clips, the team at June Forteene Enterprises could live with that. True, Edward seldom had paper clips—or a stapler, or a tape dispenser—but it was a very low priority.

Of course, that wasn't the case with the rest of what they considered a suite of offices, although "suite" never seemed like quite the right word to describe a string of two rooms—half of one of which was a supply closet—that shared nothing but a bleak common hallway on the fifth floor. But the only other tenant on the floor—a shady Bulgarian talent manager who barely spoke English—had vacated his office a few months earlier, and as long as that office remained vacant—and she possessed all the bathroom keys—she was going to take over the hallway and consider it a suite.

Of course, despite an abundance of desks and computers, she was also running a place she called "Enterprises" with an unpaid part-time intern and an almost-unpaid assistant, so she was well versed in the art of deception. Would the Big Boys—and Girls—take her even slightly seriously if she was a private citizen blogging from home in her pajamas? No, they would not.

Despite the flesh trade on the building's first floor, the Eighth Avenue office offered some benefits, chief among them cheap rent for a convenient location. Cheap rent was important; even though controversies like the Times Square Mosque had built a large readership—and therefore higher ad rates and occasional speaking fees—she was hardly in the same league as Drudge. It was a goal but not yet a reality.

But there were downsides, too, and when it came to all-important security, she knew those old wooden doors and frames could present a problem. But once the problem was identified, it was quickly resolved.

June was practical enough to know—as a prominent and controversial blogger—that one break-in could put her out of business for a long time. Political paranoia alone would have done the trick, but the sketchy patrons on the ground floor with their Live! Nude! Girls! made her especially cautious. As a blogger, she depended on immediacy to spread her message, and if she were to go out of business for even a few short days while replacing computers and files when the Next Big Story Broke, she might as well consider herself as outdated as the typewriter. Her philosophy was, "Lose a story, lose a career."

The doors couldn't easily be retrofitted, but one of her more conspiracy-oriented acquaintances—a security consultant who once allegedly did some work for G. Gordon Liddy but wouldn't discuss details about that or any other aspect of his past—assessed the situation and resolved it to her satisfaction. Better yet, he did it as a gift from a devoted reader of her blog. The alarm system he installed was state of the art; if anyone tried to open one of the office doors after hours without the security code, not only would a backup dead-bolt system kick in, but the consultant would know right away...and he'd alert June and the police. Someone could still get in, but they'd have to work fast...faster, that is, than June, the consultant, and the police. And the consultant, June, and the police would work pretty damn fast if someone was breaking in.

June Forteene now slept soundly at night knowing her office was secure. It was with that sense of reassurance that she prepared to leave work that evening. It was only 6:00, and no one but Republicans had humiliated themselves that day; therefore, there was no blog-worthy news.

"Time to lock up, Edward," she said, laptop bag over shoulder and keys in hand.

He was sitting at the desk in the hall. The one with only three paper clips left in the top drawer and no stapler or tape dispenser.

"Do you mind if I work late?"

She narrowed her eyes, suspicion being her default reaction whenever someone said something she wasn't expecting them to say, and almost as often when they did. "Why?"

"I'm still trying to figure out this database program." June's eyes were still narrowed, and Edward felt a flutter of panic in his stomach. "I'm not asking for any overtime. I just want to be able to do right by you."

That eased her mind. Not much, but enough. She appreciated ambition and industriousness.

"Do you remember the alarm code?"

"I do." He recited it back to her. "And I'll make sure the office is locked up nice and tight before I leave."

June raised an eyebrow. Her gut still told her she should be suspicious, but damn if she could find anything concrete behind it. His earnest, corn-fed demeanor was alarmingly disarming.

"Okay, then." She pressed the elevator button.

Edward smiled cheerfully. "See you in the morning!"

After June disappeared into the elevator and the doors closed, he waited, studying the database with close to no interest. Two minutes passed…then three…He began to think she had really left for the night when a *ding* announced the elevator's return.

The door opened and June's head poked into the hall.

"Did you forget something?" Edward asked.

She looked at him, sitting diligently behind the desk and studying the database just like he said he'd be doing. So much for her suspicions. One of these days she'd learn to trust people.

"I thought so, but…I guess not."

"Well…good night, then."

"Good night again, Ed."

"Ed*ward.*"

She smiled and the doors slid closed.

When he was sure she was gone—really, truly gone this time, and not out on the sidewalk waiting for another opportunity to try to catch him at something—Edward made a beeline for June's computer. It was password-protected, but that was no obstacle for him. The password was REAGANGIRL; June wasn't nearly as spontaneous or imaginative as she thought she was. Plus, she had the password written down on the first card of her Rolodex, something he'd noticed during his first day of work but never thought he'd need to know until now.

It took only a few clicks until Austin Peebles's erection filled the monitor.

He forwarded the image to himself, did what he could to erase evidence that he'd been on the computer at all, wiped his fingerprints from the keypad, and returned to his desk.

Edward Hepplewhite was a recent graduate of the Southern Pennsylvania Bible College and proud of it. He was even more proud that his very first job was as an assistant to the legendary June Forteene, a true goddess and role model. He was pretty sure she was born Jewish, but so was Jesus, so he could forgive.

Everyone—his family, his friends, his instructors and classmates at SPBC—had warned him about moving to New York City at such an impressionable age. Actually, they'd warned against moving to New York at *any* age, but especially at a relatively impressionable twenty-two years. Edward wasn't stupid, and knew their concern had less to do with this modern Sodom than his own former proclivity toward sodomy, which gave him all the more reason to go. He had to prove—to them, and more importantly to himself—that he had conquered the homosexual demon that lurked within. Thanks to the recent "Beyond Sin" conference he'd attended in Washington DC sponsored by the Moral Families Coalition's Project Rectitude, he was confident he was now right with God.

But just to be safe, he rented an apartment in New Jersey and commuted into Sodom. There was no sense offering too much temptation to Satan. Weehawken was still far from heaven, but it was much more saintly than, say, the Lower East Side.

And he had been saintly for the entire one hundred forty-four hours since he'd moved north…until he'd walk in on the singular temptation of Austin Peebles's manhood on the screen of June Forteene's computer.

Edward Hepplewhite still didn't understand why that image was there or whom it belonged to, although he was confident June was not viewing it for prurient reasons. No doubt it was the private thingie of a liberal or some other sort of America-hater, and she would use it to destroy them. Therefore, Edward reasoned, it was all right to take a nice long look, because the image wasn't a form of devilish erotica, but rather a tool to be put in the hands of righteousness.

That's what he told himself, at least.

And so Edward sat dutifully at his desk in the hallway of the fifth floor, staring at the dingle-dangle on the screen and silently cursing its symbolic evil. And maybe touching himself every now and then.

He stared at it for the next hour, as a matter of fact.

If plans had gone as expected, June Forteene might have encountered three shady-looking men entering the lobby at the same moment she exited for the second time.

But Grant, Chase, and their newest associate—Nick Donovan— were running late that evening.

One of them needed a costume change.

Nick didn't live far from June Forteene Enterprises, so Grant and Chase agreed to meet him down the block from the apartment he shared with his mother to review what needed to be done on the job before actually *doing* the job. The explanation would be simple and straightforward, and take no more than five minutes. Then they'd get to work.

That was Grant's plan, at least. What happened next, though…

"What the hell is that?" Chase caught a glimpse of something yellow and blue approaching from a half block away.

Grant squinted. "Oh, hell no. It can't be."

"I think it is."

And it was. Nick Donovan swaggered toward them, exuding confidence, determination, and strength. All of that was good.

What wasn't good was that he was wearing light blue tights and a yellow cape. And a black mask, but Grant and Chase almost overlooked the mask because it seemed comparatively normal.

When Nick finally reached them, it took Grant a few beats to find the right words for the occasion. Then they came.

"What the fuck are you thinking, kid?"

Nick smiled, lifting his cheekbones a bit at the edge of the mask that covered his dark eyes until it almost disappeared beneath the dark wavy hair cascading over his forehead. He had an Irish surname but his DNA seemed to have come exclusively from his Italian mother.

"Like it? I call myself..." He paused for dramatic effect. *"Cadmium!"*

Chase swallowed hard. "Cadmium?"

"You called?"

"No, I meant..." Chase sighed and looked up into the canopy of tree branches. "You can't wear this on a job."

Nick looked puzzled. "But you said we'd be like superheroes."

"I did?"

"Don't you remember? I said I didn't think my mother would like me going on a job with you, and you said it was all right because we'd be stealing from bad people, and we'd be—"

"Like superheroes," Chase said, remembering. "But I didn't mean that literally. That was figurative, is all."

Grant snarled. "You and your figurativing."

"If anything," Nick said, "I think *you two* look underdressed." He put his hands on his hips—a studied, super-heroish pose—and glanced back down the block toward his apartment. "My mom won't be home for another hour or so. Let's go back to my room and see if I have anything that will fit you."

If they were so inclined—and they weren't—it stretched credulity to think Nick Donovan might have any tights and capes that would fit them. He was small and thin, the wiry type they might need on the job.

Grant clenched his jaw and took a quick scan across the four corners of the intersection at Tenth Avenue and West Forty-ninth Street.

"You're making a scene. Everyone is staring. Go home and change."

"No one's staring." That was true, because, while most pedestrians and motorists had indeed watched Nick Donovan out of the corners of their eyes, they pretended they hadn't seen a thing. Because they were New Yorkers, and that's what New Yorkers did. A mugging, Madonna making out with Bieber, a naked screaming crazy person, a kid in light blue tights and a yellow cape...they'd always pretend they hadn't seen a damn thing.

Grant tried again, this time with more than a growl to his voice.

"We're not having a discussion here. You go to this job dressed as Cadbury—"

"Cadmium."

"Don't say another word. You go dressed like that and we're all gonna get arrested. Follow?"

"But—"

"Dammit, it's still daylight! You stick out, and sticking out is a bad thing in this business. Didn't your mother teach you anything?"

Now it was Nick's turn to sigh. "You *know* she hasn't, Grant. Once she got out of the business, she stayed out. If she even *knew* I was here with you right now…"

The older men had pulled a few jobs with his mother in the past, until she decided to go legit and become a lawyer. After that, she told them to forget her number. But they kept her kid's, just in case the crime thing was in the genes. Apparently it was, although it came costumed.

Grant looked at the ground. "Okay, since your mother was a bad parent who failed to educate you about how to make a living in this business, I guess I'm gonna have to be your father figure. First thing—"

Nick looked confused. "*Father figure?* You're not planning to marry my mother, are you? Look, no offense, but even though she's been married nine times and it hasn't worked out yet, I still can't approve of her marrying a gay guy. And I say that as a gay guy!"

Grant looked at Chase. "Did we know that?"

"Know *what*?"

"Did we know the kid's gay?"

Chase shrugged. "*I* knew it. Just figured you did, too."

"We really need to start meeting new people," said Grant. "It's getting so everyone we know is gay. It's like we're trapped in a gay criminal ghetto."

"Well, there's Farraday. And, uh…" Chase paused, unable to come up with another name. "Yeah, maybe we should meet some new people."

Grant turned back to Nick. "First thing you gotta know is to dress to be invisible."

"Invisible?" Nick was excited about that idea. "I wish!"

Grant puffed out his cheeks and turned to Chase. "Why are these jobs always harder than they should be?"

"Let me," said Chase.

"Least you can do since you brought him on board."

Chase tossed a dismissive glance at Grant and turned to Nick, putting one paternal hand on his caped shoulder. "Here's the deal. Anyone who sees you dressed like this is going to remember you, and the idea is to not be seen. I mean, this Cadmium costume is great, and I'll bet it'll go over big on Halloween. But for now, for tonight, I have to ask you to go home and dress more appropriately."

"Appropriately." Nick turned those dark eyes and heavy lashes hopefully toward Chase. "Like a darker-colored cape? 'Cause I have black, dark red. I have green, too, but your coloring is too pasty to pull that off."

"Ah, jeez," Grant muttered, but otherwise stayed silent.

Chase tried to steer Nick away from Grant. "Appropriately as in jeans, sneakers, and a dark-colored shirt. No tights, no cape…not even an eye mask. Understand?"

Nick frowned. "I won't feel very powerful."

"If it helps," Chase said with a hopeful smile, "it'd be fine if you wore your Cadmium underwear."

"Cadmium does *not* wear underwear. See?" Nick stepped back to give him a full view of the costume. *Too* full of a view.

"Ah, jeez," Grant said again, before taking a step forward. He wasn't as inclined toward diplomacy as his partner. "Here's the deal, kid. Go home and change into *real* clothes like Chase just said. If you do that, you can go on the job. If you don't do that, I am gonna personally kick your metallic ass all the way to the West Side Highway. *Capisce?*"

Nick nodded. The Italian reminded him of his mother and made the conversation suddenly seem a lot more serious.

"When I ask you something, you say 'yes, sir' or 'no, sir.'"

"Yes, sir," Nick mumbled. Without another word he turned, and the cape rustled in the light breeze as he walked back toward his apartment.

When Cadmium was out of earshot, Chase said, "Very impressive. You almost sounded like a father. Or a drill sergeant."

Grant shook his head. "Can you believe that costume?" He took a glance at his watch. "And now we're behind schedule."

Chase probably would have said something reassuring about how they had flexibility in their scheduling and the job wouldn't take too long anyway, but he didn't have time before catching something out of his peripheral vision and dragging Grant into the bodega at the corner before he had a chance to object.

"What?" Grant hissed.

"It's Kelly!"

"Kelly…? Uh…uh—damn, she's been married so often I can't remember her last name. You mean Nick's mom?"

"That's the one."

Which is when Kelly Marinelli Dennison DuFour O'Rourke Donovan DuFour Bell Spencer DuFour Capobianco pushed open the door to that very same deli and walked inside.

They ducked around the aisle, trying to figure out which way she was walking from her footsteps and barely avoiding her when they guessed wrong and she turned the far corner. She would have seen them if she hadn't been studying the label on a soup can.

Grant and Chase moved and would have bolted for the front door but she reappeared, this time scanning the shelves for something, so instead they retreated to their original position.

"Can I help you?" asked the clerk, an older Puerto Rican woman who'd been watching them bob and weave in the small bodega, and acted like it was something she saw every day.

Chase popped his head out from behind the shelving, smiled, and nodded no, but Kelly's voice called out, "Flour?"

"Against the wall over there," said the clerk, pointing directly at Chase. Kelly's footsteps approached, and they scrambled to the rear of the store and around the center shelving units. Spotting a curtain separating the store from the stockroom, they ducked inside.

"Gentlemen, you cannot go back there," they heard the clerk call out from the front counter.

Chase tried to mask his voice. "Just looking for the bathroom."

"No bathroom! You go to McDonald's!" She pointed out the window. "Two blocks!"

And things should have only gone downhill from that point, but then they heard Kelly ask, "Can I pay for these?"

"I'll call the police!" yelled the Puerto Rican woman. But first they heard her agree to ring up Kelly's soup and flour.

Back behind the curtain, Grant whispered, "She still looks good."

Chase nodded. "Curvier than I remember, but she wears it well."

Grant agreed. "She used to be so great on the long con. Too bad she became a lawyer. A *legit* lawyer."

"Probably trying to set a good example for her son." Chase giggled. "You know, *Cadmium*."

Grant didn't think that was very funny at all.

They waited until she was gone, and then the two men emerged from behind the curtain.

"Sorry." Grant shrugged to the clerk as he walked past the counter.

"What? No sale?"

In return, she got a smile from Chase. "Nice store you've got here." Then he, too, was outside on the sidewalk. The clerk eyed them warily through the dusty front window.

They watched Kelly Capobianco's curvy frame as she carried her plastic grocery bag away from them. They had dodged that bullet but knew their problems were far from over.

"If she gets home and figures out her son's on his way to a job, she's not gonna let him leave," said Chase.

That was exactly what Grant had been thinking. "Maybe we'll be finding out if this is a two-man job after all." He felt at his pants pocket and was reassured at the slight bulge his fingers found. "Of course, we could always drug her."

"Yeah, right." Chase laughed, but then he saw Grant's face and the laugh vanished. "Uh…what exactly are you talking about?"

Grant was matter of fact about it. "I brought that knock-out stuff."

Chase's eyes widened. "The drug? You brought the *drug*?! I thought we discussed that!"

"We did." Grant patted the pocket again. "And you lost the argument. Sorry, I forgot to tell you." When he realized Chase was angrier than he'd expected, he figured maybe he should try to calm him down. "No one says we're gonna use it. I just figured I'd bring it in that one-in-a-hundred chance that June woman is working late."

Chase shook his head. "I do *not* approve of this."

"I know." Grant stared down the street and watched Kelly—about the same height as her son, just curvier now—climb the stairs to the front door of her brownstone. "For the record, I would prefer to keep it and drug Jamie Brock again someday. That was kinda funny. But it's a tool we might need. That's all."

Chase fumed in silence for another fifteen minutes while Grant repeatedly checked his watch, mostly because there was nothing else to do but look at Chase fuming. He was about to suggest they give up on Nick and try to do it alone when he saw the young man drop to the sidewalk from the fire escape in front of his building.

"Looks like Spider-Man escaped his mother and is ready for business."

Chase stopped moping long enough to look, half-afraid he might indeed see Nick in a Spider-Man costume. But, no, he appeared to be dressed as instructed: jeans, a black shirt, and sneakers.

"Almost didn't make it," he said, after jogging the last stretch. His thick hair seemed to keep bouncing long after the jog. "My mom came home."

"We saw," Grant said.

"She didn't want me to go out, so I told her I'd be playing video games in my room. Locked the door, came down the fire escape, and here I am!"

"And about time. Let's roll."

They were almost an hour behind schedule. It was time to stop fooling around and get to work.

The "getting into the building" part of the job was almost *too* easy. It was a few minutes before seven o'clock, and while many of the building's employees had left for the day, there were still enough people moving around the lobby that it was no chore to blend in.

But when the elevator doors opened onto the fifth floor offices of June Forteene Enterprises, they could see that the rest of the job could be a bit more difficult. It was apparent the place hadn't closed up shop for the night. The lights were all on and, somewhere in the background, a radio talk-show host was ranting about something or another. No one was sitting behind the front desk, but the door leading into the main office was wide open.

Grant motioned Chase and Nick back into the elevator and they rode it to the lobby.

"You think she's up there?" asked Chase when they were standing outside the sidewalk watching the occasional, slightly embarrassed man slip into see some Live! Nude! Girls!

"I don't know if she's there, but *someone* is. The thing is, I can't go back up there. If it's that guy from this morning and he recognizes me, there can only be trouble."

Chase nodded at his predicament while Nick studied a man walking out of the very adult storefront and adjusting his fly.

"You think men just go there to meet women?" he asked. "Or do they maybe meet other men, too?"

"Find out on your own time." Grant got back to the matter at hand. "You two are gonna have to go up alone and assess the situation. If you run into a guy with a stupid red sweater vest and stupid hipster glass frames, I can't be involved. If anyone else is there—especially if that someone is June Forteene—you'd better come get me."

Chase, trailed by Nick, took a few steps toward the building entrance when Grant stopped him.

"Here," he said, offering up the baggie full of chalky powder. "You might need this."

"Grant, you know how I feel—"

"I do. I just said you should take it. Whether you use it or not is your call."

Chase frowned and reluctantly stuck the baggie in his pants pocket.

The desk was still empty when Chase and Nick returned to the fifth floor. But this time, without Grant, they felt a little more comfortable taking a look around.

And the first thing they saw was a giant erect penis on the laptop monitor sitting on the desk in the hallway.

"My, my, my!" Nick put his face close to the screen and studied it so closely that his mother might have warned him he'd go blind for at least two reasons, only one of which his optometrist might have thought to warn him about. "What's this?"

"That," said Chase quietly, "is what we've come to get." And then he thought, *It can't possibly be this easy, can it? Grab the laptop and run, and be done with the job?*

He shook the thought away. Of *course* it wouldn't be that easy. It never was.

Nick finally pulled his eyeballs back a half inch or so from the screen. "So we're here for a photo of a penis? Why? There are millions of them on the Internet."

"That's not just any penis. That's what you'd call a famous penis. That's the picture we're here to erase. Y'see, if you zoom out there's also a face in the picture."

"Cute?"

Chase feigned disinterest. "He's okay, I guess."

Nick reached for the keypad. "Let's see." He zoomed the photo back. "Oh, he's *really* cute! Wow!"

"Ya think?"

The younger man kept staring at the monitor. "Hell, yeah. I'd totally do him. He's really hot for an old guy!"

That stopped Chase. "Wait...*old*?"

Nick didn't bother lifting his head. "I'm twenty-one. My old is a lot different from yours."

Chase didn't like that but supposed he had been there once.

"How's about we get to work?" Chase took a look around the hall. His eyes settled on the open office door. "I suppose we'd better take a look and see who's still here. Don't touch anything."

Nick finally averted his eyes from the monitor and whispered, "I hear ya, Grandpa."

Chase didn't say anything, but thought, *I'm beginning to understand how Grant became Grant.*

They stealthily slipped across the threshold and into the office, which was—unsurprisingly—nothing more than a room full of desks, computers, and paper. Although given the ground-floor tenant and the first image they'd encountered when entering June Forteene Enterprises, they'd be forgiven for expecting otherwise.

The disembodied voice of the radio host blathered something inflammatory about a trade agreement with the Solomon Islands as they crept through the room. Chase, who actually knew what they were looking for, saw nothing that struck him as the single repository for images of Austin Peebles's manhood, and that depressed him a little bit. It would mean that every piece of electrical equipment would have to be taken out that night.

Usually, a job like that would have made Chase a very happy man, and would have paid the rent for the month. But this night they had two jobs, and dragging a half dozen computers and God knew how much other crap around Manhattan would only slow them down.

And they still didn't know who was in the office: June Forteene, or the guy in the red sweater vest, or someone else. *Someone* was there, and they'd have to figure that out before making another move. It wouldn't do to be caught walking off with the computers.

They didn't have to wait long for the answer to that question, because—over the radio blather—they soon heard a voice.

"What are you doing in there?!"

Chase's instinct, as an experienced criminal, was to drop his frame below the closest desk. *Try to stay compact; try to hide.* Those were the instincts and experiences of a professional kicking in.

The newbie stood frozen like a deer in headlights in the middle of the office, unprotected and open.

Which is why Nick—standing as tall as someone Nick's height could stand, and unprotected by anything but bare floor—was the one who got caught.

Chase, compact and hidden on the far side of a desk behind the door, was safe…for that moment, at least.

The pro wondered how the newbie would handle himself. He wished only professional curiosity was at stake, but knew that both of them—and Grant—had too much riding on it for this to be an academic exercise.

To his credit, Nick played it cool, never once glancing in Chase's direction. Meanwhile, a man who could only have been the one Grant encountered earlier that morning—red sweater vest and all—entered the office from the hall.

"I asked what you're doing in there," he said again, setting the bathroom key on top of a desk. He was trying to act tough, but sounded more skittish than they were.

Chase moved his head just enough to see Nick. He was smiling and had somehow made himself look like the most innocent man in the tri-state region.

"Do you work here?"

"Of course. Why?"

Improbably, Nick's smile seemed to broaden. "I'm here as a concerned citizen. Did you know there's an adult video establishment in your building?"

Red Sweater Vest blushed slightly. "Of course I do. I have to walk past that den of perversion every time I enter or leave the building. But what about it?"

"We need to shut it down."

The man eyed him warily. "Who are you again?"

"A concerned citizen." Nick coughed into his hand. "A *very* concerned citizen."

"I meant your name."

"Oh. The name is John."

"John *what*?"

"John, uh, LaMarca." Behind the desk, Chase frowned. "Did you know that men are receiving sexual favors in that peep show?"

The blush spread until Red Sweater Vest's face matched his clothing. "I have no idea what goes on down there. I don't *want* to know."

"And not just from the Live! Nude! Girls!" Nick exclaimed every exclamation point.

There was a long pause before Red Sweater Vest could speak again. "You mean homosexual gay sodomy is occurring in this building?"

Nick nodded vigorously. "We have to stop it."

"But how can I...?" Red Sweater Vest leaned against a desk and fanned himself with a floppy hand. "Mr. LaMarca, I appreciate your concern, and I will definitely discuss this with my boss. But now you'll have to go. I need to lock up..."

Nick stood his ground. "Don't you care?"

"Of *course* I care. But this really should be dealt with at a higher level. I mean..." Some of the color began to fade from his cheeks. "I haven't been in New York City for a full week. *I* certainly don't know where to turn."

"Less than a week? Wow! Maybe you need a buddy to show you around the city."

Nick's voice had taken on a slight purr, which came as more than a little surprise to Chase. With much of the action blocked from his hiding spot, he wondered what, if anything, had inspired Nick to lay on the seductive tone and think it might help...although he supposed the fact that Red Sweater Vest had been looking at a photo of a phallus before they walked in was as logical a starting point as any.

For his part, the other young man—the one who actually belonged there—sounded increasingly flustered.

"I, uh...That's very kind of you. But as you can see I'm very busy, and, uh..."

"Are you sure?" The purr deepened, and Chase began to wonder when Nick would go full-on Eartha Kitt. "Because I really know my way around."

"I...I..."

"Around and around and around…"

"Uh…I, uh…" Chase didn't have to look to know that Red Sweater Vest was in full blush.

And then Nick—who'd already pushed quite a bit more than Chase would have pushed—took it another step further.

"By the way, I couldn't help but notice the dick shot on your computer screen." A long, awkward pause followed before he asked, "Is it yours?"

To which Red Sweater Vest said something that sounded like, "Gahhhhh!" Which was followed by the sound of two feet stumbling toward the desk in the hall. He'd just listened in on either the best attempted seduction or the best mind-fuck—or maybe *both*—ever.

Chase lifted his head from behind the desk, and this time saw Nick's face not six inches away.

"How'm I doing?" the kid whispered.

Chase bobbed his head agreeably. "You've got game." And then, because they were dealing with a man—a self-righteous one at that, who also seemed to be a hypocrite, not that the combination surprised him much anymore—he decided that maybe Grant's drug might come in handy after all. It was an impulse he knew he would not have had if they'd been interrupted by a woman, and that sort of bothered him. It was sexist and unprofessional to treat some victims better than others, even if the fairer sex had been represented by June Forteene herself. But that was the way he'd been raised. He was an Old-Fashioned Gentleman when it came to stealing things and drugging people.

He slipped the baggie into Nick's hand. "Put some of this into his drink."

Confusion clouded Nick's face. "I have to take him out drinking?"

Chase shook his head. "Water…coffee…Anything."

"Oh! Gotcha." Nick's face disappeared and Chase slid back to the floor behind the desk.

The conversation that followed was hard to hear, since almost all of it took place out by the elevator, but after a few minutes voices were raised and Chase was sure he heard a scuffle. He started to emerge from behind the desk, only to take a step back into the shadows when Red Sweater Vest staggered into the office and slammed the door behind him. He shuffled to a panel on the wall and punched in a few numbers, and then—mission already accomplished—stood stiffly and swayed a few times before crumpling indelicately to the ground.

It was only when the guy was flat on his back that Chase approached and saw that he was out every bit as much as Grant and Jamie had been out. Red Sweater Vest wouldn't interfere with them for at least the next five hours.

And then Chase heard the sound of Nick's voice, looked up, and saw him leaning through the still-open transom window.

"Don't open the door," Nick warned. "I'm pretty sure he set the alarm."

Chase, perplexed, glanced at the wooden door. "He set the alarm?"

"I think so. When he figured out I drugged him, he made a dash for it. Said something about locking things down. Also that I'd be going to hell." Nick looked down from his perch at the comatose assistant splayed across the floor. "Gotta give him credit for being a loyalist."

"Why didn't you stop him?"

"I tried—didn't you hear us wresting out here?—but he got away from me. Sorry about that." Nick shrugged the best he could, considering his narrow shoulders were the only things holding him in the transom frame seven feet above the hallway floor. "That's one of the disadvantages of being on the small side."

Chase looked at the narrow transom window where Nick was perched. There was no way he was getting up there, let alone through it.

"You'd better go get Grant."

Chapter Eight

Grant Lambert took one look at the lock and decided he wouldn't even risk it. All that wiring meant he might get through, but someone would be there before any of them had a chance to do much except get arrested.

"So what am I supposed to do?" Chase called out in the direction of the transom. "Stay in here with the drugged guy until someone turns off the alarm in the morning? That doesn't sound like a very good plan."

He heard Grant's voice on the other side of the wooden door, but had a hard time making out his words. So he hollered at the transom again.

"What was that?"

Nick appeared, with a smile on his face that expressed how much he was enjoying being the small, wiry young guy, and therefore the only one of them who didn't find the transom an insurmountable obstacle.

"Grant says you should start handing equipment to me through the transom while he goes and finds a handcart."

Chase thought about that. "Still doesn't answer the question about how I get out of here."

Nick turned and conferred with Grant before continuing. "He says he'll figure that out."

Chase leaned against June Forteene's desk and said, mostly to himself, but maybe also to God if He existed, "Perfect. Just perfect."

Over the next half hour, in the downtime when he wasn't climbing up on the desk he'd pushed in front of the door in order to hand Nick a computer or monitor or stray cell phone or whatever else he could find, Chase used the last computer in the office to search June's files. He was afraid it'd be almost impossible to log into her computer, but she'd helpfully left her Rolodex open to a card that could only be her password: REAGANGIRL. Chase was more a Clinton man, but appreciated her devotion.

He found a few copies of Austin Peebles's dick pic stored on the hard drive and in some network folders, then followed one of her bookmarks to an Internet file storage site and found a few more. He carefully deleted each one, and then deleted them again from the trash directories. Finally, he spent another twenty minutes carefully inspecting his work, going back and forth until he was as confident as possible—which was closer to 90 percent than 100 percent, but it was the best anyone who *wasn't* June Forteene could shoot for—that he'd done what needed to be done.

One thing bothered him, though. Based on her bookmarks and a careful review of various passwords and web addresses she tried to hide in her Rolodex, June didn't seem to have a secure site on the Internet to store files. That didn't seem right.

Then again, maybe she'd never needed one. Her thoughts were immediately accessible to the world when she blogged. It was reasonable to think that Austin Peebles's cock shot was the first top-secret file she'd ever stumbled upon.

"Grant wants to know what's taking so long," said Nick, once again propped in the transom.

"Tell him I'm updating my Facebook status." With that, he pulled the power cord from the outlet and walked June's computer and monitor over to the desk, climbed up, and passed them through the window to Nick. "These are the last pieces. Now…how am I supposed to get out of here?"

He waited a minute while Nick handed off the merchandise to Grant on the other side of the transom and relayed the question, and then Nick was back in the opening.

"He wants to know if you're absolutely sure you can't fit through the transom."

"Tell him I'm *more* than absolutely sure. And ask him, if he's so limber, how come he's not climbing up to the transom to tell me himself?"

"Hey," said Nick, with the same tiny shrug, one he could carry off while his legs dangled a half-body length above the floor. "Don't get angry at *me*. I'm just the messenger."

"Then tell the guy who I'm angry with to figure a way for me to get out of this fuckin' office."

Another minute passed before the young man returned. "Grant says you should give us a ten-minute head start to get the equipment out of here, then open the door and run like hell."

"That's the plan?" Chase didn't like it.

Nick smiled. "That's *his* plan. We'll wait for you at Forty-sixth and Ninth, outside that Thai place."

Chase wanted to ask which one—there were approximately seventeen Thai restaurants near the intersection of West Forty-sixth Street and Ninth Avenue—but Nick disappeared again and the next noise Chase heard was the sound of a very heavy handcart being wheeled away.

He waited ten minutes, and—when it was time—moved the desk away from the door, took a deep calming breath, and prepared to sprint.

Chase turned the handle and yanked. The door gave maybe a quarter-inch before it stopped and he heard what sounded like dead bolts clicking. When he looked into the narrow gap between the door and frame, he saw that, sure enough, two shiny dead bolts now held the door firmly in place. He was pretty certain those locks hadn't been locked earlier.

Grant and Nick were gone and Chase was locked inside a fifth-floor office he'd just burgled. With a drugged young man in a red sweater vest sprawled across the floor. And no doubt in one or two or twenty nearby locations, an alarm was now ringing.

He regarded none of that as good.

People called Joseph Enright "Captain" in recognition of his former careers as a Virginia state trooper and chief of security at the Virginia Cathedral of Love, which—unlike the state police—was not an official state institution, but was as close as any private institution had managed to get.

But the mega-church fell on hard times—mega-churches tended to do that when their pastors were charged with several dozen state and federal felonies—and Captain Enright needed a source of income. Fortunately he had skills, foremost among them that he considered himself a top-notch security consultant.

How he ended up living in Manhattan was another story, and one

Captain Enright didn't talk about. Some thought that maybe he was more involved with whatever had happened at the Virginia Cathedral of Love than he wanted people to know. Others thought he might be chasing a dream. And there were even people who suspected Enright enjoyed the relative anonymity afforded in a huge metropolis because he was hiding from darker secrets than any of them could ever guess.

One thing people seldom considered was that he moved to New York because it was where the money was, and people who had constant concerns about security—from terrorists to street thugs—were often all too willing to part with that money.

Enright had heard all the rumors but did nothing to dismiss them or stop their spread. He even encouraged some of the shadier ones. In his line of work, a little mystery was usually a good thing. The G. Gordon Liddy rumor? Bullshit! Would he stop it? Never!

There was little mystery about one aspect of his character, though. Captain Joseph Enright was a slave to his political convictions. When he wasn't working—and sometimes when he was—he did little but listen to conservative radio hosts. He didn't need validation for his beliefs—he'd held them since the days pre-dating talk radio—but it was always nice to have new ammunition in his arsenal. Through the radio shows, he discovered right-wing bloggers. And the rest fell into place.

When the Times Square Mosque was first proposed—let the mayor and cowardly power elite of the city argue that the mosque was on Eleventh Avenue and almost a mile from Times Square; that was just their mollycoddling rhetoric—the blogger June Forteene was the first and loudest voice to stir the opposition. Enright attended one of her rallies in the heart of Times Square and was immediately struck by her bravery...so struck by it that he feared for her safety. With her office strategically positioned on Eighth Avenue—equidistant between Times Square and the Times Square Mosque—he believed June's stance had placed her in danger.

And so he offered to do something he'd never done before. He gave away his professional services for free.

Now the offices of June Forteene Enterprises had state-of-the-art security. If anyone tried to get in without entering the code, backup dead bolts would click into place and an alarm would go off at Enright's home office. If someone attacked during working hours, she or her staff could press a panic button and an alarm would go off at Enright's home office. He was even designing her a safe room, and in return he asked for nothing but her personal safety, and maybe an occasional free mention on her blog. He'd once checked out her blog ad prices after the Times Square Mosque issue made her popular and—*whew!*—better to get a free plug than pay.

June hadn't needed an alarm to go off to know Enright had given her a good deal and as much peace of mind as anyone had in a crazy city full of wild-eyed granola-chomping liberals, angry blacks, illegal Guatemalans, militant married homosexuals, godless Muslims, knife-wielding Puerto Ricans, Italian and Russian and Chinese mobsters, inscrutable Hasidim, surly teenagers, the chronically homeless, homeless advocates, and aggressive stroller moms from the Upper West Side and Park Slope.

Ironically, for all that peace of mind, when the alarm first sounded that night Captain Joseph Enright thought the noise was coming from the TV.

It took almost a full minute before he realized the sound was a *real* alarm. And, checking the panel in his home office, he saw that someone had tried the door at June Forteene Enterprises.

Enright holstered a pistol and prepared to go to work.

Chase was getting too old for this.

Once he made peace with the fact he was locked in and alone, he shoved the desk back in front of the door—figuring if push came to shove it'd buy him another fifteen seconds before the inevitable arrest—and tried the windows. The sheer drop to the ground wasn't inviting. Then there was the furniture, but it was one thing to hide from Red Sweater Vest, and quite another to hide from the cops or private security or whoever would inevitably show up. The ceiling...No, there was no drop ceiling; it was just flat plaster and pipes.

That left the transom.

The *fucking transom.*

The opening would have been a tight squeeze for Nick Donovan had he gone all the way through instead of just hanging there, showing off his relative youth and limberness. Chase was taller, thicker, and quite a bit older. There was no way he was going to make it through that small window.

But there were also no other options.

Chase took a deep breath and committed to the only possible escape route he could imagine, as unlikely as it was.

❖

Captain Joseph Enright lived a short five-minute cab ride from June Forteene's office. Although—since it took him five minutes to hail a cab before starting that ride—he was actually ten minutes out. He wanted to be the first man on the scene, so his plan was to wait until he was a few blocks from his destination before calling 911 to report the attempted break-in.

The cab was getting close. He had tapped the 9 and a 1 on his phone's keypad when the driver slammed on the brakes. Enright looked out the front windshield and saw two clowns trying to cross mid-block with a handcart overloaded with computers and accessories that kept slipping off and crashing to the asphalt. It would have been funny if they weren't causing him an inexcusable delay.

"Thees peeples," said the exasperated driver.

"I hear ya, Omar," said Enright. The driver's name wasn't Omar; it was just something he called everyone who looked like they were born in a place where everyone didn't look Nordic. "Hit the horn."

"Beg pardon, there ees fine to honk."

"If they catch you, I'll pay it."

Thus unburdened, the cabdriver happily laid on the horn, and the clowns—shocked at the sudden noise—knocked another computer off the cart.

"Idiots," Enright muttered.

There was a full-length mirror propped against one wall in the office, and Chase paused—very briefly—to admire his reflection. For his age, the stomach was fairly flat and the body was fairly taut. Sure, everything had been flatter and tauter once, but he was holding it together for a guy in his mid-forties.

He could notice these things because he was standing in a pair of gray—"dove gray," the box had said—boxer-briefs and nothing else, having tossed the rest of his clothes—pants, shirt, shoes, even socks— over the transom. There had been a moment when he wondered if he'd made a mistake, but the clothes were already gone and there was no turning back. And if he was going to make it through that tiny opening, he couldn't risk that anything would get snagged...or add as much as an extra millimeter of girth to an already impossibly tight fit.

Chase climbed onto the desk one last time and grasped the frame of the transom, straining his biceps as he hauled his body toward the window.

Enright, still having only dialed 9-1, held his finger over that final "1" and ordered the cabbie to blast his horn again.

The good news, Chase supposed, was that his body was now more out than in. What was left inside was mostly just bare legs, kicking in the air and trying to find traction.

What was outside was his entire upper body and the top half of his bare buttocks.

It was what was stuck in the middle that was the problem.

That is where those dove gray boxer-briefs had snagged on the frame, half-exposing his ass and leaving him dangling upside down over the hallway floor. He tried rocking, but nothing came loose. He tried lunging, but nothing gave.

And this, Chase thought, as blood rushed to his head and made him think the situation was sort of funny, *is how my criminal career will end: upside down with my ass half-exposed and dangling out of a...*

Then there was the sound of ripping cotton-polyester blend and Chase didn't have time to finish the thought before his taut—and now naked—body plummeted seven feet to the very hard floor.

Enright charged through the lobby and pressed the elevator call button. He was frustrated, but at least he'd beat the NYPD to the scene of the crime.

When the doors opened, he stepped aside to let a limping man hobble out before boarding. He thought the guy looked too young to be in such rough shape, but then again this wasn't a pretty city and it especially wasn't a pretty block.

Enright pushed the button for five.

Chase LaMarca, mostly clothed except for the boxer-briefs he'd had to leave behind, stumbled onto the sidewalk, propped his ass on a fire hydrant, and rued the day he chose a life of crime. It would have been too easy to blame Grant Lambert, but…well, yes, it *was* Grant's fault, now that he thought about it.

It had been eighteen years since they both decided on the same night to break into the Groc-O-Rama where Chase worked and—before the next morning dawned—began the relationship that soon made them partners in life *and* crime. For Chase, the Groc-O-Rama job was only going to be a one-time thing, a way to compensate himself for a lousy job and a worse boss. For Grant, this sort of thing was a career.

To the extent Grant had drawn him in for almost two decades, Chase thought it was fair to lay the blame for this latest debacle at his feet. *Grant* had turned him into a professional criminal. He thought briefly about how the Church had pushed the concept of free will, but he didn't like that thought, so he pushed it away and continued to blame everything on Grant Lambert.

He could have done more blaming while he free-willed his sore body to not be so sore, but that's when Chase caught a glimpse of flickering blue and red lights approaching up Eighth Avenue. The lights were roughly four blocks away; he figured he had about thirty seconds before they pulled up in front of him.

He also figured a middle-aged guy who'd just taken a nasty headfirst, seven-feet fall would look sort of obvious staggering away from the scene of the crime. For that matter, he'd also look obvious propped against the fire hydrant, especially if anyone cared to ask him about missing underwear.

Chase looked around for an escape route.

Captain Enright punched in the security code and tried to open the office door. The dead bolts retracted, but it was blocked. He put his shoulder into it and finally felt movement.

The lights were still on inside the office—on the entire damn floor, for that matter—and as the door slowly opened he saw he was fighting a very heavy desk. *An old-school but clever way to block the entrance*, he thought, putting his shoulder to the door and shoving with just a bit more force.

Once he'd moved it enough to squeeze through the threshold he took a step inside and stopped. A young man's body was sprawled across the floor.

Enright checked for a pulse. Reassured he wasn't dealing with a stiff, he finally called June Forteene.

His call went to voice mail.

"Miss Forteene, this is Enright. It looks like there's been a break-in at your office. I can't say for sure, but this appears to be drug-related, based on the junkie passed out on your floor. Please call me back so we can ascertain if anything is missing."

He clicked off as a half dozen of New York's Finest swarmed out of the elevator.

"Who're you?" asked the first cop who'd managed to squeeze through the door, his hand hovering near his holster.

The captain puffed out his chest. "Enright. I'm the guy who called you."

Cop One was wary, and that was *before* he saw the man in the red sweater vest eating industrial carpeting. His eyes shifted back and forth between the alive guy and the maybe-not-alive guy before he decided the alive guy was the one he'd rather deal with. There was less paperwork involved with alive guys.

"Got ID, Enright?"

Enright did and presented it.

Cop Two had now shoved his way through the narrow entrance into the office. He took a glance at Edward Hepplewhite and asked, "Who's the deceased?"

Enright puffed up again. "He's not deceased. I got a pulse. Figure he's a junkie. I saw another one get off the elevator when I arrived. This building must be *crawling* with them, like it's a shooting gallery or something."

"You say you saw another junkie?" asked Cop One, still eyeing Enright's credentials.

"Affirmative. Limping like a sick old man."

"Well, was he?"

Enright scoffed. "Nah, he was around forty years of age. White; brown hair with highlights—"

Cop One interrupted. "Kind of old for highlights."

"True." Enright got himself back on track. "Five-nine, five-ten, something like that. But stumbling like an old man at forty, well, that's what drugs'll do to you."

Cop Three had now entered the office. He rubbed his nose and gave out a little half laugh. "If you say so." Then he rubbed his nose again and let out a cackle. Enright thought the cop was being ironic; he wasn't.

From the hallway, Cop Four called out. "Hey, you guys see these underpants?"

"What underpants?" asked Cop Two.

"Stuck in that window over the door."

They all looked up and saw the gray fabric.

"Gray underpants," said Cop Four.

"Nah," said Cop Five. "That's what they call 'dove gray'. See, you've got your 'gray,' your 'dove gray,' your 'dark gray,' your 'storm cloud gray'…"

Enright's face scrunched up and he looked at comatose Edward with contempt. "What kind of sick junkie bastard *are* you?"

After the paramedics wheeled the junkie in the red sweater vest—who may have been wearing dove gray boxer-briefs over his clothing, a form of perversion that made even cops who thought they'd seen it all on these mean streets shake their heads in disgust—Cops One through Three and Six thought they'd better have a look around.

Thanks to Enright, they now knew the junkie had broken into June Forteene's office. Some cops loved her; most cops loathed her; but all cops knew who she was. And all cops also knew that she'd use her blog to rip apart the entire force—from the commissioner to the rookie beat cop—if they came up with nothing but a junkie in a red sweater vest and a ripped pair of underpants.

Ripped pair of underpants. *Sick bastard…*

"Where the hell is Chase?" Grant asked for the fortieth time in twenty minutes. After spending far too much time loading, dropping, re-loading, and re-dropping their haul, he and Nick had finally managed to stow the computers, paraphernalia, and handcart in a friend's basement a few blocks away where—for a C-note—no questions would be asked. Grant hated to part with the money, but it was safer than wheeling a load of electronics around the streets of New York all night.

But…

"Where the hell is Chase?"

Nick pondered that. "What if he's trapped?"

"I worry," Grant acknowledged.

A twinkle came to Nick's eye. "It sounds like you're in love."

Something less than a twinkle came to Grant's eye. "Of course I love him. Think we've been together for eighteen years just so I don't have to do my own laundry?"

That sobered Nick, but maybe not enough. "You know who can save him if he's trapped?"

"I'm listenin'."

"Cadmium!"

"I'm not listenin' anymore."

When Cops One, Two, and Six walked into the storefront advertising Live! Nude! Girls! in full uniform, they couldn't have killed the buzz more quickly if they'd lit the place on fire. The moment they entered, the music died and the only sound was that of zippers zipping and the clicking heels of a few Live! Nude! Girls! as they ran to the closets that passed as dressing rooms before the lights went up and their patrons realized they were watching forty-eight-year-old grandmothers taking it all off for their carnal enjoyment.

Chase stood away from the handful of other patrons near a rack of magazines featuring women with breasts the size and shapeliness of bags of concrete. He'd only been in the place for a few minutes but had already had no fewer than three invitations to join other men in the buddy booths. So much for posing as a breast man. In any event, he wouldn't even consider those invitations. He was totally devoted to Grant Lambert. It also helped that two of the asks came from men who reminded him of his grandfather—who'd been dead for twenty years; at least one of the guys looked like he might have died at the same time—and the third came from a guy who was maybe thirty-five but probably hadn't had teeth in twenty years.

The cops seemed nice enough, though, so he was happy to talk to them. Not that he had a choice. He shelved the copy of *Mega-Mammaries Monthly* he'd been browsing and flashed them a smile.

"Name?" asked Cop Two.

"Charles LaMarca." He hated his birth name—hence his almost exclusive use of "Chase"—but this was not the time to object. And he wasn't going to lie, which had far less to do with morality than the repercussions of being caught in a lie.

"And why are you here, Mr. LaMarca?"

"Why does anyone come here?" Chase nodded at the magazines. "I like breasts."

"Mmm-hmm." The Cop Six made a few notes on a pad. Chase didn't like the fact they had his name and didn't seem to believe he liked female breasts, but he had no priors and there was nothing illegal about hanging out in an adult video store. It was skeevy, maybe, but perfectly legal.

"Have you seen anything suspicious tonight, Mr. LaMarca?"

Chase pretended to think about that. "This probably has something to do with that ambulance, right?"

"We'll ask the questions."

"Of course." He pretended to think again. "No, I can't really think of anything."

The cops nodded. "Okay, thank you, sir…"

"Except…"

They turned back to him. "Go ahead."

"Except there was this guy wandering around outside acting sort of strange. He might've been drinking. Or…" Chase pantomimed shooting a needle into his arm. "That."

"Can you describe this man?" asked Cop Six, who already had his notepad out again.

"Hmm. Glasses…red sweater vest…"

The cops looked at each other knowingly. "Thank you, sir. That's helpful."

Chase shrugged. "So am I free to go?"

They said he was, and so he did. As quickly as his bruised, aching body could get away from Live! Nude! Girls!

"Where the hell is Chase?" Grant asked for the forty-ninth time. But then he saw him across the street outside one of the many Thai restaurants that weren't the one where they were waiting and called out to him. Soon he had his answer.

"What took you so long?"

Chase didn't say anything. He just sort of glowered, even staring down Grant.

Grant finally caved. "I take it something went wrong."

Nick happened to glance over at a moment when Chase moved his legs and noticed something was off. Or at least off center.

"How come you're not wearing underwear?" Not that Nick didn't approve; but since he'd noticed…

Grant's brow furrowed. "You're not wearing underwear?" Chase *always* wore underwear. Even to bed. Furthermore, Grant disapproved of Nick's approval of this situation.

Finally, Chase spoke. "Long story. Someday—*if* I ever decide to forgive you—I'll tell you all about it."

"Fair enough." Grant didn't really agree—he wanted to know what happened to his partner's underwear—but he swallowed his jealous impulses and glanced at his watch.

"We'd better get over to the East Side and take care of the second half of this job."

"Let's go," Chase agreed, and he managed to hobble a few yards before reeling into the side of yet another Thai restaurant.

"You okay?" There was a hardness to Grant's voice that didn't sit well with Chase, who was in no mood to placate him.

"Fine as a guy can be after he was abandoned."

Grant knew there was more to that. "And?"

Chase sniffled. "And therefore had to crawl through a teeny tiny transom window."

"And?"

"And ended up ripping his underwear off and falling to the floor. And then had to run into Live! Nude! Girls! to try to avoid the cops, 'cept they found him there anyway so he had to lie his way out of the place after they interrogated him and got his name."

Grant finally got it. He patted Chase on the shoulder. "Sorry."

Chase sniffled again. "Thank you for finally understanding."

"Yeah, I get it now." Grant's eyes darted around and then returned to his watch. "But, you know…"

Chase took a step away from the wall. "The East Side job. Yeah. I'll do my best."

"I'll try to make this easy on you."

Chase hadn't quite forgiven him but still kissed Grant under the garish yellow awning advertising Pad Thai. "Thanks."

Grant smiled. "Next leg of this job, we'll make Nick do the hard stuff."

CHAPTER NINE

While Chase had been hanging upside down by his underwear—and then crashing to the floor *not* in his underwear—June Forteene had been having a much less memorable evening. The crowds and traffic congestion that accompanied the annual United Nations General Assembly made her neighborhood practically uninhabitable between early morning and late evening for two weeks at the end of each September, so she decided to wait it out by seeing a movie.

Which meant her phone was turned off when Captain Enright called...and for quite a while afterward.

It was only when she was walking back toward her apartment that she finally picked up the message in which Enright informed her that a junkie had broken into her office, and his follow up message reporting that the police had said junkie in custody. He had also, she noted, managed to pat himself on the back repeatedly for designing and installing the alarm system that had detected the perp. No doubt he was fishing for more publicity on her blog.

Maybe she'd give it, maybe not. That would probably depend on what freebie extras he'd throw in to ensure this never happened again. In any event, promoting Enright's business was one of the last things on her mind when she called him back.

"What do you *mean* there was a break-in?"

"Just that. There was a break-in."

"Did they take anything?"

Enright was standing outside the building hunting for an empty on-duty cab, so he wasn't in the position to take inventory. But he had to tell her *something*.

"I couldn't really tell, but since we caught the perpetrator on the premises I can't see how he would've had an opportunity to steal anything."

She fumed at the corner of Park Avenue and East Forty-second Street, across from Grand Central Terminal. "And how, exactly, did someone get into this fortress you designed for me?"

Since his client deserved an answer, Enright waved off the first free cab he'd seen in seven minutes of waiting. "The transom."

"The *transom*?!" Rage was making her shake; in turn, the shaking was making other pedestrians swing wide to avoid her on the busy sidewalk.

"We didn't wire it. Figured it wasn't big enough for a human being to get through it."

"Well…how do you know that's the way he came in?"

Enright swallowed hard. "Are you sure you want to know?"

"Tell me!"

"We found his underwear snagged on the transom frame."

June braced herself against a light pole. "You mean this burglar was naked?"

"No, ma'am. Fully clothed."

"But…"

"We figure he was wearing the underwear on the outside of his clothes."

June Forteene closed her eyes tightly. She felt violated. "What kind of *sick bastard*…I should come over there."

Enright sat himself on the same fire hydrant Chase had sat on less than an hour earlier. "You can if you want, but I'm sure we nailed the guy before he could steal anything. Just another pathetic junkie who passed out before he could commit the crime."

The cold metal against the light pole seemed to calm her. "In your professional opinion, he didn't steal anything?"

"In my professional opinion, if he did it'd have to be in the ambulance with him. Meaning he couldn't have taken much but—if he stole anything—it'll be waiting at Roosevelt Hospital in the morning." He chuckled. "That or The Tombs."

She was wavering. She wanted to be reassured, but she was also so used to being in control. "You're sure?"

Enright nestled his butt into the fire hydrant cap. "Listen, I've been in this business—in one capacity or another—for over thirty years. Nothing's ever one hundred percent, but trust me when I tell you this feels like ninety-nine-point-nine percent to me."

June didn't like that stray one-tenth of one percent. "But—"

"Go *home*," Enright pleaded as another empty cab passed him. "Anything that has to be cleaned up can be cleaned up tomorrow."

So she did. Not happily, and not contentedly, but she did it.

Worst-case scenario, she thought, *I still have my laptop. With my tools, no one can stop June Forteene.*

If she'd known who was plotting against her, she might have felt even *more* self-confident.

The super was wasting time in the lobby by the time she weaved a path through the mob of cops and people hanging around to see what the cops were doing and reached her building.

"Evening, Hillary." He said it politely, but it still made her cringe. June Forteene had so taken over her identity that she barely remembered there was a Hillary Morris buried somewhere inside her.

She nodded pleasantly and went to collect her mail, since there was nothing to be gained by lashing out at her super for using her legal name, and wasn't really paying attention as he talked to her.

Not until she heard the letters UPS.

Her eyes were focused like lasers when she turned toward him. "I'm sorry, what did you say?"

"Just that there's been a lot of craziness around here today. Glad you got through the—"

"There's *always* craziness during the General Assembly. But what did you say about UPS?"

He laughed. "Yeah. Someone stole a delivery truck right off Second Avenue this afternoon. Can you believe it? The driver doubled-parked and ran into a building down the block. Wasn't gone for three minutes, but then the truck was gone. You'd think with all the cops around here…"

She stopped him before he could ramble off on another tangent. "What did this UPS driver look like?"

He had to think. "Young black woman. Short hair." That sounded right to him. "Why?"

As soon as she heard "young," "black," and "woman," June lost interest. "No reason. Just curious." She added a shrug. "Just wondered if I could use the story on my blog as another example of lawlessness in this liberal city."

The super shook his head. "It's big news for the block, I suppose. Especially for the folks who didn't get their packages. But I don't think the nation would care."

She pushed the button next to the elevator and tuned him out again, which is how she almost missed hearing him say:

"And then there was the other UPS driver today. The one who came looking for you."

The elevator opened but she didn't step inside.

"A UPS driver was looking for me? A *different* one? Not the young, black woman?"

"Nah, this guy was white. Maybe mid-fifties...hard to tell. Needed a shave. Nice guy, but kind of seedy. Maybe he's a temp or something."

Her eyes darkened. "By any chance, was that driver—the seedy one; not the young, black female—wearing an *old* uniform?"

He blinked a few times, as if conjuring up the image. "Now that you mention it, I believe he was. Yeah, it had some loose threads and it didn't fit right." He thought about that a second. "Yeah, I guess he *was* a temp. Poor guy, probably starting his life over at an advanced age..."

The super prattled on and June stabbed at the elevator button, not listening. It was impossible to believe all of this—the seedy UPS driver showing up at her home and work, and then the break-in—was a coincidence. She'd get Enright on the phone again as soon as she was back in her apartment and safely locked behind a sturdy door.

Minutes later, Grant's face looked through that lobby window. The super was still puttering around.

"That's a guy who needs a hobby," he said, motioning Chase and Nick to the stoop next door.

He'd filled them in on his plan on the shuttle train that ran from Times Square to Grand Central and fleshed it out on the walk downhill to Second Avenue. It sounded easy enough. Chase would get June out of her apartment and down to lobby under some pretense—the UN General Assembly offered them a multitude of excuses, so they might as well try to use it to their advantage—and Grant and Nick would break into the apartment and grab her laptop, cell phone, and anything else they thought might contain that photo of Austin Peebles being indiscreet. And then they'd get the hell out of there.

Chase had decided he should pretend to be a cop, so they stopped at a shop in Grand Central Terminal and picked up a cheap tie. He looked more like a crook wearing a tie—and no underwear—than detectives on the screen, but since it didn't make him look much different from most real-world NYPD detectives, it'd do.

But first they had to get the damn super out of the lobby. A few minutes passed, and it didn't look like he was going anywhere.

After another few minutes, Chase had an idea. He walked into the lobby and flashed his wallet at the Guy Who Obviously Needed a Hobby. "Bailey, NYPD United Nations Special Detail." His fake badge gleamed in the lighting, which was no surprise since the super seemed to have time to dust the fixture every day. "I'm looking for the building superintendent."

The man pointed to himself. "That's me."

Chase's expression was severe. "Do you know the name 'General Abudhabi'?"

The super scratched his ear. "Can't say I do." He scratched again. "Should I?"

Chase's expression deepened from "severe" to "life-and-death." "General Abudhabi is in charge of United Nations General Assembly security, and he needs to talk to you."

"Me?" The super was confused.

"You." Chase leaned close to his ear. "You didn't hear this from me—because I'm not supposed to tell a soul—but tomorrow night the leaders of the world's superpowers will be having a secret meeting at the United Nations Building. It's very hush-hush, and won't even be announced to the public until days after it's over." He scowled. "Maybe weeks. Maybe *never*."

The super was still confused, but now at least understood he was somehow becoming involved in perhaps the biggest single event in world history. That sure beat polishing and re-polishing the brass handrail on the lower level of the staircase.

"So remember," Chase continued. "Don't tell anyone. The safety of our country—maybe the world—depends on your silence."

"I promise." The super swallowed. He understood he was about to play an important role in history, one he *might* be able to share with a grandchild one day if either of his kids ever took the time to procreate. "I *promise!*"

Chase clasped his shoulder. "That's fantastic. You're a good citizen." Then, leaning into his ear again, he added, "General Abudhabi will be contacting you within the hour. It's important for you to stand by your phone and wait for the call."

"But my phone number is unlisted."

Chase winked. "That's no obstacle for the leaders of the world's superpowers, citizen. Now you'd better get to your apartment. And remember: Don't leave until the general calls."

"I won't!" The super saluted and proudly walked off to his basement apartment. Usually he thought of it as dark and depressing and sad, but tonight General Abudhabi would be calling!

When the lobby was empty, Chase opened the door for Grant and Nick.

Grant was wary. "That looked a little too easy. What's the catch?"

"No catch." Chase rolled his shoulders, which were still sore from the fall, and tried to work out a few kinks. "I have a gift—the gift of being convincing—and I use it for your benefit."

"Okay, Rain Man." Grant pushed the elevator button. "And now we're gonna finish this job, right?"

The three men bumped fists and got on the elevator.

Enright, quite proud of himself, had June Forteene on speakerphone so Bernadette could hear her voice. That Bernadette was a cat really didn't matter; at least he could share his close personal relationship with this famed blogger with another living being.

He had wanted to start with self-congratulations for his capture of the comatose junkie, but she was all over a different topic.

"I'm being stalked by a fake UPS driver."

Enright stroked Bernadette. "A...*what*?"

"I'm telling you—wait, am I on speaker?"

Enright responded with something between throat noise and "yes."

"Take me off."

"Sorry. I had it on speaker so Bernadette could listen in."

"Who's Bernadette?"

"Never mind. So you were saying..."

"There's a guy dressed in an old UPS uniform who's stalking me. He showed up at my office this morning, and this afternoon my super ran into him in my apartment building lobby."

"Are you sure it was the same man?"

"Well...no. I haven't personally seen him yet. But how many seedy-looking bums wearing old, frayed UPS uniforms can there be out there?"

A lot, Enright thought, because—unlike June and most other people—he'd seen some scary things. But he wisely kept the thought to himself.

"I'll start staking out your office and apartment building tomorrow. I had already planned to ratchet up security to protect you in that building after the break-in tonight. This stalker just makes it more imperative."

"So what should I do now? He knows where I live."

"First stay calm. As long as you're locked inside your apartment, you're safe." He thought it out a bit. "Would you like me to come over?"

The tone in her voice made it clear she'd like nothing less. "That won't be necessary."

He coughed a few times for no other reason than to deflect attention from the fact she had just rejected his services. "Okay, well, it's too late to hire outside help tonight, but I'll arrange to have someone at your office and outside your apartment door first thing tomorrow."

"In the meantime—" She stopped again. "Am I still on speaker?"

"Uh...no."

"Take me off!" Enright stopped petting Bernadette—she wasn't happy about that—and pushed a button on the phone. And finally June continued: "In the meantime, what am I supposed to do?"

"Stay calm, stay in your apartment, and call me if anything is the least bit suspicious."

That was it? She could have figured that out on her own.

June hung up without saying good-bye, took a deep breath, and powered on her laptop. This new wrinkle in her life—how she'd been targeted several times today by a shadowy conspiracy—would no doubt make compelling reading for visitors to her blog.

She had a half dozen paragraphs written of a first draft—tentatively titled How the Vast Left-wing Conspiracy Silences Its Foes—when there was a solid rap on her door.

She glanced at the bottom of her draft, where her courage was spelled out in a sixteen-point font: "My Daily Affirmation is to love myself even more." And so she did.

June Forteene looked at the screen and thought how ironic it would be if the fake UPS driver killed her while she was in the middle of writing a blog post about him. Now, *that* would be news! Drudge and Malkin would rue the day they'd stopped talking to her if that happened.

The downside, of course, was that she would be dead, and therefore unable to enjoy the media frenzy. She sighed; there was always a downside.

The rap came again. June was reluctant to leave her laptop—before editing, her first draft read like a self-pitying mash letter to herself—but she could always work on it later. She saved the file before creeping up to the door and looking through the peephole.

A fortyish man with highlights wearing a dark shirt and bad tie stood in the hallway, holding a wallet in his hand. He looked more like a casually dressed police detective than a hit man, but she couldn't take any chances.

"I've already called the police!" Her shout echoed against the metal door, the only thing protecting her from the potential assassin. "If you're smart, you'll leave before they get here."

The man in the hall smiled. "Ms. Morris?"

He used her old name; she didn't care for that, but it *did* make him sound less like the stalker-killer she'd half expected. "Didn't you hear me? I called the police!"

"I heard you. Ma'am, I *am* the police. Detective Bailey, UN General Assembly Special Detail."

Oh. June Forteene hadn't expected that response. "Let me see your badge."

The man slipped the wallet open and smushed it so close to the peephole she couldn't see a damn thing except darkness. Still, he wouldn't have made the gesture if he didn't have a badge, would he? If he didn't have a badge, he would have given her some lame excuse or gotten the hell out of there.

No, she told herself. *Don't trust. See the badge.*

"I need to see that badge."

The wallet was pulled back a few inches until it came into focus.

"Back up," she demanded, and he took a few steps toward the opposite wall. "You carrying a gun?"

The man patted himself around the midsection and lifted his pant legs to show that nothing was strapped on his ankles. That made her feel better until she thought about it and...

"Hey, if you're a cop, how come you don't have a gun?"

That didn't seem to faze this cop. He leaned close to the door so he didn't have to shout. "Guns are a very sensitive issue on the UN

Detail. For example, if I'm carrying a service weapon I'm not allowed near most western European delegations, or even Canada. I'd be stuck with Mexico, Syria, Russia, and the United States. For me, not carrying a weapon is a career move."

A long pause followed. She still wasn't quite sure.

"For what it's worth," he added, "I wish I was carrying. I value the Second Amendment more than any other amendment. In fact, it's probably my favorite amendment."

On her side of the door, June Forteene still debated whether or not she should open the door. The guy had all the right answers—and if this had been a first date, his passion for the Second Amendment would have guaranteed another—but something felt a little off.

Then again, he was a detective with the New York Police Department. Wasn't that to be expected?

Having weighed every angle and having come up with nothing but paranoia, she took a leap of faith and unlocked the dead bolt.

June still wasn't sure she trusted this alleged cop. Maybe his credentials passed the test, but there was something off about both the man and the situation. And it wasn't just her certainty that he wasn't wearing underwear.

Fortunately, she had a degree of power he lacked.

She never dreamed she would have pulled a gun on a cop, but there she was. The nine-millimeter came out of her purse as he stood in the threshold between the hallway and her apartment.

"Hands up."

The cop smiled. "'Hands up?' You're Edward G. Robinson now?"

June was twenty-nine years old and therefore not quite sure who that was. "I said, hands up."

So his hands went up, and her hand—the one that wasn't holding the nine-millimeter—grabbed the phone and dialed.

"It's June Fortee—" She stopped herself. "It's Hillary Morris in 7-F. I have a guy here who claims he's a cop." She paused and listened to the voice on the other end of the line. "Really? Really? Well, all right, then."

"So?" asked Chase as she hung up the phone. He had been nowhere near as casual about having a gun pointed at his chest as he'd tried to let her believe.

"The super vouched for you." The nine-millimeter went back into her purse. "So maybe you're a real cop."

Chase exaggerated a sigh. "I appreciate your skepticism, Ms. Morris. Especially in *your* position. But we don't have much more time to waste. If it'd put your mind at ease, I can go outside and find my supervisor and have him talk to you, but you *really* don't want to wait."

She squinted. "I don't?" He nodded. "Why not?"

A sober, just-the-facts-ma'am expression was on his face. "We have reason to believe your life is in danger."

June reached for her purse and almost had her hand on the gun before Chase was able to grab her wrist.

"There'll be no need for that, Ms. Morris." They struggled a bit, but finally the gun dropped from her hand back into the bag. "The NYPD is all over this."

That didn't exactly fill her with a sense of security. "But who...?" She gasped. "The fake UPS driver!"

"The *who*?"

"There's been a seedy guy in an old, frayed UPS uniform who's been shadowing me all day. He was at my office this morning and then showed up here this afternoon."

Chase nodded. "Seedy, you say?"

"A real lowlife. Shifty-eyed. Shady-looking. And very old."

He knew she was talking about Grant—who *was* all of those things, except maybe not *that* old—and he couldn't help but feel defensive. "I'm sure he wasn't *that* seedy."

She disagreed. "Worse." June hadn't actually seen him, of course, but based on the descriptions by Edward and the building superintendent, her mind had captured a vivid image. "Shady, shifty-eyed, seedy, and old."

"Well...hmm." Chase took a deep breath. Mostly, he wanted to calm himself and forget she was describing his partner, but he figured it might make his detective act a little more believable if it looked like he was considering her information. "In that case, it's all the more imperative you leave this apartment right now."

She shoved her hands to her hips. "What?"

"Ms. Morris..." He took another deep breath, and all those slights to Grant dissipated with the fresh air. "I don't think you appreciate how serious this situation is."

Her nostrils flared. "What I understand is *this*!" She grabbed for her purse, but Chase once again slapped her hand away. "Ow! Why do you keep doing that?"

"Why do you keep reaching for your gun?"

"I thought you loved the Second Amendment!"

"I do. I just don't love it when the Second Amendment is pointed at me."

The back-and-forth could have gone on forever—probably *would* have—but four sharp knocks stopped them.

Chase sidled close to the door. "Identify yourself."

"It's Rafferty."

Chase winked at June. "My partner. Can I let him in?" She scowled. "Okay, then."

He opened the door, and June saw a casually dressed man in his late fifties tapping his foot impatiently. Unlike the first cop—the one with the highlights he was getting too old to pull off—the second cop looked old, sloppy, and tired. Now, *this* was what she thought a seasoned police detective should look like.

And, like a seasoned detective, he got straight to the point.

"You Hillary Morris?"

"I am."

"You gotta get out of here." When a glimmer of hesitation crossed her face, he doubled down. "Now!"

"But…"

The veteran cop was inches in front of her before she could react. "This is not negotiable, Ms. Morris. Detective Bailey here is gonna get you to safety, and I'm gonna make sure your apartment doesn't explode and you're not killed in a bloody inferno."

She was close to panic, but she still had the presence of mind to point a fingernail in his direction. "You mean a *fiery* inferno."

He cleared his throat. "What I mean is, if this place goes up, it's gonna be fiery *and* bloody. So *go!*"

June reached for her bag. "Okay, I…"

He shook his head. "That stays."

She looked at her bag. It was her constant companion. "But…But I *need* my bag."

"You mean the bag some terrorist might've lined with explosives, according to NYPD intelligence? You wanna carry *that* bag around with you?" While June stared blankly at him, the older cop offered up a seen-it-all sigh and gingerly picked it up. "Sorry, but the purse stays here."

She wasn't happy about that but thought it might be better than dying in a fireball. "Can I at least have my phone?"

"You mean the phone that might be rigged to explode at any minute?" The cop studied his watch. "Like, in seconds? Or maybe in a few minutes when you're standing out on Second Avenue and it not only blows your head off your shoulders, but also kills everyone around you? Is *that* the phone you want?"

"But—"

"Lady, I appreciate your concern. Hopefully this is a false alarm and you'll be back in business in less than an hour. For now, though, I can't let you leave with anything 'cept yourself. Got it?"

She nodded. She still wasn't happy, but she got it.

But if that seedy, shady-looking, shifty-eyed old fake UPS driver was anywhere outside, she might have to take her chances with the explosion.

"Christ, I thought she was never gonna leave." Grant stood in June's living room, Nick at his side, and sized the place up. He could see nothing worth fencing. "Guess this blogging business doesn't pay much."

"Think of it as a time-saver for you." Nick eyed a prehistoric boom box, trying to figure out what it was until it occurred to him it was June's stereo. "You won't be slowed down stealing her stuff."

"I guess there's that." He set the purse on the keypad of her still-open laptop. "I'm just gonna take a quick look around for jewelry or whatever, then we should get out of here."

And not that either of them knew or cared, but the heavy side of the purse—the side holding her cell phone, Kindle, gun, and makeup—pressed down on just the right keys to publish a blog post that began How the Vast Left-wing Conspiracy Silences Its Foes, went on to rant about a seedy UPS driver who'd been stalking her across the city, and ended with "My Daily Affirmation is to love myself even more."

Within seconds, readers around the world—friends and foes alike—were saving screen-captures of the not-intended-for-publication blog post.

Hundreds of them.

❖

Out on the sidewalk, June took in the usual General Assembly traffic chaos before turning her attention to Chase. "So where's the rest of the bomb squad?"

"Finnerty can handle this by himself. He's the best man we've got."

She started to say something but stopped, because there was a new something that suddenly seemed much more important. "*Finnerty?* I thought you said his name was *Rafferty*."

"Uh…that's right. Detective Finnerty Rafferty. *Junior*." He had no idea where the 'Junior' came from, but for some reason he thought it added a touch of verisimilitude.

June did not. "Finnerty Rafferty is not a real name."

"Lady, you named yourself after a holiday. You shouldn't be talking."

She fumed over that comment. It was bad enough her neighborhood had been invaded by cops and diplomats from scores of nations that officially hated American freedom; she didn't also need to be insulted by a police detective.

And even though she tried to respect the badge, she was about to call him out on the insult—and would have, because she was trying to love herself even more—had the building superintendent not suddenly appeared at the top of the stoop.

"Detective Bailey!" he hollered, and a half dozen cops who'd been standing nearby were suddenly paying attention to the trio on the sidewalk. Chase signaled for the super to lower his voice, to no avail. "Detective Bailey, I still haven't received that phone call!"

June's eyes darted back and forth between the two men. "What phone call?"

"He can't tell you," said Chase.

"Oh, that's right! I can't. Anyway, Detective Bailey—"

"No need to keep using my name," said Chase as softly as possible, which really wasn't all that quiet since the men were standing ten feet apart. He felt the eyes of the real police officers watching carefully. Fortunately, a police force with tens of thousands of officers offered a high degree of anonymity. "Now go back to your apartment. I'm sure the call will come at any moment."

"Wait!" June had also noticed the interest of the real police officers, which only deepened her own suspicions. "Why are you sending him back into the building if there might be a bomb in there?"

"A *bomb*?!" The super was the opposite of discreet as he hurried away from the apartment building he loved, just not enough to die inside.

There was something about the liberal use of the word "bomb" at high volume on a street swarming with cops already jumpy about terrorist threats that drew a lot of attention, all of it bad. As the police sprang into action, Chase realized that his continued presence on the sidewalk was most certainly a very bad idea.

"Did you hear them?" Chase asked, with authority in his voice, to the first three officers who rushed up. "They're saying there's a bomb in the building. Clear the area!"

"But…no…*He* said…" June sputtered.

Her sputtering didn't matter. Chase's three sentences had created enough chaos to allow him to melt into the crowd, and he kept melting until he was a block away and safely hidden around the corner.

Unfortunately, the same could not be said for Grant Lambert and Nick Donovan. The super was no doubt already leading the police to June's apartment.

Chase pulled his phone out of his pocket.

If Chase had been able to keep June and the super quiet for just a few more minutes, there would have been a clean getaway. They were *so* close.

But, of course, things didn't work out that way.

Alerted by Chase and knowing that the elevator would trap them without an escape route, Grant and Nick decided to take the stairs back down to the lobby. They were between the second and third floors when they heard a commotion below, and then the door at the lobby level opened with a bang and the voices of a half dozen very edgy cops were coming toward them.

At the second-floor landing, there was a half-open window looking out to the gloomy air shaft…

Grant went first, followed by Nick, who threw himself through the opening moments before the lead cop rounded the turn in the staircase. At any other time, someone would have noticed the open window, and maybe even heard them when they landed twelve feet below that window. But this wasn't one of those times. This was a time when a half dozen loud, duly-sworn police officers pumping adrenaline were rushing to investigate a possible bomb, not stealthily trying to catch a couple of burglars.

So they missed the open window. And they also missed the sound two adult bodies make when they hit the ground twelve feet below with a god-awful thud.

Grant didn't move for quite a while, but when he finally dared to turn slightly he was surprised to discover that nothing seemed to hurt too much.

"Kid?" he asked the darkness.

"I'm here," said Nick.

"You hurt?"

"Nope."

"Good." Grant realized he had landed on something sort of squishy, no doubt the reason he was still alive. "You mind telling me what I landed on?"

Nick came closer, until Grant could finally make out his dark features. "Are you sure you want to know?"

Grant's lip curled in. "Is it a body?"

"No. Just a mattress. But…just don't look."

"Trust me, I ain't gonna look. Nothing good ever came out of a mattress at the bottom of an airshaft."

"Yeah, you might also want to take a shower as soon as you can."

They heard something rustle along the ground.

"Is whatever's moving down here another thing I don't want to know?" Nick nodded. "Okay, this time don't tell me."

After it was clear there was no bomb in June Forteene's apartment, and after she'd proven the nine-millimeter left on the kitchen floor was hers and she had a permit, and after she realized her phone and laptop had been stolen and filed a report, the building began to empty out what had become a massive police presence.

A half hour after that, Grant and Nick slowly eased open the window that led from the airshaft to the mailroom, and then exited the building through the lobby, carrying the laptop and phone as if nothing out of the ordinary had occurred that night and their limps were just something that had happened.

Chase, who'd been keeping in touch with them by text message the entire time they were hidden in the airshaft, was waiting down the block. They sent Nick back home to Hell's Kitchen, and then Grant and Chase stole a Ford Taurus—so tired they didn't even bother disabling the GPS—and headed home to Jackson Heights.

After Grant took a thirty-eight-minute shower, he and Chase helped each other liberally apply Bengay to bodies that were both too old for the abuse they'd received that night. Then they finally settled into bed.

"If there's a silver lining," said Chase, "it's that we got the goods. Best I can figure, we've recovered every picture of Austin Peebles's penis except the one on his own phone."

Grant was silent for a while until—in the darkness—he said, "I underpriced this job. I should have charged forty thousand."

"Fifty," said Chase.

"Sixty…"

The number kept rising until they finally fell asleep in each other's arms.

A few minutes later, some cop called June's cell phone and asked if he could vouch for one Edward Hepplewhite. Grant didn't know the name, but had a good idea who this Hepplewhite was, so he told the cop he was Mr. Forteene and that neither of them had ever heard of him. That's what they *both* got for waking him up.

After he shut down the phone, Chase took it from his hands and removed the battery. It wasn't just so they could get a decent night's sleep. It was also to keep the police from tracking the stolen phone back to their apartment.

That Austin Peebles's penis and face appeared in both their dreams that night was never discussed. That was for the best, especially considering the violence in Grant's dream and the eroticism in Chase's.

CHAPTER TEN

Her office and apartment had been burgled, she'd been invaded by fake cops, there had been a bomb scare, a seedy guy in an old UPS uniform was stalking her, and the goddamn UN a block away was making her life a living hell. So it was understandable that June Forteene had been unable to sleep.

Not to mention her cell phone had been stolen, which left her feeling especially isolated. Sure, she had a landline, but the only number she had memorized was the super's, and the bomb scare had rattled him enough to send him to his daughter's place in Brooklyn Heights for the night. Not that she would have been even slightly tempted to call him for solace.

If she'd had her cell phone, she could have at least called a friend for a shoulder to cry on. Maybe Pamela...or Ann...or even Karl. But no. Instead she paced the apartment, alone and more than a little paranoid.

What she didn't know was that Pamela, Ann, and Karl—not to mention tens of thousands of other people—had already had quite a laugh at her expense that night. One leftwing blogger had already launched JuneForteenesDailyAffirmation.com, which rose into the top hundred in web traffic rankings overnight and generated hundreds of comments, most of them vicious.

There was nothing like letting the world know you had a daily affirmation to incite that world to create their own for you.

"I'm June Forteene and I'll deny global warming until the inevitable day I'm roasting in hellfire."

"I'm June Forteene and I'd go lesbian for Michele Bachmann."

"I'm June Forteene and I want Santorum inside of me."

And so on.

Of course, she knew none of that at the time. She also knew

nothing of the Huffington Post–Gawker–Drudge–Kos–National Review Online–TMZ mockery.

There was yet another thing she didn't know. The police had tried to reach her hours earlier to confirm the identity of the now-awake Edward Hepplewhite. The groggy guy who'd answered her cell phone told the cops he was Mr. Forteene and no one had ever heard of this Hepplewhite character, so that was that. The cops weren't surprised— all his raging about seductive tiny burglars and penises and date-rape drugs were a sure sign of drug-induced mental illness—so they thanked Mr. Forteene, apologized for waking him up, hung up the phone, and got out their Tasers.

It was still dark—*very* dark—when Grant nudged Chase.

"Wha...?"

"It's time to get up."

"I'll call in sick."

"I'm not talkin' about the Gross. We've gotta get to Manhattan."

Chase—eyes firmly closed—fumbled around in the sheets. "What time is it?"

"Four forty."

"'Nother hour." Chase's head settled back against his pillow.

Grant jabbed an elbow into his partner's very sore shoulder. "Now!"

When he stumbled out of bed, Chase remembered to add, "I really wish you'd call Groc-O-Rama by the proper name."

"Get in the shower."

At 6:32 a.m., June was walking north on Eighth Avenue toward her office. Sleep-deprived, she didn't notice the two men in a taxi duck down as she passed. She would remember fake Detective Bailey and fake Detective Finnerty Rafferty Jr. until the day she died—even after a night without sleep—but missed the encounter. It was just the latest in a string of very unfortunate circumstances that had befallen her in less than eleven hours.

But it was the only thing she missed that morning.

When she opened her office door, her first instinct was to say, "What the fuck?!"

Her second was to say, *"What?! The?! Fuck?!"*

Captain Joseph Enright and Edward Hepplewhite were both *so* fired!

But first she needed caffeine.

Grant and Chase finally found a cab driver who would transport them— and a trunk load of computer equipment—to the Upper East Side for an extra twenty dollars.

They were loading the trunk when Chase said, "Put the monitor in front of your face."

"Huh?"

"Just do it."

Grant did, and a few seconds later June Forteene stormed past, making a beeline toward the Starbucks across the corner. When she was out of their way, they finished loading the last few items and snapped the trunk closed.

One of the landlines was ringing when June returned with her Venti Caffè Americano. *But of course it's a landline*, she thought. *What the hell else is left?* Also, *Who the hell is calling before seven o'clock in the morning?*

She answered the ringing telephone crisply. "June Forteene Enterprises."

"Yeah, this is Sergeant Robins, Midtown North Precinct."

Oh, great. Another fake cop. That's what she thought. What she said was, "Go on."

"I'm trying to check on one Edward Hepplewhite. Says he works there."

"Fired."

"'Scuse me?"

"Edward was fired."

"You sure? 'Cause he says…"

"Don't believe a word he says." She hung up, and when the phone repeatedly rang over the next half hour, she refused to answer.

On Manhattan's Upper East Side—less than a half mile from the address Grant and Chase were directing their cab driver to—Austin Peebles heard a knock on the door to what had been *his* bedroom ever since

Penelope had kicked him out of *their* bedroom when the penis picture came to light. He hid the Craigslist "Casual Encounters" screen he'd been viewing behind a spreadsheet he hadn't looked at since college, slipped his sweatpants down just enough to show the arc of his ass, and said, "Come in, baby!"

The door opened a crack and Triple-C looked inside.

"Oh, sorry." Austin pulled up his sweats. "I thought you were Penelope."

Catherine Cooper Concannon took a step into the room and pretended she hadn't seen her son-in-law's ass. Nor the slight bulge at his lap. That was none of her business, and she was thirty years too old for any of it to have been intended for her.

Although...*No*, she was *definitely* too old.

She smiled at him, very motherly. "I've tried talking to her, Austin, but she's still very angry. Maybe if you tried."

He rolled his shoulders, close to not caring at all. "She'll get over it."

Triple-C was, for the briefest moment, resentful of his cavalier attitude toward her daughter. But then she sensed that attitude was his way of protecting himself from Penelope's harsh treatment—kicking him out of their bedroom and refusing to speak to him—and let go of that resentment.

"I'm sure she will." The U.S. Representative looked approvingly at the spreadsheet on his monitor. "I see you're applying yourself. And I'm impressed you're up so early in the morning."

He saw no need to bother her with a few details; like, say, he had a sinus cavity caked with cocaine and hadn't been to bed yet, and the fact that an exciting Craigslist "Casual Encounters" lurked behind the spreadsheet. Those were just minor issues that need not concern her.

"Thank you, Mother. I'm trying."

She didn't smile; she beamed. "You're more than trying, Austin! You're succeeding!"

When Triple-C finally left his bedroom, Austin returned to the Casual Encounter profile. The twenty-four-year-old WILD'N'HOT girl lived somewhere nearby on the Upper East Side, so she could be a constituent! And since she'd only posted her ad a half hour ago, she'd no doubt had a night like he had.

Which made this the *only* way to campaign.

❖

Sometimes, June Forteene now knew, your best friends *won't* tell you.

She waited outside until the minute the closest office supply store unlocked its front door to buy a laptop, and then ran across the street to the cell phone store while the office supply employees got her up and running. An hour later, she was mostly back in business.

That was when she first discovered she had become a target of Internet mockery overnight.

After her third panic attack, she knew what she had to do. June got her breathing under control, logged onto her website with the new laptop, and started typing.

> *Dear Friends:*
>
> *As you know, I have taken some highly controversial positions over the years: opposing open borders, opposing the Times Square Mosque and Islamofascism, opposing the liberal agenda. These actions to protect American freedom and exceptionalism have now made me the target of liberal, Jihadist hackers...*

It took less than fifteen minutes for the story to go viral.

Her Daily Affirmation? "When in a corner, lie like hell."

She'd used that one a few times before.

Grant and Chase helped Kevin Wunder move the computer equipment up to his office at the far end of U.S. Representative Catherine Cooper Concannon's suite on Second Avenue. Or maybe it was the other way around, since Wunder wasn't a lot of help. Whatever; the job was finally done.

"Thanks." The lack of a smile on Wunder's face mirrored the lack of enthusiasm in his voice. "You can expect payment in a few weeks. Just as soon as we get the invoice, we'll process it."

"Expedite it, Wunder." Grant fixed him with one of his harder stares. "Don't make us come back."

An hour later, Catherine Cooper Concannon sat behind her desk in that very same office and watched Kevin Wunder fidget in front of her.

"Yes?"

He held out the cell phone that had once belonged to June Forteene. "It's done."

"*What* is done?"

"You wanted me to get those pictures of Austin's, uh…" He looked at her seventyish face. "Uh…the, uh…"

"The pictures of his penis?"

"Yeah, that." He shrugged. "Anyway, I took care of it. Every single computer, cell phone…whatever June Forteene owned is now stashed in my office and ready for disposal."

Triple-C—a woman who'd been shocked by and disapproved of many things in her life—still mustered a fresh look of shock and disapproval. "Kevin! You can't hide stolen goods in the office of a Member of Congress!"

"But…"

She shook her head. "I expected better judgment from you. Kevin. Now, get rid of it."

"But…"

The discussion was over. "Get rid of it *now*!"

On the surface, Kevin smiled pleasantly and agreed to obey her command. Inside, though, he was throwing the biggest hissy fit American politics had seen since the day Newt Gingrich had to ride in the back of Air Force One.

The only reason he kept his cool was his knowledge that he had the upper hand.

And he was ready to use it.

Kevin Wunder was done being the obedient Concannon Family lackey. It was time to spread his wings.

If they'd expected a break—and a few weeks to relax and heal and slather themselves in Bengay—they didn't get it. They got something like twelve hours.

Chase's phone rang, and he glanced at the caller ID. "It's Jamie."

"Ignore it." Grant rubbed more Bengay on his ass. "I'm never a fan of Jamie Brock, and I'm especially not a fan right now."

Chase ignored the call. And the next one. And the ones after that. It was only when Jamie called for the sixth time in four minutes that curiosity got the better of him and he answered.

"What's up?"

"Kevin Wunder just called. He wants to see us right away."
Jamie's voice kept disappearing behind street noise. It sounded like he
was calling from a cab.

"Us? As in *all* of us?"

Through the uneven signal, it sounded like he said, "Yes. And
right away."

Chase waited until a horn stopped blaring on Jamie's end. "You
think he's paying us already?"

"I'd bet on it." Jamie's voice vanished into noise and was in mid-
sentence when it returned. "—is the sort of thing they'll want to put
behind them as soon as they can. It's too seamy for a campaign to be
involved in blackmail and...Hey! *Hey!*"

"What's the matter?"

"Not you. *Hey!* Take Park Avenue! Fifth's too slow!"

Chase got it. "Cab?"

"Yeah. This idiot doesn't know where he's...*Hey!* I said *Park!*"

Chase ignored the directions. Those were Jamie's problem.
"Where does Wunder want to meet?"

"The place on Second Avenue."

"Where we met before?"

"Yes...*Not Fifth*, dammit!"

"Got it. Second, not Fifth. Wait—did I say Fifth?"

"Not you! This idiot driver...*Hey!*"

Chase clicked off without saying good-bye and turned to face
Grant, who was sitting at the kitchen table in a T-shirt and pair of baggy
boxer shorts that were once a much whiter shade of white.

"Looks like it's pay day, partner."

Grant rubbed Bengay on his right knee. "How do you mean?"

Chase smiled. "Wunder just told Jamie he wants to see all of us,
and he wants to see us *now*. So throw on some clothes and let's get to
Manhattan."

Grant nodded unpleasantly. "This doesn't feel right. Didn't they
tell us this was gonna take four to six weeks, or something like that?"

"Your problem," said Chase, "is you're too pessimistic. We told
the guy we wanted our money right away, we did the job, and now he's
doing what we told him to do. So why the suspicion?"

"It comes from many years of having things go sour on us. You've
been right there with me, so you should feel it, too."

"What I feel is that we're gonna be thirty thousand dollars richer
in an hour. So put on some pants and let's go."

Grant appreciated Chase's optimism and wanted to believe. His churning stomach and aching back were less charitable.

Jamie met them outside the white-brick building on Second Avenue and they were buzzed inside. They took the elevator up, and—as before— were met by Kevin Wunder, holding open the door leading into the congresswoman's suite of offices.

"Inside," he said brusquely, and they followed him.

And, as before, Wunder went through the process of unlocking and relocking doors, except this time after the second door, he veered off and opened a different door. It was the one leading to what Grant had earlier assumed was the congresswoman's—*Representative's*, he mentally corrected himself—personal office, what with the semicircular throw and lack of wear and tear outside the door.

The light was already on when Grant, Chase, and Jamie entered the room. A tall blond woman—improbably young, even with a severe expression etched on her face—commanded the center of the office, watching them through cold blue eyes that never broke contact. Her perfectly tailored navy blue suit and high-collared white top were designed to let people know she was supposed to be at the office or a board of directors meeting or something like that. Her clothes said she meant business.

Two large young men in black suits and white shirts flanked her and gave the impression they *also* meant business…and could deliver, despite the ducks decorating one guy's tie. Neither of them was less than two hundred pounds and both looked like recent members of a particularly vicious college football team. If some college had a team nicknamed "The Decapitators," these guys were probably the star players.

But the blonde was scarier. The Decapitators would only separate your head from your body; the blonde looked like she'd separate a lower, more delicate body part. It was clear no one was going to mess with her. Ever.

Jamie, close to oblivious, whispered in Chase's ear. "Look! They brought in the campaign team to say thanks."

Chase took a look at the welcoming committee and rather doubted that.

The blonde took charge, which was no surprise.

"Close the door, Kevin." He did exactly that, and they also heard him throw a dead bolt. No one was getting in and—if Grant read the situation correctly—no one was getting out until their business was concluded.

"These are the men." Grant thought he heard a slight quaver in Wunder's voice.

She had a tiny nose—most likely courtesy of an Upper East Side plastic surgeon, maybe the same one who did Jamie's—but still managed to look down it at them.

"Take a seat."

"If you don't mind," said Grant, because his body was still sore. "We'll stand."

"I *said* to take a seat." She sort of smiled, but it wasn't a real smile and it wasn't an invitation. There was a three-second standoff before the men gave in and sat. Her tiny nose wrinkled. "And which one of you is wearing the bad cologne?"

Grant half raised a hand. "It ain't cologne. It's Bengay."

Only then did she lean back against the desk at the center of the room. Grant could see enough of the nameplate behind her to confirm they were borrowing Representative Catherine Cooper Concannon's private office, and wondered if that made this a federal case. The thought didn't help calm the stomach that had been churning and back that had been aching since before he left Jackson Heights.

The blonde stood there for a moment, sizing them up with those icy blue eyes. Finally she spoke again.

"You don't know me, so let me introduce myself." She let the pause hang for a full ten seconds. "My name is Penelope Concannon Peebles."

Grant hiked an eyebrow. This wasn't something he had been expecting, but it helped explain why Peebles was twittering or tweetering or sexting or swexting or whatever to random anonymous women who were probably a lot nicer to him.

He nodded at The Decapitators. "And who are they?"

"None of your business." She continued, "You already know Mr. Wunder." They muttered an affirmation, and she picked up something that looked an awful lot like a check from the blotter centered on Representative Catherine Cooper Concannon's desk. She glanced at it. "Which one of you is Jambro Enterprises?" She pronounced the word with a long A.

Jamie raised his hand. "Jambro." He used a short A. "It's my company. Jambro is short for Jamie Brock. Get it?"

She didn't care; no one did. "So you're here to collect your check?"

Jamie leaned forward and began to reach. "Yes, thanks, and let me just say it's been a pleasure…"

Her eyes flashed. "Not so fast."

She held the check just out of reach. From the corner of his eye, Grant saw Chase studying the piece of paper with a perplexed expression and thought he was about to say something, but then Jamie said something instead.

"We get the check, right?"

Penelope Concannon Peebles answered by ripping the check in half.

Then she ripped it into quarters.

Then eighths.

Jamie's smile disappeared. "But…"

It was time for Grant to take over. He slowly and painfully rose from his chair and dropped his voice to the lowest level in his register. "Listen, lady, we did the job, and we've got the bruises to prove it. So now you've got to pay the fee. Those are the rules."

"Except," she said, letting tiny pieces of what had been the check flutter to the carpeted floor, "you *didn't* do the job. *You failed.*"

Deep down, Grant had expected the campaign would try to cheat them. But he hadn't expected to be told he'd failed. Not when he knew he hadn't.

"What do you mean, sayin' we failed? We got the pictures back. Every one of 'em."

She turned and wordlessly nodded at one of the large silent men— the one with the duck-tie—who stood scowling behind her. In turn, he produced a laptop. It was already connected to the Internet.

"Does this look like success, Mister…Mister…?"

"No last names necessary," muttered Grant.

"Fine. I'll just call you Mr. Criminal."

"Fair enough. And I'll just call you Missus…"

"Grant." Chase's hand was abruptly on his elbow, a sign he should quiet down.

Grant, Chase, and Jamie strained to see the tiny screen on the laptop but had to get out of their chairs to catch a closer look. That hurt, but they toughed it out.

"What are we looking at?" asked Grant, squinting to make out the screen.

She sneered. "You're looking at that horrible June Forteene's blog. And if we scroll down…" She nodded again, and the man with the duck tie scrolled at her unspoken command. June's open letter detailing how her blog had been attacked by imaginary hackers appeared.

Mrs. Peebles said, "Scroll," and soon large lettering promised:

A PREVIEW OF COMING ATTRACTIONS

"Yeah?" grunted Grant. "So?"

"Scroll." The monitor now showed something that looked flesh-like and…

Grant and Chase sank back to their chairs. Jamie continued to examine the picture.

"Hey!" he finally said. "It sorta looks like part of that picture of Austin's penis!" He looked away from the screen only to discover that no one else was shocked by his pronouncement.

Austin Peebles's wife shook her head. "That's brilliant. Just *brilliant*. You should be a private detective." She slammed down the laptop lid, not bothering to order Duck Tie to do it and—in the process— came within a quarter inch of costing Duck Tie three fingertips.

"That is indeed a cropped version of the photo. If you didn't know what you were looking at, you wouldn't know exactly what it was. Or *whose* it was. But *we* know, don't we? *We* know it's my husband's cock shot." Her icy blue-eyed glare focused on Jamie, who was clearly the person she liked the least in a room full of people she didn't like at all.

Grant couldn't figure it out. "That's impossible. We stole her computers. We stole her phone. We stole her assistants' computers. We cleaned out her apartment. How in hell's name…?"

They looked at each other in silent befuddlement until Penelope Concannon Peebles again took charge.

"I don't know. I don't know how she has a copy of the photo. I don't really *care* how she has a copy of the photo. All I know is that June Forteene states on her blog that, if a certain unnamed candidate doesn't withdraw from his congressional race within the next five days—and pay her a substantial amount of money to compensate her for her losses—she'll make the entire photo public." She stood up straight and managed to seem even taller. "And, as you know, the entire photo shows more than a penis. It also shows a face."

"Wait!" Jamie was suffering from another unfortunate brainstorm. "If she's threatening an *unnamed* candidate, maybe she isn't after your husband after all!"

Penelope Concannon Peebles eyed Grant and Chase and nudged

a shoulder in the direction of Jamie. "I hope that one isn't the brains of your operation."

Grant slumped back in his chair. "Never seen him before in my life."

They managed to ditch Jamie at the Fifty-ninth Street subway station and eventually made it home to Jackson Heights, wondering the entire trip how they'd managed to screw everything up. They'd cleared every piece of equipment out of her office, searched her online storage, and emptied her apartment, but *still* June Forteene had managed to hold on to one of the images. That didn't make sense.

And now they were out thirty grand. Days of lost work and considerable risk with nothing to show for it except a dressing down by the candidate's wife.

When they reached their stop, Grant turned to Chase. "This is why I hate working for other people. From now on, we only work for ourselves."

"Deal," Chase agreed.

They'd trudged a half block down the street in the direction of their apartment building when Chase said, "After the game with the fake check, I'm surprised you didn't walk away."

Grant stopped dead in his tracks. "Huh? What fake check?"

"The one she ripped up in front of us."

"What about it?"

Chase studied him, trying to figure out if his leg was being pulled. "You saw it, right?"

"Saw what? The check? Sure."

"The *fake* check."

Grant stared blankly in another direction. "I don't know why you keep saying that."

"Because…" Chase paused. "Wait, you didn't see it?"

"See what?"

Rather than go around that circle one more time, Chase paused to collect his thoughts before continuing. "That check Penelope whatsername ripped up. It was *blank*."

Grant's neck made a snapping sound when he jerked his head to get a clear look at Chase, who he hoped to discover was kidding. But wasn't. "You mean…blank, like the amount was blank?"

"Blank like *everything* was blank. They didn't even bother making it payable to BroJam or JamBro or whatever Jamie's scam company is called."

Grant returned his gaze to nothing, allowing the full realization of how much Wunder and company had screwed them—premeditatedly screwed them, at that—to sink in. Because if that hadn't been their plan all along, why even bother having a prop like a fake check on hand? Why not just never call them back? That's what Grant would have done.

"So they never intended to pay us a dime."

"Not a penny," Chase agreed.

They walked in silence the rest of the way back to their apartment, which gave Chase a solid ten minutes to contemplate a few things, none of which had to do with that fake check. Over their years together, he'd grown used to Grant's bad back, his slight touch of arthritis when the weather turned, and his increasingly frequent trips to the bathroom at three in the morning. And, yes, there was also that unsettling *snap* his neck sometimes made, which sounded like it should hurt a lot, but so far didn't seem to.

But if Grant's eyes were now slipping—and the intentionally blank check, while not obvious, was something the younger Grant Lambert would have spotted a half mile away—they were going to have to rethink their line of work. Not to mention Chase's Groc-O-Rama paycheck wasn't big enough for both of them to live on.

While Chase was thinking things through, Grant was listening to much the same inner monologue. *How could I have missed that? Am I getting too old for this career?*

But for both of them, pride in their work won the day. Getting older was one thing; probably getting screwed over by a client was something altogether different.

So by the time they reached the front stoop of their run-down brownstone, they said the same thing at the same time.

"Those bastards can't get away with this."

CHAPTER ELEVEN

Neither of them got much sleep that night, but Grant finally nodded off around four in the morning, roughly an hour after the last time he had to get up to pee. Not that Chase was keeping track. Too much.

When Grant awoke an hour later—because his body woke up; not because his bladder did—the other side of the bed was empty. He found Chase on the computer, staring at June Forteene's blog.

"You know," Chase said, hearing Grant shuffle out of the bedroom, "I have an idea."

"Does it involve hiring someone to kill Jamie Brock?" Grant tried but failed to stifle a yawn. "Because then it would be a very good idea."

"Yeah, it would. But that's not what I was thinking." His eyes stayed focused on the monitor. "What I was thinking is we take another shot at getting the picture back."

"Ugh." Grant shuffled into the kitchen. "You'd better hold that thought until I make coffee, 'cause I'm gonna need caffeine in my system before I tell you to go to hell."

Chase kept talking, mostly to himself. "Did you see this post on June Forteene's blog? Kind of crazy and paranoid. Makes me think she might be cracking up."

A few minutes later Grant returned with two mugs of hot coffee. Chase was still staring at the penis fragment on June Forteene's blog, but looked up when he smelled coffee. Grant handed him a mug.

"So want to hear my idea?"

"No." There was silence for a while until Grant half sighed and half yawned. "You still sore?" Chase nodded. "Me, too."

"Is this a competition?"

"Nah. Just trying to figure out if I should have sympathy and listen to your idea. I still feel bad for you, so go ahead. You've earned it."

"Okay, so—"

"Wait."

"What?"

"I feel bad for you 'cause you fell maybe six feet out a transom, but I fell...I dunno, maybe twenty, twenty-five feet down an airshaft. Don't I get some sympathy, too?"

"Oh, jeez." Chase rolled his eyes. "Okay, I'm sorry your six-foot fall hurt more than my twelve-foot fall. Better?"

Grant nodded. He didn't care about the actual footage; he only cared that his plummet was acknowledged. Especially since Chase was making such a big freakin' deal over his own fall of maybe three or four feet.

"So whatcha got?"

"You're not gonna like this."

"No doubt."

Chase kept his eyes on the prize. Or, in this case, the penis. "I figure we go back to June Forteene's place and steal everything again."

There was more silence, and this time for a lot longer than a while. In fact, it went on so long that Chase, eyes still locked on the monitor, started to wonder if Grant had somehow silently slipped out of the room behind his back.

"Did you hear—"

"I heard you." Grant no longer cared if Chase was sore or how far he'd fallen. "I also think it's such a stupid idea you make me worry." He eased himself onto the arm of the couch. "Not to mention, I think I've heard this before, and I seem to remember I didn't like it *then*, either."

Chase blushed. "You did. Remember Jamie's idea about how we could maximize our income by stealing the picture over and over again? I sort of modified that to meet our more immediate needs."

Grant wasn't happy. "Sweet. So now you're stealing ideas from Jamie Brock. Next thing, you'll start going to the Hamptons with him to pick over the carcasses of the rich and elderly. Because Jamie Brock is like the Einstein of crime. He could be a Bond villain."

Chase looked up from the penis fragment featured on the blog as a A PREVIEW OF COMING ATTRACTIONS. "You have a better idea?"

Grant sipped at his coffee. The humiliation of the previous

night had somewhat dissipated; also, he was too bone-tired to dwell on revenge. "The best idea is that we forget this entire episode ever happened. Make it disappear from our lives."

"But I want that thirty grand." Chase set his jaw firmly. "We worked hard for it."

"Yeah, we did." Grant stared off, his eyes as unfocused as his thoughts. "But pulling the same risky job twice doesn't make sense. June will be waiting. June will have more security. Plus, if we didn't get it the first time, even after stealing every piece of equipment June Forteene has—er, *had*—how are we gonna find it on the second run? I hate to say this, but it's impossible."

"But thirty thousand dollars…"

Grant put his hand on his partner's shoulder and squeezed gently. "So we'll steal thirty or forty more cars or something. Now it's not our problem. It's Austin Peebles's problem…it's that bitch of a wife's problem…it's Boy Wunder's problem…but it's not—" He stopped himself. "Wait a minute."

"What?" Chase had almost allowed himself to be talked out of revenge, but if Grant now wanted to pursue it…

Grant rubbed his chin with the hand that wasn't on Chase's shoulder. "It's *not* Boy Wunder's problem, is it?"

Chase didn't follow. "What do you mean?"

Grant set down his coffee cup next to the computer and started pacing, thinking out loud as he walked. "Who benefits from this? June Forteene? Sure, because she gets attention and maybe makes some more ad money, but big deal. In a week, no one will remember she broke the story, and she'll be rutting around for her next exposé. It's worth money to her, but certainly not thirty Gs. So beside her, who benefits?"

Chase thought that over. "Not Peebles. And not his wife."

"True and true." Grant stopped pacing and stood behind the desk, his hands gripping the edge of the monitor. "The way I see it, only one guy gets a boost out of this. And that guy's name is…" He paused for dramatic effect. *"Kevin Wunder."*

"Wunder? But how…?" Before Grant could answer, Chase's brain flipped into full-on criminal mode. "I get it. Once Peebles has to end his campaign, there's no logical candidate to replace him on the ballot. *Except* Kevin Wunder."

Grant stroked his chin again. "Exactly. Wunder already told us he wanted to be in Congress, didn't he? This works to his advantage, and *only* to his advantage. In fact, I'll bet he was the one who sent the pictures to June Forteene in the first place."

Chase knitted his brow. "You think he'd do that?"

"Motive and opportunity," said Grant. "Isn't that what the cops are always looking for? Well, us, too. It'd be easy enough for him to get on Peebles's phone and send out that picture and make sure June got the twixter."

"Tweet."

"Whatever."

A thought clicked in Chase's sleep-deprived brain. "When I was going through June's computer, I couldn't find a secure online storage space. Couldn't figure it out *then*, but I get it now. If Kevin Wunder is her source, she doesn't need to protect the images. He can keep the cock shots coming."

"That's what I'm thinking." Grant began pacing again. "Here's how I figure things. Wunder sends the pictures to June and the family panics. Maybe Peebles...maybe the wife...maybe even the congresswoman. Maybe *all* of 'em. So who do they turn to take care of the problem?"

"Wunder!"

"Exactly. So he hires us, because he has to. But he never had any intention of leaving it at that. He was always planning to double-cross us."

"What about Peebles's wife? Think she's in on this, too?"

"That...That I can't figure out. Maybe."

Chase continued to warm to the idea. "Which means we really *did* get all the pictures when we raided her office and apartment. We just didn't count on Kevin Wunder double-crossing us by sending her another one." He thought some more. "Which means we really *did* earn our thirty grand!"

"Didn't we sort of come to that conclusion last night?"

Chase waved him away. "Last night it wasn't making a lot of sense. But this morning it is."

Grant walked around the desk and leaned over Chase's shoulder, where he could study the penis fragment on the screen. "That's exactly what's going on here. Wunder screwed us. And nobody screws Grant Lambert and Chase LaMarca except Grant Lambert and Chase LaMarca. *Now* this is about revenge."

Chase looked up at his partner. "I hear something in your voice that's very scary...and maybe a little bit sexy."

Grant's smile was broad; it seemed incongruous on his face. "If there's one thing I understand, it's revenge."

Chase grabbed his arm and led him toward the bedroom. Revenge could wait another hour.

Knowing something and doing something about it were two different things, of course, and Grant and Chase understood that. They also understood that they had only a few days to somehow bring down June Forteene's operation, ruin Kevin Wunder's plan, and—if possible—make back their thirty thousand dollars. If everything else would be more than difficult, the last component would probably be impossible. But they could hope.

They also knew they'd need help.

They had been fortunate during the foray into June's office and apartment, but they'd also had the element of surprise. Not to mention a lot of luck, although Grant and Chase—still bruised and limping two days after taking falls of somewhere between eight inches and forty feet, depending on who was telling the story—could be forgiven for scoffing whenever someone mentioned luck.

This time June Forteene would be prepared.

And this time they'd not only have to burgle June's office and home, they'd also have to burgle Wunder's office and home.

And maybe the campaign headquarters.

And maybe U.S. Representative Catherine Cooper Concannon's district office.

And they had four days if they were lucky; maybe less if June Forteene was an impatient woman. Which they figured could very well be the case.

If there was a positive aspect to the job at hand, it was that they'd at least be working for themselves. Working as a contractor for other people, as Grant had long believed and had just proven again, was never a good idea.

They'd also need to find help without much money to buy it, and no one liked doing things for free—especially criminal things—so it would be a challenge to bring together the right people willing to take on a laundry list of risky jobs as a favor. Fortunately, Grant had an idea about who they could use on the inside.

"Grab your Metrocard," he said as he picked up a windbreaker from the back of a chair.

"We going somewhere?" asked Chase.

"Manhattan. I think we need to pay a quick visit to someone who's gonna be very important to us if we're able to carry this off."

"Who?"

"Austin Peebles."

Chase smiled, but didn't move from the computer. "Peebles? The man behind the penis?" He laughed; Grant did not. "Seriously?"

Grant began putting on his windbreaker. "Of course I'm serious. He's the one with everything on the line. *And* on the Internet. I figure we need an insider, and who better than the guy with the most to lose?"

Chase nodded and looked back at the monitor. "If you say so..."

"Are you coming?" Grant asked impatiently.

"Do you even have any idea where to find him?"

"I figured his campaign headquarters—"

"At this hour of the morning?"

Grant glanced at his watch. It *was* very early. "So we'll wait for him."

Chase clicked the mouse, and a window that had been hidden behind the blog popped up on the monitor. "Try across the street from Bloomingdale's."

Grant squinted. "How'd you figure that out?"

Chase tapped the screen. "They post his public schedule on the campaign website, and it says here he'll be meeting the voters across the street from Bloomingdale's later this morning. So if you wanna talk to him, we can either find him on Fifty-ninth Street in a few hours, or pay two thousand dollars each to see him at his fund-raiser at the Friars Club tonight. Your call."

Grant took off the windbreaker. "Free and Fifty-ninth Street works for me." He tossed the jacket on a chair. "What time?"

"He starts his meet-and-greet at seven thirty. By eight he should be bored with meeting and greeting."

Grant looked at the photo on the monitor. In his Official Campaign Photo, Austin Peebles still looked ridiculously young, but not as young as he looked in his Official Penis Photo. "I can't believe we're helping a child get himself elected to Congress. He'll probably be the first one whose youthful indiscretions *are* youthful indiscretions."

He studied the official campaign photograph, which—to Grant—looked like it might as well have been taken at high school graduation. The image captured on the screen—with his youthfulness and elfin hair and long lashes and mischievous half smile—didn't look like a congressman. Austin Peebles looked more like he should be posing shirtless on the cover of *Tiger Beat*.

The candidate's youth and general *prettiness*—the word popped into his head because Peebles was definitely pretty, not handsome— did help underscore a few things, though. Like, why Kevin Wunder resented him so much, and why in hell's name this candidate was stupid enough to take a picture of his penis with his face in the background and send it out. When God was giving out common sense, Austin Peebles had obviously missed the announcement, probably because he'd been tweeting pictures of his junk.

"I have a very hard time taking this guy seriously."

Chase laughed. "The good news, I guess, is we don't have to take him seriously. That'll be a mistake for the voters. All we have to do is use him for a while."

Grant scowled. "If this guy can be a congressman—I mean *Representative*—then Nick Donovan should be mayor."

"Don't give Nick any ideas." Chase looked back at the screen. "You want a mayor called 'Cadium'?"

"Cadmium," Grant said, surprising them both.

Austin Peebles stood outside the subway entrance at the southeast corner of East Fifty-ninth Street and Lexington Avenue, directly across the street from the Bloomingdale's flagship, surrounded by a half dozen campaign volunteers who were still in or barely out of their teens. Meaning not much younger than he was.

The kids—an equal mix of cute, enthusiastic white boys with perfect haircuts and cute, enthusiastic white girls with perfect haircuts— wore blue T-shirts that read PEEBLES FOR THE PEOPLE; Peebles for the People wore a charcoal gray suit, light blue shirt, and blue-and-red rep tie, along with an expression that made it clear he'd rather be in Aruba wearing board shorts and nothing else instead of this grown-up costume that made him feel a little too much like his father and grandfather. And, come to think of it, his *great*-grandfather, too.

Of course, he knew he'd have to get used to the idea that he'd be dressing this way for the rest of his life. There was roughly a 100 percent chance—give or take a thousandth of a percent, in case something weirdly Libertarian happened on Election Day—he was going to be elected to Congress, and this was the way he'd have to dress. He was *not* disinclined to ask the Speaker of the House if perhaps a sharp blazer, stylish jeans, and an open collar could be allowed on the House floor, but figured he should wait on that until after he was sworn in.

The kids handed out palm cards featuring the same blue-and-red PEEBLES FOR THE PEOPLE theme as their shirts, while the candidate made a halfhearted effort to meet those PEOPLE he hoped to represent in Washington. He'd started out trying to campaign full-heartedly, but the fact that almost every voter, non-voter, tourist, and illegal alien—or was that undocumented worker? He couldn't remember how the Democratic Congressional Campaign Committee had encouraged him to refer to them—who'd crossed his path over the previous hour had brushed past him in a rush to get to work or Bloomingdale's had sapped at least 80 percent of his enthusiasm.

The typical exchange went like this:

"Hi, I'm Aust—"

"Outtamyway!"

"Nice to meet you!"

"Shuddup!"

He'd had occasional success, mostly from voters who already knew he was the new Concannon-by-marriage and would continue the family's long tradition of public service. A fair number of people—most of them women—were drawn to him, too, but that was something he'd grown used to since his childhood. Having sailed through life as an adorable baby who grew into an adorable toddler who grew into an adorable teenager—yes, he was even adorable as a teenager, without a trace of acne or awkwardness—who grew into an adorable young adult, he took it as a given that women would flock to him.

There weren't too many Concannon- or adorable-young-man-loving admirers that morning, but there were enough to keep him going. That would continue for at least the next hour promised on his public schedule, he hoped.

When he spotted the two men coming up the stairs from the subway platform, he'd already had enough experience to know they'd pretend he wasn't there and push past him. There was a rough, no-nonsense look to them, especially the older one. The younger one, with highlights a bit too obvious to pass in polite society, was probably gay—that was good; gay men seemed to love him as much as women—but he figured they'd both brush past. They probably worked in the basement of one of the nearby office towers and were late getting to their jobs.

Instinctively, he turned away from them and searched the crowd for less certain rejection.

But then one of the Peebles Kids was tugging on his elbow, saying, "Austin, these gentlemen would like to meet you." He turned and saw it was the two rough, no-nonsense men.

Okay, so it takes all kinds, he thought, and plastered on his smile. And then Austin Peebles went into Candidate Mode.

He smiled and batted his lashes. "Hi, I'm Austin Peebles, and I'm running to be *your* voice in Congress."

Grant and Chase sized him up. Based on his campaign photo— and the face behind the penis in that *other* photo—they were expecting young and cute, but they were getting a lot more of both than they were prepared for. Austin Peebles was one of those people who photographed attractive, but not as attractive as they were in flesh and blood.

"Ah…uh…" Chase stammered until Grant nudged him. "*You're* Austin Peebles?" Grant didn't like the soft smile that accompanied the question.

"I am. So what issues are important to—"

Chase put a hand on the candidate's shoulder and maybe squeezed it a tiny bit.

"Can we talk to you a second?"

"Well…sure." Austin mustered another, brighter smile. Someone actually wanted to talk to him! It figured it was the gay one with the bad highlights, but still… "I'm always happy to talk to the people about the important issues of—"

"Privately." Before Austin had an opportunity to answer, Chase was leading him down the sidewalk away from the subway entrance. When they were standing in front of an H&M display window and had as much privacy as one could expect to find on one of the busiest sidewalks in Manhattan, he continued.

"We know about the picture."

"The…?" Confusion clouded Peebles's face, but only momentarily. Then he got it. Still, he had to be sure. "The picture?"

"The sweet," said Grant.

"Sext," Chase corrected.

"Whatever." He fixed Austin with a stare. "We know about it."

If they'd expected that would rattle him, they were disappointed. Instead, he smiled, as if he were proud of his little escapade. "How do you—?"

"'Cause we're the guys Wunder hired to steal it from that June dame. And we did it."

Chase nodded. "Right. Which is why we've got to talk to you.

Someone isn't playing straight with us. And the way we figure it, that means they aren't playing straight with *you*."

Austin Peebles remained silent, but his face began to redden. He pondered their words. "*Kevin* hired you to steal the picture?"

Grant and Chase nodded.

"Seriously?"

"Seriously."

"But…you couldn't have stolen that picture, because June Forteene still has it. It was on her blog this morning." He thought some more, and then annoyance crept into his voice. "Listen, if this is some cheap blackmail attempt, you won't get away with it. I know the district attorney."

"You do?" asked Chase.

"Well…okay, my mother-in-law does. But still…"

Grant bounced a glance off Chase and sighed. "We aren't trying to blackmail you, Peebles. We just want what was promised to us, and also to let you know your friends aren't necessarily your friends."

Austin wasn't following, and it showed in the confusion on his face. "Promised? What was promised? And by who? Uh…*whom?* Uh…Wait, maybe I was right the first time. Who?" He thought again. "No, *whom*."

Chase talked, mostly to stop the who/whom thing that was going on. "Your campaign manager. Kevin Wunder. He promised us thirty grand if we stole the picture from June Forteene, which we did. Then he ripped us off."

"Him and your wife," added Grant.

Austin Peebles's thick eyebrows arched.

"Yeah," Chase said. "And the two of them refused to pay when we went to collect. But the thing is, we did what Wunder said he'd pay us to do." Confusion continued to cloud Austin Peebles's young, well-formed face, and Chase suddenly felt bad that they'd delivered such devastating news. He also sort of wanted to muss Austin's hair and tell him everything would be all right, but fought back the impulse. "Don't be upset. We're only here to help."

Grant stared at his partner. "Why would you care if he's upset?"

But Peebles half turned from them, eyeing the Kids still shoving palm cards into the hands of uninterested passersby not twenty feet away.

And he wondered, *How did everything get so complicated?*

Life was so simple just a few weeks ago, when I could do whatever I wanted.

What he said, though, after squaring his shoulders, was, "I don't know what you guys are up to, but if you've got a problem with Kevin—or with my wife—you'll have to take it up with them."

"Here's the thing, kid," said Chase, who smiled and put an affectionate hand on the candidate's shoulder before thinking to ask, "Mind if I call you Austin?"

"I..." He faltered. "I don't mind."

"You see, Austin, like we told you, we were hired to do this job. So we did it, and then we got screwed out of thirty thousand dollars. But that's not why we're talking to you right now."

Peebles made a face. "It isn't?"

"It *is*, but it isn't," said Grant. "Your campaign *does* owe us thirty Gs, but we'll take care of that on our own."

"Then why are you bothering me?" He looked around at the sea of indifferent and/or hostile passersby that kept streaming out of the subway. "I'm supposed to be meeting people...and, uh, doing...uh... campaign stuff."

To Chase, Grant said, "He thinks *this* is bothering." Then he smiled darkly and addressed Peebles. "We've thought this through a hundred ways, and the only possible way that picture got back to June Forteene is if your buddy Wunder sent it to her."

Austin crossed his arms defiantly. "Kevin Wunder is a friend and political ally. On top of that, he's my mother-in-law's most loyal aide! He would *never* sabotage my campaign."

"Or so you think," said Grant. "But here's something I want you to ask yourself: If you have to get out of the race, who's the logical person to run for Congress in your place?"

"*And,*" added Chase, "who wants to be a congressman, but got passed over because he isn't a Concannon?"

"*And,*" Grant said, but stopped. He looked slightly confused. "Wait—there was one other thing, but I forgot it."

Chase didn't miss that. First it was Grant's back, then the neck *snap*, then his bladder, then his eyes, and now his memory. But he could worry about that later. "I remember. If Wunder isn't the guy who keeps sending your cock shots to June Forteene, who is?"

Austin Peebles—who fully expected to be sworn in as a United States Representative in three short months and trusted Kevin Wunder—

wasn't impressed by their reasoning. He couldn't conceive of Kevin double-crossing him, and he certainly wasn't going to play games with these lowlifes. Why, they probably weren't even enrolled voters in the district.

"The answer to your last question is that you must have failed to do what you *claim* you were hired to do. This is just a cheap attempt at blackmail. I should call the police right now." He began fumbling in his coat pockets for his phone, hoping they'd just go away and end this incident right now. Mostly because he'd really prefer the police not be involved, but also because he wasn't used to wearing a suit and couldn't remember where he'd tucked his phone.

"Here's the thing, Peebles." Grant was pretty sure the guy was bluffing but also was confident they could disappear into the subway if Peebles really did call 911. "Wunder had the motive, and he had the opportunity."

Austin found the phone in a breast pocket and pulled it out, but didn't punch in any numbers. "So you say."

"If we're lying," said Chase, "then why would we have been at your mother-in-law's congressional office last night? Want me to describe it?" Austin didn't answer. "And how did we know your wife was there with Wunder?"

"I...I..."

Seeing the young man finally falter, Grant added, "Did you even *know* your wife was there last night?"

"I don't believe you." Austin slipped the phone back into an inside pocket and hoped they wouldn't notice. They did. "If my wife was there, describe her."

"Tall blonde," said Grant. "Young, attractive, doesn't take bullshit from anyone...And no offense, but she looked like, if you poured warm water in her mouth, you'd get ice cubes back."

Austin nodded involuntarily. That *was* Penelope. And then he allowed himself to think, *Maybe...*

He pushed that glimmer of doubt away. The world was full of maybes, and if you thought about any impossibility long enough, it could seem possible.

There was a tiny bit of logic in the words these hooligans were saying, but the facts still didn't add up. Maybe Kevin *did* want to be the candidate, and maybe he *was* frustrated when Mother Concannon bypassed him to keep the congressional seat in the family. Maybe—and it was a stretch—Kevin had hired these men to try to steal the image back. And maybe Kevin had even somehow gotten Penelope involved.

But maybe Austin was out of the loop because he was the candidate and didn't need to know some of the ugly truths that were part of any campaign's backroom operation. His father had never dragged him into it, nor had his grandfather. Nor had Mother Concannon, for that matter.

Of course, that could have had something to do with the fact that he'd been indiscreet enough to take and send the picture in the first place. It *was* a really awesome photo—his face, body, and penis looked *perfect*—although he could understand why taking it and tweeting it could result in his banishment from the campaign decision-making process.

However, to connect all those suppositions and come to the conclusion that Kevin Wunder—*his own campaign manager*—was trying to cut his legs out from under him? That seemed impossible.

The truth, as Austin Peebles saw it, was this: Maybe these guys were hired to do this job. But they failed, because June Forteene still had the photo. Still, they wanted their thirty-thousand-dollar fee, which they had never really earned. So…

Grant and Chase had been standing silently, eagerly awaiting the moment Peebles recognized they were telling the truth and Kevin Wunder was the real enemy. What they got, though, when the candidate was finished mentally sorting through the facts, was quite the opposite.

Austin Peebles offered up a seductive smile, smoothed his tie, and leaned toward them to deliver the harshest words he'd ever uttered in his life.

"If I ever so much as see you again, I'll have you both arrested."

And then he strutted off to meet the unwelcoming public.

Those words didn't sound right coming from a guy whose dick they'd seen. Grant and Chase were stunned for a moment.

Grant elbowed Chase when he caught him following Austin Peebles's butt as he walked away.

"I wasn't, uh…I wasn't looking at that," said Chase.

"Shuddup."

❖

Back on the subway platform, Grant said, "I think he needs a little more convincing."

Chase raised an eyebrow. "Ya think?"

"By the way, I saw you flirting. You weren't exactly subtle."

"I wasn't flirting." Chase rolled his eyes. "*Please!* He's a baby! Like, what, twenty-two?"

"Wunder said twenty-seven. Anyway, you have to be twenty-five to be a congressman. I mean, *Representative*."

"Close enough. And *whatever*."

"We'll talk about it later at home." Grant paused and leaned forward to see if a train was coming. "But you were definitely flirting."

"Oh, jeez…"

"Anyway, you've got a reprieve, because we aren't going home right now."

Chase jammed his hands in his pockets. "No? So where are we going?"

"First we're gonna grab some breakfast. And then we're gonna pay some people a visit." Grant leaned forward again, and this time saw the distant light of an approaching train.

Chase thought he understood. "Because we'll need backup."

As the train roared into the station, Grant leaned close to Chase's ear and raised his voice.

"More than backup. If this guy isn't going to cooperate, we're gonna need an entire gang."

CHAPTER TWELVE

L isa Cochrane was a savvy real estate agent and knew a deal when she saw it. That's why a few years earlier she became a refugee from Manhattan, settling across the East River in the Borough of Queens. Her apartment at Aquaterra Tower II was on a high floor that faced the river and, of course, the Borough of Manhattan, with all the scenery it had to offer.

The cruel irony of Manhattan residential space was that you either had to make millions a year or forfeit a view. Lisa made hundreds of thousands of dollars and wouldn't have minded making millions, but wasn't quite there yet. Still, she wanted a million-dollar view, and knew she could get that—and more—through the simple act of moving off the damn island.

Now the Queensboro Bridge—she refused to think of it by its rechristened name, the Ed Koch Queensboro Bridge; not because of politics, but because she was a traditionalist—was the view from her terrace. The United Nations Building was the view from her bedroom. If she looked down, she saw the backside of the iconic Pepsi-Cola sign that had been an East River landmark for decades. She could see the Empire State Building, the Chrysler Building, Roosevelt Island...

Better to pay a lot of money to have the view of Manhattan, she firmly believed, than pay even more to actually live in Manhattan, but have a view of an airshaft. Lisa refused to pay a lot of money to look at an airshaft.

Her partner, Mary Beth Reuss, had bitterly objected to the notion of moving to Long Island City, insisting they would lose the prestige that came with a Manhattan address and be stranded in some sort of homophobic wilderness. But when Lisa—who paid all the bills for the necessities, not to mention most of Mary Beth's monthly credit card debt—informed her she was free to stay in Manhattan, but on her own dime, Mary Beth decided she'd learn to love living in an Outer Borough. After several years, she'd managed to at least get used to it. For the most part. But it wasn't worth arguing about, especially because she loved Lisa but also because she'd never worked—not even a single day—and therefore had no idea how she'd pay rent, eat, drink, and shop at Dolce & Gabbana, Hermès, Valentino, Calvin Klein, Barneys, Bloomingdale's, and Giorgio Armani if she were on her own.

Even Mary Beth had to agree—albeit begrudgingly—that Aquaterra Tower II was a nicer building than they would have found in their price range in Manhattan. The units were spacious and bright, the residents were professional and polite, and the security was top-notch.

So top-notch, in fact, that the doorman was eyeing Grant Lambert and Chase LaMarca warily on a closed circuit camera even *before* they'd walked into the building lobby, and came damn close to calling the police.

"Can I help you?" he asked as they approached his desk, one hand still poised anxiously over the phone.

"We're here to see Lisa Cochrane in 28-C." Grant tried to give him a friendly smile; on Grant, it didn't come off as particularly friendly. "No need to announce us. We know the way."

"You *have* to be announced," said the doorman.

"Have to?"

"It's policy!"

"You don't understand. Lisa and me, we're close friends." Grant edged away toward the bank of elevators, Chase following reluctantly.

"Sir!"

"Like I said, we know her…"

The doorman stood, doing his best to look intimidating. It worked about as well as Grant's friendly smile. "Sir, if you don't let me call up, I'll have to call the police." He looked at the panel on his desk. "I'll lock the elevators, too."

That stopped them. Even when they weren't pulling a job, they had a natural aversion to the police and twenty-seven flights of stairs.

Grant looked at the doorman, shrugged, and said, "Go ahead and call up. I'd hate to violate building policy."

While the doorman dialed, Chase whispered, "What if she won't let us up?"

"I thought about that. Which is why I didn't want him to call."

As the phone rang in 28-C, the doorman continued to eye them warily. Finally, he heard a voice on the other end. "Ms. Cochrane, this is the front desk. Two gentlemen are here to see you." He listened to her, nodded, and then looked at Grant. "She said she isn't expecting anyone."

Grant snatched the phone from his hand, dismissing him. "Let me talk to her."

"Sir!" the doorman squawked, but left it at that and didn't try to grab the receiver back.

The phone talked back at Grant in a gravelly voice that, disembodied, almost sounded like it came from a hard-edged man. "Lambert? I know that's you. I recognize your voice."

"Yeah, it's me. I need to come up and talk to you."

"Not today. I've got guests."

"Just for a few minutes. Then we'll be on our way."

"Didn't you hear me? I have guests for brunch, and they're not the type of people you're used to dealing with."

Grant smiled at the doorman and winked. "Great! I'll be right up!"

"Lambert!" she screamed. "Don't you dare—"

He cradled the phone and said to the doorman, "We know the way."

For his part, the doorman was embarrassed he'd been rude to a tenant's guests. "I apologize, sir, but I *do* have to announce visitors."

Chase smiled. On him, it worked. "We understand. You were just doing your job. It's policy."

"Yes, sir. Exactly. Just policy."

They took the elevator to the twenty-eighth floor, found Lisa's door, and knocked. The door opened a crack. Just enough to show angry eyes and flaring nostrils.

"Go away!"

The door closed in their faces. If she hadn't had guests, no doubt it would have been slammed.

Grant and Chase looked at each other and shrugged.

"I guess she really doesn't want to see us," said Chase.

"Guess not. That's a shame." Grant knocked again.

This time, Lisa was more polite, but her cool greeting was, to be charitable, unenthusiastic. "What the hell are you doing here?" Her voice was paying the toll for decades of cigarette smoke and hard liquor.

"We're here to see you." Grant added a shrug that said, *But you knew that.*

"How many times do I have to tell you to call first? I'm in the middle of brunch, Lambert. With guests. *Nice* guests."

"Brunch? Oh, fancy."

Her hiss was not unlike that of a coiled snake. "I. Have. Guests. If you had called, I would have explained that and saved you a trip. But, of course, you don't call."

He glanced at the floor. "Yeah, well...you know."

Lisa shook a head of short-cropped blond-going-gray hair. "I understand people being afraid of spiders. Or flying. Or the dark. Not phones."

"I'm not afraid." He tried not to sound defensive and failed. "I just don't like 'em."

"You, my friend, are a phone-aphobe."

"Hey, I called from the lobby."

"You yanked the phone out of the doorman's hand. That's not the same thing."

"Look, can we just talk for a few minutes?"

Seeing no other option, she finally opened the door wide enough for the men to enter. It was that or try to wait them out, and Lisa Cochrane knew Grant had such a stubborn streak he'd stand in the hallway for a week if he had to.

"Go directly to my office," she commanded. "Don't even *look* at my guests."

They would have done just that, but Lisa's brunch guests had their own ideas.

"Oh!" A plump, pink-faced man with thinning white hair, holding what looked like a mimosa, reacted with too much enthusiasm when Grant and Chase walked through the front door. "More guests? I should help put out place settings!" He looked at the new arrivals again. "By the way, I'm—"

"They're not staying long enough for you to bother introducing yourself." Lisa's smile was so tight it threatened to fracture her cheekbones.

Seated next to the plump, pink-faced man at the table, a short middle-aged woman sized them up with a bad attitude most people would cross the street to avoid. She then turned to him and said, "Keep your hand on your wallet."

Grant heard that but pretended he didn't. Instead he looked around and asked Lisa, "Where's Mary Beth?"

"She's out shopping, but she should be back soon. So let's try to get this over before she gets home. None of us need *that* drama." With that, she began herding Grant and Chase toward her home office.

"I'd really like to see her."

"Just *move!*"

The short woman would have none of that. "These guys are criminals, aren't they." It was a statement, not a question.

The plump man tried to shush her. *"Margaret!"*

Lisa, still trying to herd, shook her head. "Of course not. They're, uh…they're…"

Grant stopped and gave the short woman a hard look. It was meant to be withering, but she simply stared back, unblinking. "Who's she? And why is she calling us names?"

Now it was the plump man's turn to speak. He leaned forward, suddenly intrigued by—and maybe a little bit proud of—his companion's outburst. "If anyone can spot a criminal, it's this woman."

"Oh, hell," muttered Lisa. She shook her head at Grant. "You couldn't call first."

Ignoring Lisa, the short woman continued. "I wasn't calling you a name. I was just identifying your occupation."

"Who *is* this woman?"

The plump man held his mimosa but didn't drink. "Perhaps you've heard of Margaret Campbell. *People* calls her the Grande Dame of the American Mystery Novel."

Grant didn't get it. "Which people?"

The man sighed. "I was referring to the magazine." He then thought to add, "I'm David Carlyle. I'm Margaret's—and now *Lisa's*—editor."

"Yeah, okay," were the first words out of Grant's mouth, until his brain processed David's words. Then he stared at Lisa. "Why did this guy say he's your editor?"

Lisa wouldn't answer him. So David Carlyle took it upon himself.

"Our company will be publishing Lisa's book next month!"

"Huh?"

"Celebrity Boudoirs I've Known…And the Walk-In Closets, Too!"

"Huh?"

Lisa heaved a deep breath. Her little secret wasn't so secret anymore, and she truly regretted that. Was there anything more embarrassing than being outed as a writer? "It's not really a book… well, not a *book*-book, that is. It's more of a coffee table book, with a lot of photographs of houses I've sold." She suddenly, desperately, needed a cigarette, finally spotting her pack on a kitchen counter. "It's really no big deal."

Grant shook his head slowly. "That's why you didn't mention it?"

"That's why I didn't mention it."

His shoulders slumped. "And here I thought we were friends."

"Yeah, well, you'll get over it." She lit up then nodded down the hall toward her home office. "Let's get this over with."

When they were out of range and could talk privately, Grant asked, "How'd that short woman make us?"

She looked him over. "As criminals? Gee, I don't know…let me think. Maybe it's the entire aura of *criminality* you project."

A sour expression came to his face. "Really? We look like criminals?"

Lisa glanced at Chase. "He doesn't." Back to Grant. "You do."

To which Chase said, "I've been telling him he needs a better hairstyle."

She nodded her agreement, even though she thought Chase's own highlights were getting a little over the top for a man whose age was starting to catch up with him. Still, this was about Grant right now.

"A new wardrobe wouldn't hurt, either. After that, we can start working on the personality. And then the phone-aphobia."

Grant's sourness deepened. "Can we get to business please?" Lisa shrugged consent, the better to get him out of her apartment quickly. "I got this job, and I'm gonna need help."

"I figured as much. Unlike the old days, we never just meet up for good times. These days, you only come to me when you've got a job." She ground out her cigarette in an ashtray. "Okay, how much?"

Lisa Cochrane was very successful in her line of work, which—unlike Grant and Chase's line of work—required her to file tax returns and go to an office every day. She was good, which meant she made good money, which meant the only times she really saw Grant Lambert in recent years was when he was looking for a banker for one of his jobs. Such as *this* time, she assumed.

But at this particular moment, she was wrong.

"I'm not looking for money." Both Lisa and Chase—who had not yet been fully brought up to speed on Grant's budding plan—reacted with surprise.

They waited for him to continue, but he let the words hang in the air.

"You're not looking for money?" She didn't quite believe him.

"Well, yes, I'm looking for money. But not from you. Somebody owes Chase and me thirty grand. *That's* the money I'm looking for."

She still didn't believe him, but didn't have a choice. "Go on."

"Yeah." Chase was also wondering where Grant was going with this. "Go on."

Grant locked Lisa in with his eyes. "I need a woman."

She couldn't stop the laughter, which erupted in a throaty burst that was even more just-drank-a-glass-of-lye than her normal speaking voice, which was pretty damn rough. "That's twice in less than a minute you've said something I thought I'd never hear."

"Uh…Grant?" Chase was thoroughly confused.

Lisa calmed herself, although a few throaty giggles threatened to creep out. "Please satisfy my curiosity—and it looks like you've lost your boyfriend, too—and tell me why you need a woman."

"Y'see, there's this horny candidate running for Congress…"

"You'd better give me a moment to recover from the shock."

He ignored her gibe. "He's campaigning over by Bloomingdale's right now. Just the other side of the river here…"

"I know where Bloomingdale's is."

"…and we just went to see him. I need him to see the wisdom in working with us to get some money his campaign owes us. Follow?"

"Of course not. I usually don't. But keep talking."

"So we try to tell him that his campaign manager is trying to destroy his campaign…"

She stopped him. "Why would his campaign manager try to destroy his campaign? Isn't that sort of the opposite of what a campaign manager does?"

"Usually, I figure. I don't really know these things. But we know the campaign manager wants to be the candidate, so he's trying to destroy the real candidate. Got it now?" She nodded distractedly. "So we went over to Bloomingdale's to try to tell that to the candidate, but he shooed us off."

Lisa Cochrane looked at Grant and then took a quick glance at Chase, who nodded to confirm it. Then she pulled another cigarette from the pack, pausing to light it and take a very deep drag before continuing.

"So what's your angle? You don't do politics, Grant, so when do you get to the part where you're trying to make some money? And why do you need a woman?"

"I was gettin' to that. See, the candidate sent this picture of his, uh, his…" He didn't discuss male genitalia often with lesbians, and wasn't sure how delicately he should proceed.

She squinted through the smoke drifting near her eyes and, thanks to his discomfort, figured out where he was heading before he got too tongue-tied. "His *penis*?"

Grant blushed slightly. "Yeah, that. Anyway, the picture got in the wrong hands, and the campaign manager hired us to get it back."

"You? Why you?"

He looked more than a little ashamed. "Jamie Brock brought us the job."

"Oh, Lambert. You should know better." She shook her head admonishingly at him, then at Chase. "And you let him take the job?"

Chase was every bit as chagrined as Grant. "It sounded like an easy thirty grand. And it would have been, except this campaign manager double-crossed us."

She took a drag from her cigarette and blew the smoke at the ceiling. "Now I'm starting to get the picture. Stupid Jamie Brock brought you a stupid job—of a stupid cock picture, of course, because I'd expect nothing more from stupid Jamie Brock—and you were stupid enough to take it. So you pulled the job, and they refused to pay up. And somehow, with all the stupidity involved, you're still surprised."

Grant nodded. "That's about it. And now we're out thirty grand."

"Why don't you let it go? I know it's a lot of money for you, but…" She shrugged, and the fact it would have been a big-but-not-devastating loss to her, while it was both big *and* devastating to Grant and Chase, went unsaid.

Much as Lisa might have hoped she was being subtle, Grant got it. He also didn't care. He knew who he was, he knew what he wanted, and he knew why he wanted it.

"It's a matter of pride. Word gets around the street that you can screw over Grant Lambert, my career could be over. I might even have to go legit, which I've got no skills for."

"Another thing," added Chase. "This isn't over."

"What do you mean?"

Chase explained. "It's not *just* that we didn't get paid. It's that this campaign manager turned right around and sent the uh, the, uh…" He was no better at it than Grant, so Lisa had to once again take control.

"The picture of the penis."

"Yeah, that. Anyway, he must have sent it right back to the person we stole it from, which is how we figure he's trying to destroy his own candidate."

Grant took over, back in control of his hoped-for destiny. "So we went to Bloomingdale's to try to warn this candidate…"

Lisa was ahead of him. "And get the thirty from him?"

"Well, yeah. Sure. We earned it, so we would have taken it if he offered. But it didn't get that far. Anyway, we went to talk to him, but he didn't believe us. The thing is, if we're gonna make this all right with everyone—especially us—we'll need someone on the inside of the campaign. Meaning, we'll need the candidate's cooperation."

She stubbed out the cigarette after a few puffs, but only after making a point of blowing the last of the smoke into Grant's face. To her great regret, he didn't even cough. "I think you should give up and write it off as a loss. But if you insist on this plan to avenge yourselves, why not do what we've done before? Just plant someone in his campaign, let a few weeks pass until the plant works his or her way into position, then—voilà!—revenge!"

Grant leaned forward, shoulders on knees. "I would if I could, except I don't have a few weeks. I have something like four days before the person who got the photo releases it to the world on her blog. After that, the campaign goes up in smoke, the campaign manager becomes the new candidate and ends up in Washington, and we *still* don't get our thirty grand."

Lisa glanced at her watch. She was getting impatient and motioned for him to wrap it up. "Okay, now tell me why you need a woman."

"Because we already know the candidate, the one with the, uh, uh—"

"Penis picture."

"Yeah, that. He must have what they call a zipper problem. Otherwise, why's he sending those pictures? So I figure if we get an attractive woman close to him, maybe she can work the job on the inside."

She tapped her foot. "Seduce the candidate, convince him to help you…Is that where you're going with this? Because that's the only logical direction. Oh, and also? It's probably the most idiotic idea you've ever had. And—as someone who's watched you try to rob a mega-church, steal a yacht, blackmail an actor, and tunnel into a bank vault—I think I know an idiotic Grant Lambert idea when I hear one."

He folded his arms defiantly. Not that he looked, but he knew Chase was backing him up. "Got a better idea?"

"Take the loss!" She knew he wouldn't, so was compelled to add, "In any event, I'm far too old to be seducing married congressional candidates…"

He stopped her. "No offense, but I wasn't thinking about you."

That offended Lisa Cochrane, even though she tried not to show it. "You weren't? Why not?"

Grant tried to be gentle. "I was thinking younger. And more…uh, less…uh…I was just thinking *different*, is all."

"Then who?"

Grant couldn't believe he was about to tell her, let alone that he had conceived the idea in the first place.

"Your girlfriend."

Lisa thought her ears were playing tricks. "Mary Beth?" She paused and replayed the conversation in her head. "You're here for *Mary Beth*?"

"Yeah."

She tried and failed to wrap her head around that. "But…you *hate* each other."

"True," Grant said. "But I have to admit she's good. When she wants to be."

This was all news to Chase, too, and he was having every bit as hard a time as Lisa believing he was hearing Grant right.

"Are you sure? I mean, Mary Beth is, uh…" Chase looked apologetically at Lisa, but he was about to speak the truth and knew they all knew that truth. "She's a bit difficult, Grant."

"She's a bitch," Grant said.

"And," Lisa added, without objecting to Grant's very accurate characterization of her partner, "she's never quite forgiven *any* of us for the last time she had to seduce a man during a job. I had to go a month without sex after that incident, which now that I think of it, was *also* a job brought to you by Jamie Brock! Believe it or not, Lambert, most lesbians aren't longing to seduce men."

Grant held out his hands and stopped her. "I don't need Mary Beth

to seduce him. I just want her to get close to him. Lead him on a little…
that sort of thing."

"Seduction!"

"No. More like a friendship. A teasing, flirtatious friendship. Then
all she'll have to do is convince him that Chase and I are on his side,
stop the campaign manager, get our thirty thousand dollars, and that'll
be the end of it."

Lisa wasn't happy. "You make it sound so easy. And she'd have
only a few days to take care of that. It's…it's…why it's a walk in the
park! And I think *everyone* knows how easy it is to meet a congressional
candidate and quickly become his confidante."

Grant scrunched his face. "Is it really that easy? See, I figured that
might take some work."

She was done being nice and gave him a cold stare. "You are *such*
an idiot."

David Carlyle and Margaret Campbell waited until Lisa and the
newcomers were closed behind the door of the home office before he
whispered, "Do you *really* think those men are criminals?"

"C'mon, Carlyle." She took a gulp from her tumbler of bourbon.
The Grande Dame of the American Mystery Novel—according to
People magazine—was the only one drinking the hard stuff during
brunch and that didn't bother her one bit. If straight bourbon wasn't
known as a brunch drink, that just meant the rest of the world had yet
to catch up with her. "Did you get a look at them? Especially the older
one."

David fussed with his napkin, folding and refolding it. "Well, he
does look rather unsavory. But I'd *swear* the younger one was gay."

She raised an eyebrow. "Gay hoodlums? *Puh-leeze!* Just because
the young one has bad highlights doesn't make him gay."

"At *his* age, it does."

"Hmm." She thought that over and realized that, after twenty-six
novels, she'd never written a gay criminal as a character. It was an
idea…

She downed another gulp of bourbon. "I've been writing mysteries
for decades, David. I've done jailhouse interviews and visited precinct
houses from Tacoma to Tampa. Trust me: I know a crook when I see
one, and these guys are the real deal."

They continued in that vein for a while and listened as muffled voices occasionally rose and fell in the other room, only stopping when the office door was reopened. Lisa, looking more than a little annoyed, paraded the group back down the hall, followed by the older guy who looked like a criminal with the younger one who was too old for his bad highlights bringing up the rear.

Lisa forced a smile in the general direction of her lunch guests. "I apologize for the interruption. These gentlemen are leaving now."

Margaret Campbell was having none of that. "You," she said, fixing Grant with an intense stare that almost made him shiver. "Sit down for a second."

"But..." Lisa's protest was waved away before she could utter it.

Grant held his ground. "I'll stand, if you don't mind."

"Are you sure?" Her stare seemed to intensify. "Because I want to talk shop."

"Then I'll sit." Grant took Lisa's seat at the table, leaving her to lean against the counter that divided the kitchen from the living room/dining room. There was one more chair at the table, but Chase opted to rest his back against a wall.

"How long have you been in the business?" asked the writer.

"How long have you been in *your* business?"

"Twenty-three years. Now, back to you."

Grant looked at her unpleasantly. "I don't know what you're talkin' about."

She peered at him over the rim of her half glasses. "Let's see. You're around fifty-five years old, so I figure forty years in the business. Am I right?"

He squinted. "You think I look like I'm fifty-five?" He turned to Chase for support, but got little more than a weak smile in return, so he turned back to the author. "Not that you need to know this, but I'm in my mid-forties."

Margaret again peered over her glasses and studied him closely. "Are you sure?"

"Of *course* I'm sure. I'm the guy who lived it!"

She tilted her head and reached for her bourbon. "I'll take your word for it." She gulped. "So anyway, what's your specialty?"

Grant planted his hands palm-down on the table. "Listen, lady, I keep telling you this, and I want you to get it. We're *not* criminals."

"I told you so," sniffed David Carlyle. He nodded at Chase. "They're obviously gay."

She ignored him and kept talking to Grant. "I'm not making any value judgments. This is just professional interest. I write about criminals, so I like to get into their heads. So you're...what? A car thief? A second-story man? Blackmailer? Lock-breaker? What's your specialty?"

Grant leaned back. Pretty much every one of her guesses was correct, but it was still none of her business. "What makes you think I'm not a hit man?"

She rolled her eyes. "Oh, please. Respect me enough to take me seriously."

"I could be a hit man."

"Tell me a story, not a myth."

A sigh escaped as a frown appeared on his lips. "If I was a criminal—and I'm not sayin' I am—I think I'd be the type of criminal guy who plans the heist and brings a gang of experts together to pull it off."

"Ah!" she said, as if that was a satisfactory answer. "Very Westlake!"

"Huh?"

"Don Westlake. He was an old friend of mine. Wrote these very funny crime capers."

None of this information interested Grant, and he let that be known. "I'm just sayin' that's the type of criminal I'd be. But since I'm *not* a criminal..."

Chase stepped away from the wall where he'd been leaning. "I've got a question for the author."

"Who, me?" Margaret Campbell pointed to herself, even though she was the only *real* author—Lisa *hardly* counted with her picture book—in the room. "What's your question?"

Chase took a deep breath and refused to look in Grant's direction. "Remember, this is hypothetical." She nodded. "I was wondering how you'd solve a case like this. Say there's a guy being blackmailed over something, and these crooks are hired to get this thing back from the blackmailer. And they do the job, except the thing ends up right back in the blackmailer's hands."

Margaret mulled over Chase's scenario for maybe five seconds. "Obviously, someone close to the victim stabbed him in the back."

Chase slapped one hand against the other. "Exactly!"

"Chase," Grant warned in a low voice that was ignored.

"So now the crooks that did the job don't get paid, and the victim is still being blackmailed. But the victim doesn't want to believe that his friend stabbed him in the back."

She nodded and gave it another five seconds. "What you'll want to do—"

"Not us." Chase only then realized he might have already said too much. "This is just hypothetical."

The Grande Dame of the American Mystery Novel—according to *People*—smiled knowingly. "Of course it is. What these *hypothetical* crooks would want to do is go back and steal the thing one more time. Except...no, wait."

"What?"

"I have to think this through." She did and then continued. "The problem is that the blackmailer's already been robbed once, so he'll be better prepared for the second robbery."

"She."

"Excuse me?"

"The blackmailer's a she." Grant groaned and Chase stopped himself. "Uh...hypothetically."

"Okay." She brushed that away. "*She's* going to be ready, which means these *hypothetical* crooks will need help. Maybe someone inside. Or maybe a gang." She smiled. "Or maybe you'll have to kill her!"

Chase's eyes widened. "Kill her? Oh, *no*. Not even hypothetically."

"Too bad. That would be quick and easy. Make it look like a mugging. The problem is solved and the crooks walk away." She jiggled the ice in her almost empty tumbler. "That's how *I'd* do it."

Grant put his own spin on the hypotheticals. "How 'bout if the crooks got a woman to seduce the victim?" Lisa rolled her eyes. "Get her close and friendly with the victim, and maybe convince him to cooperate."

Margaret didn't like that idea, much to Lisa's relief. "I *suppose* that could work, but there are too many variables. Like, how do you know the victim can be seduced? How do you know the woman won't double-cross the criminals? Crime fiction is rife with double-crossing femmes fatales. I've created a few myself. Next thing you know, the woman's the one who's doing the killing, and she walks away with everything."

Grant looked up at Lisa. "Yeah, that's true. Some women ain't very trustworthy."

"Give it a rest, Lambert."

The author finally drained the last trickle of bourbon. "You could try, but I'd think the premise only works if there's a larger gang working several angles. You've got to take out the blackmailer, take out the backstabber, and compromise the victim. It's complicated, but I suppose it could work."

"So any thoughts?" asked Chase.

She laughed. "Are you kidding? Now you're talking about a caper, like Westlake wrote. I write edgy, hardboiled crime novels, not capers. And why would I? There's no money in it. No one reads that crap." She held one hand above her head. "My sales." The hand dropped out of sight below the table. "Caper sales. You do the math."

Lisa stole a glance at the clock on the wall and saw that time was running short. "This has been fun, but our uninvited guests have to be going."

"I think we should wait for Mary Beth." Grant didn't look like he intended to go anywhere.

"And *I* think you're deranged. Get out!"

But between their lengthy talk in the office, and especially Margaret Campbell's interrogation, what Lisa feared the most had happened. With the sound of a key in the front door lock, she knew she had finally run out of time.

Then Mary Beth Reuss was standing in the living room, clutching only a half dozen shopping bags. Which meant it had been an easy day on Lisa's American Express card, by normal standards.

Mary Beth politely greeted David Carlyle and Margaret Campbell, and sort of smiled when she nodded in Chase LaMarca's direction. Then her eyes found Grant Lambert and she didn't have to fake it anymore.

"What the hell are *you* doing here?"

There was company—*polite* company—so Lisa tried to defuse the situation. "Grant and Chase were just leaving."

Grant settled back in his chair and smiled. "No, we weren't. We were waiting for you."

"Me?" Mary Beth dropped the bags on the floor of the entryway. "Now you've seen me, so you can leave."

He *did* stand, but then started walking in the opposite direction of the front door. "I need to talk to you in private." He punctuated the sentence by snapping his fingers at her. "In the office."

Chase followed Grant down the hallway; Mary Beth did not. No one had *ever* snapped their fingers at her.

"I'm not talking to him," she informed Lisa. "And I hope you didn't, either. I don't know what he's got up his sleeve or how much money he wants from you, but the last thing we need is another one of his dumbass schemes."

"Uh, honey?" Lisa stopped her partner with a nod toward their non-criminal guests. "The sooner you talk—in *private*—with Grant and Chase, the sooner they'll leave."

Mary Beth frowned, but lowered her voice a decibel so as to not disturb the brunch guests. That decibel dropped her volume from the equivalent of a jackhammer to that of an approaching airplane. "I'd rather chew glass."

From the table, they heard Margaret drawl in a Southern accent she'd largely lost unless she was into the bourbon, which, of course, she had been, "If you aren't going to talk to them, *I* will. It'd be great research to watch criminals plot a crime."

"*Hypothetical* criminals." Lisa turned back to Mary Beth. "Now see what's happening? If you don't talk to them, not only are Grant and Chase never going to leave, but no one else will, either." Her eyes darted back to Margaret and David. "We barely had a chance to discuss *my* book before Grant and Chase got here, and suddenly they're the only ones anyone wants to talk to. *Except* you."

Mary Beth made a face. "Your book?" Then she remembered. "Oh…right…Okay, I'll talk to them. But I can't guarantee the next sound you hear won't be the noise a man makes when you kick him in the balls."

Leaving the shopping bags where she'd dropped them, she walked away. Moments later they heard the sound of the office door not quite slamming, but certainly not being closed with tenderness.

And as it turned out, the next sound they heard was not that of a man wailing in almost unimaginable pain. Nor was it the sound of shattering sheetrock or breaking glass or fracturing bone.

It was a squeal of delight.

Even more incomprehensible, it was a squeal of delight coming from Mary Beth Reuss.

She practically skipped down the hall upon her return before checking her happiness long enough to directly address David Carlyle and Margaret Campbell.

"Sorry, but brunch is over, and you have to leave."

They looked at her in confusion.

"Now!"

"Mary Beth!" Lisa couldn't remember the last time she'd seen her like this. Oh, she was used to the sort of rude behavior that would lead her to abruptly tell guests to leave, but not when accompanied by such a sunshiny mood. She wondered what Grant and Chase had pulled back in the office and glowered at them as they returned to the living room.

David burbled to Mary Beth, "We were talking about book publicity!"

"What? Publicity for *what* book?"

"Lisa's, of course."

"Oh, right. That. Well, it's not coming out for another month. That gives you plenty of time."

"Not real—"

Mary Beth handed him his flute, which still held maybe an eighth of an inch of champagne and orange juice. "Bottoms up!"

David Carlyle and Margaret Campbell were gracious enough about the hasty end of what had been an enjoyable brunch until various criminals began arriving. They left with tentative plans to get together in a more professional setting within the next few days. And then only Lisa, Mary Beth, Grant, and Chase remained in the apartment.

Lisa sized up the others. "Okay, what's going on?"

Grant shrugged. "Just what we talked about. Except it turns out you don't seem to know your girlfriend as well as you think you do."

She didn't blink. "I don't know what kind of game you're playing, Lambert, but I'm gonna find out. Mary Beth, these clowns *did* explain to you how they want you to seduce a man, right?"

"Sure they did." She smiled blissfully, and Lisa wondered if she should check the office for a pod, because this was definitely not her girlfriend. "And I said I'd do it."

"You said...?" None of this added up. "Could you run that past me again? 'Cause the last time I checked, I was pretty sure you were a lesbian and you hated Lambert and every plan he's ever come up with."

Mary Beth nodded her agreement on those items—she was indeed a lesbian, and she certainly hated Grant and his schemes, and barely tolerated Chase—but couldn't manage to erase the smile on her lips. "All true. But then they told me *who* they want me to seduce."

She had Lisa there; that was information she didn't have and hadn't been interested in. Maybe it was time to get interested in it.

Lisa turned to Grant. "So who's the mark?"

Grant started to tell her, but Mary Beth talked over him.

"Austin Peebles!"

Lisa—not a stranger to newspapers, unlike the rest of them—said, "The guy who's running for Congress?"

"That's the one," said Grant.

"But…" She glanced again at Mary Beth, who was still grinning like an idiot. "I don't get it. What's so special?"

Mary Beth clasped her hands in front of her, slightly pushing out her breasts, which didn't really need any help. "He's just *adorable*!"

"Still a lesbian, right?"

"*Of course* I'm still a lesbian! But Austin Peebles is just so cute and seductive and sexy, and…well…dreamy."

Dreamy? Had her very lesbian girlfriend just called a man "dreamy?" She had a hard time wrapping her head around that.

"Are you having Bobby Sherman flashbacks?"

Mary Beth cocked her head. "Who's that?"

"He was a teen idol in the sixties."

"*Way* before my time."

Lisa's eyes dropped. "Never mind."

Chase, though, readily joined Mary Beth in the Church of Austin Peebles-as-Elvis. "We just met him! He's even cuter in person!"

"Oh my God!" Mary Beth squealed again and looked like she was going to melt.

Grant and Lisa looked at each other. They seemed to share an imperviousness to Austin Peebles's charms.

"'Oh my God' is exactly the phrase I was looking for." Lisa downed what was left of David Carlyle's mimosa.

When they finally left—and Lisa could not get rid of them fast enough—Grant turned to Chase in the elevator.

"One down, more to go. And let's hope they all go as well as this did."

"What's next?"

"We're going to Harlem."

"Ah." Chase put a finger to his lips. "Gotcha."

They passed back through the lobby and exited the building, and Grant squared his shoulders. "I need you to do me a favor."

"What?"

"I get that you've got a crush on Peebles—I don't understand it, but I *get* it—but try to keep a more professional demeanor, okay?

Upstairs you and Mary Beth were acting like I promised to take you to a Justin Bieber concert."

Chase frowned. "I wasn't like that. Not at all." He paused. "Was I?"

"Yeah, more than a little. I hate to break this to you, lover, but your teenybopper days are far in your past."

Grant walked off, and Chase followed a few steps behind. And as he watched Grant's backside, he convinced himself that his boyfriend was only jealous because his ass no longer moved the way Austin Peebles's ass moved. It used to, but…no more.

Back, bladder, eyes, memory, weird neck *snap*, ass…Getting old was a bitch.

CHAPTER THIRTEEN

"Hello, Dr. Walters? This is Betty from Guest Services. First, sir, I wanted to make sure you're enjoying your visit to our hotel and the room is satisfactory." While she listened to Dr. Walters complain that he needed more pillows, the middle-aged black woman typed gently on the keyboard in front of her. She was updating her Facebook status, but he didn't have to know that.

"I'll have housekeeping take care of that within the hour, Dr. Walters. Please accept the apologies of the hotel." She paused and gently cleared her throat. "Now, there's one tiny thing I need to resolve. There seems to be a problem processing your credit card." She let him speak before continuing. "Between us, Doctor, this isn't the first time we've had a problem today. There seems to be a glitch with the computer, and you're the fourth guest I've had to hand-process. I'm *very* sorry." Another pause. "So could I get your card number again? Or information for an alternative card?"

Betty from Guest Services waited while the guest retrieved his wallet, then took down his information. "And the expiration date? Thank you. Oh—and the unique card code?" She paused. "That's the four-digit number on the front of your American Express card." He read it to her, and she typed it on the keypad before triumphantly announcing, "*This time* it went through. Thank you so much, Dr. Walters. I'm sorry for the inconvenience, and please enjoy your stay."

The woman ended the call. And then she ended the Betty Ruse.

Before five minutes had elapsed, Constance Price had ordered $16,852 in merchandise on Dr. Walters's American Express card, directing it to be delivered to an address where no one would ask any questions and no one would *answer* any questions on the off-chance law enforcement officials ever went looking for the goods. And since she was a savvy shopper with a keen eye for consumer demand, every dollar she had spent could be easily fenced—or even sold on eBay—for close to forty percent of retail, meaning one phone call would soon gross her close to seven thousand dollars.

That, she thought, was not a bad salary for less than ten minutes of work. And she was just getting started.

Or rather, she would have been just getting started. The ring from her doorbell changed her plans.

Constance peered between the slats in the blinds covering her window, frowning when she saw Grant Lambert and Chase LaMarca standing at the top of her stoop.

She was going to pretend she wasn't home, but—after another five minutes of doorbell ringing—realized they weren't going to leave. Grant Lambert was stubborn that way.

Her voice was weary when she finally broke down and answered the door. "What is it, gentlemen?" She did *not* invite them inside, a point that wasn't lost on Grant and Chase. "This had better be good, because I'm very busy today."

Grant sized her up. "A scam?"

He probably thought he appeared friendly, but she was having none of it. "None of your business, Grant Lambert."

He didn't seem to notice. "You should be happier to see us. We almost didn't pay you a visit, 'cause word on the street was you were working for the feds."

Constance looked at him coolly. "Gossips gotta gossip."

He shrugged. "Well, yeah, except in *our* business that kind of gossip is sorta important. You don't want to pull a job with someone who's turned legit."

"You think I'd turn legit?" She scoffed. "And here I thought you knew me."

Grant eyed her top to bottom and side to side. "So you're not working for the feds?"

She crossed her arms. "I am a free agent, Lambert. I do what I have to do to earn a living. Nothing more, and nothing less."

He was willing to believe her. They'd known each other and occasionally worked together for a long time. That didn't mean he had to believe every word out of her mouth—Chase was just about the only person he *mostly* believed—but if she said she hadn't turned, he'd have to accept that.

"Can we come in?"

She shrugged. "You here to pay a social call? Or are you working a job?"

There was no reason to play coy. "Working a job."

"In that case..." She opened the door wide enough for them to pass. As they did, she added, "I just don't know why you can't call before dropping in."

Grant shook his head. "Yeah, well..."

"I know. Because you're a phone-aphobe."

He scowled. "I wish people would stop saying that."

Constance motioned Chase through the door. "And why can't *this one* call?"

Chase answered for himself. "Solidarity."

She sighed. "White boys."

The particular block of Harlem where Constance lived could be a bit rough, but the interior of the apartment was prim and ordered. It looked more like any stereotypical grandmother's home than the home of a middle-aged lesbian con artist.

"So what's the job?" she asked, getting down to business. Constance was very no-nonsense when it came to their line of work.

"It's a bit complicated," said Chase.

"Simplify it."

Chase attempted to do just that. "We got double-crossed on a job and screwed out of thirty thousand dollars. So now we've got to make things right."

She shook her head. "That wasn't simplifying. That was *over-*simplifying."

On his second attempt, Chase took more time. When he was finished, she didn't look happy.

"Correct me if I'm wrong," she said. "But it sounds like all you're gonna get out of this job is revenge."

Grant shrugged. "Maybe. I mean, we're hoping once we get the picture back this Peebles guy will pay up, but if he doesn't... Yeah, all we get is revenge."

She sat in the middle of her couch, not inviting them to join her. "I don't know about you, Grant Lambert. Have you considered just walking away from this?"

"Not at all."

"We *did* earn that money," Chase noted. "We deserve something."

"Even if that something is just revenge?" They both nodded. "You two are the biggest fools. You'd risk going to Rikers Island for revenge?" They nodded again.

"The thing is," said Grant, "if we get screwed and take it, that sets a very bad precedent. Pretty soon everyone is gonna start to think they can take advantage of our specialized services without paying. They could do it to you, too."

She wagged a finger at him. "Oh, no, Grant Lambert. No one would dare do that to me."

"That's what you think."

"That's what I know. It's also why I never contract out my services, unless I know and trust the person I'll be working with. You *used to* be in that category, but now I think you must be getting a little soft in the head."

"Hey!"

Constance ignored him. "And let's say I decide to work this job with you. How are you gonna pay me? You expect me to do this for free?"

"Well…" Grant frowned. "Remember, our plan is to collect the thirty grand from Peebles. You'd get a cut of that."

"And if he turns you down?"

"We'll still have that indiscreet photo he took."

She frowned. "That's just great. You get no money—maybe you even end up going to Rikers—but at least you'll have the peace of mind knowing you own a picture of a politician's penis."

Chase changed the conversation so abruptly it threw off both Grant and Constance. "So what's your current scam, Constance?"

She cocked her head. "That's *my* business."

"Oh, c'mon."

"Where are you going with this?" His answer was nothing more than a knowing smile. "Okay, fine. I've got a friend at the front desk of one of the Times Square hotels. He used to feed me credit card numbers for wealthier guests, but management started sniffing around and scared him. But when he gets the chance, he still passes me names and phone numbers that connect directly to the rooms. Then it's up to me to con the guests into giving up the rest of the information. It's safer for him—'cause if anyone complains, management figures the guests gave their information to a random grifter working the tourist crowd—and it still pays off for me. I just have to do a little more work to make it pay off. Satisfied?" Chase nodded. "So why are you asking?"

He held an index finger in the air. "What do you do with the credit card numbers?"

"I order shit. And then I fence it or sell it. What do you think I—"

"And where do you have the merchandise shipped? Not here, I assume."

"Of course not. I know this guy…" She frowned. "You want to tell me where you're going with this?"

Chase smiled. "You have it shipped somewhere. To a friend."

"Not really a friend, but you're on the right track."

He was ready for his triumphant moment. "Suppose this non-friend decides to keep the merchandise for himself. Then what?"

Constance opened her eyes widely, finally understanding the reason for Chase's long, convoluted, seemingly pointless string of questions. "I get it! You're trying to draw a parallel between what happened to you and Grant with what *could* happen to me."

Chase was feeling very proud of himself. "That's it! It's all about the breakdown of trust."

"Except…" Her mouth fell into a scowl. "Except I would never let that happen to me. Someone fucks with me—even once—I know these Dominican guys that'd happily and permanently take care of the problem just for the fun of it."

That deflated Chase.

Grant, who was born deflated, asked, "So this credit card fraud gig. How's it working out for you?"

She smiled. "It's like fishing, Lambert. Or sex. Some days you sit there and do nothing but hold your pole, and some days they're biting. Why?"

There was no need to tell her he was already thinking about the next scam. "Just wondering."

With that, Constance looked at the grandfather clock tucked in the corner of her living room. "Now, if you'll excuse me, I have to get back to work."

Back out on the stoop, Chase said, "I really thought she'd see the light."

Grant never really expected success and was far less surprised than his partner. "We've got another person to talk to—and maybe a few more, if we can figure out what we need—but we'd better start preparing to pull this job on our own."

"We still have Mary Beth on our side. And Lisa, sort of."

"That's a very iffy 'sort of.'"

"And Jamie."

Grant stared at the sky, silently praying that a falling air conditioner would put him out of his misery.

They were one-for-two. A great percentage for batters, but not so great for criminals.

It was time to visit Brooklyn.

Paul Farraday's tiny basement apartment in East Williamsburg was not meant for entertaining. It was meant for a lot of things—writing unreadable, bleak poetry, drinking alone, lamenting one's irreversible mistakes in life, attempting suicide—but not entertaining. That's why Farraday was pretty much the only person who'd ever been inside the front door.

Grant Lambert and Chase LaMarca were two exceptions, and even *their* visits were few and far between. Yet there they were again, on the sort of warm day that didn't feel like the end of September.

He parted a tattered curtain and watched them ring the buzzer until Chase noticed the curtain moving and an eye peering out, at which point he figured he'd better let them come inside.

Farraday's bulk filled the doorway when he opened the door and greeted them with an unhappy groan. "What?"

"Is that any way to invite a pal inside?" asked Grant.

"How do you figure I'm gonna invite you inside?" He eyeballed the visitors for a few seconds before he caved. "Okay, come in. But make it fast."

"Why? What's doing?"

"Getting ready to drink."

"That's friendlier."

"Don't push it, Lambert. I'm on a schedule."

"Your first mistake," Farraday said, after they'd given him their pitch, "is that you took a job referred to you by Jamie Brock."

Grant's shoulders slumped. "No argument there."

Farraday leaned against the bar, the only item in the apartment that showed a pride of ownership. "The guy is useless."

"I get that. But it sounded like a good idea at the time."

"Jamie Brock can sling the bullshit. I'll give him that. But you should be smart enough to see through it. Nothing he's ever come in with has been worthwhile. Remember the Caymans bank scam?" Grant hung his head. "Remember the time he wanted to blackmail that actor in the Hamptons?" Grant's head dipped a little bit more. "Remember when he had the bright idea how we should rob Henry Kissinger—"

"Okay, okay!" Grant had lived through all of it and didn't need to relive it, especially in this dingy apartment where even positive things sounded depressing. "Would it help if you knew that Lisa and Mary Beth are very excited about this job?"

Farraday weighed that. Lisa was an operator, and Mary Beth was a bitch, and they wouldn't just buy into any old half-baked scam. "What do you mean by excited?"

Chase leaned forward, more to get away from a spring in the couch that had started poking his ass than to get closer to Farraday. But whatever worked.

"Let's just say the excitement level is through the roof. Especially Mary Beth."

"Mary Beth?" Farraday had to think about that. "She don't get excited about much except shopping."

"But she's excited about *this* job! See what I'm saying?" Chase snapped his fingers for emphasis.

"I dunno." Farraday shifted and—Farraday not being a small man—the movement disturbed the stale air in the apartment. "Anyone want a drink?"

Grant and Chase passed, so Farraday poured himself a triple in their honor. He was on a schedule, after all.

While their host filled a rocks glass—minus the rocks—Chase continued. "Like Grant's been pointing out, if people start to think they can take advantage of our criminal talents, well…there's just no justice."

Farraday set down the bottle of scotch and raised the glass to his lips. "You might want to rethink your terminology. Seems to me 'justice' isn't the word you were looking for." He sort of sipped, sort of gulped. "Here are some of the things I don't get…"

"Go ahead," said Grant.

"I was gonna." Hostility flickered across Farraday's face but he forced it away, reminding himself these guys were almost friends, or as close as he had these days. He took a big gulp of scotch—this time there was no half sip—and let the booze burn the inside of his throat. "First, correct me if I'm wrong, and I hope I am, but do I understand you want me to do this job without a set fee?"

"C'mon, Farraday." Grant leaned forward, feeling the twin brother of the spring that had attacked his partner. "Hopefully, this job clears thirty grand. So if things work out, there'll be some money for you. Hopefully."

"I keep hearing you say 'hopefully.' That isn't one of my favorite words."

Grant shrugged. "It's not like we've never worked together before. When I say 'hopefully,' I mean—"

"You mean I might make two hundred dollars. Or fifty. Or nothing."

"Well, no...but..." Grant sat back against the spring, defeated. "I suppose that could be a possibility."

"Okay, so there's that problem. And then there's another one..." Farraday stopped and looked around the room. "Is it too bright in here?"

"It's fine," Grant and Chase said at the same time, since the level of light seemed to be about what you'd get if you were buried alive.

"If you say so. Anyway, like I was sayin', I got another problem." He paused; the next words were going to be awkward. "I'm thinkin' of leaving the business."

They looked at him, uncomprehending. If Farraday had said he was going to take his almost 290-pound frame over to the Lincoln Center and join the ballet, it would've made more sense.

"Could you say that again?" Chase finally asked after the silence stretched for an uncomfortably long time.

Farraday frowned. He didn't want to say those words again if he didn't have to. "You heard me."

"But that doesn't make sense..."

"Damn right it doesn't make sense." Grant sounded indignant. "What are you thinking? You don't know how to do anything else."

That sort of pissed Farraday off. "In case you've forgotten, before I got into this business I used to be the best cab driver in the city. *Not* one of the best. *Not* in the top ten. I was *the* best."

They nodded. What he said was true. Farraday was a legendary cab driver until he realized he had to make a choice between the keys and booze, and the keys lost. Since then, he'd become even more legendary in the circles in which a skilled driver who could start, steal, and maneuver anything with four wheels was highly regarded.

"I'm sorry," said Chase, "but I still don't get it. I mean, if you go back to driving—legit driving, that is, with long hours and responsibilities—you'll have to give up the booze."

Farraday looked up from the bar where he was refreshing his triple scotch. "What makes you think I can't do that?"

Grant cleared his throat and almost said the wrong thing, but decided against it. "All right, Farraday, tell us what's going on."

"I did."

"Tell us what's *really* going on."

If he was going to do that, he was going to need more fuel in his system. So he drained the glass in three swallows and refilled it before taking a seat in a broken recliner across from where Grant and Chase sat on the couch. The chair squealed a protest and the footrest popped out a few inches.

"Remember Mrs. Jarvis?"

Grant didn't. "Who?"

"Mrs. Jarvis. That neighbor of ours from the time we pulled the job in Virginia."

Now it was coming back to him. It had been surprisingly easy for Grant to suppress the memory of Farraday in puppy love. "What about her?"

Farraday fidgeted in the recliner and the footrest popped out another couple of inches. "We've been staying in touch."

Grant and Chase saw where this was going and began to feel even more uncomfortable than their host.

"Are you trying to say," said Grant, "that you've got something going with this lady in Virginia?"

"Yeah." Farraday was relieved he didn't have to spell it out. "First time I've been happy since the divorce."

"But the booze…"

"I'm thinking of moving to Nash Bog, Virginia, Lambert. And if I make that decision, nothing you or Chase can say will change my mind. Me and Mrs. Jarvis figure if I can move there and quit drinking, maybe I could get a job as a school bus driver or something."

Farraday stood—the recliner sighed with relief—and walked back to the bar.

"You know," said Grant, "maybe I'll have a drink after all."

"Pour one for me, too," added Chase.

Farraday poured as he talked. "There's another reason I can't do a job right now."

Grant didn't really want to hear it, but figured if it made him happy…"Why's that?"

"My schedule is really booked these days with flying lessons."

Grant scratched his head. "What, in an airplane?"

"No, I flap my fuckin' arms."

"Sorry…I just…"

Farraday handed his unwelcome guests their drinks. "Of course I mean an airplane. What else would I mean?"

"So…" Grant was having a hard time wrapping his head around this revelation. Sure, Farraday was the best wheelman in the Northeast, but that was a lot different from piloting a plane. Also, planes were expensive. "So you pay an instructor?"

"Who said anything about an instructor?"

"Well, how…?" He caught the tiniest hint of a sly grin on Farraday's lips. "Are you telling me you steal planes to practice flying? With no experience?"

"Exactly."

"And you fly in skies that are above *me*?"

Farraday raised his glass. "Bottoms up."

Grant Lambert considered himself a realist, and so—realistically— he knew there was no way he would be able to pull off a series of synchronized burglaries with only Chase, Lisa, and Mary Beth. Even with Constance and Farraday on board, he'd be shorthanded.

"We could bring Nick back," Chase suggested as they trudged down the block after leaving Farraday's apartment.

"Maybe. But that mother of his worries me. Kelly gets wind of this and I can see her running to the cops. We're already pushing it."

Chase shook his head sadly. "She used to be the best on the long con."

"That's the truth. But I'll tell you, becoming a lawyer is the worst thing for a former criminal to do. A total three-sixty."

"One-eighty."

"Huh?"

"A total three-sixty would mean she'd come back around to being a criminal again. A one-eighty would mean she'd be the opposite of a criminal."

Grant waved him away. "I'm not interested in fractions right now."

"Not fract—" Chase stopped himself and decided it'd be best for both of them to drop it.

"So is Nick in or out?"

"He's a maybe. Got any other suggestions?"

Chase shrugged, knowing that Grant wouldn't like the only name that came to his head. "Jamie?"

"Maybe." Grant saw the surprise on Chase's face. "I didn't say yes. Just maybe. He's pretty worthless, but I'm gonna need more bodies, and at least he's a body."

Chase almost laughed as they neared the subway. "Yeah, I guess he *is* a body."

"Might be a good man to have along," Grant added, as they began descending the stairs to the platform. "In case we need to leave someone behind."

That evening they sat in their kitchen in Jackson Heights and continued into a fifth hour of trying to put a gang together. Grant had a pad in front of him listing almost thirty names, twenty-five of which he'd crossed out.

"How about that Pete guy?" asked Chase. "The one from Hoboken?"

"In jail."

"Really? They catch him boosting an ATM again?"

"Nah. Pete got himself elected to the city council and the feds nailed him on a corruption rap."

"No kidding."

Grant shrugged. "That's New Jersey for you." He looked at the remaining names on the list. They belonged to the few people who they hadn't rejected or who hadn't rejected them. "Better get Jamie Brock and Nick Donovan on the line and get their commitments."

Chase hiked an eyebrow. "Are you sure?"

"I can think of a lot of people I'd rather have on the job, but they'll have to do. At least Nick's already familiar with June Forteene's office, which will be helpful. And Jamie knows the layout of Concannon's congressional office...not that I trust him to carry off a burglary."

Chase dialed and Grant stared at the list again and thought, *Ah,*

Hoboken Pete, why'd you have to go and get yourself elected to city council? I could've used you about now.

One name that wasn't on Grant's list—for many reasons, but especially because he'd never met her before—was that of Angelina Ortiz.

Grant *had* heard the name before, but it hadn't registered with him and was gone in seconds. She wasn't in their business.

And yet, when things looked bleakest—when Grant's gang consisted of himself, Chase, Lisa, Mary Beth, and *hopefully* Jamie and Nick—Angelina Ortiz was the woman who came to his rescue.

At the same time Chase was working the phones, she arrived home from a long shift waiting tables at a Midtown diner. She was bone-tired and wanted nothing more than to sit and unwind over a glass of something strong.

"Hi, baby," she said to her longtime partner as she shuffled into their very orderly living room.

"Hi backatcha," said Constance Price, looking up from the computer screen. "I just ordered you a present."

Angelina smiled. "*You* did? Or is it courtesy of one of your victims?"

"It's the thought that counts." Constance logged off and gazed lovingly as Angelina poured herself a glass of red wine. Neither of them was as young as they'd once been, but she admired the way Angelina had eased into middle age. Her face showed only the finest lines; the hair that had once been lustrous and black was now gray and cropped short. That those were the only visible signs of a life that hadn't always been easy was nothing short of amazing.

If only her own face and body had held up half as well…Not that Angelina ever complained.

Angelina carried her wineglass to the couch and sat. "So how was your day?"

"Fairly profitable." She joined her partner on the couch. "I had to waste some time with Grant and Chase, but otherwise I had a good day."

"What did Grant and Chase want?" They might not have known *her* name, but she certainly knew theirs. Even though Angelina Ortiz wasn't a practitioner, she knew everything about Constance's career. "Did they have a job for you?"

"They got screwed by a client, so they're looking for help getting revenge." Constance chuckled. "Dumbasses."

Angelina curled one leg beneath her. "So are you gonna help them?"

"Hell. No."

"But they're your friends."

Constance leaned back against a throw pillow. "Calling them friends is stretching it. We're business associates, and business is business. They took a bad job and got burned, so why should I volunteer my time to help them?"

Angelina shook her head disapprovingly. "Hope nothing like that ever happens to you. If you won't help your friends when they're in a jam, nobody's gonna be around to help you in the same situation."

"The difference is, I would never put myself in the same situation. If a fool like Jamie Brock brought me a job retrieving pictures of a penis, I'd kick his ass down the front steps."

"Wait…pictures of a penis?"

"You heard me." Constance laughed. "Some guy running for Congress—Pebbles or Peebles; something like that—took a picture of his junk and…"

Angelina jerked upright, almost spilling her wine in the process. "Peebles? Austin Peebles?"

Constance raised an eyebrow. "You've heard of him?"

"He's *adorable*!"

"Yeah, well, that adorable man got himself into trouble taking pictures of his—"

Angelina bounced on the couch. "You've got to take that job!"

Now it was Constance's turn to jerk upright. "I certainly do not."

"Come on! It'll be fun. You'll be helping a friend *and* helping Austin Peebles at the same time!"

"I'm not—" Constance paused mid-objection. "And why the hell should I give a damn about Austin Peebles's penis?"

In her enthusiasm, Angelina ignored the objection. "I'll even help!"

That stopped Constance cold. In all the years they'd been together, Angelina Ortiz had never shown any interest in working with her. "You will?" It didn't seem right. "What's so special about this Peebles guy that's got you so boy-crazy?"

"He's just…I don't know, I guess 'adorable' is the word."

"It's certainly the word you keep *using*."

"I've been reading about him in *The Daily News*. He looks like such a heartbreaker, but he's such a nice boy. He even reads to blind orphaned puppies!"

Constance eyed Angelina. "You're a little too excited about this guy. Are you sure you're a lesbian?"

Grant sat, depressed and alone, at his kitchen table. Chase was working a late shift at The Gross, which cut him off from the world. He supposed he could pick up his phone and try to round out the gang, but... *nah*. Jamie was now on board—for all the good *that* would do—and Nick would be getting back to them. That was a start, if not quite the manpower he'd need.

He stared at his cell phone resting on the counter next to the sink. He was definitely not a phone-aphobe—no matter what an increasing number of people seemed to think—but saw no need to actually pick it up and talk to someone. Whatever thoughts he had could wait until Chase came home from work and—

The phone buzzed, startling him. He gripped the edge of the table and stared at it again, watching it move a half inch with the vibration. When the noise and movement stopped, Grant finally took a breath.

And then it happened again.

He stood and cautiously approached, transfixed as the phone danced along the countertop. From a yard away he tried to read the screen to see who was calling. That didn't work, so he took another step closer.

The screen read *Constance Price*.

Grant took a deep breath, closed his eyes, and reached for the now-silent phone, hoping she'd hung up.

"That you, Lambert?" Constance's voice asked the dead air.

"Yeah."

"Look at you, answering your phone! I'm so proud of you!"

He sighed. "Is this important?"

"You think I'd waste my time on bullshit?" He didn't say anything, so she continued. "I'm calling to tell you we're in."

"You're in what?"

"Christ, Lambert, why do you have to make this harder on me than it already is? We're in on your revenge job. But let me tell you—"

"You're in? That's great." He felt more enthusiastic than he sounded until his head rewound her words. "Wait—who's 'we'?"

"Me and Angelina."

"Who's…?" He thought for a moment until something buried far back in his memory glimmered. "Angelina? Isn't she your girlfriend?"

"We prefer 'partner,' but yes, that's the one."

Grant didn't like that idea. "But she's not in our business. She's never pulled a job before, has she?"

"No."

"Ever helped you on a scam?"

"No, and that's why I'm not happy about this. She wants to do the job because of this Austin Peebles. I don't understand it, but she's infatuated with him."

"There's a lot of that going on. My partner was flirting with him, and even Mary Beth seems ready to switch teams."

It was Constance's turn to be surprised. "Mary Beth? Mary Beth *Reuss*? She hates everyone!"

"Everyone except Austin Peebles. Go figure." He tapped a finger on the countertop. "I met the guy. Nothing special."

"I'm going to have to see him for myself," Constance said. "I don't think I like the effect he's having on my lesbian community."

"I don't like the effect he's having on anyone. Especially if that effect is bringing rookies in on the job."

"Don't worry about Angelina. If she wants to come along I can't stop her, but I'll make sure she stays out of the way. Anyway, another pair of hands—and eyes—are a good thing, right?"

"If those hands know what they're doing and those eyes know what they're looking for."

"Don't worry, Lambert. I'll keep Angelina out of the way."

"You'd better," Grant grumbled.

He didn't need a five-bar cellular connection to hear indignation from the next borough due west. "Is that any way to show appreciation to me for saying yes?"

He mumbled an apology and was grateful a few minutes later to be able to put the phone back on the counter.

Then he thought better of it and stowed the phone in the silverware drawer.

The next time a phone rang in the apartment, it was morning again and the phone belonged to Chase.

"It's Nick," he announced to Grant, who was once again at the kitchen table, this time with a tube of Bengay in hand. "Want to take the call?" Grant's response was a cold stare, which didn't surprise Chase at all. "He can't come to the phone right now, Nick. So what can I do for you?"

The kid spoke for a few seconds, and then Chase informed Grant, "He's in."

"Okay, tell him—"

"But he wants to know if he's a villain or a hero?"

"Oh, jeez." Grant rubbed some ointment on his shoulder. "Tell him it's the same deal as before."

Chase spoke to Nick, and Nick spoke back.

"He says he'd rather think of himself as a supervillain."

"Ugh." They didn't make crooks like they used to. "Okay, fine, tell him whatever he wants to hear. If he wants to think of himself as a villain—"

"*Supervillain.*"

"Supervillain, then. If that's what he wants, tell him it's okay. Whatever it takes to seal the deal."

So Chase did. It was only after he hung up that he thought to ask Grant, "Do you think that was wise?"

"Whatever. We need him. He already knows the layout of June's office, and he's the only one who can fit through the transom."

"Hey, *I* fit through it!"

"Yeah, but you're running out of underwear. Anyway, the kid has already been educated on how to dress and conduct himself. Which his mother *shoulda* done, but that's what happens when you go legit." He was reminded how he could have used Kelly whatever-her-most-recent-married-name-was right now, but that ship had sailed. "I figure we shouldn't have any problems with him this time."

One of Chase's eyebrows inched up. "You're sure?"

Grant heaved a sigh. "If I have the chance, I'll talk to him again when we get the gang together to go over plans. *If* we get a gang together, that is. Right now, we're not where we need to be."

He figured they needed two more people: someone to drive and someone with the fast hands of an expert pickpocket or shoplifter.

And he had no idea where he was going to find those people.

CHAPTER FOURTEEN

Grant and Chase might have been stalled on their end, but the same was not true for Mary Beth Reuss.

She had an assignment and was determined to carry it out. True, on those rare occasions she'd been drawn into past schemes, she'd been a reluctant participant. But this was different.

On past jobs, she'd only become involved for her beloved Lisa. Lisa gave her everything and asked for little in return except Mary Beth's indulgence in the kicks she got committing crimes alongside Lambert and LaMarca. It *had* to be the kicks, because she didn't need the cash, and when Grant Lambert came up with a plan, you could guarantee any payoff would be small change.

Mary Beth got that, even if she didn't share Lisa's apparent faith in Lambert and his idiotic schemes.

She'd been born into money and cultivated expensive tastes until Dr. Gerhard Reuss—once known to her as "Daddy"—offered her a "be my daughter or be a lesbian" ultimatum, and she felt the temporary thrill of being her own woman. Daddy—no, it was "Dr. Reuss" now, and he was only a podiatrist, not the guy who was going to cure cancer—lost his "Princess" that day.

That should have been devastating for Mary Beth, but she found it thrilling.

Or it was for maybe forty-eight hours. Until the moment she realized she'd never be able to survive on hand-me-down clothes or figure out how to turn on a stove burner without singeing her hair.

It was a fortunate circumstance when she met Lisa Cochrane a short time later. Lisa offered her those thrills she thought were gone forever, and that was before Mary Beth realized Lisa was rich. That they were still together was a matter of love, not money, but Mary Beth was not above settling for both if she could.

So Mary Beth indulged Lisa's thrill crimes—there was really no other way to describe them—because she had experienced her own thrills of loss and discovery. Not that a wallet full of credit cards hurt.

She knew everyone considered her a pampered bitch, and she agreed with them. She saw it as self-protection but was comfortable enough in her own skin to let other people think what they wanted to think. Lisa got her, and that was what was important.

Maybe that was what attracted her to Austin Peebles.

From watching him on the occasional newscast, she got the same sense about his background. Maybe he hadn't been disowned by his family—or maybe he had; she never got that far into his life story—but Mary Beth sensed damage beneath his charming façade. Somehow this poor lost puppy had been thrown to the sharks and was flailing in open seas.

Wait…puppies? That reminded her: Any man who would read to blind orphaned puppies melted her heart.

She knew Lisa would object, so Mary Beth waited a full half hour after her girlfriend left for the office before showering, dressing, and making her way to the Austin Peebles campaign headquarters to volunteer…or whatever she'd improvise to get close to the candidate.

No, Grant had not yet authorized her to put the plan in motion.

No, she didn't care.

When she walked into the campaign headquarters on Lexington Avenue, every male—and a few of the females—turned to look. She couldn't blame them.

For a woman of fairly small stature, Mary Beth had very large breasts…and knew how to use them to her advantage. The dress she'd selected for this foray to the campaign headquarters was cut to emphasize breasts and curves. It wasn't the sort of outfit one would wear to church, but she wasn't going to church.

She was going hunting.

"Can…can…?" stammered the first young man she encountered.

"Can you help me? Yes, you can. I'm looking for Austin Peebles."

"He's…uh…" The man took his eyes off her chest and managed to control himself. "He's not here."

She looked at him and shook her head. It was more than pathetic the way most straight men turned into idiots at the sight of a rack, but that was *their* problem.

Repositioning her body back into his line of vision, she asked, "Do you know where I can find him?"

"He's…uh…" The young man shifted his eyes until he was looking at a wall. "He's campaigning at a senior center."

She moved again, this time giving her upper body a little jiggle. "When will he be back?"

"He won't be back today." The young man focused both eyes on his stapler. "He has events on his schedule all day, and a fund-raiser tonight."

By the time he looked back up he only caught a rear view of the woman as she walked away.

One year earlier, Chase had pulled a few jobs with a shoplifter from Staten Island who came off like a hockey mom, not a criminal. He'd been impressed with her fast fingers and introduced her to Grant, just in case they needed someone with her talents one day.

This was that day.

When she heard Chase's voice on the other end of the phone line, Chrissy Alton's first impulse was to say no before she knew what he was proposing. Because she actually *was* a hockey mom, and the boys had practices and games lined up on an almost daily basis for the next ten years or so. Since Staten Island had limited mass transit—no subway; just buses and a train with tracks running nowhere near where she'd needed to be—and her husband the dentist was too busy to drive them everywhere, the burden fell on Chrissy.

But she was a sport, and decided to hear Chase out. She could always turn him down later.

Chase started with the blow to his and Grant's honor inflicted by Wunder's double-cross. Surely any criminal would understand their need to avenge a thirty-thousand-dollar slap in the face.

She was unmoved.

So he promised her cash if the job was successful and the Peebles campaign paid up.

She laughed. "Three thousand dollars? Seriously?"

"Hey, that's ten percent of the take."

"No offense, Chase, but I can make more than that in four minutes just by shoplifting from Walgreens."

So Chase went back to "honor," and she remained unmoved.

The conversation had almost drawn to a close when one last thought popped into Chase's head. "Too bad I won't have this opportunity to show Grant what you can do."

"Yeah, well, maybe someday—"

He interrupted. "We pull big heists from time to time, and I figured if he saw you in action he might bring you into a gang. But…"

After the briefest silence she asked, "How big are these heists?"

"Couple of hundred thou…sometimes a few million." That information was true, although Chase left unsaid that the money they tried to get and the money they counted at the end of a big heist didn't necessarily correspond.

"A few…" She swallowed. "Million?"

"Yeah."

"Let me think about it." Chrissy hung up and a few minutes later her husband Karl walked through the front door.

"Hey, babe," he said, by way of greeting. "What's for dinner?"

She'd been thinking of millions of dollars and his question brought her out of it. "I hadn't planned anything…"

"That's okay. I'll order a pizza."

She looked around her very pleasant middle-class house in her very pleasant middle-class neighborhood, and then at her very pleasant middle-class husband—the dentist—who worked hard and left her to drive the boys to an endless number of ice rinks.

Then she looked down at the Manolo Blahniks she'd swiped the week before.

Which was the moment Chrissy Alton decided it might be a good idea to show Grant Lambert just how good she was at her craft. Because hockey and pizza and Walgreens didn't seem to cut it anymore.

There was nothing wrong with being a hockey mom married to a good provider. There was also nothing wrong with wanting more excitement and disposal income.

June Forteene stood in the middle of her office, paralyzed into inaction by, well…*everything*.

To the best of her knowledge, Edward was probably still in jail.

Her only other paid help—a researcher named Gretchen who seldom worked out of the office but could be called in a pinch—had told her just minutes earlier she was pregnant and taking a job with benefits, effective immediately. Her office had been broken into by some pervert who had left his underwear behind. And a scruffy man in a UPS uniform was following her.

No assistant, no researcher, and no sense of security. How was she supposed to handle all that? She was almost at the moment of her greatest triumph and everything was falling apart.

The blogger dropped a hand into her purse and felt the handle of her nine-millimeter. At least she still had *that*.

She finally forced one leg to move, and then the other, and soon was walking. That helped. She was incapable of blogging or doing much besides alternating between extreme bouts of anger and paranoia, but at least she could walk.

And she decided she hated Gretchen. How dare she get pregnant like that? June suspected she'd done it out of spite. The girl knew by quitting she'd leave June all but alone. She could manage without a researcher for a week or two, but not much longer.

What was worse was the realization that without Edward and at least the possibility that Gretchen might come in every now and then, she was now the only person on the entire fifth floor. A burglary had been committed, the Live! Nude! Girls! and their patrons were spreading their diseases below, and Captain Enright reported junkies in the building, but she was alone. If something happened, there'd be no one to help her.

For the first time ever she wished the Bulgarians were back in their office.

She felt again for the pistol, and again was reassured.

June saw only one immediate option. No others came to mind.

For at least the short term, she needed Edward Hepplewhite back.

She could fire him—*would* fire him—later and fill the position with someone more competent and, hopefully, better able to defend her office. But that would take time. June Forteene could not afford the time to hire and train a new employee right now…not with the photo of Austin Peebles's penis about to go public. When that happened, the phone wouldn't stop ringing and the e-mail wouldn't stop flowing into her in-box, and she'd have to be ready.

She picked up the phone before she had an opportunity to doubt her own judgment and hoped he wasn't still in jail.

It hadn't been difficult for Mary Beth to find the PEEBLES FOR THE PEOPLE campaign fund-raiser. It was posted right on the website. The Friars Club, six to eight p.m., two thousand dollars per person. And she wouldn't even have to change out of her breasts-and-curves-enhancing dress. She left a vague note about a campaign event on the kitchen table. Then she went to work.

As she waited in line to pay her for her ticket, she debated telling Lisa about the money. Two thousand dollars was a large enough amount that she'd probably notice. But if Mary Beth told her, there was a good chance Lisa would object—she was already acting inexplicably strange about Austin Peebles—so she decided it would be a better idea to keep it to herself for the time being.

After they ran her credit card there was no turning back, and Mary Beth walked into the Milton Berle Room and took a look around. The crowd wasn't the type she was used to mingling with, but it was definitely the type she aspired to mingle with, if on the old side.

And then she spotted him across the room.

Austin Peebles stood in the middle of a knot of people, smiling shyly while one guest after another talked his ear off. He looked young enough to be the grandson of most people in the room.

And she thought, *The poor thing...*

Ironically, Austin was thinking the same things. Both "poor thing" *and* "these people are old enough to be my grandparents."

These events used to be tolerable when Penelope was speaking to him—she wasn't always pleasant, but his wife could be a delightfully catty companion—but she couldn't even be bothered to show up at this event. For that matter, even Mother Concannon had taken a pass, leaving him at the mercy of Kevin Wunder and approximately one hundred senior citizens.

Ah well, he thought. *Start the day campaigning at a senior center, and* end *the day campaigning with the seniors.*

The circle of elders seemed to tighten around him, some of the women tenderly touching his arm as if he were a favored grandchild.

It was intrusive, but it wasn't the first time he'd been the center of attention. He figured he could stick it out until eight o'clock and act happy to be there…but then he saw the beautiful young woman in the low-cut blue dress standing across the room and thought he might not have to act after all.

If Penelope Peebles had known who her husband was ogling at that moment, she might not have cared. Even without knowing Mary Beth was a lesbian, she might not have cared.

Less than two years earlier, she'd entered the marriage with her eyes wide open. Austin had many less-than-admirable qualities, but guile and manipulation were not among them. Penelope knew exactly what she was getting: a bad boy husband who, not coincidentally, would bring her greater public exposure and double the number of potential clients for her financial management firm.

It was like they had an unwritten—and unspoken—contract. Until something voided that contract, they would present a unified front and prosper. It would be a win-win situation for both of them.

It was also unwritten and unsaid that sexting a photo of your *freakin' erection* to some *stranger* on the *Internet* was a contract-killer.

She thought she'd probably stay with him through the election, but it was hard to imagine life with Austin past November. Penelope had a career to build, and no time for her immature husband's shenanigans.

If the photo went public—and thanks to the incompetent thieves Kevin Wunder had hired, that seemed likely—the marriage was definitely over. Austin's private dalliances were his own business; publically humiliating his wife was another thing altogether.

Her mother might try to convince her to save the marriage, but Penelope could be very determined. And if her mother loved the man-child so much, *she* could marry him.

She looked at the clock and realized she was wasting too much time obsessing over the situation, so she buzzed for her assistants—the same large young men who'd given her a hand a few nights earlier when she had a completely blank check to rip up in front of a very disappointed trio of burglars—and announced it was time to get back to work.

❖

When Mary Beth arrived home late that night, Lisa was waiting up.

"You wore *that* dress?" were the first words out of her mouth. "You wore *that* dress to campaign with Austin Peebles?"

"It's a long story," she said but realized she should elaborate when she saw the hard, unhappy expression on her partner's face. "I wanted to make an impression."

"I'll bet that did it."

Mary Beth smiled. "Yeah, he definitely knows who I am now." When Lisa started to say something, Mary Beth cut her off. "He *also* knows I like women. I made that clear right up front."

Lisa believed her but couldn't quite put all the pieces together. "So why the dress?"

"Look." Mary Beth pulled a chair away from the kitchen table and sat. "We know Austin Peebles is a horndog, right?" Lisa nodded. "That's why I wore the dress. We don't have a lot of time, and I needed him to notice me right away. It worked!"

"Go on…"

"We ended up having a long conversation, and—"

"Did you convince him that his own campaign manager is trying to stab him in the back?"

She shook her head. "Not yet. First I had to get my foot in the door. I'll take care of the other business tomorrow."

"Tomorrow? Do you have another date?"

"Now, Lisa…"

Lisa frowned. "I don't like this."

"But it's working. I'm in." She held up her cell. "I even have his phone number."

"So how did it come up you're a lesbian?"

"Well…" Mary Beth gulped and knew this already not-so-pleasant conversation was about to go in an even less pleasant direction. "You see, he sort of…tried to seduce me."

"What?!"

Mary Beth scrambled to get the words out before Lisa had a complete meltdown. "Which is when I told him I'm a lesbian. So you see? It was all very innocent."

Lisa looked away and tried to remind herself that Mary Beth was home and nothing could have happened and those were the only things that really mat— "I can't believe that horny motherfucker tried to seduce you!"

Mary Beth now had two secrets from her girlfriend. The first was the two thousand dollars she'd spent to access the fund-raiser.

The second was that Austin Peebles now had a pet name for her. *Kitten.*

CHAPTER FIFTEEN

Grant Lambert pondered the dozen sheets of paper on the kitchen table in front of him for a while, made a few jots, made a few more, contemplated a while longer, and then squeezed his eyes closed. His head throbbed. Worse than that, it was never all going to come together with the precision he needed for the plan to work. His gang was going to have to simultaneously burgle and/or rob five different locations, several of which had already been robbed and burgled and several others which seemed as secure as Fort Knox.

And what a gang. Some weren't even professional criminals, and one was only a few years above the age where he'd have to get his mommy's permission.

What struck him, though—what made him so pessimistic that he had a hard time concentrating—was that they were missing one key component.

They still didn't have their inside man.

Despite the fact his thus-far unidentified penis fragment was out there on the Internet for the world to see, Austin Peebles wouldn't believe him. Grant knew Wunder was setting up Peebles, but until Peebles came to realize it, there was no hope to bring him on board.

And with just days to go before June Forteene released the entire photo—consisting of an entire penis *and* an entire Austin Peebles head—they didn't have time to integrate anyone into the campaign. If he'd had a month, it'd be tough enough; it was an impossible task to pull off in mere days.

He kept diagramming ways in which there might be a one-in-a-million possibility of doing the job and hoped that Mary Beth could turn on the charm.

❖

In fact, Mary Beth *was* turning on the charm.

Austin had a small, partitioned corner in the rear of the campaign headquarters, affording him some privacy. It was the quiet space where he was supposed to make campaign fund-raising calls, although he more commonly used the seclusion to take pictures of himself making faces and forward them to old college friends from Brown.

The campaign staff respected Austin's corner—few had even been on the other side of the partition—which made it somewhat galling when Mary Beth, a new volunteer on her very first day, was invited in by the candidate. If it had been anyone but Austin, there might have been some hard feelings.

She posed for a few photos with him—they puffed their cheeks; they stuck out their tongues—and waited for him to send them to his friends before getting down to business.

"I need to talk to you about something important."

Austin frowned just a bit. He didn't like "important." "What is it, kitten?"

Mary Beth nodded at a nearby space, identically partitioned. "Is that where your campaign manager sits?"

"Kevin? Yes, but he doesn't usually arrive until late afternoon. Why?"

"Because he's what I need to talk to you about."

That confused him. "Kevin?"

Her expression was grave and she delicately took one of his hands. "He's not your friend, Austin. He's trying to destroy you."

He laughed. "Oh, c'mon. Kevin's my campaign manager!" He waited for her to let him in on the joke, but quickly saw no joke was coming. "Why would you—?"

"He's the person who's been sending the pictures to June Forteene!"

Austin shook his head. "So weird you would say that! Just the other day these two guys came up to me when I was campaigning outside Bloomingdale's and said the exact same thing!"

She squeezed his hand. "I'm with them. We're trying to protect you."

"Wait." He pulled his hand away. "You're working with those thieves?"

She grabbed his hand and held it firmly. "You can't do this alone."

He tried to pull away again but there was no way she was letting go, so he gave up. "But why would Kevin do something like that?"

Mary Beth stared deeply into his eyes. "Because he wants to be in Congress. But first he needs to get rid of you."

"But…"

She tightened her grip. "Listen to me. You're down to two options: Work with us to stop Kevin Wunder, or sit back and watch him destroy you."

"But…"

"No no no no no! There's no 'but.' You already know he hired my friends and then stabbed them in the back. That should tell you something right there about his character."

"Wow." Austin sat back in his chair, a look of confusion on his face. "It just doesn't make sense."

Nodding toward Kevin Wunder's partitioned retreat, she said, "Let's take a look."

Mary Beth walked to Wunder's workspace first, and Austin obediently followed a few seconds later. It didn't take them long to find the smoking gun.

"That's brazen," she said, holding a yellow Post-It bearing the message *Call June*. "It's like he's *trying* to get caught."

He shook his head, lost in thought. "I can't believe it."

"But there it is, all spelled out for you." She embraced him gently and whispered, "But we're here for you, Austin. We'll take care of you."

When he finally looked at her, his eyes were clear and his voice was determined. "What do you need me to do?"

She slipped the Post-It in a pocket—because it wouldn't do any good for anyone to find a yellow Post-It reading *Call June* in Mary Beth's handwriting on top of Kevin Wunder's desk—and put her arms around him again. "I'll fill you in on everything. In the meantime, don't worry. We'll take care of you, Austin."

"Thank you, kitten."

Shortly after Chase arrived home from Groc-O-Rama, the doorbell rang. He looked out the peephole and saw nothing but mass.

"Grant!" he called. "Farraday's here."

The response came from the kitchen. "You sure?"

Chase took another look through the peephole. "That or someone parked a truck in front of our door."

When Farraday was standing in their living room, Grant said, "I thought you were going to Virginia."

"I don't wanna talk about it."

Chase looked at him with sympathy. If Farraday hadn't gone south to Virginia, it meant things had probably gone south with that Jarvis woman. "Okay, we'll respect your privacy. But just so you know"—he placed a hand on the big man's shoulder—"we're here for you if you want to talk."

Farraday scowled and swatted the hand away. "What part of 'I don't wanna talk about it' didn't you understand?"

Chase backed away, ceding the floor to Grant.

"So if you're here, that must mean you're looking for work."

"Why not? I've gotta keep myself occupied." He paused. "You still need a driver for that job?"

"That's the *only* thing I need."

Farraday grunted. "Before I make any commitments, who else is in?"

"Lisa and Mary Beth, but I told you that already." Farraday indicated he wasn't impressed. "Constance Price and Angelina Ortiz."

"Angelina Ortiz? Who the hell is that?"

"Constance's girlfriend."

The driver's mouth pulled downward. "What is this, on-the-job training?"

"Constance vouches for her, and that's good enough for me." Grant hoped it really was and got himself back on track. "Jamie Brock, of course." Farraday made a face. "Nick Donovan."

"Who?"

"Remember Kelly Marinelli?"

"No."

"I'm sure you worked with her." Grant thought it over. "Maybe she was married to someone at the time. Marrying men is sort of a common thing she does."

Farraday snapped his fingers. "Hold on. Do you maybe mean Kelly DuFour?"

Grant nodded. "Yeah, she married that DuFour guy something like three or four times. They were like the Burton and Taylor of small-time crime."

Farraday searched his memory. "I thought I heard she went to law school and was legit now."

"She did. But Nick Donovan's her son, and not so legit."

"Her son?" The Kelly DuFour he used to work with seemed to be too young to have a grown son. "How old is he? Twelve?"

"He's a kid, but old enough to work."

"You ever use him on a job?" Farraday asked, not quite buying it.

This question, at least, Grant could answer honestly. "Yeah, we used him the other day. He did a good job."

"If you say so." Farraday paused. "Anyone else in this gang of yours?"

Grant shrugged. "One more person, but you wouldn't know her."

"Try me."

"Chrissy Alton."

Farraday smiled, which is something both Grant and Chase found unsettling. "Chrissy Alton is *great*!"

"You've heard of her?" asked Chase. "I've worked with her once or twice, but didn't think she was very well known outside Staten Island."

"That's where I met her. I worked out on Staten Island last year, and she was in on some of the jobs." He shook his head with admiration. "That woman's got a light touch and quick hands."

"That she does."

Grant reviewed the roster in his head one last time, hoping he hadn't forgotten anyone. "So that's the gang. And I've already explained the job to you."

Farraday shook his head. "I still don't feel good about it. We're talking about politicians! Those are like superhuman criminals!"

Grant's face was dead serious. "In that case, they've met their match."

"Sure, Lambert." The scowl was back on Farraday's face. "Now that the small talk's done, how about pouring me a drink."

While Grant poured, Chase remembered one name Grant had forgotten. "We also have an insider on the job."

"Yeah?"

"Yeah. Austin Peebles. The candidate himself."

Farraday stared at him. "How'd you manage that?"

"Mary Beth brought him on board."

"Yeah?"

"Yeah. She can be very convincing when she wants to be."

That night, the gang sat in Lisa and Mary Beth's well-appointed apartment in Long Island City and drank coffee—except Farraday, who drank something amber and strong—while they went over details of the following day's game plan. This was the time to ask questions and make sure everything was clear; tomorrow would be too late.

"We start the first job at six thirty in the morning," said Grant, who'd commandeered Lisa's favorite chair. "Farraday, you're gonna get a truck and drive over to June Forteene's office on Eighth Avenue. Nick and Jamie will meet you there."

Jamie scrunched his face. "Six thirty in the morning? Can't you put me on one of the later jobs? I'm not really a morning person."

"Just be there," growled Farraday, shutting Jamie up before turning his attention to Grant. "What kind of truck you want?"

"I don't know. Just a pickup, I guess. We'll need something big enough to hold all the computers and other crap we've gotta collect. But nothing too obvious. I figure something like a moving van would look obvious."

Farraday nodded. "I know what we need, and it's not a pickup. It's a garbage truck."

"A garbage truck?" Over several decades of criminal activity, that was one form of transportation Grant had never considered. Leave it to Farraday...

"We can mash everything we collect." Their wheelman sounded a little too enthusiastic. "Grind it to a pulp."

Grant didn't think that was a bad idea. "Okay, then, grab a garbage truck. Nick's already been to June's office and knows the layout. Plus, he can fit through the transom."

Farraday nodded toward Jamie. "Why him?"

"'Cause I make it for a three-man job. Also it's the place he can do the least amount of damage."

"Hey!"

"No offense." Grant continued, "You guys clean out her office, toss it in the back of Farraday's garbage truck, and drive over to Peebles's campaign headquarters on Lex. Any questions?"

Nick raised his hand. "I can be a supervillain, right?"

"Knock yourself out, kid."

Chase, who'd been leaning against a wall, stood forward. "Just to clarify, he means you should wear your supervillain *attitude*."

"Right," Grant agreed. "Attitude."

Nick ran a hand through his thick, wavy hair and nodded his agreement. If anyone thought he didn't fully grasp what they meant by "attitude," they might have been correct.

"Any other questions?"

"Do I have to—" Jamie started to ask before Grant cut him off and pointed to Mary Beth and Lisa.

"You two are gonna meet Peebles at his campaign headquarters at seven." The women nodded in unison. "You've confirmed he's got the keys?"

"He texted me an hour ago." Mary Beth held up her phone. "He's got the keys and he's psyched."

"Great. By the time Farraday gets there, you should have everything packed up and ready to throw into the truck. Any questions?"

Angelina raised one hand and pointed at Mary Beth with the other. "I've got a question. How come she gets to spend all this time with Austin Peebles? Maybe some of the rest of us would like to…"

Grant brushed her comment off. "We don't have time for this now. If you ladies want to fight over Peebles after the jobs are over, go right ahead." He looked at the list in his hand. "Next up is Chrissy."

"Here!"

"You're gonna meet me and Chase around the corner from June's apartment on Second Avenue near the UN. Be there at seven twenty and bring a big empty handbag."

"Got it."

"We're gonna have to grab her cell and laptop out on the street. It'll be a little tricky, 'cause the General Assembly's going on and there's a lot of cops in the area, but we'll work it out. Worst-case scenario is we make it look like a mugging, hand her stuff off to you, and keep running. If there are cops, they'll chase *us*, not *you*. All you'll have to do is disappear into the crowd."

"Got it," she said. "Disappearing into crowds is my specialty. But I'm not crazy about the thought of you guys playing cop bait."

Grant wasn't crazy about that, either. "Let's hope things run smoothly so it doesn't come to that." He glanced back down at his outline. "After you've got June's stuff, head up to Kevin Wunder's apartment on East Eighty-first Street."

Angelina smiled at Constance. "Here comes our part!"

"Right," said Grant. "And here's an opportunity for some improvisation. Wunder leaves for work on the early side, so we don't want to just steal his stuff, we have to slow him down. You're gonna have to interrupt his routine somehow. Create a diversion or whatever."

Constance nodded. "You want a big show, I'll give you a big show."

"Whatever it takes. You and Angelina get the ball rolling, and Chrissy can help when she gets there."

"Help?" Constance was offended. "I don't need any help. I've been in this business longer than you have, Grant Lambert."

He sighed. He hated it when criminals got their backs up at an inappropriate moment. "That's not what I meant. It won't do us any good if he gets to work while we're robbing the place. We wanna make sure we have a lot of people in his way."

She still wasn't happy—she preferred to work alone—but got it. "I'll make sure he has a lot to clean up after we're done with him. Police reports and all that jazz."

"Good, good." There was only one more item on his list. "And then, no later than eight o'clock, we're all gonna meet outside Congresswoman Concannon's office on the Upper East Side. Wunder's the only one who gets there before eight thirty, but he's gonna be delayed. All we have to do is go up the elevator, pick a few locks, and steal some computers. Farraday will meet us with the garbage truck, we'll throw everything inside, and we should be out of there in fifteen minutes. Maybe less."

"A piece of cake," said Chase.

"As long as no one drops the ball."

Farraday shook his head. "If you can pull off five jobs in an hour and a half, you'll be legendary, Lambert. The delinquents down in Juvie will all know your name."

Grant slumped a bit in Lisa's favorite chair. "Let's worry about the work, not the legends." He looked around the room. "Any last questions?"

No one piped up.

"Are we good on this?"

The gang nodded their assent, keeping any private doubts to themselves.

"Okay, then…" Grant Lambert took one last look around the room. "Get some sleep and be ready to roll out very early tomorrow morning."

Fifteen minutes later, Grant and Chase were the last people to leave Lisa and Mary Beth's apartment. As the elevator descended, Chase smiled.

"I feel really good about this job."

"You do?" Grant frowned. "'Cause I feel terrible. Someone's going to screw this up."

"Stop being such a pessimist. Everyone seems to be on the same page."

"I hope you're right." He stared at the descending numbers on the panel above the door. "I just don't trust people."

It was still on the early side and Jamie Brock saw no reason to rush home. Fortunately, when he found his way back to Manhattan he realized he was only a few blocks away from the Penthouse, one of his favorite East Side gay bars.

But he knew he had to be responsible. He would have two drinks and go home. Just enough to unwind; not enough to disrupt his life.

What could possibly go wrong?

CHAPTER SIXTEEN

Grant Lambert hadn't slept all night. Neither had Chase LaMarca. Some members of their gang had managed an hour or two of slumber, but—with one exception—that was all.

They were getting their game on, keyed up from the exciting anticipation of The Job. They were practicing their skills, memorizing their timing, and making mental contingency plans for that inevitable moment when something threatened to disrupt the script.

There was no alcohol involved, with two exceptions. One was Farraday, which was to be expected. But even Farraday was drunkenly slumbering and dreaming about the job. He was a professional; like the rest of them, he knew how to work in his sleep.

The other was Jamie. But when he stopped at the bar after leaving Lisa's place, he'd been very controlled about shutting himself off after two vodka-sodas.

Unfortunately, that was where his self-control had ended.

Grant looked out the kitchen window into the pre-dawn darkness, then at his watch.

It was finally 5:30.

He turned to Chase, who sat quietly at the table, huddled over a cup of very black coffee.

"It's time."

Chase looked at the clock on the wall. "So it is."

"Let's hope everyone is on the ball, 'cause if they aren't, this day is *not* going to turn out well for us. Pulling five jobs in less than three hours...Ugh."

"It'll be fine," said Chase. But in his head he was saying a silent prayer.

❖

All around New York City, people were getting ready to go to work. Among those millions of people yawning and stretching and brewing and toasting were the members of the Lambert/LaMarca gang.

In Greenpoint, Paul Farraday turned a key in the ignition of a large blue garbage truck and was rewarded with the sound of a low rumble as the engine came to life.

In Harlem, Constance Price and Angelina Ortiz fed the cats before walking outside, taking care to triple-lock the front door before turning in the direction of the subway.

In Long Island City, Lisa Cochrane and Mary Beth Reuss carefully reviewed their assignments for the day before making their way to the elevator.

In St. George, Chrissy Alton fidgeted with an extra-large handbag that currently felt far too light on her shoulder and waited for the approaching Staten Island Ferry to dock.

In Hell's Kitchen, Nick Donovan crept silently through the dark apartment, careful not to wake his mother or catch his cape on the furniture.

On the Upper East Side, Austin Peebles—not technically a member of Grant's gang, but driven to associate membership by circumstances—got out of bed in the bedroom he did not share with Penelope and began the deliberate process of selecting that day's tie. Austin didn't quite *get* ties, so it wasn't an easy process, but the Hermès showed promise.

And in the bedroom of a Financial District penthouse belonging to some guy he'd met the night before whose name he'd promptly and permanently forgotten, Jamie Brock, well…

Jamie had been the one member of the gang who'd managed to sleep soundly that night, mostly because he'd been up far too late getting to know that penthouse bedroom—and living room…and kitchen…and terrace—far too well.

So as New York City—and the gang—prepared to go to work, Jamie continued to dream sweet dreams that had absolutely nothing to do with a series of crimes depending on pinpoint precision timing.

There was inevitably a moment when something threatened to disrupt the script.

This would have been one of them.

❖

At 6:25 a.m., Paul Farraday was in Manhattan, backing the stolen garbage truck into the narrow alley behind the Eighth Avenue building that housed June Forteene's offices. A series of beeps warned pedestrians away as the truck slowly eased between the buildings, backing toward the Dumpsters. A patrol car passed, but Farraday wasn't concerned. He'd stolen a lot of vehicles in his life—cars, tractor-trailers, delivery vans, and of course a plane or three—without breaking a sweat. He was even less concerned about *this* vehicle. He doubted there'd *ever* been an APB issued for a stolen garbage truck.

When the truck was perfectly positioned, he turned off the ignition and waited.

A few minutes later, Nick's head popped up at the window.

"Are we ready?"

Farraday gazed out the grimy windshield. "Almost. As soon as Jamie gets here we'll get moving." He glanced at the clock in the dashboard. "And he'd better get here pretty damn soon, 'cause we got a full day ahead of…"

That was when Farraday took another look out the window at Nick. He'd missed it a few seconds earlier in the dim light of dawn, made dimmer because he was parked in an alley, but now his jaw dropped.

Nick's eyes narrowed. "Is something wrong?"

"What…? What…?" He swallowed and his voice came back. "What the *hell* are you wearing?"

Farraday had worked with a lot of oddballs before, but not this odd. Not on the surface, at least. The kid stood in the alley wearing something that looked like dark blue tights and black boots…and if that wasn't unconventional enough, he also sported a blood-red cape and a black mask over his eyes.

"Like it?" Nick made a little twirl in the alley, quite pleased with himself. "It's my supervillain costume!"

"Your…?" Farraday wondered for a brief moment if maybe he hadn't woken up yet. Then he decided he *was* awake, which made it worse. "Kid, what the hell are you thinking? Didn't anyone tell you you're supposed to be discreet when you pull a job?"

"But I told Grant that I'd go into full supervillain mode for this job!"

"I'm pretty sure he thought you meant attitude. Not costume."

Farraday shook his head. "You've gotta go home and change your clothes. You look like…Oh, hell, I can't even put it into words! You look ridiculous! Worse than that, you're gonna get yourself arrested." He thought about that. "And even worse than *that*, you're gonna get *me* arrested!"

Nick puffed out his lower lip. "Mr. Farraday, I wish you wouldn't worry about things like that. You're in the presence of…The Conundrum!"

Farraday, stunned into a stupor, could only mutter, "Holy shit, what a fuckin' disaster."

"Anyway, I can't go home to change clothes. My mom will be up by now, and if she figures out I'm working with you guys, she won't let me go on the job."

"A real fuckin' disaster," he muttered again, and he slumped behind the wheel of the garbage truck that was almost the color of The Conundrum's dark blue tights.

Constance Price, dressed very conservatively and holding a clipboard, looked over the list of names next to the door buzzer. First, she found Kevin Wunder's name; next, she found the building superintendent's name. That was the buzzer she finally pushed.

"What?" was the gruff reply several minutes—and pushes on the buzzer—later.

"Mr. Robles?"

The gruff voice wasn't happy. "What?"

Her own voice mimicked every bureaucrat who'd ever worked for every government agency. Ever. "This is Constance Brown from the New York City Department of Health. If I have reached Mr. Robles, I need to speak to you right away about this building."

There was silence from the intercom, and Constance was afraid Robles had seen through her ruse until the voice returned. "Lady, you got any idea what time it is?"

"I do indeed, Mr. Robles. It's six forty-five in the morning for *me*, too. But you have a very serious building condition, and I *must* speak to you. *Right away*."

She heard him sigh through the intercom. "Give me a few minutes to put some clothes on."

"Take your time, Mr. Robles." Then, to keep it real, she added, "I'll give you five minutes."

❖

Farraday flipped open his phone and punched in Chase's number. He would have called Grant, but knew that even on a day when a series of jobs depended on heightened coordination, Grant wasn't the man you wanted to try to get on the phone.

Chase answered on the first ring. "What's up, Farraday?"

"We've got a few big problems. Brock ain't here, and Donovan is…" He glanced out the window and saw Nick delivering karate kicks to imaginary foes, no doubt fracturing their imaginary eye sockets and saving the world. "I can't even begin to describe it. Let's just say we got a few big problems."

Chase dialed, and Jamie's cell phone began buzzing.

Unfortunately, Jamie's cell phone was buzzing inside Jamie's pants pocket, which was in the living room of that Financial District apartment belonging to the guy whose name Jamie had forgotten, which was one room and a long hallway away from the bedroom where Jamie still slept soundly, dreaming contentedly of warm breezes and soft sand and a marriage proposal from David Geffen.

In other words, it was a moment that passed the "threatened to disrupt the script" stage.

At 6:50, Mary Beth and Lisa met Austin Peebles at the front door of PEEBLES FOR THE PEOPLE headquarters on Lexington Avenue. His hair had been carefully arranged to make it look as if he'd just crawled out of bed. If he hadn't spent forty minutes on it and had come straight from bed, it would have looked exactly the same.

They grunted barely awake hellos at each other as he unlocked the front door and went inside.

"Nice tie," said Lisa through a yawn, although her limited knowledge of men's accessories wouldn't allow her to put a price tag on it.

He smiled; only Mary Beth smiled back. "Thanks. Hermès."

That—even more than Austin Peebles's smile that dimpled his cheeks—drew Mary Beth's attention. She, too, couldn't put a price tag on men's accessories. But she *could* put a price tag on Hermès.

"We should grab the tie when we grab the rest of the stuff," she whispered to Lisa, who responded with a nod.

Austin stood near the front window of the darkened headquarters, looking out over rows of tables covered with posters, phones, computers, and voter enrollment printouts. It made him nostalgic for a simpler past, one which he suspected was now gone forever, and all because he had allowed himself to follow the Peebles and Concannon call to public service. But he managed to shake off the nostalgia for the good old days, when he could get away with whatever he wanted, and got down to business.

The women also scanned the room. Bare linoleum floor, maps and posters tacked to the wall, folding tables, telephones, and at least a dozen computers. It was designed for temporary functionality, not style. This wasn't the sort of place anyone would come to relax.

"The campaign staff doesn't start coming in until around eight thirty, unless I have an event. Do you think we'll be done by then?"

"The truck is supposed to be here at seven forty-five," said Lisa. "That should give us plenty of time, right?"

"Right. There's not that much we'll have to take out of here." Austin glanced with affection at a folding table, upon which he'd come a little too close to bedding a campaign volunteer until she'd panicked that her fiancé might find out. And also that anyone passing by on Lexington Avenue would be able to see them in the act, even though Austin thought of that as a bonus. "I assume you just want all the electronic equipment, right?"

Lisa nodded. "All the computers and whatever else is in Wunder's desk. Just in case he's hiding something in there."

"Anything else?" He hoped she wouldn't want the table; it had sentimental value.

Mary Beth eyed a poster hanging one wall next to a map of the Upper East Side marked up by volunteers to show where they'd dropped brochures. It prominently featured the Official Campaign Photo—a slightly more mature-looking, still ridiculously young Austin Peebles—against the backdrop of an American flag. "Can I have one of those, too?"

"Sure, kitten." He smiled and dimpled again.

"Absolutely not," said Lisa, who neither smiled nor dimpled.

Austin finally turned on the lights, and the room began to glow with a sickly fluorescence. He walked toward the far end of the office, motioning to them.

"Follow me," he said over his shoulder. "I'll show you where Kevin has his desk."

Chase pocketed his phone. "He's not answering."

That didn't help Grant's increasingly gloomy mood. "What do you mean he's not answering?"

"What I said. I called four times, and he didn't answer." He looked absently out over the traffic gridlocked on Second Avenue from the sidewalk across the street from June Forteene's building. "Maybe he's stuck in a tunnel."

"I got a tunnel for him," Grant muttered.

Chase frowned. "I'm not quite sure what you meant by that, but I wish you'd reconsider the metaphor."

Grant wasn't listening. "Don't make excuses for him."

"I'm not making...Okay, I can tell you're in a bad mood, so I'm gonna back off."

"I'm not in a bad mood."

Chase tossed out a mocking laugh. "You are in *such* a bad mood!"

Grant was about to angrily tell Chase that he was not only *not* in a bad mood, he'd punch him in the neck if he claimed he was in a bad mood one more time. But then he saw something out of his peripheral vision that stopped him.

"It's her." He said it just loud enough for Chase to hear over the traffic. They ducked behind a parked car.

Chase looked at his watch. "It's not even seven! She can't be leaving her apartment already! We're not ready!"

"So much for our timing. As usual." Grant crouched and watched her walk past on the other side of the street, blissfully unaware she was being observed and discussed just fifty feet away. "You'd better tell Farraday to abort the job at her office. Too risky now, and we're getting behind schedule."

"I think they have time to pull it off."

Grant shook his head. "Not with two people. Unless Jamie gets there in the next few minutes. She could get there while Farraday and Donovan are in the middle of robbing her, and I can't see how that helps anything."

"Well, then how will we—"

"I don't know." Grant eyed June as she approached the corner.

Chase took the phone from his pocket and started to dial while Grant rose a bit from his crouch to get a better view of June from behind the parked car. And then he said, "Wait a minute."

With one digit left to dial, Chase let his finger hover. "What?"

"She went into Starbucks."

"Which one?" There were three in view. Grant pointed. "So…do I tell Farraday and Nick to abort?"

"I'm not sure." Grant strained to see through the glass window of Starbucks before giving up. "I need to get a better look."

"Bedbugs?"

"Bedbugs," Constance said again.

Robles wasn't buying it. "Lady, I *live* here! I'd know if this building had bedbugs."

Constance adopted a very officious tone, even more officious than the tone she'd already been using. "Mr. Robles, I understand your concern about alarming your tenants, but I can assure you the Department of Health has received a number of complaints, and I assume those have come from the people who live here, so your tenants are *already* alarmed."

The superintendent folded his arms across his chest. "I'm gonna need to see some identification, Miss…?"

"Brown." She pulled a wallet out of her purse, opened it, and handed him a laminated card identifying her as a special inspector for the New York City Department of Health. Whether or not that was a real job title at the agency was beside the point, as was the fact that, had Robles examined her other forms of identification, he could have found similar cards claiming she was an official with the New York City Department of Finance, the New York City Department of Parks and Recreation, the New York State Department of Agriculture, Weight Watchers, and the Church of Scientology.

"I still don't believe this," he said, handing the card back.

She nodded at the white van she'd double-parked outside before pushing the buzzer. A van she'd borrowed from a street corner in Morningside Heights less than an hour earlier after scouting it out the night before.

Constance stared down Robles. "There's one sure way to find out if those complaints are legitimate. The department's special bedbug inspector is inside that van."

Robles looked at the white van and a middle-aged Latina with close-cropped gray hair waved back at him.

Grant crossed the street alone and approached the coffeehouse, taking pains to stay behind other pedestrians. It would be a very bad thing if June Forteene spotted him. When he reached the front window, he stood at a far edge and scanned the crowd until he spotted her waiting to order, and kept an eye on her until she claimed an empty table and opened her laptop. It looked like she was going to make herself at home for a while.

He hustled back across the street and explained the situation to Chase.

"Call Farraday. I think they have some time, but the two of them are gonna have to try to pull it off without Jamie. Tell him to listen for his phone, though, in case June surprises me and doesn't stay long."

Chase began punching in the digits.

Ninety minutes earlier, in an immaculate penthouse apartment on Water Street in Manhattan's Financial District, the darkness had been interrupted by a loud *Bzzzzzzzzzzzzzzzzzzzzzzt!*

An arm emerged from under the comforter and felt blindly for the clock on the nightstand. Finally, the hand attached to that arm found a button and the alarm stopped.

And Jamie Brock returned to a particularly vivid dream in which he'd convinced a wealthy and famous and dying retired actor to not only add him to his will, but also make him executor.

Then there was the Steve Jobs dream...the Olivia de Havilland dream...the Barry Diller dream...even the Wally Cox dream, although that was a recurring dream so it really didn't count.

The dreams still felt real—and highly profitable—when Jamie awoke. He stretched in bed and glanced at bright sunshine pouring through the window, and almost fell asleep again before his brain sparked and he realized bright sunlight shouldn't be streaming through the window at 5:30 in the morning.

He was afraid to look at the clock.

And then there was the man suddenly stirring next to him in the bed, murmuring, "Good morning."

Jamie racked his brain, but—like the night before—still couldn't remember his name. He remembered he was a stockbroker, and he remembered that the rent on this apartment was $4,212 a month, but the name? That was gone.

So Jamie did what Jamie always did at moments like this.

"Good morning, *baby*." He rolled over, planted the briefest of kisses on the man's forehead. "How'd you sleep, *baby*?"

"Oh, wow," said the man, blinking his swollen eyes. "Look at the time! I'm already late for work."

Jamie squeezed his eyes shut. "I hope you're about to tell me that it's five o'clock."

He laughed. "Try seven ten...uh...*baby*."

Jamie bolted upright in bed. Neither "seven ten" nor "baby" were what he'd hoped to hear. One was an insult—how *dare* whatsisname forget Jamie's name?!—but the other meant he had *really* screwed up.

Angelina Ortiz, clad in white coveralls that could almost pass for a hazmat suit if you weren't paying close enough attention or weren't aware that hazmat suits and painting coveralls were extremely different things, walked out on the front stoop gingerly holding a tiny plastic bag in one hand. She presented it to Robles, who inspected the tiny insect inside.

"Is that a bedbug?"

Angelina nodded her head, with the grimmest expression—one usually reserved for coroners and oncologists—fixed on her face. "It's not just a bedbug, Mr. Robles. This is an Argentine Leaping Bedbug."

"Huh?"

"In the Department of Health, we call these the Bedbugs of Bedbugs. This is the *worst* kind of bedbug to have. They reproduce daily. In extreme cases, some cities in Argentina have had to burn down entire blocks to eradicate the pests."

"Whoo boy!" Constance fanned herself. "I sure hope the city doesn't have to burn down East Eighty-first Street because of this. *That* won't make the mayor look good."

Robles studied the bug. "Argentine—"

"Leaping Bedbug." Angelina looked at the plastic baggie with disgust bordering on hatred. "They call them that because they don't only crawl like normal bedbugs. They can also *leap*!"

Her almost-shouted "leap" made both Constance and Robles leap themselves.

Robles steadied himself against the building. "They leap?"

Angelina nodded. "Some have been known to leap more than ten feet. That's why the department considers containing this problem to be a priority."

Robles finally looked away from the bug in the plastic bag, still not realizing he was looking at a very small raisin. "Then how come I never heard of 'em?"

Angelina rolled her eyes just enough to indicate she wasn't rolling them at Robles, but at the government. "The bureaucrats downtown want to keep this hush-hush. The city doesn't want everyone to panic."

That didn't sound right to Robles. But he'd never dealt with Argentine Leaping Bedbugs before, so maybe…

"And I've got worse news for you," Angelina confided, leaning closer. "This poor bug…before she died, she gave birth. Which means on top of whatever problem you already have, you've now got a litter of at least twelve newborn Argentine Leaping Bedbugs burrowing through your house."

Constance stepped forward, assuming full authority. "I've heard enough. Mr. Robles, I need you to evacuate this building right now."

"But…"

"That's an order." When he wavered, she added, "If you don't do it, *I'll* do it. On order of the New York City Department of Health!"

Robles scrambled inside, leaving the women on the stoop. When he closed the door behind him, Constance leaned close to Angelina's ear.

"You are *so good*! I never knew you had this much talent!"

Angelina beamed with pride.

When the elevator doors opened, Nick nodded at the office door and told Farraday, "This is the place."

Farraday growled. "You know, I'm supposed to be the driver. I don't do breaking and entering."

"C'mon, Farraday!" Nick was almost giddy with nervous energy. "Your part is easy. All you have to do is stand here while I do the hard stuff. I'm the one who has to go through that transom window and steal everything. You just have to collect it when I hand it to you."

"Sounds like a job better suited for Jamie Brock."

"Yeah, well…He's not here. We *are*."

Farraday eyed the narrow transom window warily. "You sure you can even fit through there?"

Nick scoffed. "If Chase made it through, I can make it through." Then he looked at what he was wearing and thought things through a bit more. "Although this costume might not be practical."

He began the process of stripping to his underwear.

Farraday averted his eyes. "I'm not gettin' paid enough to see this."

June Forteene was in Starbucks, Chrissy Alton had not yet arrived, and Grant and Chase were getting nervous.

"June's been sitting there for twenty minutes," Grant muttered. "If Chrissy doesn't get here soon, we're gonna have to grab the laptop and cell ourselves. Since she's already seen both of us, I really don't like that idea, but I don't think we have a choice." He put a hand on Chase's shoulder. "If something has to be done, you're the man to do it."

"Me?" Chase didn't like the idea very much. "Why me?"

"You're a decent pickpocket, and I figure running in there and stealing her laptop and phone are just a variation on that theme."

"I think I disagree."

"Plus, you can run a lot faster than me."

Chase still didn't like it, but he couldn't argue with that. "Okay, let me size things up."

He made several subtle passes in front of the coffeehouse, once even sticking his head inside the door to take a look around, but couldn't figure out how he was going to be able to waltz up to June Forteene and steal her stuff. It would have made things easier if June wasn't typing on her laptop and taking phone calls every time he stole a peek, but not *much* easier.

"Just bolt in there, grab the stuff, and run," was Grant's advice when Chase relayed his concerns.

Chase looked at the ground, hoping to maybe divine a plan through gum-stain patterns or something. "That'll work for maybe forty seconds." He looked up and into his partner's watery hazel eyes. "You'll come visit me at Rikers, I assume?"

"I'll think about it."

Chase steeled his nerves. He wasn't happy, but he was finally committed.

"Okay, if that's the way it's gotta be…"

He would have done it, too, but then there was salvation.

It came in the form of a five-foot-two blond woman who parted the crowd as she pushed her way down the sidewalk in red-soled Louboutin heels, an oversized handbag bouncing limply against one hip.

"Ready?" asked Chrissy Alton when she approached them.

"You're late," said Grant.

Chrissy put a hand on one defiantly cocked hip. "I come all the way from Staten Island, and it's not *my* fault the trains are screwed up this morning. And anyway…" She glanced at her watch, which not too many days earlier had been part of a display at Harry Winston. "Why am I apologizing? You told me to be here at seven twenty, and it's seven eighteen. I'm not even late!" She would have hit him with the bag, but—empty—it wouldn't have the desired impact.

Grant mumbled something like, "You coulda been," but kept it mostly to himself.

Chase pretended nothing was wrong. Nothing really *was* wrong, but that attitude made things easier when dealing with temperamental people. "Ready for the score?"

"I'm ready," she said.

He thought to add, "And I assume you see cops all over the place?"

She eyed the massive police presence. "Good. I love a challenge."

Grant checked the time. "You think you can wrap this up quickly— very quickly—and get uptown to help Constance and Angelina take care of Wunder?"

She looked disappointed in him. "This shouldn't take any time at all." Looking across the street at the plate glass window, she asked, "The woman with the dark hair? The one on her laptop?"

"Uh…" Chase looked in the direction of the window, but his eyes weren't as sharp as hers. "That probably describes half the customers."

Chrissy laughed at that, even though Chase was only telling the truth. "The one in the blue top?"

That much he'd seen from behind the parked car. "That's her."

"Let me go inside and size it up." She took a step toward Starbucks but paused. "If it looks like anything's going wrong, get the hell out of here." She took another step but paused again. "Not that anything *will* go wrong, of course. But if something does, I don't want you guys slowing me down."

Chase was impressed by her cool. "How are you gonna pull it off?"

Chrissy shrugged and played with the strap hanging limply over her shoulder. "Every job is all about improvisation, Chase. Don't worry about it. Leave the tough stuff—and the thinking—to me."

With that—Chrissy Alton's very own Daily Affirmation—she was through the front door.

June Forteene hated sitting in Starbucks so early in the morning, but there was no point in sitting around the apartment. She hadn't been sleeping well since the burglaries, and those apartment walls seemed to close in on her over the long, sleepless nights.

Inside the coffeehouse twenty-three minutes earlier, she had typed, *Daily Affirmation: I killed Hillary Morris and she's never coming back.* Then she wrote a rant about something or other for the next nineteen minutes between sips from her far-too-strong cup of coffee. As June Forteene rants went, it was a four on a scale of one to ten, but she reread it and was pleased. She was just coming off a major humiliation; now was the time to ease back into the pool of controversy, rather than plunge.

She read over her words one more time...

Her stomach fluttered. Right there on the screen—at the very *top* of the screen—was spelled out *Daily Affirmation: I killed Hillary Morris and she's never coming back.*

She deleted the line and castigated herself for being slow to learn a lesson. She'd already become a mockery for something like this; it was careless and foolish for her to not delete it earlier.

But now it was deleted, and no damage had been done. Close call, but no harm.

June Forteene switched to a new tab and her blog appeared on the screen. She scrolled until Austin Peebles's partial penis was in view.

It was *his* fault she'd been distracted lately. It was *his* fault her world was falling apart. That bastard—who, if elected, would represent her in Congress—had to go down!

She took a sip from her cup. It was almost empty, and what was left was cold. But the clock at the corner of the screen told her she had plenty of time for another.

It wasn't as if the office on Eighth Avenue held any more appeal this morning than Starbucks.

"Here goes," said Nick Donovan. With that, he started to make his way through the transom window.

Holding The Conundrum's costume in his arms, Farraday watched Nick's slim upper body slide through the opening out of the one corner of the one eye that wasn't queasy about looking at mostly naked men and thought, *I've been on some bizarre jobs before, but* this *one...*

The Superman underpants were just icing on the cake.

That thought stopped when Nick stopped wriggling through the window.

"Hey, Farraday! Little help?"

Farraday glanced up at two hairy legs kicking helplessly eight feet above the floor. It looked like the kid was trying to swim in air.

"What's the problem?"

"I think I'm caught on something."

The driver looked up. From his vantage point, it was hard to see anything but kicking legs. "So whaddya want *me* to do about it?"

"Help me get unstuck?" When Farraday didn't immediately answer, Nick added, "My underwear's snagged on something. Maybe on the frame." Nick sort of giggled; the blood rushing to his head as he hung upside down on the other side of the transom wasn't doing him any favors. "Shit, now I know what Chase went through. If you could just climb up here and get my underwear unsnagged, that'd be a help."

"You mean—"

"Yeah, just unhook me."

Farraday didn't quite know how to respond to that request. "Uh... Lambert told you I'm not like the rest of you, right?"

"What do you mean?"

He was going to tell him that, as a confirmed heterosexual, he was uncomfortable climbing up to the transom window and playing around with Nick Donovan's Superman underwear, but in the end he didn't have to give him an answer.

Because there was a sudden ripping noise, followed by a thud, followed by Nick saying, "Ow."

A woman's shriek filled the air. Not only inside Starbucks, but also out onto the sidewalk and beyond; far enough that a few cops looked in the direction of the scream, even though that was the extent of what they did about it.

The second shriek that followed seemed to almost form a word.

And that word was *"Pornography!!"*

Grant and Chase stood at the curb across the street and watched chaos unfold through the plate glass window. It was impossible to tell exactly what was going on, and they both thought that was for the best.

Less than a half minute passed before Chrissy Alton emerged from the front door. Without so much as a glance in their direction, she walked briskly in the direction of Grand Central Terminal. The oversized bag she carried now seemed a lot heavier than it had been when she walked into Starbucks.

"You follow Chrissy." Grant's eyes shifted up and down the sidewalk. "I'll keep an eye on this situation. If June gets the cops after you, I'll call."

"Gotcha." Chase was a few steps away before he stopped and turned back. "Did you say you'd *call*?"

Grant fumed. "I am *not* a phone-aphobe!"

As nonchalantly as possible, he walked across the street and positioned himself at the edge of the Starbucks window, watching cautiously as things began to settle down on the other side of the glass. June Forteene was nowhere to be seen for a while—she wasn't at the table where she'd been sitting, and he couldn't spot her in the crowd of customers—but he soon caught a glimpse as she made her way through the crowd, pushing her way back to where she'd camped out before the screaming started.

But now June seemed confused.

She looked at her table. Then she looked at the neighboring tables. And finally she spun around, making made a wide, careful scan of the interior.

Grant stepped away from the window, figuring she was just beginning to realize her stuff had left without her. He was right, because a few seconds later she burst out the front door and ran directly to one of New York's Finest as he halfheartedly tried to move the hopelessly gridlocked traffic.

If the morning had already had its share of disasters, Grant thought, at least this part went off without a hitch.

Wisely, he crossed back to the other side of the street.

Chase returned a few minutes later, passing June and a couple of cops as they discussed the situation outside Starbucks before crossing Forty-second Street to where Grant stood.

"Let's take a walk," Grant said, and they casually moved around the corner onto Second Avenue. When he was sure no one had paid attention to their inordinate interest in June Forteene, he asked, "Did you catch Chrissy?"

Chase nodded. "She's gonna hold the laptop and phone until we're ready to dispose of them."

"She did good." Always interested in improving his skills, Grant asked, "She tell you how she pulled it off?"

His partner laughed. "Chrissy saw that June was working on her blog, meaning the penis picture was on display..."

"Ah. Now I get all that yelling about pornography."

"Right. She screams. She points it out to some of the mothers and old people that were there. And then..." Chase smiled. "Well, we saw the results. The manager asks to have a word with June, Chrissy grabs the computer and phone when June's talking to the manager and her back is turned, and the job is over in less than a minute."

"A real pro." Grant approved of Chrissy's performance so much he started to believe he—not Chase—was the one who'd brought her in on the job. "I only wish the rest of these misfits we call a gang could get their acts together. We're trying to pull five jobs in one morning, and as far as I know only one has been completed."

"Three. Well, two and a half." Chase held up two fingers and bent a third at the knuckle. "While I was with Chrissy, Constance texted to let us know that the job at Wunder's apartment building is coming together perfectly. And Lisa said they're ready at the Peebles campaign headquarters whenever Farraday gets there with the garbage truck."

"That's a big *if*." He blinked a few times. "And why's everyone contacting *you*? What about *me*?"

"Because of your phone thing."

"I don't have a—" Grant decided to drop it in mid-sentence and changed the subject. "Have you heard from Farraday?"

"Not yet."

"Until I know him and Nick got into June's office—*and* got back out—I'm not considering that job or the Peebles headquarters job to be even close to done."

Chase sighed. "You're never gonna see the glass as half-full, are you?"

"A few decades in this business has provided me with a lot of shattered glasses." He patted Chase on the shoulder. "Okay, let's get ready for the big job."

"Sure you're ready?"

Grant took a deep breath of exhaust. "Ready as ever, lover."

Most of the residents of the building on East Eighty-first Street were standing on the sidewalk as Constance Price paraded in front of them, trailed by Angelina Ortiz in her not-all-that-convincing—but convincing-enough-for-the-moment—hazmat suit.

"Settle down, people! Settle down!" The residents were confused and annoyed, but not angry, so there was little settling to be done.

Constance stood on the second step of the stoop and continued. "As Mr. Robles has informed you, the Department of Health has issued an EFO for your building."

"What's this EFO thing?" asked a middle-aged man who'd been evacuated in a sweatsuit. His face still bore patches of un-toweled shaving cream.

"Emergency Fumigation Order." The tenants grumbled, but she waved them down. "You will be allowed to return when our inspection is complete."

"Why?" A woman holding a baby, who'd escaped from her apartment wearing only a robe, was on the verge of tears. Constance figured it was a postpartum thing and wanted to be sympathetic, but work was work.

"I'm sorry, miss, but agency rules prohibit me from revealing that. Trust me that this is in your best interest." And then she thought to add, "The best interest of your baby, too."

A young man in a T-shirt and bike shorts piped up. "Robles said something about Argentine Leaping Bedbugs?"

Constance offered him a smile she hoped conveyed "bureaucratic reassurance" and "ecological disaster" at the same time, and bit her lip to give weight to the serious nature of the problem. "There's no need to panic."

The young mother squirmed and scratched at an imaginary itch. "Bedbugs that leap?"

As the perceived authority—the white coveralls helped with that perception—Angelina stepped forward. That surprised Constance—she wasn't in the business and was only supposed to be a prop—but when Angelina nodded a "May I?" Constance nodded a "Go for it" back to her.

And Angelina did, finding an authoritative voice and using it. "Everything will be fine, folks! Please listen to Dr. Brown and don't panic! These infestations are seldom fatal!"

The tenants collectively stepped to the other side of the curb.

"According to Dr. Brown, less than five percent of Argentine Leaping Bedbug infestations result in fatalities."

The tenants collectively stepped to the middle of East Eighty-first Street. A few passing cars had to slow and weave their way through.

Constance whispered in Angelina's ear. "Doctor?"

"I thought it gave you more authority."

"Okay, then. Let's run with it." Constance looked back to the crowd huddled in the middle of the street. "Is there a Mr. Kevin Wunder here?"

Robles, standing slightly away from the tenants in his own private no-man's-zone between the agitated residents and his responsibility to the building, spoke. "He hasn't come out of his apartment yet. I told him, but he said he'd leave when he's good and ready."

"If he isn't out in five minutes, I'll have to call the police so they can force him out."

"Force out Kevin?" asked the young mother. "Why?"

Constance's face grew deadly serious. "His apartment is ground zero of the Argentine Leaping Bedbug infestation."

The young mother blanched and began scratching. "Oh my God! I live next door to him!"

Chapter Seventeen

June Forteene hadn't had much of a chance to re-equip her office after the first break-in, which meant that Farraday and Nick had to swipe only a few laptops and someone's cell phone that had been left behind. It was a nice easy job and, Nick now realized after two appearances at the same location, an easy one for two people. Even if he was now darting around that office wearing nothing but a mask, his ripped Superman underwear still hanging where it had snagged on the transom frame. He'd miss that pair—it was his fourth favorite—but supposed he'd be able to buy a lot of new underwear when he got the payoff from this job. Maybe even the entire special-edition X-Men collection!

Out in the hallway, Farraday kept watch over the laptops that had been passed through the transom and dreaded the coming minutes between when Nick made his return passage and when he'd be back in his costume. The blue and red outfit was one of the more ridiculous things he'd ever seen, but at that moment he knew he'd rather see Nick *in* it than *out of* it.

The Naked Conundrum's masked face appeared in the transom window next to the dangling briefs. "We're done here."

"Does that mean what I think it means?" Farraday grumbled.

"Yeah. I might need a hand coming down."

Farraday turned his back on him. "Sorry, kid. You're on your own."

Nick heaved a dramatic sigh. "You seriously won't help me out? Just because you're afraid you'll see my penis?"

"That about sums it up."

"But…"

Farraday turned his back.

❖

By the time Kevin Wunder finally exited his East Eighty-first Street apartment building, the crowd standing in the pavement thought of him as no less than Public Enemy Number One. He was no longer the respectable congressional aide who'd lived quietly in the second-floor, one-bedroom apartment for the past eight years. He was now the man who harbored Argentine Leaping Bedbugs in their building and had exposed them to an Emergency Fumigation Order, or EFO as the tenants now familiarly called it, because they were quick to pick up on Government-Speak.

When she heard the booing start, Constance knew she'd found her man.

"You Wunder?" she asked.

He stood at the top of the stoop, perplexed at the jeers. "Uh…yes." His eyes shifted toward her, and then toward the gray-haired Puerto Rican woman wearing what appeared to be coveralls. "I'm Kevin Wunder. What's the meaning of this?"

Constance flicked her wallet. "Dr. Constance Brown, Department of Health."

He stopped her before she returned the wallet to her purse. "May I?"

"Knock yourself out."

He looked at her ID, found nothing objectionable, and handed it back. "What can I do for you, Ms. Brown?"

"*Dr.* Brown." She affected indignation. "Why didn't you leave when Mr. Robles asked you to vacate?"

"I was getting ready for work." Wunder looked at more than a dozen tenants of his building who now blocked traffic, some of whom booed when he caught their eyes. "What's this all about? Robles said something about bedbugs?"

"Not just *ordinary* bedbugs." Constance's expression told him that ordinary bedbugs were trivial compared to what she had discovered. "Mr. Wunder, this building is about to be condemned. We've found an infestation of Argentine Leaping Bedbugs, and ground zero seems to be your apartment!"

First he was befuddled; then he was enraged.

"Listen, lady…"

"*Doctor.*"

"Doctor! Listen, there are no bedbugs in my apartment!" With that, he began descending the stairs to the sidewalk.

"Stop right there, Mr. Wunder! By order of the *New York City Department of Health*!"

He had been determined to keep going—to walk straight through that crowd of jeering neighbors and go to work—but the authority in her voice brought him to a halt. Because even though this all sounded like bullshit, her *voice* sounded like the real deal.

That didn't mean he had to be happy about it.

Wunder huffed. "What is it now?"

Constance approached from one side, Angelina from the other.

"Are you carrying any electronic equipment on you, sir?" Constance asked.

He glanced at the laptop bag hanging from his shoulder. "Well, yes, but…Wait, what business is that of yours?"

Angelina, eager to prove to Constance just how much a natural she was, stepped forward. "Argentine Leaping Bedbugs are particularly attracted to electronic devices. Computers, cell phones…things like that. Ordinary bedbugs like fabric and wood, but ALBs…"

"ALBs?"

She rolled her eyes. "Argentine Leaping Bedbugs."

It was his turn to roll his eyes. "I think you're making this up."

She ignored him. "ALBs like electronics. That's where we find ninety-two percent of them hiding. If you're carrying a laptop, you could be unknowingly transporting these bugs."

"None of this makes sense." Wunder held his laptop bag close to his hip. "I don't know what you're up to, but…"

Angelina eyed him evenly and raised her voice just enough to carry to the huddled masses standing in the middle of East Eighty-first Street. "Your laptop may be home to dozens—even *hundreds*—of these pests. If you get on a subway, you could end up spreading them throughout the city. We'll have an epidemic on our hands!"

Wunder had tried to be patient, but his patience was gone. "Get out of my way." He swatted at Constance and Angelina as he passed.

He made it several yards down the sidewalk toward Third Avenue before Constance shouted to the crowd, "Somebody stop him! Get that laptop!"

Kevin Wunder spun around. "What?!"

That's when Robles tackled him.

❖

Farraday stood at the far end of the hall—with his back still turned—as Nick gingerly squeezed his naked body through the narrow transom. He positioned himself so the torn underwear would protect his most sensitive region, and then shifted slightly when the threat passed.

Roughly half his weight was soon outside and Nick gripped a pipe that ran along the ceiling. That had been his mistake going in; he let gravity take control until he was helpless and flailing away without traction. He wouldn't make the same mistake again.

Gripping the pipe, he inched his midsection through the frame and wondered how someone the size of Chase LaMarca—hardly a big man, but nowhere near as small and wiry as Nick, had managed to get through. He supposed fear of being trapped in the office he'd just burgled until the police arrived was a powerful motivation to help cram a 170-pound mass through a hole barely big enough to accommodate 130 pounds.

Nick's buttocks finally squeezed through the transom. He felt the unpleasant scrape of hard metal against tender flesh, but ignored it until he was home free. With one last yank on the pipe, he pulled his legs and feet through the opening...

Those were the circumstances leading up to the moment when Nick Donovan dangled naked from an overhead pipe, wearing only a black mask, and the elevator doors opened.

Edward Hepplewhite stepped into the hall. He had only intended to get into work early; he hadn't intended to step onto the fifth floor and immediately be confronted by a naked masked man. It took a few seconds for the realization that there was, indeed, a naked masked man suspended from a pipe in the fifth floor hallway to kick in, but when it did...

The last thing Edward remembered was the room spinning.

June Forteene stormed out of Starbucks. She was beyond angry.

Neither the manager nor the cops seemed to be especially interested in the fact she'd been violated once again. The cops more or less said they had better things to do, and the guy at Starbucks more or less said it happened all the time, and it was mostly her own fault for leaving her laptop and phone unattended.

Once, in the past, she would have accepted those excuses. But she wasn't that woman anymore.

Hillary Morris was dead. Dead *and* deleted.

"You think he's dead?" Farraday asked as he held an armful of laptops and looked at Edward Hepplewhite sprawled across the floor, and definitely *didn't* look at the naked young man standing next to him. "You coulda given him a heart attack or somethin'."

Nick nudged Edward with his toe and was rewarded with the twitch of a muscle. "Nah. Just passed out."

"In that case, put your damn clothes on before you give *me* a heart attack."

Chrissy Alton walked toward East Eighty-first Street from the Seventy-seventh Street subway station. Her progress was slower than she'd hoped, but that was always a problem when a person was trying to navigate the mean streets of New York City in a pair of Louboutin heels.

And it probably would have been a good idea to have shoplifted the right size in the first place. But she was in a rush that day, so the shoes she grabbed were close, but not quite perfect.

Oh, sure, her husband Karl could and would be a dentist forever, so they'd never want for food or shelter. But his practice was on Staten Island—not in Manhattan—so they'd probably want for everything else. *She* would, that was; Karl was fine with what they had. Chrissy had always wanted more.

Fortunately, she had a talent.

Shoplifting had proven a good way for her to get the finer things in life without busting the family budget. She was good—hadn't been caught yet, which was important because Karl definitely would not approve of her sideline—and after a dozen years in the business she'd not only perfected her skills, but she'd started to meet professional associates like Chase LaMarca, which broadened her career prospects.

Although, she thought as she sat for a moment on a half wall outside a tony apartment building to give her feet some brief relief, *if I'm gonna shoplift to get the things I want, I should probably pay more attention to size.*

❖

Kevin Wunder struggled under the weight of his own building superintendent. "What the hell are you doing, Robles?"

The super—already envisioning the headlines and public acclaim for having helped save New York City from the Great Argentine Leaping Bedbug Epidemic—tried to force the bag out of Wunder's hand. "I'm making sure you don't infest this entire city with those things."

Although most of the other tenants kept their distance—those bedbugs *leapt*, dammit!—Wunder felt other hands on him. Still, Robles was the one he always tipped during the holiday season, and he had been the one who'd tackled him, so he was on the receiving end of his anger.

"You moron, there's no such thing as—" He realized his hand was no longer gripping the bag handle. "Where the hell is my laptop?"

From beneath Robles, Kevin Wunder glanced along the ground. He saw a few random knees and a pair of red-soled shoes walking quickly away, but no trace of his laptop bag.

Red-faced, he hollered, "Call the police!"

"Stand back, everyone!" Angelina demanded. "He's out of control."

The crowd moved to the opposite sidewalk.

Farraday drove the garbage truck out of the alley and onto Eighth Avenue. Without looking at Nick he turned onto a eastbound side street.

"This job is all screwed up." He said it more to himself than Nick, and was surprised when the kid answered.

"It's all coming together, Farraday. Remember: *The Conundrum* is on this job."

"Jesus Christ," Farraday muttered. "Shoulda listened to my instincts and told Lambert to get the hell out of my life."

At that moment, the out-of-breath Jamie Brock barreled out of an elevator and fell over Edward Hepplewhite, who was still on the floor but had regained consciousness.

"Ow!" they both said as Jamie landed on the floor next to Edward.

Jamie looked over at him. "Who the hell are you?"

Edward looked back. "Don't hurt me!"

"Hurt you?" Jamie picked himself up from the floor. "Why would I hurt you?"

Edward shrank back, afraid to stand. "Are you with the other guy?"

Jamie wasn't quite sure how to answer, so he decided to stay vague. "Which other guy?"

"The naked guy who was hanging from the pipe."

Jamie was pretty sure he wasn't with that guy. "No. I think I'm on the wrong floor. Or, uh, something like that." He scrambled to his feet and pressed the elevator's down button before something colorful up near the ceiling caught his eye. "What's that?"

"What's *what*?" Edward followed Jamie's pointed finger. And then he recoiled.

"Is that—" He squinted. "Underwear?"

"Oh my God!" Edward had to look away. "What kind of sick bastard—"

"It's *Superman* underwear!"

Edward almost retched. "I have…to go back…to Pennsylvania…"

Grant sat on the same bench in the Roosevelt Island Tram Park where he'd worked out the plan a few days earlier and, again, he stared at traffic. Chase sat next to him, working his phone. He had been painfully pessimistic, but—bit by bit—most of the jobs were coming together. Yes, they were behind schedule, and that would make things much more difficult, but at least they were making progress.

"Farraday and Nick pulled it off at June's office, although Farraday said something about Nick being naked. Not sure what that's all about."

Grant closed his eyes. "Let's hope he found his clothes."

"The thing is, Farraday said something about his clothes being almost as bad." Chase shrugged it off. "They're on the road now and should be meeting up with Lisa and Mary Beth in about ten minutes."

Grant took a look at his watch. "They'll still finish up before people start arriving at the campaign headquarters, so I guess that job can almost be considered done. How's Constance doing with Wunder?"

"They're about to close up shop. Somehow—don't ask, 'cause I don't know—they got Wunder's own super to take him out. Chrissy got his laptop and she's on her way to meet up with the garbage truck."

"What about his cell?"

"Constance lifted it from his suit coat after the super tackled him. She's gonna dispose of it."

Grant shook his head and allowed himself a tiny smile. "Wish I coulda seen that job play out. Sounds like they put on quite a show."

"Doesn't it?" Chase ticked off the jobs on one hand. "So we got June's cell and phone; Wunder's cell and phone; cleaned out June's office; about to clean out the campaign headquarters…" He paused and looked out at traffic, trying to figure out if he'd forgotten anything. "That's it, right?"

Grant stretched and some parts that weren't his neck cracked. They both noticed. "Everything except the last job. The biggest job of them all."

"Oh yeah." Chase frowned. "Concannon's office."

Grant looked at his watch again. "That's the one. Of course, now that we're running so far behind schedule we're gonna have some big problems with that one. There's no way we're gonna get in and out before her staff arrives for work."

"So…" Chase looked at him. "What should we do?"

"Exactly what I've been sitting here trying to do. Come up with a perfect Plan B." Grant Lambert sighed. "Which is easier said than done."

The dark blue garbage truck lumbered to a stop at the corner of Lexington Avenue and East Fifty-sixth Street outside the temporary PEEBLES FOR THE PEOPLE storefront, and Farraday lumbered out of the driver's seat.

Seconds later, The Conundrum stood at his side, drawing stares from a handful of otherwise jaded early-morning New York pedestrians and causing Farraday no little amount of embarrassment. He tried to ignore the supervillain who shadowed him and pushed the door. Tried to ignore him so much, in fact, that he shoved the door closed in Nick's face as soon as he was over the threshold.

Or maybe that was on purpose.

Lisa looked at them impatiently. "You're late."

"Tell me about it. Jamie Brock never showed, meaning we had to pull the job on June Forteene's office with just the two of us."

"Oh." She might have said more, but that's when she saw The Conundrum in his black mask and blue tights and black boots and blood-red cape and was rendered speechless.

Mary Beth, approaching from the back of the room, did not have the same reaction.

"What the *fuck*?!" She stopped mid-stride and her hands went to her hips. "What the hell is *he* supposed to be?"

None of this fazed Nick Donovan. No one was more comfortable inside his skin—not to mention inside his supervillain drag—than Nick. "I'm The Conundrum."

Lisa finally found her voice. "You certainly are."

Farraday shook his head. "I hope things are coming along here, because I've had a very bad morning."

Lisa couldn't take her eyes off Nick, but managed to answer him. "Yes, we've been a model of efficiency." Her hand pointed at nothing specific toward the rear. "Got the computers stacked and everything that was in Wunder's work area has been boxed up for the trash. We're ready to go."

Hearing a rustling noise, Farraday glanced behind him just long enough to see Nick's cape whip through the air as he again practiced karate kicks. He tried to will himself to ignore it and was almost successful.

"Okay, then let's get it in the truck and get outta here." He looked around. "Ain't Peebles supposed to be here?"

"Little boy's room," said Mary Beth, who—like Lisa—couldn't take her eyes off The Conundrum.

When Austin Peebles emerged from the bathroom at the rear of the office a few minutes later he didn't seem to even notice Nick's supervillain attire. He finished wiping his hands with a paper towel and sized up the garbage truck parked in front of the building.

"That truck's illegally parked."

"When did *you* start to mature?" asked Lisa, not caring if she sounded too sarcastic.

Mary Beth managed to take her eyes off Nick long enough to focus them on Peebles. "That's *our* truck."

"Ours?" Peebles thought about that, then finally got it. "That's how you're carting everything away?"

"That's right," said Farraday.

"And when it's gone?"

"It's gone, Peebles. And it ain't never coming back."

Austin smiled. "That's awesome." He looked to the women for further guidance. "So will you be needing me for anything else?"

"You're free to go," said Lisa, with a tone indicating he could leave *immediately*. "Expect a phone call in forty-five minutes or so when your campaign staff discovers the burglary."

He was growing giddy. "I'm already looking forward to that."

Mary Beth put a hand on his bicep. "Do you have to run off already? There's one more part of the job we'll be pulling." She tucked her head a little closer. "Maybe you'd like to come along."

Austin smiled and touched her hair. "That's tempting, kitten, but I'd better make myself scarce. Especially since the shit's about to hit the fan."

"Exactly," Lisa added icily. "Also, since you're stroking my girlfriend's hair, which could cause the shit to hit the fan a lot sooner than you're expecting."

Mary Beth pouted. "I didn't say I wanted to sleep with him. I just enjoy his company."

Austin fluttered his lashes. "I enjoy your company, too, Mary Beth. Maybe when all of this craziness is over—and before I have to be a congressman and do all that responsible stuff—we can get together and hang out."

An involuntary shudder ran down her back. "That'd be fun."

Lisa's gravel-voiced grumble interrupted them. "Oh, for crying out loud…"

Farraday and Nick loaded the back of the garbage truck with computers and the box of everything that had belonged to Kevin Wunder. Austin took a long look around the campaign headquarters. He felt relief; it seemed as if this nightmare was finally coming to an end.

Chrissy Alton arrived with Wunder's laptop bag and June's laptop and phone, all of which promptly went into the back of the truck. And with those final items, everything they intended to steal to that point had been stolen. If they didn't know there was one more job ahead of them, it would have been time for a celebration.

But there *was* that last bit of business that still needed to be addressed. It was going to be a tough job, but they were feeling confident.

Inside the now-emptier campaign headquarters, the gang—and Austin, their official mascot—turned at the sound of a loud groan from the street outside. It was the truck's compacter. Farraday stood on the curb smiling at the grinding noise a dozen computers made as they were pulverized.

Austin smiled, too. Or at least he did until he realized that The Conundrum had his eyes locked on him.

"Uh…can I help you?"

"Oh, sorry. I didn't mean to stare. It's just that you look younger in person than in your cock shot."

Most men would have been repelled by that statement, but Austin Peebles was not most men. He knew how to accept a compliment.

"Thank you." It finally occurred to him to ask about the costume. "So what's the deal with the getup?"

"It's my supervillain look. I call myself The Conundrum." Nick realized that sounded silly and figured he'd better explain. "Just so you don't get the wrong impression, I don't walk around the city dressed as The Conundrum all the time."

"Of course you don't…"

"I have a bunch of *other* costumes at home, too."

"Oh." Austin thought about that. "So…do you always wear a costume?"

That thought made Nick laugh. "Hell, no. A costume is only useful when you need to protect your identity. So I have normal clothes for the times I'm not fighting crimes—or *committing* crimes—and I have the costumes for special occasions. Like today!"

Austin touched his shoulder. "That's reassuring. You make me feel just a little bit safer."

A few yards away, Mary Beth turned to Lisa. "You see the way that freak Nick Donovan is flirting with Austin? It's disgusting."

Lisa didn't bother responding.

The grinding noise outside stopped, and Farraday walked back inside. "Okay, time for the last job. I'm gonna take the truck over to that place on Second Avenue now and…"

All their phones vibrated at the same time.

"No you're not." Lisa had been the fastest among them to retrieve the text message. "Lambert says it's too late." Farraday reached for his own phone to confirm.

"So…wait a sec, here." Austin Peebles wasn't the type of man who was concerned about much, but this turn of events concerned him a great deal. "If you don't get into my mother-in-law's office and steal Kevin's computer, what's to stop him from sending that picture to June Forteene again and putting us back in this mess?"

"Us?" growled Farraday.

"Well…okay, just me."

"Calm down." Lisa was reading the most recent text message from Tramway Park. "We're still going to pull the job. It's just too late for us to get there before her staff shows up for work this morning, meaning plans have changed. We need to regroup and figure out a new scheme."

Farraday looked at Nick. "That gives you time to go home and change clothes."

"Do I have to?"

"*I* say you do. And put on some underwear while you're at it."

The others found their eyes focusing on Nick's tights.

Lisa's phone vibrated again, drawing her attention back to more important things. "Grant wants us to meet up at the Roosevelt Island Tramway Park as soon as we can get there. And then we're gonna figure out what to do."

Farraday shook his head. "No can do. I know it's just a garbage truck, and no one's probably looking for it, but it isn't a smart thing to spend all day driving around in a hot vehicle full of stolen computers and cell phones. I got a place to dump it in Jersey where no one's gonna trace it back to us or Peebles. Leaving it out on the street for a few hours while Lambert figures out a new plan is a very bad idea."

She texted back, and the reply came almost immediately.

"Okay, Farraday, get the truck out of here. And you"—she pointed at Nick—"get home and put on *real* clothes. And underwear."

"Grant texted that?"

"No, I'm telling you!" Nick nodded; he didn't want to mess with her. "Meet us at the Tram as soon as you're properly dressed."

"What about me?" asked Austin.

Lisa sized him up. She didn't share Mary Beth's enthusiasm for the kid, although she supposed he could be kind of charming in a certain way… *No!* She shook the thought out of her head.

"Go somewhere and stay out of our way. We'll be in touch."

Jamie was not a regular patron of the New York City subway system, which is why what should have been a short ride across town on the E Train turned into a long ride to Harlem on an A Train. But he finally made it to the Lexington Avenue station and mounted the stairs two at a time until he was at street level.

He was a half block from PEEBLES FOR THE PEOPLE headquarters when he saw Farraday steer the dark blue garbage truck around a corner.

Damn! He had missed *another* job!

Jamie mentally kicked himself a few times before realizing there was still time to play a role in the last big job of the morning: the burglary of United States Representative Catherine Cooper Concannon's district office on Second Avenue. If he could catch up with Farraday, he'd still be part of the action.

It didn't occur to him that Farraday had turned west off Lexington, when Second Avenue was east. The only thing that occurred to him was that he had to catch up that garbage truck.

He broke into a run.

In the shadow of the Roosevelt Island Tram, Constance and Angelina had just finished telling Grant and Chase how they'd robbed Kevin Wunder and caused a panic on East Eighty-first Street when Lisa led Mary Beth and Chrissy into the plaza. So Grant made them tell the story again, which produced a lot of laughter and almost as much scratching at imaginary bedbug bites.

Chase looked around when the laughter subsided. "Where's Nick?"

Lisa shook her head. "I sent him home to change his clothes." Grant started to ask, but she stopped him. "Trust me, you don't want to know."

There were some things Grant was fine with not knowing, and it sounded like this was one of them. He brought up another unpleasant topic instead. "I see you don't have Jamie with you."

"Nope." She shook her head. "Jamie Brock is useless. But we already knew that."

"The guy brings us a bum job and then doesn't help pull it off. In my book that makes him worse than useless."

Something about the route didn't look right to Jamie. It seemed the truck was heading in the wrong direction.

Then again, from where he stood perched on the rear bumper of the garbage truck, holding on to the handle next to the compactor for dear life, it was hard to get a good read on the scenery. At one point the truck stopped for a red light, and he'd attempted to hop off and climb into the truck's cab, but before he reached the ground, the truck suddenly accelerated and almost threw him. He figured he was better off staying where he was than risking being left behind and missing the final part of the job.

He knew Grant didn't respect him very much, but Jamie was determined to prove him wrong. He would not only be present for the final part of the job, he would be the member of the gang who made a difference.

Farraday made a right turn and Jamie tightened his grip on the handle as the truck lurched and his body swayed. And then...

The truck started to speed up.

It took him a while—at least several miles worth of thinking about this situation—before he realized the truck was speeding north on the West Side Highway. And there was no way he was going to jump off the back of a moving garbage truck as it traveled down a highway at fifty-five miles per hour.

But he had great views of the Hudson River as the truck crossed the George Washington Bridge. That was something, at least.

Fifteen miles into the state of New Jersey, Farraday took a look to see if Jamie was still hanging on to the back of the truck. He didn't really care much either way but figured it was probably for the best when he saw an arm waving in the rearview mirror.

If Jamie could hold on for the last five miles until Farraday could ditch the truck, he'd have one hell of a story to tell some day.

The deck was stacked against them, Grant thought, as he sat on the bench and stared at nothing. They'd had a little bad luck and a little incompetence—he was being kind in thinking Jamie was incompetent; it seemed more likely he'd taken a powder on the job—and the combination was leading to failure.

It wasn't enough that four jobs had been pulled off. Unless all five were completed, they wouldn't succeed.

Worse than that, if all five weren't completed, they'd either have to walk away with nothing, or...

He refused to think through that "or." Because the only option other than walking away was to plan and execute the entire thing all over again.

With every passing moment, a successful fifth burglary moved a bit further out of reach. First he'd lost Farraday and his garbage truck. Now he was about to lose Lisa.

"I'll be back." She lit a cigarette in defiance of the municipal code. "Just call."

He didn't like that. "I don't know that we'll have much lead time once I sort this thing out in my head. Are you sure you can't stay?"

She took a drag. "Positive."

"What could be so important?"

"I have to make a living, Lambert." She leaned down until they were at the same eye level. "Look, I think I've been a good sport about this, but I've got a real estate business to run and a book coming out in a few weeks. I don't have free time to sit around and wait for you to come up with a plan."

He grumbled; she didn't care.

"You'll be fine. I'll see you soon." Lisa disappeared down East Fifty-ninth Street.

Ah, well. Grant still had Chase. And Mary Beth and Constance, as well as the apparently naturally brilliant Angelina. He supposed it was better than nothing.

A few pros, a bitch, and a rookie. What could possibly go wrong?

Seven minutes later, Nick Donovan reappeared and reminded him.

"Ta-da!"

Grant looked up, expecting the worst, but Nick wasn't wearing a goofy outfit. That was progress.

Then Nick had to go and shatter the illusion. "Underneath my clothes, I'm wearing a Spider-Man suit!"

"A…a…?" Grant's head began to ache.

Nick pointed at the incoming tram. "C'mon, you've seen the movie, right? That scene where Spider-Man had to save the Roosevelt Island Tram?"

Grant was thinking maybe a good punch to the throat would shut the kid up but didn't follow through.

Because he had a sudden inspiration.

"Okay," he announced. "I've got a plan."

CHAPTER EIGHTEEN

S o if you don't mind me asking," said Chase as he waited with Grant for the light to change, at which point they'd cross Second Avenue, "what's your brainstorm?"

"Nick Donovan is wearing a Spider-Man costume under his clothes." He said it so matter-of-factly that Chase wondered if maybe Grant had snapped under the stress of the job.

"And?"

"And that got me thinking." The light changed and they continued walking. "See, I'd been planning on doing this the traditional way and coming from the inside—go through the front door, pick the locks, and so on—but what if we come from the outside? That's what Spider-Man would do, right?"

Yeah, thought Chase, *he's snapped.*

They reached the now-familiar white brick façade of the building that housed Triple-C's district office, and Grant kept walking to the north side of the building. He pointed down the narrow alley next to it, the same passageway where a few days earlier Wunder had led them when they upped their fee to thirty thousand dollars. That seemed like such a long time ago.

"If I've got my bearings right, Wunder's office looks out on this alley." Grant's finger counted up to the fifth floor window, three below the roof, and studied it in silence.

"So what's the plan?" Chase finally asked.

"Hmm." Grant took a step to the side and studied the building opposite Wunder's window. "We have to either access Wunder's office from the roof…or from the window across the alley."

Chase didn't like those options. They both sounded like someone was going to get hurt, which is what he told Grant.

"If Farraday was here he could steal us a cherry-picker," said Grant. "But he's in Jersey with the garbage truck, so we're stuck with those options."

Chase figured the alley was eight feet wide. He pointed to the window opposite Wunder's. "How are we supposed to get across?"

"I dunno. Build a bridge out of something, I guess." Grant took another look at the top of the building. "You don't want to go over the roof?"

"Hell, no." Chase shook his head. "The only one of us I'd trust dangling from a rope one hundred feet above the pavement is Nick, and I don't even trust *him* that much."

Grant nodded. "I suppose you're right." That settled, he turned to his partner. "Call Lisa and tell her it's time to get to work."

Margaret Campbell—the Grande Dame of the American Mystery Novel, according to *People*—had been waiting for David Carlyle in the reception area of Palmer/Midkiff/Carlyle's office on Sixth Avenue for a half hour before he finally stepped off the elevator at 9:00 a.m. He saw her before she saw him and briefly considered trying to escape but knew he'd have to go into the office eventually…and she'd still be waiting. Like a trip to the dentist, it was preferable to deal with the pain of Margaret Campbell as quickly as possible, before it got worse. Then, God willing, she would go back home to Chapel Hill, North Carolina, and leave him alone for a while.

"Margaret!" he gushed and forced a smile to his pink face. "How is my favorite author?"

She shot him down with a stare. "Cut the crap, Carlyle. You know why I'm here."

"Do I?" A hand fluttered to his face. "I'm afraid I have to plead ignorance."

"Really!" It was a declaration, not a question. "Did you even *look* at what your copy editor is trying to do to my manuscript?"

He had, and he had agreed with the copy editor. Margaret had been getting a little sloppy lately, no doubt due to an unfortunate combination of too much writing and too much bourbon. He wouldn't tell her that, of course.

"I'll talk to the copy editor." David's hand smoothed back a stray strand of thinning white hair that threatened to fall over his face. "I'm sure we can make you happy. But now, if you'll excuse me, I have an appointment..."

Margaret Campbell stared him down. "And is that appointment with someone more important than Palmer/Midkiff/Carlyle's top-selling author?"

He was tempted to inform her that no fewer than six other PMK authors now outsold her, including Glenda Vassar, a romance novelist who tragically seemed to have a fresh nervous breakdown every six months. But, tempting as that was, Margaret's books still made a lot of money for the publishing house his grandfather had co-founded, so he held his peace and hoped she wouldn't bolt to Simon & Schuster.

"If you *must* know—"

"I must."

"I'm going to *finally* sit down with Lisa Cochrane to discuss publicity for her book."

Margaret frowned. "Who?"

"There! I told you it wouldn't interest—"

"Calm down, David. I know exactly who you mean. The real estate lady, the one who consorts with criminals."

He looked around to see if anyone was listening. No one was. Still, he leaned close to her. "We don't know those gentlemen were criminals."

"They *weren't* gentlemen. And they *were* criminals. Meaning she's probably one, too."

"A gentleman?"

She hit him in the shoulder, and not in an affectionate way.

A few moments later the *ding* of an elevator announced Lisa's arrival. David welcomed her and began escorting Lisa down the hall. Margaret—uninvited and not going anywhere—followed, much to their chagrin.

If there was payback, it was how boring the next half hour felt to her, because the editor and the picture-book author actually talked book publicity. It was so painfully boring she eventually couldn't take it anymore.

David droned. "And then you're booked at the Barnes and Noble in Albany..."

That's when Margaret decided to interrupt. "I still want to meet those criminals you associate with."

Lisa sold real estate and therefore lied a lot and quite expertly. She knew how to handle people like Margaret.

She smiled. "I have no idea what you mean."

David's head bobbed in vigorous agreement. "Neither do I. Margaret, you're being—"

He would have continued, but Lisa's cell phone rang. She grabbed a blank notepad from in front of David, jotted something down, and disconnected the call, ripping off the piece of paper and tucking it inside her blazer pocket.

"Gotta go!"

They waited until Lisa was far away from the office before speaking.

Margaret spoke first. "Did you see that? I'll bet you anything she's about to commit a crime with those crooks she hangs out with."

He leaned forward, a bit too excited at the thought. "You think so?"

"I *know* so." Her smile was almost blissful. "Trust the mystery writer in me, Carlyle."

David spun in his chair until he looked out his window. "I have a confession to make."

"Spill."

"Remember that time years ago when you and I got ourselves in the middle of that, uh, little adventure?"

"Which...? Oh, you mean the thing with the Mafia?"

"Exactly. And the FBI. All that running around and danger and, uh, sexual tension..."

She frowned. "*What* sexual tension?"

"Okay, maybe I'm confusing things. Anyway, it was all so exciting!"

She remembered it a lot differently, and that was even before he mentioned sexual tension. Mostly, she remembered a lot of talking without action. She thought she might have met an FBI agent and was pretty sure she'd met the son of a mob boss, but—as usual—David Carlyle was glamorizing the adventure.

But still, he was right. "Those were some good times."

He slammed his palms on the desk and Margaret jumped. "Dammit, I never felt as alive as I did then! That was amazing." He shook his head slowly and sadly. "Sometimes I feel as if life is passing me by, and, well...I wish Lisa had taken us with her. If she's really going to meet up with those criminals, that is."

Margaret Campbell's smile was tight. "So you agree with me now?"

"I do."

She scowled. "Not good enough."

"I *do*! I *do* believe!"

"So let's follow her. She can't exactly stop us."

A quizzical look came to his face. "We don't even know where she went."

She sighed and wondered why she was always the person who had to do *all* the thinking. "Give me a pencil."

He doubled up on the quizzical expression. "I don't think I—"

"Look in your drawer."

Eventually, he found a pencil tucked beneath packets of catsup and Chinese mustard. He handed it over, and Margaret lightly brushed the graphite over the notepad until the impression of an address emerged on the sheet below the one Lisa had written on.

"Let's grab a cab."

Before Lisa arrived, the rest of the gang had taken a few steps in the direction toward turning Grant's plan into a reality.

With a boost, Chase raised Nick up to the fire escape so he could access the building opposite Triple-C's offices. Nick slid open a window, then scrambled down the stairway to the ground floor, where he expected a sign would warn him of alarms. But there were no signs, so he held his breath and pushed it open to let them inside.

It was the building's emergency stairwell, and because people who belonged in the building would be using the elevator, that meant there was a good chance no one would be interrupting them while they were trying to work.

But they still needed something to bridge the gap across the alley. Leaving Grant behind, they propped open the door, split into teams, and dispersed through the neighborhood to forage for materials.

Chase and Nick returned first, carrying a few sections of metal scaffolding pipes they'd borrowed from a construction site a few blocks away. Grant looked them over and figured they'd reach the other side, but couldn't see himself crawling on hands and knees over a fifty-foot drop with only two flimsy metal rods to support his weight. So maybe the pieces of scaffolding weren't the best idea.

It was a better idea than Mary Beth and Chrissy had, though. They were the next to come back to the stairwell, bearing a couple of two-by-fours that would never support the weight and girth of a full grown man…or even Nick Donovan, for that matter. Not to mention, the pieces of wood were only six feet long.

Constance and Angelina did much better. They spotted a ten-foot long wooden extension ladder propped against a building façade on First Avenue and borrowed it, figuring the guy whose feet were dangling out the second-floor window would probably feel for a rung before he put his weight down and gravity dropped him to the sidewalk. If not, it would be an important lesson for him to learn.

Grant sized up the ladder and figured it would do the trick.

Outside, Lisa paid her cab driver and stood on the sidewalk in front of the alley, where she lit a cigarette before looking up. Five stories above her head, she watched as a ladder poked out of a window in the building to her left and was slowly extended across the gap until…

She winced at the sound of breaking glass and took a long drag on her cigarette.

Yeah, she'd found them, all right. Who else could it possibly be?

They ducked below the window frame when the ladder broke through the window on the other side of the alley, but—when nothing happened and no one started shouting, "What the hell did you do to my window?"—finally got up the courage to peek outside.

Chase stated the obvious. "He must not be in his office."

"Must not be." Grant eyed the darkness through the broken pane of glass warily. "I'm going over."

"You?" It wasn't only Chase who asked him that.

"Yeah, me." Grant gave the members of his gang an accusatory look. "Why not? You think I've never done something like this before?"

Constance slowly shook her head. "I'm sure you have. But a *long* time ago."

"A *long* long time ago," added Mary Beth.

He snarled. "I've still got it. Just hold this end of the ladder so it doesn't move."

Grant inched his way across the ladder suspended fifty feet above very hard pavement. It shook with every movement, and he wondered if he maybe should have sent Nick. When he reached the middle, it sagged under his weight and his stomach did a somersault. Despite his claim when he'd been on steady footing in the stairwell, he'd never done this exact thing before. He probably should have taken into consideration that a wooden ladder was going to have at least a *little* play in it, and this one seemed to have a lot. But every time he took a look at the far end, where it rested unsecured against shards of broken glass, he was reassured to see it didn't look like it was going anywhere.

He finally reached the other side and looked through the broken glass, which is when he realized they'd punched a hole through the wrong window.

Grant inched his body backward until he could get a look at the windows facing the alley and counted them again. Which is when he realized they'd counted wrong, adding a small window near the ground to their tally when they shouldn't have.

They were still one floor below Kevin Wunder's office.

Kevin Wunder sat behind his desk and heard the sound of glass breaking out in the alley. *Damn punk kids.*

Ordinarily, he would have taken a look, but ordinarily he wasn't on his cell phone trying to talk June Forteene off a ledge.

Not literally; figuratively. Although the way she'd been carrying on, the literal might not be that far in the future.

It hadn't been a good morning for either of them. First he'd been robbed of his cell and laptop in the middle of that ridiculous bedbug panic—and the building management company would definitely be hearing from him about that—and then he'd had to wait in line for almost an hour to get a replacement phone programmed. Then word came of the break-in at campaign headquarters. And now June Forteene was on the phone telling him she'd been robbed in Starbucks and her office had been burglarized again. Even if computers and phones hadn't been the only things stolen from all four locations—and they were—it would have been all too easy to trace the crimes back to the source. This was payback.

It was harder to explain why June kept finding underwear hanging from her transom, but no one paid him to do that.

He listened as she ranted about fake cops and real cops and unhelpful Starbucks managers and fake UPS drivers and underwear-free burglars until it became so much white noise. But then—just as he was about to hang up—she said something that caught his attention.

"Today's the day, Kevin."

"The day for what?"

"Today's the day I destroy Austin Peebles. I can't take this anymore. By the close of business, I'm posting the photo and ending his career before it begins." She paused. "But, of course, I'll need the photo…"

He smiled at the stack of computers still sitting in one corner of his office. "I'll get that photo back to you within the hour."

"And I need my computers back. It's hard to run this operation on a single laptop."

He doubted that—all she did was *blog*, after all—but he eyed the stash in the corner of his office, the one he'd assured Triple-C was no longer there. "They're waiting for you. Come and get 'em."

Lisa smoked and waited for Grant to plummet to his death. When he didn't, she watched him back his way to the building on the north side of the alley and vanish back through the window. She flicked her cigarette to the gutter, where it landed next to her two previously discarded filters, and then found the stairwell door propped open at the sidewalk level and let herself inside.

"You catch all that?" asked Margaret Campbell, sitting next to David Carlyle in the back of a cab parked across the street.

"How could I miss it? Breathtaking! For a moment there, I was *sure* he was going to fall."

She opened the door. "We need to get in on this action."

David was so enthusiastic he almost forgot to pay the driver. The cabbie wasn't quite as forgetful.

"Oh, right!" He peeled the fare from a wad of bills in his pocket, paid the driver, and followed Margaret across the street and through that door.

"That's the right office."

Mary Beth frowned. "Are you sure this time?" She was answered with a hiss.

Grant stood in the window across the alley and stared at the back of Kevin Wunder's head through the open window, recognizing that round bald spot. "Soon as he's out of there, we're going in."

Chase started to ask, "Who do you want to—" but Grant heard something and shushed him.

"Someone's coming up the stairs."

Sure enough, footsteps slowly approached. But when Lisa appeared they collectively took a breath.

"Easy for you to do." Her normally gravelly voice had acquired a fresh coating of gravel, and she leaned against the wall, gasping for air. "If there are any more stairs on this job, I'm going to lose a lung."

"You should quit smoking," said Nick.

"Shut the hell up, kid." She took another couple of deep breaths. "This isn't the fault of the cigarettes. It's the fault of all these stairs."

"So anyway," said Chase again, eager to get back to business. "Who do you want to—"

Grant shushed him, and again they heard approaching footsteps.

"*There* you are!" Margaret Campbell said as she reached the landing and spotted the knot of people trying to loiter next to an open window and ladder and not look suspicious. "Christ, those stairs almost killed me." She turned to Lisa. "You have a spare cigarette?"

The exertion had deepened David Carlyle's usual pink hue into a frightening maroon. "We apologize for inviting ourselves along—"

"Who the hell are these people?" Constance wasn't happy.

Grant had to answer because Lisa was still catching her breath. "Lisa's editor and some writer."

"*Some* writer?" Margaret coughed as her lungs rebelled. "If I don't let *Publishers Weekly* refer to me like that, I certainly won't let some two-bit criminal do so!"

David's coloring was frightening, but at least he could breathe. "Now, now. Simmer down." To Constance—and the others to whom he'd not yet been introduced—he bowed slightly. "I'm David Carlyle, and this is Margaret Campbell, and we're here to—"

Angelina interrupted. "Wait a minute. The *author* Margaret Campbell?"

David nodded. "One and the same."

She clapped her hands with excitement. "*Murder in Mount Kisco* is my favorite book *ever*!"

"Ah, jeez," Grant muttered as he sank to the floor. He stared at the people crowded onto the landing in the stairwell—including him, they now numbered nine—and longed for the days when the job was understaffed. Especially since they had work to do, and he was losing the gang's attention to an impromptu book club discussion. "Okay, hey, everyone shut up for a minute!"

It took a full thirty seconds and a few more shouts, but they quieted down.

He continued. "We need to stay focused here and solve some problems. Starting with Problem Number One: How are we gonna get Wunder out of his office?"

"Who's Wunder?" asked David.

Grant didn't appreciate that the newcomer expected him to recap the plot for his benefit and let that be known through a scowl.

Chase, more amicable, filled in the gaps. "As long as you're here, you'd better make yourself useful." David nodded his agreement. "The office across the alley belongs to this congresswoman. Concannon's her name."

"Catherine Cooper Concannon?" David was impressed. "She's a legend! And that son-in-law of hers—Austin Peebles—is just adorable!" Normal coloring began to return to his face. "*We're* breaking into *her* office?"

"What's this 'we'?" snarled Grant. "Who said anything about the two of you—"

"Grant, let me." Chase spoke while his partner stewed. "Not *her* office, really. But this guy that works for her has some things we want. *His* is the office we're breaking into."

Margaret, having mostly regained her lung capacity, stepped forward. "Is it safe for me to assume you intend to access that window— that window way over there—with this flimsy ladder?"

"That's the idea," said Grant.

She folded her arms across her chest. "That's not the way *I'd* do it."

"Lady, you just write books. I do the real thing. This is how I make my living, so with all due respect—"

"Okay, you two." Chase stood between them. "Save the second-guessing for later. Right now, we have to get Wunder out of his office. Otherwise, we don't need to worry about the ladder."

David cleared his throat. "Tell me about this fellow Wunder." After Chase gave him the basics, he had an idea. "I believe I can get him out of the office."

Chase eyed him skeptically. "You're sure?"

"I think so. As long as it doesn't involve any more stairs."

Grant nudged his shoulder in Margaret's direction. "Take her, too."

"No way." She stood her ground, planting her feet firmly on the landing. "I came to see you pull a job, and I'm going to watch this unfold all the way through to the disastrous end."

He sighed and looked at Lisa. "I blame you." He didn't have to say that; she already blamed herself.

David departed, and they knew they'd have time to kill. Maybe ten minutes, maybe ten hours. That gave Grant a lengthy opportunity to regret almost everything about the job. Sending this guy he didn't even know to the building across the alley to try to convince a guy *he* didn't even know to leave his office was just the latest seat-of-the-pants wrinkle in a stunningly ill-fated plan.

He was surprised to find himself wishing their Insider had been present, and even more surprised to hear himself say it out loud.

"I never thought I'd say this, but I wish Austin Peebles was here right now."

Before he had the chance to clarify the thought, Mary Beth, Angelina, Nick, and Chase had their cell phones out and fingers poised to dial.

Grant didn't think anything could surprise him anymore, but this did. "Seriously?" He stared down Chase. "You, too?"

Chase shrugged abashedly but didn't bother trying to explain.

"I've got an assignment for you."

Edward Hepplewhite looked up from his sudoku to see his boss standing in front of him. She didn't look good. Her hair was wild, not carefully coifed, and there were dark circles under her heavily lidded eyes. He tried to hold her gaze while discreetly hiding the puzzle under a manila folder.

"Yes, ma'am?"

"I need you to go to the Upper East Side and pick up some computer equipment." She chose her words carefully; it wouldn't do for Edward to know too much. "Some surplus equipment to get us up and running again."

"Okay."

"Here's the thing." She leaned in closely. "And I'm taking you into my confidence on this. No one must ever know."

"My lips are sealed."

"My source works for the enemy."

He had to think about that. "The enemy?" He thought some more and his voice dropped to a conspiratorial whisper. "You mean, the Democrats?"

June Forteene nodded and matched his whisper. "The Democrats. My source is about to turn on them and dish enough dirt to ruin the party, and *I'll* have the exclusive story. It'll be live on my blog before Drudge has a chance to get off the toilet. Which is why we've got to keep this a secret."

"You can count on me, Miss Forteene."

She smiled. "I know that, Edward. I know that."

Farraday sat behind the wheel of a 2011 Lexus that had belonged to a dentist from Saddle Brook up until nine minutes earlier and fiddled with the radio. He wasn't ordinarily the kind of man who listened to the radio while driving, but he figured the noise might drown out the whining from his passenger.

That passenger—Jamie Brock—sat back in his seat sulking, and said for maybe the twentieth time since they'd ditched the garbage truck, "I can't believe you didn't see me back there."

Farraday found the traffic report. "I know. Can you believe that? Those trucks don't have good rear views. I'm sorta surprised they aren't involved in more accidents."

"I was waving and everything!"

"No kidding." He increased the volume on the traffic report.

They traveled in silence through northern New Jersey on Route 46 until Farraday nodded to the right. "There's Teterboro Airport. Wanna fly the rest of the way home?"

Jamie, who thought Farraday was joking, slumped back in his seat. "I could have fallen off and been killed."

"That woulda been a shame…"

No one was more surprised than Grant to look through the window across the alley and see the pudgy form of David Carlyle appear.

"Son of a gun. He got through the door."

But getting through the door and making his pitch convincing enough to get Kevin Wunder out from behind his desk were very different things.

❖

"Immortalize?" Wunder pointed his thumb at his chest. "Me?"

"You," David confirmed. "You see, Mr. Wunder, I have a lot of friends in the political field. When I told them Palmer/Midkiff/Carlyle wanted to publish a book about a consummate political insider, yours was the first and *only* name to come up."

Wunder drummed his fingers on the top of his desk. "It's true that I've been around a while and have seen a lot, but…Hmm." He was naturally cynical—he'd been burned too many times, and the Austin Peebles insult was an especially fresh wound—but he also knew that what this editor was telling him was probably the truth. If someone was asked who knew where the bodies were buried, the first name on their lips would probably be his.

David could see the criminals massed in the open window across the alley over Wunder's shoulder. "Maybe we could step out and grab a cup of coffee, and I can explain my proposal in greater depth."

But Wunder didn't move. He sat behind his desk and thought of the consequences—good and bad—of being, well, *immortalized*.

"Mr. Wunder?"

The consummate insider smiled. "Please, call me Kevin."

CHAPTER NINETEEN

Austin felt he was finally making progress with Penelope—she'd even looked at him without hate in her eyes, although also without words, when he walked into the library upon returning from robbing his own campaign headquarters that morning—but it didn't take long for the frost to return.

He took Kevin Wunder's call reporting the burglary and acted appropriately shocked. When he shared the news with her, she simply shrugged indifferently and that was that.

Things only got worse a short time later when his phone rang and—while she was in earshot—he answered with, "Hello, kitten."

Austin listened while a breathless Mary Beth insisted he get to his mother-in-law's office right away and help someone he'd never heard of try to get Kevin out of the office for a while. He tried, but couldn't get her to expand or explain, and when he hung up he still knew nothing he didn't know the night before.

"Kitten?" Penelope's voice dripped with contempt. It had been days since he'd heard her voice, and he wondered if she'd always sounded like that.

"Just a campaign volunteer." There was no need for her to know more than that. "And don't worry about it. She's a lesbian, and it's a pet name."

She didn't buy it. "Nice try, Austin, but you're just digging yourself in deeper."

Twelve minutes later, he walked into Mother Concannon's office, still not quite sure why he was there. That made answering the first question posed to him even more difficult.

"Austin!" said Catherine, spotting him in the reception room. "Why are you here?"

"Uh...To, uh...To see if Kevin would like to get a cup of coffee."

She shook her head. "We've already had this conversation, Austin. As a candidate, it doesn't look good for you to be here. The ethics purists would have a field day if they thought we were advising you out of a government office rented by the taxpayers. In the future, I have to insist—*again*—that you phone ahead and have Kevin meet you outside."

"Yes, sorry."

She smiled at him indulgently. He wasn't always the sharpest person she'd ever worked with, but his apology was so sincere. "Go downstairs and I'll have Kevin meet you."

"Uh...okay."

She walked in one direction—toward Wunder's office—and he walked in another—toward the elevator—but Austin paused when he heard the receptionist on the phone as he passed her desk.

"I'll tell Mr. Wunder that you'll be here to pick up the computers at noon. Thank you."

Noon? He checked his watch. If that call was what he thought, they had less than fifteen minutes. After that, that awesome picture of the candidate and his penis would be back in the hands of June Forteene and soon spread across the globe.

Once out on the sidewalk, the candidate in question nervously paced for a few minutes. Mary Beth and the criminals weren't going to be happy with the way he had bobbled the assignment. Worse, all of this—the series of crimes leading up to this moment—would be an exercise in futility.

When he paced past the alley running along the far end of the building, a noise attracted his attention. He glanced up.

Mary Beth and Nick waved to him from an open window. An open window that seemed to be across the alley from Kevin Wunder's window. That still didn't make complete sense, but it did start to fill a few gaps in the story.

Austin had no idea how they planned to get across the alley and steal the computers. They didn't seem like the type of criminals who shimmied along ropes strung over open spaces, but what did he know? He hoped they could do whatever needed to be done in less than fifteen minutes.

❖

Catherine Cooper Concannon knocked but didn't wait for an answer before opening Kevin Wunder's office door. Both Kevin and the pink-faced man on the opposite side of his desk looked at her expectantly.

"I'm sorry to interrupt, Kevin, but Austin has come by to see you."

Kevin squinted unhappily. "He's not supposed to come here."

"I reminded him of that."

"So where is he now?"

"He's waiting for you outside the building."

David, who'd been making no headway getting Wunder out from behind his desk and was almost out of small talk, said a silent prayer of gratitude for the intervention of Austin Peebles.

They watched Kevin Wunder and David Carlyle leave and waited a cautious amount of time to make sure no one returned. No one did. Then the ladder slid slowly and steadily out the window until it touched down on the ledge outside Wunder's office.

This time Nick went first. He was halfway across when Chase began to follow.

Grant pulled him back by a belt loop. "One at a time, lover. I think this is sturdy enough, but let's not test it under the weight of three people at the same time."

One by one they crossed the alley until Grant, the last man over, scrambled through the window and into Wunder's office. He locked them inside—or rather, locked everyone else *outside*—then examined the computers still stashed in the corner where he'd left them.

"That's a lot of equipment," he muttered. "Six computers we stole from June Forteene's office, plus the two on Wunder's desk. I don't know about you, but I don't feel like making multiple trips across that ladder. It'll be dangerous and take too much time."

Chase was lost. "So how do you want to handle it?"

"I have an idea…"

The cab pulled to the curb and Edward double-checked the address before stepping out and paying the driver, making sure to tell him to keep the sixty-five cents in change as a tip.

He eyed the white-brick building and steeled himself. He was going into the belly of the beast—the office of a Democratic Member of Congress—and had to be prepared for whatever debauchery he'd encounter. No doubt it would even be more frightening than naked masked burglars dangling from the ceiling.

After saying a silent prayer, Edward looked skyward for reassurance and...

...and thought, *Why is there a ladder stretching between the buildings?* That *is odd.*

He took a few steps toward the alley, trying to figure it out. He didn't have long to think about it.

Because seconds later, a computer came hurtling out a window toward him.

"What the hell are they doing?" croaked Lisa after the second computer toppled out the window.

Constance stood next to her. "They're making noise and a big mess. That's what the hell they're doing. Are they *trying* to get caught?"

Margaret Campbell stood with her arms folded. "That's not the way *I'd* do it."

Minutes later, Constance and Lisa were outside, alternately dodging computers and throwing the shattered remains into a Dumpster.

Wendy Hyer-Romanov was returning from one of the most dreadful client meetings she'd ever had the displeasure to attend and wanted nothing more than to get back to work. Her firm—WHR Associates—was located on the fourth floor, just below the office of United States Representative Catherine Cooper Concannon.

She waited impatiently for the elevator doors to close until she saw a young man wearing hipster frames rush toward her through the lobby, at which point she jabbed the Close Door button a few times. He managed to squeeze inside before the elevator obeyed the buttons, so she pretended she hadn't done what she did and stood aside to give him room.

She exited on the fourth floor and took out her key as she approached the single-room office with a fake-wood plaque outside the front door reading WHR ASSOCIATES, then let herself inside.

The first thing Wendy Hyer-Romanov noticed was the broken window and shattered glass all over her desk and floor.

The next thing she noticed was something large and gray tumble past that broken window.

She approached cautiously and looked up, where a wooden ladder stretched between the buildings.

Then she looked down and saw two women furiously collecting broken pieces of something gray in the alley.

Wendy Hyer-Romanov couldn't make sense of any of it, but somehow the ladder, the hurtling items, and the activity in the alley added up to a broken window and glass all over her office. It could be vandalism, or it could be an accident, but—after the morning she'd had—she wasn't in the mood to deal with it.

She called 911.

When the office was empty of everything electronic, Grant said, "Let's get out of here."

He went out onto the ladder first, followed by Chase. Nick—the youngest and lightest—was to be the final man out the window.

"I don't know if I like going last," he said, when Grant gave him the instructions.

"Don't worry, kid. It'll hold."

Under that scalp of thick wavy hair, Nick focused his dark eyes on the ladder. "But what if it doesn't?"

"If it doesn't…uh…"

"We'll catch you," said Chase with a wide smile he hoped was reassuring.

Grant nodded. "Yeah, that."

Edward pushed his way into Representative Concannon's office without so much as a consideration of the debauchery inside. He was *that alarmed* by what he'd just seen.

"Excuse me!"

The receptionist, slightly bored, eyeballed him and took him for another crazy constituent. "Can I help you?"

"Someone is throwing computers out a window."

Yeah, she'd pegged him. "If you'll take a seat, one of the Representative's aides will help you in a few minutes."

Because he was an obedient young man, Edward took a few steps toward a row of chairs lining one wall, until he remembered he wasn't here to see an aide. He returned to the reception desk.

"Ma'am, my name is Edward Hepplewhite, and I'm supposed to pick up some surplus computers from a Mr. Kevin Wunder."

"Oh." She jabbed a long nail in his direction. "You're the one who called."

"That's right."

"Kevin's not in right now, but I'll have someone see if they can help you." She picked up a phone and buzzed someone.

While she did, he kept talking. "You see, I'm supposed to pick up these computers, but people are throwing computers out of the building, and, well...I'm wondering if those events are connected."

She wasn't paying attention. "Marie, could you send Randy out front. Kevin promised some computers to this gentleman, but he's not here right now. Thanks!"

"As I was saying..."

She smiled and tuned him out. They didn't pay her enough to deal with the crazies. "Randy will be right out."

Although the delay was tying Edward's stomach in knots, Randy was with him in less than thirty seconds. He smiled pleasantly, exchanged eye rolls with the receptionist, and led Edward back toward Kevin Wunder's office. Randy didn't stop until the door refused to open for him.

"That's strange. Kevin hardly ever locks his door." He yelled over the partitions, "Marie, do you have a key for Kevin's office door?"

Marie hollered back, "Kevin's got the only key."

Randy gave Edward an apologetic smile. "Sorry about that, but he should be back soon."

"But...what if those computers are the ones being thrown into the alley?"

Randy smiled, but behind that smile he was thinking, *Oh, damn, I've got a crazy constituent on my hands.*

Grant crossed the alley, and Chase followed as soon as his weight was off the ladder. The wood groaned beneath him, but he progressed steadily until he reached the window into the stairwell.

In Wunder's office, Nick crouched in the window frame and slowly reached for the ladder.

His fingers were inches from it when it slid away from the frame and the men—as well as the other members of the gang and a handful of passersby—watched in horror as the ladder plummeted, bouncing off both buildings before breaking in two and crashing to the ground.

The ladder shattered what remained of Wendy Hyer-Romanov's window, sending a spray of glass through the room. She shrieked and put in another call to 911.

One floor above, Randy and Edward paused at the sounds of rumbling and breaking glass.

"What was that?" asked Edward.

Randy shook his head and tried the doorknob one more time before hollering, "Marie, you'd better call Kevin and tell him to get back here! I think something is wrong."

On the other side of that locked door, Nick—framed in the window and left behind—mouthed some words.

"What did he say?" asked Grant.

"Sorta looked like he said, *What the fuck?!*"

"That's what I thought." Grant looked down at the ladder and then back at Nick. "Now we've got a problem."

When Marie called, Wunder was sitting in a booth in the corner coffee shop. Austin sat next to him on the outside, penning him in, and David sat on the other side. Much as he liked the idea of being David's consummate insider, he resented the way the editor invited himself along, as well as Austin's eager acquiescence. He had no idea what the candidate wanted to talk about—the burglary, or his penis photo, or the price of soybeans—but clearly none of it could be discussed in front of David Carlyle. By the same token, neither David nor Kevin could discuss the book idea in front of Austin.

And so they sat nursing cups of coffee and not talking about much besides the weather until Wunder's new phone buzzed. He took the call and grew visibly alarmed.

"I've got to get back to the office," he said after disconnecting.

"Is everything all right?" asked Austin.

"Yes, perfect. But if you'll just let me out—"

David raised his voice. "Oh, but I was just about to tell you about the time I saw James Franco at an event at the Guggenheim!"

"I really have to—"

Austin didn't move. "Sit for a minute, Kevin. This sounds like it'll be a great story."

"Could you let me out? I've got to—"

"Go on, David," said Austin, still planted firmly in the booth. "I love James Franco!"

Kevin nudged; Austin didn't move. Kevin shoved; Austin didn't move. Kevin kicked under the table; Austin didn't move. And as for the story? *Really!* So he saw a stupid actor across the room one night. He didn't even *talk* to him!

"Are you going to let me out?" Wunder finally snapped.

Austin looked at him as if he'd just spoken for the first time. "I'm sorry, I was listening to David's story. It's *fascinating*!"

"Oh, ferchrissake." With that, Kevin Wunder hauled up his stocky body until he was standing on the cushioned seat and crawled over the back into the neighboring booth. It wasn't occupied, and he wouldn't have cared if it was.

David threw a few bills on the table, and he and Austin set off in pursuit.

Edward thought she'd never pick up, but finally he heard June Forteene's voice on the phone.

"I'm at Congresswoman Concannon's office," he told her. "And something's going on."

Figures, she thought. *I can't even trust Edward to complete a simple errand. I should've left him in jail.*

He continued. "Mr. Wunder's office door is locked, and we can't get at the computers."

"Can't someone call him and tell him to come back?"

"They did. But here's the thing: When I got out of the cab, someone was throwing computers out a window."

"Someone… Wait, say that again." He did, and her head began to pound. "Were they throwing them out of Wunder's window?"

"I can't say. All I know is there was a ladder stretched between the buildings—"

"A ladder?"

"Yes, and I went to look at it and then a computer almost hit me. And then another one! And then I ran inside Congresswoman Concannon's office to tell them about it and we checked Mr. Wunder's door but it was locked and people say he never locks his door." His run-on sentence left him winded.

June put her head on her desk. Nausea was beginning to overtake her sudden headache. She saw where this was going.

The same people who'd burglarized her home and office, stolen Wunder's cell phone and laptop, and emptied out the Peebles campaign headquarters were now involved in a direct assault on Triple-C's congressional office.

It made sense. It would be the last logical place pictures of Austin Peebles's penis might be stashed. Even as June Forteene sunk to the floor, facing the strong possibility that all the copies of that photo were now gone forever, she knew she had to give credit to the geniuses who'd planned the job.

"Miss Forteene?" Edward's voice came from her phone—her second replacement phone in a week—and sounded so far away. As it should, since the phone was on her desk and she was now horizontal on the industrial carpeting with her eyes firmly pressed closed.

"Excuse me," said a man's voice—not Edward's; this man was standing a few feet away—and she turned and opened her eyes.

When June Forteene saw the brown UPS uniform, she burst into tears and lost her battle with nausea.

The banging grew louder, but Nick did his best to tune it out and barricaded the door with Kevin Wunder's heavy metal desk.

Unlike Grant, he already had his Plan B.

He didn't know if Plan B would work, but at least he had it.

Five stories below, Grant, Chase, and their associates looked expectantly at the window, hoping that Nick could get himself out of this jam. Because *they* sure as hell couldn't figure out how to do it.

Grant turned to Chase. "Maybe we should call his mother. I think he's gonna need her services."

"She's not gonna be happy," Chase said. "If you get her baby boy arrested, this could get ugly."

He might have called anyway, but then something white caught his eye as it fluttered through the air.

"What's that?" asked Chrissy.

"It looks like..." Angelina stared. "A shirt?"

The shirt was still fluttering when a sneaker landed in the alley with a thud.

"What's he doing?" asked Lisa.

And then they stood in awe as a figure that didn't seem to be Nick Donovan appeared, framed in the window.

"What are you doing?!" Wunder slapped David's hand away from the panel after he pressed the elevator buttons for the second and third floors, only to have Austin reach behind him and press the fourth floor button. "You know we're going to the fifth floor, you moron!"

"It's my fault," said David. "I like elevators to go very slowly. Otherwise, my stomach gets queasy."

Wunder ignored him and turned his venom on Austin. "And how many times has your mother-in-law told you to stay away from her congressional office?"

"Once or twice."

"So what are you doing on this elevator?"

Austin shrugged and a *ding* announced they'd reached the second floor.

Chase was multitasking, watching the fifth-floor window while speaking to Farraday. "Where are you?"

"Just crossing the George Washington Bridge."

Chase relayed the information to Grant, who didn't like it. "Okay, we'll catch you later."

"Without Farraday around, we're gonna have to steal a car," said Grant

"Fortunately, we've got skills."

Grant frowned. "Glad you feel that way, 'cause you're gonna do the stealing."

"But..." Chase looked up at the building. "If I go steal a car, I'm gonna miss this."

"Guess so," growled Grant. "Which means you might be the lucky one."

Behind him, he heard Margaret Campbell say, "This isn't the way *I'd* do it," but he ignored her.

Sixty feet above them, Spider-Man was clinging to those white bricks outside the window but not moving much.

The reason he wasn't moving was because Nick Donovan was coming to the belated realization—when a person realized things while hanging by their fingernails sixty feet above the hard ground, it was too late to turn back, and therefore belated—that some of these superhero stunts were a lot tougher than they looked in the comics.

He tightened his grip and tried to lower himself a few inches.

Kevin Wunder almost dropped to the floor and kissed the ground when the elevator finally reached the fifth floor. Even as David and Austin kept getting in his way—and what the hell was *wrong* with them?—he pushed through the crowd surrounding his office door.

"What's the problem?"

"Your door is locked," said Randy.

"No, it isn't."

"Yes, it is. I tried it about a dozen times."

Wunder had to try it for himself before he believed him, but sure enough… He pulled a key ring from his pants pocket, found the key he needed, and turned it in the lock, which responded with a gentle click.

The damn door *still* wouldn't open.

He slammed his body into the wood and it gave a tenth of an inch. "It's barricaded! Who the hell got into my office and barricaded it?!"

The receptionist was standing at the back of the crowd and pointed at Edward. "He's the only crazy we've had in here all day."

Wunder stared at the crazy and sputtered. "Who are *you*?"

"I'm not a crazy, Mr. Wunder. I'm Edward Hepplewhite."

"Is that supposed to mean something to me?"

"I was sent by…" Edward remembered he was in the middle of enemy territory. "I was sent to pick up the computers."

"Who sent you to…?" Wunder's memory finally kicked in and trumped his anger. "Oh, right, yes. Yes, yes, yes. Okay, then, Ed, I want you and…" He looked around. "Randy! You and Randy are going to help me open this door."

It took a while—Nick had done a good job of blocking it—but finally they inched it open.

The office was empty of both computers and people.

❖

"Cops," said Grant, and he didn't have to say anything else. The gang that had been staring up for so many tense minutes instantly transformed itself into small groups of casual pedestrians and neighbors.

The patrol car pulled up outside the front door and parked at a hydrant. Two officers—acting even more casual than the criminals—finished their conversation before getting out of the front seat and walking to the entrance.

Wendy Hyer-Romanov stood in the doorway of her office, wondering what was taking the police so long, when a leg appeared in her broken window.

There was a crunch of glass as the foot attached to the leg touched down on the ledge, and then she was watching Spider-Man lower himself through the opening. It had been the sort of day when that didn't seem as bizarre as it should have.

"Spider-Man?"

"Sorry to disturb you, citizen." He began crossing the small office toward her door. "I had to take care of some burglars upstairs."

He passed her in the doorway and entered the stairway just seconds before the elevator doors opened and two uniformed police officers stepped out.

"You're not going to believe this one," she said as they approached.

Kevin Wunder looked down. And then he looked up. And then he looked at Edward.

"So you're trying to tell me you saw a ladder."

"Right. It looked like it went from this window to the window across the alley."

Wunder looked back down at the ground. "And you say people were throwing computers down there?"

"Right."

"So where are the ladder and computers now? Except for that sock down there, the alley looks about as clean as I've ever seen it."

Edward started to sweat a little bit. "I don't know."

"Unbelievable," Wunder muttered. "How can someone steal eight computers and vanish into thin air?"

Down in the alley, two workers—one grabbing each side—began to wheel the Dumpster out to the sidewalk.

One block away, Chase pulled to the curb in a 1996 Cadillac. He was looking for something roomy, and the Caddy fit the bill perfectly. He popped the trunk and waited.

It didn't take them long. First to appear were Mary Beth, Constance, and Angelina, carrying the splintered ladder. Chase broke some of the larger pieces down and tucked them in the trunk.

Chrissy carried Nick's clothes. "I couldn't find a sock."

Angelina shook her head. "If he manages to get out of the building without being seen, that'll be the least of his concerns."

Finally, they heard a low rumble and Grant and Lisa appeared, guiding the Dumpster down the sidewalk until it was positioned next to the Cadillac. Concluding the procession of criminals up Second Avenue was Margaret Campbell, taking notes and telling Grant exactly what he was doing wrong.

While Chase loaded the trunk with smashed electronics, Grant turned to the author. "The job is done. You can go home now."

She smiled in a way that announced she wasn't smiling. "My home is in the state of North Carolina, so I'm not going anywhere. Let's not forget that my editor is still inside, and let's not also forget I haven't heard you negotiate to get the thirty thousand dollars they owe you."

He might have forced her into the trunk if Spider-Man wasn't suddenly running down the street toward them.

"That," said Chase, as Nick dove into the backseat and ducked down, "was a true superhero performance."

"You did good, kid," said Grant. "You did *weird*, but good."

"Here are your clothes." Chrissy handed them over. "I found everything except one sock."

"Aw, man! Those were my favorite socks!" He sat in the backseat and pouted.

Outside the Caddy, Chase pulled Constance aside. "Time for us to mop up here. I called Farraday and he says he knows a place where he can dump the car. You mind getting some of these people out of here and taking it to him?"

"I'll handle it."

"Just remember," Chase cautioned, "the car's hot, so don't attract attention."

She scowled and shook her head. "Don't insult me, Chase LaMarca."

Chrissy leaned out the window. "Sorry I have to go, but the boys have hockey practice at four."

"Not a problem," said Chase. "Your job's done here."

She winked. "This was fun. Give me a call if you have another job for me."

Chase waved good-bye as Constance pulled from the curb with a trunk full of broken things and a passenger compartment full of criminals, leaving only Grant, Chase, Lisa, Mary Beth, and Margaret behind on the sidewalk.

Grant fixed Margaret with a stare. "Okay, lady, wanna see how this is done?"

She frowned. "I'd like to see how it's done *correctly*. But your way should at least be amusing."

He squared his shoulders. "Then let's go get our thirty thousand bucks."

The staff members in the office of Representative Catherine Cooper Concannon were surrounded by chaos.

Kevin Wunder—their chief of staff, who'd been so vocally concerned about the computers stashed in his office—now claimed to know nothing about them. *Never heard of them.* He had his reasons, of course, chief among them that they were stolen property, but his sudden reversal left the rest of Triple-C's staff shaking their heads.

And then there was the presence of Austin Peebles. The staff knew he wasn't supposed to be there. If he was still in the office when the Representative eventually emerged from her closed-door meeting with trade representatives from Nigeria it could get ugly…although maybe not. Triple-C seemed to love him as much as the staff did, so he'd probably get no more than a mild rebuke. Still, it was something they'd have to prepare for.

And *then* there was the presence of the pudgy, pink-faced man, who stood observing the action but seemed to have no business being there. And the strange young man wearing hipster frames standing off to the side, quietly praying. No one had the slightest idea who these men were or why they were there, but they were present when everything was going off the rails and therefore not above suspicion.

And *then* the cops arrived and mentioned someone downstairs had seen Spider-Man in the building.

In short, it wasn't a normal workday.

Representative Concannon's loyal staff had been through an interesting day that wasn't even half over. Fortunately they had an after-work retreat for days like this—or for days less bizarre than this, because no day had ever been like this, but still… So just minutes after noon, the receptionist called and reserved them two booths in the back of the bar where they could bitch about Kevin Wunder, shake their heads over the reported sighting of Spider-Man, and otherwise speak their minds without being overheard.

But things were moments away from becoming a lot more interesting.

The office door opened, and a rough-looking older man walked in. He was trailed by a tall woman with short-cropped blond-gray hair; a young, attractive woman with dark features and a no-nonsense attitude; a man who was getting too old to pull off his highlights; and a short woman who carried a notepad in her hand and wore a sneer on her face.

On a normal day, any one of these people might raise interest. But coming in as a group they signaled "Red Alert."

"Can I help you?" The receptionist wouldn't have minded having a panic button at the moment, even though all of Triple-C's employees stood only yards away.

Grant Lambert didn't have an opportunity to answer.

"You!" Kevin Wunder stormed across the office toward Grant and Chase, shoving staffers and at least one cop out of the way as he passed. "I should have known you were behind this!"

"I don't think I know what you're talking about, Wunder." Grant shrugged and didn't look innocent at all.

Wunder stabbed a finger at him. "I want to talk to you in private."

"I'm not here to see you. I'm here to see your boss."

"In *private!*"

"Do I have to say this again?"

Wunder tried to stare him down. "You…wouldn't…*dare!*"

Grant smiled, and for the first time in years it was almost passable. "I wouldn't? Try me."

Everyone—the staff, the cops, the people who seemed to have no business being there—watched the stand-off to see how it was going to play out.

Wunder noticed that and forced his most innocent smile. It wouldn't do to have a complete meltdown in front of the staff and police. "Representative Concannon is very busy right now. And you have no reason to see *her* when you can see *me*."

"I have every reason." He held out his hand and opened his palm, revealing a flash drive.

The cops sort of watched and sort of didn't, because they were mostly waiting for the return of Spider-Man.

"Know what that was?" asked Grant.

"A flash drive."

"Know what's on it?"

Wunder's eyes flickered around the room. He was being watched by too many people to tell the truth. "I don't think so."

Grant smiled again, and this time he carried it off. "That's a shame. What's on this drive is the last image in existence of—"

Wunder grabbed but Grant snapped his hand closed.

"So…" Grant was taking his time and enjoying this. "Who do you think is gonna be the high bidder? You? June Forteene? Austin? Triple-C?"

Wunder snarled. "Give me that."

Grant wasn't impressed. "Hey, Austin!" The young man stopped flirting with the receptionist and turned around. "How much for this flare drive?"

"*Flash* drive," hissed Wunder.

"Whatever."

Peebles shrugged. "Five?"

"Is that dollars or thousands of dollars?" asked Grant.

Austin laughed. "Dollars, of course. Why would I pay five *thousand* for a flash drive?"

Wunder muttered under his breath.

At an edge of the room, Edward Hepplewhite stopped his mumbled prayers just long enough to raise his camera phone above the crowd and snap a picture, which he then texted to June Forteene. He thought she'd be interested in knowing that the scruffy UPS deliveryman was in this very room at that very moment.

At some point over the previous half hour, June had managed to retrieve her phone from the desk before sinking back to the cool floor, so it was close at hand when Edward texted her the photo along with a message telling her the image was that of the fake UPS driver.

She looked at the picture and her stomach lurched.

Detective Finnerty Rafferty Jr. and the UPS stalker were the *same man*!

June crawled into a ball. She wanted her mommy. And after all these years, she *finally* wanted her mommy's Xanax.

Kevin Wunder knew he was in a difficult situation. He also knew his temper wasn't doing him any favors, so he willed himself to calm down and assess it rationally. A couple of deep breaths came close to doing the trick.

He looked around the reception area and quickly realized that the only way out of this jam was to separate the players. The longer the criminals, the candidate, the editor, June Forteene's assistant, the other staff members, the cops, and the strange, short woman with the notepad mingled together, the greater the possibility of disaster. He needed to separate them, and he needed to do it quickly.

Some separations would be easier than others, and that's where he started.

"Everyone back to your desks," he ordered the staffers. Reluctantly, they trickled away.

"You." He pointed to Edward. "Get back to your office and tell your boss I'll be in touch."

"But I'm not suppose to return without the computers," he protested.

Wunder paused and took another couple of deep breaths. "There are no computers any more. Got it?" With a glance at the cops, he thought to add, "There never *were* any computers. Never!"

"But..."

"Never!"

And that took care of Edward.

Next it was time to get rid of David Carlyle. "I have to apologize. Things aren't normally this crazy. You should leave and we'll pick up the discussion later—"

"I find it *fascinating*!" David did the opposite of what Wunder wanted him to do and took a seat in one of the chairs lining the wall. "I'm gaining a lot of fresh insight into your career."

Okay, that one didn't work so well. He'd come back to him. In the meantime, it was time to peel the cops off the pack.

"Officers, I'm sorry we wasted your time. There seems to have been a huge misunderstanding."

One of the cops said, "Are you saying there was no crime committed?"

"None at all."

"Then why was Spider-Man here?"

Deep breaths...

Wunder managed a smile and a chuckle. "Must've had the wrong address."

But they *did* finally leave, so whatever worked.

He looked at the short woman carrying a notepad. "I don't even know who you are."

Margaret Campbell fixed him with a stare and sat next to David. "That's right. You don't."

While Kevin Wunder cleared out most of the room Grant held his silence, mostly because it was also in *his* best interest. But now that the people present had been pretty much narrowed to Wunder on one side and everyone else on the other, he figured it was time to start negotiating again.

"How about coughing up thirty grand so we can go home?"

"Shhh!" Wunder motioned at the people in the room who weren't Grant or Chase or the women who were obviously with them. "This conversation should take place behind closed doors."

"I don't know about that, Wunder. This room works just fine for me." Grant nodded at Austin. "Does it work for you?"

"Perfectly," the candidate said, and the color began to drain from Wunder's face with the realization that this *child* knew a hell of a lot more than he should have known.

It was a setup. Somehow the crooks got to Peebles, which meant... He looked around the room, and everyone—even David Carlyle—nodded a confirmation when he met their eyes.

They were all in on it together.

"Give me that flash drive!" He lunged at Grant.

Negotiations had been tense, but a deal was close at hand.

Or so Representative Concannon thought as she looked at the

trade delegation from Nigeria sitting across the desk from her. There were only a few fine points to work out, but soon she'd have a done deal to take to her good friend, the Secretary of State. The Catherine Cooper Concannon Institute of American-Nigerian Trade would be a fitting legacy.

But then the screaming started, accompanied by the sound of breaking furniture.

The Nigerians looked at each other in confusion as she rose from her chair and excused herself.

In the reception area, she found her chief of staff wrestling on the floor with an older man. As legs kicked and chairs toppled, her other staff members began to emerge from the back offices. Triple-C caught the eye of one of them.

"Randy, please break that up."

Randy, much younger, bigger, and stronger than the grappling men, waded in and had the situation under control in seconds. And then Triple-C stepped forward.

"What the hell is going on here?"

"Maybe I can fill you in, Mother." That's when she realized Austin was also in the room.

"You know you're not supposed to be here."

Kevin Wunder spit out his words. "Like that's the worst thing he's done today!"

"Kevin!" It was true she didn't like Austin's presence in her office, but she still couldn't abide her chief of staff talking that way about her son-in-law.

Chase stepped forward, careful not to step on Grant's legs. "Madame Congresswoman? Could we have a few words with you?"

When her private office was clear of the trade delegation and the entire group—including the odd woman carrying a notepad—was locked inside, Representative Concannon took a seat behind her desk. "I hope you're all happy. You've set international relations with Nigeria back weeks, if not months."

"Sorry about that," said Grant. "I'm sure that's somehow important in a way no one in the world will ever understand."

She waved a hand and dismissed him. "I think I'm owed an explanation."

Kevin Wunder knew it was now or never. This was the moment he would either save his career or see it destroyed. He pointed at Grant, then Chase. "These are the men I hired to retrieve that picture."

Triple-C turned pale. "Kevin, we do not speak of…" She caught herself. "I mean, I don't know what you're talking about."

Austin was leaning against the wall near the locked door. "That's all right, Mother. Everyone in the room knows the situation. You can speak frankly."

She didn't like this at all. It was bad enough to have an office full of hooligans; it was worse to have an office full of hooligans who knew she'd ordered Kevin Wunder to hire them to commit a crime. But she'd deal with the ramifications later. Right now it was important to clear things up and get them out of her office.

She folded her hands on her desk. "Go on, Kevin."

He wiped his brow. "So I hired them, but they didn't get every copy of the picture. And you know that's true, because June Forteene started blackmailing us again." She nodded. "That's why I refused to pay them." He paused to wipe his brow again and took the opportunity to review his story and make sure it was more or less consistent. "They mugged me this morning and stole my phone and laptop, and now they're threatening us and insisting we pay up."

The room fell silent while everyone waited for her to speak.

"Thank you, Kevin." She looked at Grant, who seemed to lead the criminals. "Do you have anything to say for yourself?"

"Just that Wunder is full of shit. Uh, pardon my language."

She wasn't inclined to believe a common criminal over her loyal, longtime aide, but Catherine was a fair woman. She'd let him have his say. "And what is *your* version of this story?"

"My version of the story is what *really* happened. We did what we were supposed to get paid to do. You want to know how June Forteene kept getting copies of the cock shot?" Triple-C reddened slightly. "Uh, sorry ma'am. Anyway, she kept getting them 'cause Wunder kept sending them to her."

"That doesn't make sense," she said. "Why would Kevin—"

"'Cause he wants to be the congressman." Grant held up the flash drive. "Wunder figures if Austin has to drop out of the campaign, he'll become the candidate."

"That's ridiculous." She stared at Grant. "Kevin is never going to be the candidate."

"What?" Wunder sputtered.

"No offense, Kevin. You're just not very dynamic."

Austin added his two cents. "Not to mention he's been working with June Forteene."

Wunder had worked himself into another red-faced rage. "I'm not working with June Forteene!"

Grant ignored him. "So in order to protect Austin, we had to go back and steal all the computers and cell phones that might have the picture of the, uh…you know…on them."

She remained skeptical. "And where are they now?"

"Gone forever."

"So no one will ever see that image?"

"Nope."

"Then what's that in your hand?"

He looked at the flash drive. "This is my guarantee that once this job is over, it's over. I don't want to see or hear from Kevin Wunder or anyone else."

Wunder snorted. "He's going to blackmail Austin! Don't you understand?"

The congresswoman did understand, and looked at Grant with a steely expression on her face. "I'll make a deal with you. If you give me that flash drive, I'll give you a check for thirty thousand dollars."

"I don't take checks."

She sighed. "I suppose I should have assumed you didn't. In that case, you'll have to give me some time to get the cash together."

Grant didn't want to repeat this episode again in days or weeks. They were already pressing their luck. "Time is something we don't have a lot of."

"Not even forty minutes? I'm afraid I don't keep that kind of cash in the office."

He reconsidered but didn't want to let her know it was no longer an imposition. "I suppose we can wait another forty minutes."

Triple-C's word was good. Forty-two minutes later he had thirty thousand dollars in his pocket.

And she had the flash drive.

As they walked out the door, Chase called out over his shoulder. "Good night, Wunder. Don't let the Argentine Leaping Bedbugs bite!"

"Why, you...!!"

The door closed between them, and they could only hear faint traces of his screams.

Because there were a lot of people and there wasn't a lot of space in the elevator, they had to make two trips. When they regrouped in the lobby, Grant approached Margaret Campbell.

"Told you I could pull this off."

Her expression conveyed boredom. "Not the way I would have done it, but congratulations."

"Thanks. Hopefully we'll never see each other again."

He began to walk away but she stopped him. "One question!"

"What's that?"

"Why'd you leave them with the flash drive?"

"They paid for a penis. Well...I gave them what they paid for."

Catherine Cooper Concannon never believed the criminal when he claimed Kevin was associating with the loathsome blogger June Forteene and knew that Austin could be easily misled. If she had believed him, she would have fired Kevin on the spot. And she certainly wouldn't have left her desk unlocked that evening.

The criminals deserved the money, and she had no doubt Kevin had tried to cheat them, but she'd made everything all right. And now Austin no longer had that X-rated image burdening him, and their lives could get back to normal, so it was worth every nickel of that thirty thousand dollars she'd paid out.

But because that desk was unlocked, Kevin could help himself to something he considered a lot more valuable than money.

He'd been taken aback when Triple-C announced he would never be the candidate, but when he calmed down he dismissed that as meaningless. He *was* dynamic and he *was* congressional material, and when Austin Peebles was out of the picture, he'd prove it.

Too bad the thumb drive he took from the unlocked desk contained only a gay porn video, which he didn't realize until he triumphantly played it for June Forteene and Edward Hepplewhite a few hours later.

As Grant had said, they wanted a penis and they got what they paid for.

They got seven times what they paid for, as a matter of fact.

June curled into a fetal position on the floor.

CHAPTER TWENTY

G rant went over the numbers again and again, muttering to himself as his pencil scratched a pad.

"I still can't figure out how we cleared less than two thousand dollars on a thirty-thousand-dollar job."

Chase, who'd been going over those same numbers with Grant through three hours and four pencils, could now repeat his lines by rote. "Twenty percent to Jamie as a finder's fee. That's six Gs off the top."

"Hate him."

"I know. Four grand to Nick; another four to Farraday. Then subtract five thousand to Lisa and Mary Beth, five thousand to Constance and Angelina..." He was forgetting someone. "*Oh*, and four thousand to Chrissy."

"How'd she earn four thousand again? Didn't we tell her three?"

"She took care of both June Forteene and Kevin Wunder, so she got a raise and we got a bargain. We should use her again."

"We'll see."

Chase ignored him. "That leaves two thousand dollars. Factor in expenses, and there's your reason why we only cleared eighteen hundred dollars."

Grant sighed and tapped his pencil on the pad before setting it down. "It just don't seem right."

"I know. Maybe the next job..."

The pencil rolled off the table and clicked on the scuffed linoleum. "If there *is* a next job. Maybe this is a sign I should retire."

"Oh, Grant!" Chase laughed and threw his arms around his partner. "There's *always* gonna be a next job." He took a glance at the pad. "And how are you going to afford to retire on eighteen hundred dollars?"

❖

"Nicholas DuFour Donovan, get your ass out here!" Kelly Marinelli Dennison DuFour O'Rourke Donovan DuFour Bell Spencer DuFour Capobianco stood outside her son's bedroom door with her hands firmly planted on her hips.

"Why?" he yelled back from behind the locked door. "I'm playing video games."

"I'm counting to five and you'd better be out here, or I'm coming in. One!"

"But I'm in the middle—"

"Two!"

The door opened a crack, and Nick's dark eyes and full head of hair showed through the opening.

"That's not outside. Three!"

He got the message. The door swung open and he stepped into the hallway. Only then did he see she was holding an envelope.

"You wanna explain this?"

"What *is* that?"

"Your bank statement, you little—" She was so angry it had taken her a few moments to even notice. "What the hell are you wearing?"

She asked because she'd realized her son was wearing a silver bodysuit and dark blue cape. Nick looked down at his outfit, appraising it. "This? Just trying out a new look."

Kelly shook her head. "*Another* superhero?"

"No." He scoffed at his mother's ignorance. "Not *another* superhero. The best superhero *ever*!" He lifted his arms and the dark blue cape spread. *"The Silver Menace!"*

She wondered if maybe she should have quit drinking the moment she learned she was pregnant, but it was twenty-one years too late for regrets.

"Wanna see a *real* menace, kid? Then lie to me when you tell me how four grand ended up in your checking account just a few days after I spotted Grant Lambert and Chase LaMarca trying to hide from me in the corner deli." She folded her arms across her chest. "You have an answer for me yet?"

The Silver Menace hung his head. "No."

"You pulled a job with them, didn't you?"

"A little bit."

That was too much. It was bad enough that *she* had been in the business, but there was no way she was going to let Grant and Chase drag her innocent boy into a life of crime. "I'm gonna kill them. But first…" Nick steeled himself for whatever was coming. "But first you're gonna give me half."

"What?"

"You heard me."

"But—"

"And you're gonna promise me you'll stay away from Grant and Chase. They're bad influences. I raised you to be better than that."

"Yes, Mother."

He figured it was the right thing to say. Also, technically the words came from The Silver Menace, and therefore Nick Donovan was under no such obligation.

Lisa Cochrane's book—*Celebrity Boudoirs I've Known (And the Walk-in Closets, Too!)*—quickly became one of Palmer/Midkiff/Carlyle's strongest-selling titles during the holiday season, and for at least a few months she acquired a reputation as a celebrity real estate professional. Both the book and reputation played off each other, although she never really saw the extra cash that was being generated.

Mary Beth saw it—and therefore Bergdorf Goodman and Saks saw it—but Lisa didn't see it.

But she could always make more money—more *legitimate* money—so that wasn't a problem. Lisa was pushing sixty, and money hadn't been a problem for decades. If Mary Beth was happy, she was happy.

Although there was that little outstanding matter of the two thousand dollars she was still owed for an Austin Peebles fund-raiser ticket.

Lisa was willing to forgive, but not forget, a lot of things. Those things did not include that debt.

"Okay, try it again. Softer this time. I don't want to even feel it."

"How was that?'

"I'm ready."

"I'm *done!*"

Constance wheeled around and looked at Angelina, who stood in the middle of their living room proudly holding a wallet that seconds earlier had been in Constance's pocket.

"Pretty good." Constance coughed into her hand. "I barely felt that."

Angelina smiled. "Don't lie to me. You didn't feel it at all. I knew that, but then you did your fake cough thing, so I *really* know it now."

Constance laughed. "You know me, don't you?" Her lips met Angelina's, and the kiss lingered for a long time. When it broke, she added, "And you're pretty damn good at picking pockets."

Angelina loved the praise but was impatient. "Thanks, but now can you explain to me one more time how that credit card scam works?"

Constance almost squealed. She couldn't have been happier.

Paul Farraday was also perfecting his skills.

In fact, he'd just had a smooth trip from Far Rockaway to Inwood and back down to 125th Street before he started to notice MTA employees giving the subway train a second look. That's why he made himself a passenger after he opened the doors, which he figured was a good thing as blue uniforms started to enter from the platform.

The cars sat in the station for ten minutes with no announcements, so passengers began cursing and filing out. Farraday joined them, walking past the confused cops and muttering about MTA inefficiency like any true New Yorker.

Up on 125th, he boosted a livery cab and drove himself home.

Most of the way, he whistled "Take the A Train."

Sure, he had six thousand dollars in his pocket that he hadn't had before, but Jamie Brock still felt disappointed. He had hoped his work cultivating Triple-C and Boy Wunder would have paid off at a higher level. He was thinking more sixty than six.

But he'd been hustling long enough to know a man had to roll with the punches. Down today, up tomorrow, and all that.

And six thousand dollars wasn't exactly nothing. It was certainly filling his glass that night at the Penthouse, his favorite East Side bar, and if he budgeted wisely it would continue to do so for...

He tried to do the math, but he wasn't good at math. Or budgeting. So he stopped.

An older, well-dressed man waved in his direction, and he thought, *Why not?*

He was brought to a stop halfway to his target when a kid half his age ran up to the codger, planted a kiss on his forehead, and said, "Helloooo, Daddy!"

Jamie had been in denial for years, but suddenly felt the decades cascade over him.

And he know only one thing could make him feel better about himself.

More Botox.

The world of political blogging expressed shock when June Forteene's site abruptly went dark. One day she was promising A PREVIEW OF COMING ATTRACTIONS; the next day visitors landed on an error page.

Many were shocked. No one was especially saddened.

Rumors swirled. Depending on the source, she had been killed by jihadists, killed by the Obamas, killed by the Trilateral Commission, or raptured.

It never occurred to anyone to track down a woman named Hillary Morris. A lot of bloggers knew her birth name, but no one cared enough to do the research. Her disappearance fed hyperbole, which increased readership and upped the price of blog ads. *That* was what they cared about.

She would have been easy to find. Even three months after June Forteene disappeared and the story faded into a non-story, Hillary Morris had barely moved off the couch in her mother's studio apartment on Long Island.

Every now and then she'd have a clear thought and vow to return. Then she'd pop another pill and realize life was nicer on the comfortable couch...

Some people weren't made for New York City. Edward Hepplewhite was one of them.

He didn't even last a full ten days.

In those less-than-ten days, he'd been drugged and fired, and experienced political corruption, Live! Nude! Girls!, Naked! Dangling! Burglars!, prison, and Tasers.

It took most people at least a full month to experience the best New York had to offer.

This was one Christian college graduate who didn't need another sign from God. Pennsylvania was calling him home, and he was only too eager to obey the command.

It was home in Pennsylvania where he would finally spread his wings and flourish.

Three years later, Edward Hepplewhite would be crowned Mr. Leather Daddy Philadelphia.

After Catherine Cooper Concannon retired and Austin Peebles replaced her, Kevin Wunder moved on.

He was never going to be an elected official. He wasn't going to be on the New York City Council, he wasn't going to be a state legislator, he wasn't going to be in Congress, and he *certainly* would never be president.

Those were disappointing realizations, even though they'd been creeping up on him for years.

So Kevin decided to move to Washington and become a lobbyist. The money was better, the hours were better, and the only downside was an occasional awkward encounter with United States Representative Austin Peebles (D-NY), who didn't trust him for understandable reasons. If that was as bad as it would ever get, he could live with it.

And, in fact, that *was* as bad as it would ever get. Kevin Wunder would live with it for a long, lucrative time.

Margaret Campbell wasn't surprised when her name was announced as the winner of a Mystery Writers of America Edgar Award. In fact, she'd bought a special gown for the evening, instead of dressing in the dowdy clothes she usually wore to these events. She didn't mind spilling bourbon on dowdy clothes, but tonight demanded a higher standard.

The gown was Versace. It brought out the color of her eyes.

When her name was called, she stood and let the applause well up around her. David Carlyle was sitting next to her in a tuxedo—tie and cummerbund matching her gown—and rose to peck her on the cheek before she made her way to the podium.

"I am...*awestruck*," she lied, and the crowd roared its approval.

She returned their applause with a throaty laugh. "If any of you told me a year ago that I'd write a crime caper novel, let alone that a crime caper would become an international best seller, I would have had you locked up! Hell, I always told Westlake he was crazy."

Her fellow mystery writers laughed along with her.

"And now that book has not only won an Edgar, but it's about to become a major motion picture starring Jason St. Clair and Matt Damon. *Unbelievable!*"

This time, the other writers in the room cheered. She was living a dream that almost none of them would ever realize. Bestseller status! Jason St. Clair and Matt Damon! Credit for reinventing the crime caper genre!

When someone asked her after the ceremony how she'd come up with the idea for the book, Margaret shrugged and humbly shook her head.

"I wish I could pretend to have some sort of secret, but the truth is…the plot just came to me out of the blue."

Two hundred-twelve days into his first term in Congress, Austin Peebles finally made the national news. On the plus side, that was remarkably soon for a freshman Member of Congress to make headlines.

On the minus side…

The New York Times called it "an indiscreet moment." *The Washington Post* said it was "a national embarrassment." *The Denver Post* wrote that the incident "was cause for Peebles's immediate resignation." Drudge had the siren up; Colbert and Stewart amped up the mockery; and even Leno managed to come up with a few passably funny jokes.

All of which was to say, Austin Peebles unwisely used his damn camera phone again.

It was another great photo—this time he managed to get the Capitol Dome in the background from the balcony of his hotel room—but people still considered it inappropriate. So much for patriotism.

Penelope had finally had enough and filed for divorce before Austin even began seriously considering the fallout, let alone the calls for his resignation. He assumed it would all go away, the way these things had always gone away in the past. This time, though, it didn't.

His father had enjoyed having his son as a colleague, but he was the person who eventually convinced Austin he'd become a laughingstock and needed to resign. It was a tough thing to have to do to a free-spirited young man like Austin, but Neil Peebles finally decided after twenty-eight years that it was time to crack the whip.

Catherine Cooper Concannon was unopposed in the special election to fill the vacancy. The public knew the old girl still had another decade or two in her. They'd miss that sweet Austin with his long lashes and seductive smile and bedroom eyes and...*mmm*...

But they were happy to have Triple-C back in office, too!

And Neil Peebles had his desk-mate back!

Chase was stocking an aisle at the Groc-O-Rama in Elmhurst when Grant appeared, almost knocking over a display of Cheez Whiz as he leaned against the shelf.

"This better be good." Chase wasn't having one of his better days at the supermarket.

"How do diamonds sound to you?"

Chase frowned. "If this is your way of proposing, you're doing it wrong."

"Oh *God*, no!" Grant laughed. Then he saw Chase wasn't laughing. "I mean, I'd be happy to make an honest man outta you, but...Well, you know."

"Yeah, I know." Most people were afraid of marriage because it was a lifelong commitment. Grant Lambert—a man the government would have been hard-pressed to prove actually *existed*—feared marriage because there was paperwork involved. "So tell me about these diamonds."

Grant tried to smile, but quickly gave up. It was best that way. "I know this guy who just got a job with Major League Baseball..."

Chase had to admit he didn't see that curveball coming.

About the Author

Rob Byrnes is the author of five previous novels, including the 2006 Lambda Literary Award–winning *When the Stars Come Out* and 2009 Lammy finalist *Straight Lies*. His short stories have also appeared in several anthologies, including *Fool for Love* (2009) and *Men of the Mean Streets* (2011).

A native of Upstate New York, Byrnes was born and raised in Rochester and graduated from Union College in Schenectady before moving to Manhattan. He now resides in West New York, New Jersey, with his partner, Brady Allen. Visit him at www.RobByrnes.net.

Books Available From Bold Strokes Books

Month of Sundays by Yolanda Wallace. Love doesn't always happen overnight; sometimes it takes a month of Sundays. (978-1-60282-739-4)

Jacob's War by C.P. Rowlands. ATF Special Agent Allison Jacob's task force is in the middle of an all-out war, from the streets to the boardrooms of America. Small business owner Katie Blackburn is the latest victim who accidentally breaks it wide open, but she may break AJ's heart at the same time. (978-1-60282-740-0)

The Pyramid Waltz by Barbara Ann Wright. Princess Katya Nar Umbriel wants a perfect romance, but her Fiendish nature and duties to the crown mean she can never tell the truth—until she meets Starbride, a woman who gets to the heart of every secret, even if it will be the death of her. (978-1-60282-741-7)

The Secret of Othello by Sam Cameron. Florida teen detectives Steven and Denny risk their lives to search for a sunken NASA satellite—but under the waves, no one can hear you scream… (978-1-60282-742-4)

Andy Squared by Jennifer Lavoie. Andrew never thought anyone could come between him and his twin sister, Andrea…until Ryder rode into town. (978-1-60282-743-1)

Finding Bluefield by Elan Barnehama. Set in the backdrop of Virginia and New York and spanning the years 1960–1982, *Finding Bluefield* chronicles the lives of Nicky Stewart, Barbara Philips, and their son, Paul, as they struggle to define themselves as a family. (978-1-60282-744-8)

The Jettsetters by David-Matthew Barnes. As rock band the Jettsetters skyrocket from obscurity to superstardom, Justin Holt, a lonely barista, and Diego Delgado, the band's guitarist, fight with everything they have to stay together, despite the chaos and fame. (978-1-60282-745-5)

Strange Bedfellows by Rob Byrnes. Partners in life and crime, Grant Lambert and Chase LaMarca are hired to make a politician's compromising photo disappear, but what should be an easy job quickly spins out of control. (978-1-60282-746-2)

Dreaming of Her by Maggie Morton. Isa has begun to dream of the most amazing woman—a woman named Lilith with a gorgeous face, an amazing body, and the ability to turn Isa on like no other. But Lilith is just a dream...isn't she? (978-1-60282-847-6)

Speed Demons by Gun Brooke. When NASCAR star Evangeline Marshall returns to the race track after a close brush with death, will famous photographer Blythe Pierce document her triumph and reciprocate her love—or will they succumb to their respective demons and fail? (978-1-60282-678-6)

Summoning Shadows: A Rosso Lussuria Vampire Novel by Winter Pennington. The Rosso Lussuria vampires face enemies both old and new, and to prevail they must call on even more strange alliances, unite as a clan, and draw on every weapon within their reach—but with a clan of vampires, that's easier said than done. (978-1-60282-679-3)

Sometime Yesterday by Yvonne Heidt. When Natalie Chambers learns her Victorian house is haunted by a pair of lovers and a Dark Man, can she and her lover Van Easton solve the mystery that will set the ghosts free and banish the evil presence in the house? Or will they have to run to survive as well? (978-1-60282-680-9)

Into the Flames by Mel Bossa. In order to save one of his patients, psychiatrist Jamie Scarborough will have to confront his own monsters—including those he unknowingly helped create. (978-1-60282-681-6)

Coming Attractions: Author's Edition by Bobbi Marolt. For Helen Townsend, chasing turns to caring, and caring turns to loving, but will love take five steps back and turn to leaving? (978-1-60282-732-5)

OMGqueer, edited by Radclyffe and Katherine E. Lynch. Through stories imagined and told by youth across America, this anthology provides a snapshot of queerness at the dawn of the new millennium. (978-1-60282-682-3)

Oath of Honor by Radclyffe. A First Responders novel. First do no harm...First Physician of the United States Wes Masters discovers that being the president's doctor demands more than brains and personal sacrifice—especially when politics is the order of the day. (978-1-60282-671-7)

A Question of Ghosts by Cate Culpepper. Becca Healy hopes Dr. Joanne Call can help her learn if her mother really committed suicide—but she's not sure she can handle her mother's ghost, a decades-old mystery, and lusting after the difficult Dr. Call without some serious chocolate consumption. (978-1-60282-672-4)

The Night Off by Meghan O'Brien. When Emily Parker pays for a taboo role-playing fantasy encounter from the Xtreme Scenarios escort agency, she expects to surrender control—but never imagines losing her heart to dangerous butch Nat Swayne. (978-1-60282-673-1)

Sara by Greg Herren. A mysterious and beautiful new student at Southern Heights High School stirs things up when students start dying. (978-1-60282-674-8)

Fontana by Joshua Martino. Fame, obsession, and vengeance collide in a novel that asks: What if America's greatest hero was gay? (978-1-60282-675-5)

Lemon Reef by Robin Silverman. What would you risk for the memory of your first love? When Jenna Ross learns her high school love Del Soto died on Lemon Reef, she refuses to accept the medical examiner's report of a death from natural causes and risks everything to find the truth. (978-1-60282-676-2)

The Dirty Diner: Gay Erotica on the Menu, edited by Jerry L. Wheeler. Gay erotica set in restaurants, featuring food, sex, and men—could you really ask for anything more? (978-1-60282-677-9)

Sweat: Gay Jock Erotica by Todd Gregory. Sizzling tales of smoking-hot sex with the athletic studs everyone fantasizes about. (978-1-60282-669-4)

The Marrying Kind by Ken O'Neill. Just when successful wedding planner Adam More decides to protest inequality by quitting the business and boycotting marriage entirely, his only sibling announces her engagement. (978-1-60282-670-0)

Missing by P.J. Trebelhorn. FBI agent Olivia Andrews knows exactly what she wants out of life, but then she's forced to rethink everything when she meets fellow agent Sophie Kane while investigating a child abduction. (978-1-60282-668-7)